"WE CANNOT DO BATTLE."

"On the contrary, Mrs. Michaelson. I'm afraid that we must. You are one Yankee to best me beyond a doubt, for I could not leave this room were I threatened with Hell's damnation itself!"

Flashes of desire, like melting stars in the sky, caught fire and danced all through her.

"Callie!"

Her name on his lips was a caress. He stood above her once again, and still he had not touched her.

"Think!" she charged herself to say once again. "I am the enemy! Vile, fearsome—"

"Never, never vile!"

She wanted him. Wanted him to come closer. And touch her.

"Really. You have to go," she whispered.

"I know," he said, and made no attempt to leave.

Just when she thought she would scream with the waiting, with the anguish, with the denial, with the desire, she felt his lips at the back of her neck. . . .

AND ONE WORE GRAY

CRITICAL RAVES FOR
HEATHER GRAHAM

ONE WORE BLUE

"A stunning achievement . . . Heather Graham does for Harpers Ferry what Margaret Mitchell did for Atlanta. Without losing an ounce of sizzling sexual tension or intense emotions, or one moment of romance, this author brilliantly entwines historical details within the framework of a glorious love story."

—*Romantic Times*

"Ms. Graham fills this book with deep emotions and excellent characters that bury themselves so deeply in our hearts we'll remember them always."

—*Rendezvous*

"Graham paints a vivid and detailed picture . . . she is an incredible storyteller, a weaver of words."

—*Los Angeles Times*

"A FIVE-STAR RATING! . . . A well-written plot, excellent characters and scenes . . . Graham creates a vivid tapestry with her words."

—*Affaire de Coeur*

THE VIKING'S WOMAN

"Heather Graham is a writer of incredible talent. Once again, she brings to life a sometimes violent but always intriguing era of romance and adventure."

—*Affaire de Coeur*

"Passionate love scenes, action and intrigue combine to make a fast-paced, well-developed story which artfully blends historical fact with romantic fiction."

—*Rendezvous*

SWEET SAVAGE EDEN

"*SWEET SAVAGE EDEN* IS A KEEPER! An engrossing, highly sensual nonstop read. You'll be captivated by the engaging characters and the fascinating portrait of early colonial life. Heather Graham never disappoints her readers. She delivers high quality historical romance with three-dimensional characters and a sizzling love story that touches the heart."
—*Romantic Times*

A PIRATE'S PLEASURE

"The sexual tension in *A Pirate's Pleasure* sizzles like the hottest summer sun. Heather Graham's sense of humor sparkles throughout this delightful and well-researched tale . . . just one more shining example of why Ms. Graham is a best-selling author. She continually gives us hours of reading pleasure."
—*Romantic Times*

LOVE NOT A REBEL

"A very, very hot, fast-paced, 'battle of wills' love story that is guaranteed to thrill Heather Graham's legion of fans . . . enough historical details, colorful escapades, biting repartee, and steamy sexual tension to keep you glued to the pages."   —*Romantic Times*

DEVIL'S MISTRESS

"The familiar and charged role of the unwilling bride showcases Graham's talents for characterization and romantic tension."   —*Daily News* (New York)

"This book may become a minor classic."
—*Romantic Times*

"One of the most exciting romances ever read."
—*Romance Readers Quarterly*

Dell Books by Heather Graham

SWEET SAVAGE EDEN
A PIRATE'S PLEASURE
LOVE NOT A REBEL
DEVIL'S MISTRESS
EVERY TIME I LOVE YOU
GOLDEN SURRENDER
THE VIKING'S WOMAN
ONE WORE BLUE
AND ONE WORE GRAY
AND ONE RODE WEST
LORD OF THE WOLVES
SPIRIT OF THE SEASON
RUNAWAY

AND ONE WORE GRAY

HEATHER GRAHAM

A DELL BOOK

Published by
Dell Publishing
a division of
Bantam Doubleday Dell Publishing Group, Inc.
1540 Broadway
New York, New York 10036

The trademark Dell® is registered in the U.S. Patent and Trademark
Office.

ISBN: 0-440-21147-6

Printed in the United States of America

Published simultaneously in Canada

April 1992

OPM   20   19   18   17   16   15

Dedication

As this is a sequel, I would like to dedicate it to those same people who were so helpful and kind when I began my imaginings for *One Wore Blue*—Mr. and Mrs. Stan Haddan, Shirley Dougherty, Dixie, and the many wonderful people of Harpers Ferry and Bolivar, West Virginia. Also, the National Park Service guides who have been so helpful over the years, very especially those at Gettysburg, Harpers Ferry, and Sharpsburg.

As this April marks my tenth anniversary with Dell Publishing, I would also like to dedicate this book to some of the very wonderful people there—to my editor, Damaris Rowland, who is simply wonderful in all things. To Carole Baron, for being both an incredible businesswoman and a more incredible human being. To Leslie, Tina, Jackie, and Monica, and to extraordinary art and marketing departments. To Barry Porter —who will always be "Mr. Romance." To Michael Terry and Reid Boyd—for having been there the longest! To Sally and Marty, thank you—actually, Toto, that was Kansas!

And very especially to Mr. Roy Carpenter, for being such a wonderful salesman, and fine gentleman.

And last, but never, never least! To Kathryn Falk on the tenth anniversary of *Romantic Times*! Congratulations, and thank you, thank you, to Kathryn, Melinda, Kathe, Mark, Michael, Carol, and everyone at *R.T.*

Prologue

CALLIE

July 4, 1863
Near Sharpsburg
Maryland

Beneath the light of a lowering sun, sometimes brilliant and sometimes soft, the woman at the well beside the whitewashed farm house seemed like a breath of beauty. Her hair, a deep rich auburn, caught the light. At times it shimmered a russet, and at times it was softer, deeper, like the warm sable coloring of a mink. It was long and free, and cascaded around her shoulders like a fall, framing a face of near perfect loveliness with its wide-set gray eyes, fine high cheekbones, and full, beautifully shaped mouth. A hint of sorrow touched the curve of her lip, and rose to haunt her eyes, but that very sorrow seemed to add to her beauty. Against the ending light of the day, she was a reminder of all things that had once been fine and beautiful, just like an angel, a small glimpse of heaven.

She stood there clean and fragrant, and though simply dressed, she seemed an incongruous bit of elegance as she watched and waited while they came.

And come, they did. Endlessly.

Like a long slow, undulating snake, they came, hundreds of men, thousands of men, the butternut and gray of their tattered uniforms as dismal as the terrible miasma of defeat that seemed to hover about them. They came on horses, and they came on foot. They came with their endless wagon train that stretched, one weary soldier had told Callie, for nigh onto seventeen miles.

They were the enemy.

But that mattered little as she watched these men now, for she was surely in no danger from them.

There was only one rebel who could frighten her, she thought fleetingly. Frighten her, excite her, and tear at her heart. That rebel would not be passing by. He could not be passing by now, for he had not fought in the battle. The war had ended for him. He awaited its conclusion behind the walls and bars of Old Capitol Prison.

If he were free, she thought, she would not be standing here, by the well, watching this dreadful retreat. If there had been any chance of his being among these wretches, she would have run far away long before now. She would have never dared to stay here, offering cool sips of water to his defeated countrymen.

He would no longer be the enemy just because he wore a different color. He would be the enemy because he would seek her out with cold fury, with a vengeance that had had endless nights to simmer and brew in the depths of his heart.

It was her fault that he lived within those walls and behind those bars and fences while his beloved South faced this defeat.

If he were free, it would not matter if she tried to run or hide. He had told her he would come for her and that there would be nowhere for her to run.

She shivered fiercely, her fingers tightening around the ladle she dipped into the deep bucket of sweet cool well water for each of the poor wretches who strayed from the great wagon train to come her way.

He had sworn that he would come back for her. She could still hear his voice, hear the deep, shattering fury in what he thought had been her betrayal.

Even if these men marching by were the enemy, they brought nothing but pity to her heart. Their faces, young and old, handsome and homely, grimed with sweat and mud and blood, bore signs of exhaustion that went far beyond anything physical. Their anguish and misery showed in their eyes, which were like the mirrors of their souls.

They were retreating.

It was summer, and summer rain had come, turning the rich and fertile earth to mud. By afternoon, the summer heat had lessened, a gentle breeze was stirring, and it seemed absurd that these ragged and torn men, limping, clinging to one another, bandaged, bruised, bloody and broken, could walk over earth so beautiful and green and splendid in its cloak of summer.

The great winding snakelike wagon train itself had not come close to Callie's farmhouse. Stragglers wandered by. Infantry troops, mostly.

It was the Fourth of July, and on this particular Fourth of July, the citizens of the North were at long last jubilant. Over the last few days, around a sleepy little Pennsylvania town called Gettysburg, the Union forces had finally managed to give the Confederates a fair licking. Indeed, the great and invincible General Robert E. Lee, the Southern commander who had earned a place in legend by running the Union troops into the ground in such cities as Chancellorsville and Fredericksburg and numerous others, had invaded the North.

And he had been thrust back.

"It were over shoes, mum," a Tennessee fellow had told her, gratefully accepting the cool dipper of water.

He was a man of medium height and medium weight with thick dark hair on his head and a full, overgrown beard and mustache. He wasn't wearing much of a uniform, just worn mustard-colored trousers and a bleached cotton shirt. His bedroll and few belongings were tied around his chest, his worn hat sported several bullet holes. "We were on our way to attack Harrisburg, but we needed shoes. Someone said there were shoes aplenty in Gettysburg, and first thing you know, on the first of July, there's a skirmish. Strange. Then all the southern forces were moving in from the North, and all the northern forces were moving in from the South. And by nightfall on the third of July . . ." His voice trailed away. "I ain't never seen so many dead men. Never." He wasn't looking at her. He was staring into the bottom of the ladle, and his gaze seemed hopeless.

"Maybe it means that the war will be over soon," Callie said softly.

He looked up at her again. Reaching out suddenly, he touched a stray wisp of her hair. She jumped back and he quickly apologized. "Sorry, ma'am. You standing here being so kind and all, I don't mean no disrespect. It's just that you're nigh onto one of the most beautiful women I've ever seen, and it's just making me think awfully hard of home. Your hair's just as soft as silk. Your face is an angel's. And it's just been so long . . . well, thank you, ma'am. I've got to keep on moving. Maybe I will get home soon enough." He handed her the dipper and started walking again. He paused and looked back. "I don't expect the war will be over any too soon. Your general in charge—Meade is his name these days, I think—he should have followed after us. He should have come now, while we're hurt and wounded. Even an old wolf knows to go after a lame deer. But Meade ain't following. Give our General Bobby Lee a chance, and he runs with it. No, the war ain't going to end too soon. You take care, ma'am. You take great care."

"You too!" she called after him. He nodded, smiled sadly, and was gone.

The next man who passed her by had a greater story of woe.

"Ma'am, I am lucky, I am, to be alive. I was held back 'cause of this lame foot of mine here, took a bullet the first day. Comes July third, and General Lee asks us can we break the Union line at the stone wall. General George Pickett is given the order. Ma'am, there ain't another man in my company, hell, maybe in my whole brigade, left alive. Thousands died in minutes." He shook his head, and seemed lost. "Thousands," he repeated. He drank from the dipper, and his hands, covered in the tattered and dirty remnants of his gloves, shook. He handed her back the dipper. "Thank you, ma'am. Thank you most kindly, ma'am."

He, too, moved on.

The day passed. The long, winding wagon train of Lee's defeated troops continued to weave its way over the Maryland countryside. Even though Callie was appalled by the stories told her by each weary man, she still held her ground. She already knew something of the horror of the battlefield, for less than a year ago, the battle had come here. Men in blue and in butternut and gray had died upon this very earth.

And he had come to her. . . .

She dared not think of him. Not today.

She lingered by the well, but toward the late afternoon Jared began to cry, and she went into the house to tend to him.

He slept again, and she returned to the well, entranced by the flow of time.

Dusk came. And still the men continued to trickle by. She heard about strange places where battle had raged. Little Roundtop, Big Roundtop, Devil's Den. All places where men had fought valiantly.

Darkness fell. Since all who had passed her way had been on foot, Callie was surprised to hear the sound of horses' hooves. A curious spiraling of unease swept down her spine, then she breathed more lightly as she saw a young blond horseman approach. He dismounted from his skinny roan horse and walked her way, thanking her even before he accepted the dipper she offered out to him.

"There is a God in heaven! After all that I have seen, still I have here to greet me the beauty of the very angels! Thank you, ma'am," he told her, and she smiled even as she trembled, for in his way, he reminded her of another horseman.

"I can offer you nothing but water," she said. "Both armies have been through here, confiscating almost everything that resembles food."

"I gratefully accept your water," he told her. He took a sip and pushed back his hat. It was a gray felt cavalry hat, rolled up at the brim.

It, too, brought back memories. "Are you a southern sympathizer, ma'am?"

Callie shook her head, meeting his warm brown eyes levelly. "No, sir. I believe in the sanctity of the Union. But more than anything these days, I just wish that the war would be over."

"Amen!" the cavalryman muttered. He leaned against the well. "With many more battles like this one . . ." He shrugged. "Ma'am, it was horror. A pure horror. Master Lee was fighting a major one for the first time without Stonewall Jackson at his side. And for once, Jeb Stuart had us cavalry just too far in advance to be giving Lee the communication he needed." He sighed and dusted off his hat. "We wound up engaged in a match with a Union General, George Custer. Can you beat that? Heck, my brother knew

Custer at West Point. He came in just about last in his class, but he managed to hold us up when he needed to. 'Course, he didn't stop us. Not my company. I've been with Colonel Cameron since the beginning, and nothing stops him. Not even death I daresay, because Cameron just plain refuses to die. Still—"

"Cameron?" Callie breathed, interrupting him.

The cavalryman started, arching a brow at her. "You know the colonel, ma'am?"

"We've—met," Callie breathed.

"Ah, then you do know him! Colonel Daniel Derue Cameron, he's my man. Never seen a fiercer man on horseback. I hear he learned a lot from the Indians. He's not one of the officers who sits back and lets his men do the fighting. He's always in the thick of it."

Callie shook her head. "But—but he's in prison!" she protested.

The cavalryman chuckled. "No, ma'am, no way. They tried to hold him in Washington, but they didn't keep him two full weeks. He was wounded at the Sharpsburg battle here, but he healed up and come right out, escaped under those Yankee guards' noses. Hell, no, ma'am—pardon my language, it's been a while since I've been with such gentle company. Colonel Cameron has been back since last fall. He has led us into every major battle. Brandy Station, Chancellorsville, Fredericksburg. He's been there. He'll be along here soon enough."

She felt as if the night had gone from balmy warmth to a searing, piercing cold. She wanted to speak, but she felt as if her jaw had frozen. She wanted desperately to push away from the well, and to start to run. But suddenly, she could not move.

The cavalryman didn't seem to notice that anything was amiss. He didn't realize that her heart had ceased to beat—then picked up a pulse that thundered at a frantic pace. He didn't seem to realize that she had

ceased to breathe and then begun to gulp in air, as if
she would never have enough of it again.

Daniel was free. He had been free for a long, long
time. He had been in the South. He had been fighting
the war, just as a soldier should be fighting the war.

Perhaps he had forgotten. Perhaps he had forgiven.

No. Never.

"I've got to move on," the cavalryman told her. "I
thank you, ma'am. You've been an angel of mercy
within a sea of pain. I thank you."

He set the dipper on the well. Bowed down and
weary, he walked on, leading his horse.

Callie felt the night air on her face, felt the breeze
caress her cheeks.

And then she heard his voice. Deep, low, rich. And
taunting in both timbre and words.

"Angel of mercy indeed. Is there, perhaps, a large
quantity of arsenic in that well?"

Once again, her heart slammed hard against her
chest. Then she could not feel it at all.

He was alive, and he was well. And he was free.

He had been there a while, just past the fence, beyond the range of her sight. He had dismounted, leading his horse, a gray Thoroughbred that had once been
a very fine mount but now resembled all the other
creatures of the Confederacy—too gaunt, with great
big haunted brown eyes.

Why was she looking at the horse?

Daniel was there.

He hadn't changed. He still towered over her, clad in
a gray frock coat with a pale yellow sash looped
around his waist, his sword at his side, buckled on by
his scabbard. He wore dun trousers and high black cavalry boots, muddy and dusty boots that were indeed
the worse for wear.

He wore a cavalry hat. It was rolled at the brim,
pulled low over his eye, with a jaunty plume waving

arrogantly from the top, laced to the hat at the narrow gold band around it.

She no longer gazed at his clothing, but met his eyes.

Those blue eyes she had never been able to forget. A blue framed by ebony dark lashes and high arched brows. A startling, searing, blue. A blue that penetrated her flesh with its fire, a blue that pierced into her, that raked her from head to toe. A blue that assessed, that judged, that condemned. That burned and smoldered with a fury that promised to explode.

They stared out at her from a face made lean by war, a handsome face made even more so by the lines of character now etched within it. His flesh was bronzed from his days in the saddle. His nose was dead straight, his cheekbones broad and well set. His lips were generous, sensual, and curled now in a crooked, mocking smile that nowhere touched his eyes.

"Hello, angel," he said softly. His voice was a drawl, a sound she had never forgotten.

She mustn't falter, she musn't fail. She wasn't guilty, though he would never believe her. It didn't matter. She simply could never surrender to him, because he did not understand surrender himself.

Breathe! she commanded herself, breathe! Give no quarter, for it will not be given you. Show no fear, for he will but leap upon it. He is a horse soldier, and so very adept at battle.

But still her fingers trembled upon the ladle. Lightning seemed to rake along her spine, and at first, it was not courage that held her so very still and seemingly defiant before him. She was simply frozen there by fear.

She had always known that she would see him again. There had been nights when she had lain awake, praying that when that time came, all that had gone so very wrong between them might be erased. Many a night she had dreamed of him, and in those dreams she had

savored again the taste of the sweet splendor and ecstasy that had been theirs so briefly, once upon a time.

She would never be able to convince him of the
truth. So very little had been left to her in this war. But
she still had her pride, and it was something that she
must cling to. She'd never beg.

Or perhaps she would, if it could do her any good!
But it would not, and so she would not sacrifice her
pride. The war, it seemed, had stripped all mercy from
him. She wanted to be as cold as he was.

She wished that she had betrayed him. With all her
heart, at that moment, she wished that she could hate
him with the same fury and vengeance he seemed to
send her now.

Angel, he had called her. With venom, with mockery. With loathing. Surely the word had never been
spoken with such a tone of malice.

"Cat got your tongue?" he said, his tone still soft, his
Virginia drawl deep and cultured—and taunting. "How
very unusual. Weren't you expecting me?"

He seemed taller even as he stepped nearer to her,
leading his gray horse. Despite his leanness, his shoulders seemed broader than ever, his size even more imposing, his supple grace of movement more menacing.

Run! Run now! Blind instinct warned her.

But there was nowhere to run.

He was a gentleman, she reminded herself. An officer, a horseman. One of the last of the cavaliers, as
the Southerners liked to call their cavalry. He had been
raised to revere women, to treat them kindly. He had
been raised to prize his honor above all else, taught
that pride and justice and duty were the codes by
which he must live.

He had been taught mercy . . .

But no mercy lingered in his eyes as they fell upon
her now. She nearly screamed as he reached toward
her, but no sound came.

He didn't touch her but merely pulled the dipper from her hand, and sank it into the bucket. He drank deeply of the fresh well water.

"No poison? Perhaps some shards of glass?" he murmured.

He stood just inches from her. The world around her was eclipsed.

For a fleeting moment, she was glad. She had thought him in prison, but she had believed, always, that he lived. No matter what he thought, what he believed, she had desperately desired that he live. Swiftly, sweetly, in a strange shining hour that had passed between them, she had loved him.

No color of cloth, no label of "enemy," no choice of flag to follow could change what dwelt so deeply in her heart.

She had loved him through the long months of war. Loved him even while the belief of her betrayal found root in his heart, nurtured by the vicious months of war. She had loved him, she had feared him, and now he stood before her again. So close that she could feel the wool of his coat. So very close indeed that she could feel the warmth of his body, breathe in the scent of him. He had not changed. Lean and gaunt and ragged in his dress, he was still beautiful. Handsome in his build and stature, noble in his expression.

He came closer still. Those blue eyes like the razor-sharp point blade of his sword as they touched her. His voice was husky, low and tense and trembling with the heat of his emotion.

"You look as if you're welcoming a ghost, Mrs. Michaelson. Ah, but then, perhaps you had wished that I would be a ghost by now, long gone, dust upon the battlefield. No, angel, I am here." He was still as several seconds ticked slowly past, as the breeze picked up and touched them both. He smiled again. "By God, Callie, but you are still so beautiful. I should throttle you. I should wind my fingers right around your very beautiful neck, and throttle you. But even if you fell, you would torture me still!''

He hadn't really touched her. Not yet. And she couldn't afford to let him. She squared her shoulders, determined to meet his eyes, praying that she would not falter.

"Colonel, help yourself to water, and then, if you will, ride on. This is Union territory, and you are not welcome."

To her amazement, he remained there, standing still. His brows arched as she pushed him aside and walked past him. Inwardly she trembled, her show of bravado just that—a show. But there was no surrender in this. That had long ago been decided between them. Regally, she walked on. She would not run. Head high, she continued toward the house.

"Callie!"

He cried out her name. Cried it out with fury and with anguish.

The sound of his voice seemed as if to touch her. To rip along her back, to pierce into her heart and soul and bring both fear and longing.

It was then that she suddenly began to run. She couldn't look back. She had to reach the house.

She picked up her skirts and scurried across the dusty yard toward the rear porch. She leapt up the steps, ran across the wood planks and through the back door. She leaned against it, her heart leaping.

"Callie!"

His voice thundered out her name again. She gasped and jumped away from the door, for he was hammering it down with the weight of his shoulders.

He had warned her.

There would be no place to run.

No place to hide.

She backed away from the door, gnawing on her knuckles. There had to be some place to hide!

He couldn't strangle her. It might be war, but Rebel soldiers didn't strangle Yankee women. What would he do to her?

She didn't want to know.

"Daniel, go away! Go home, go back to your men, to your army—to your South!"

The door burst open. He stood there staring at her once again, and there was no taunting in his eyes now, or in his smile.

"What? Are there no troops close enough to come to your rescue once you've seduced me into your bed this time?"

She had never, never seduced him!

There was a coffee cup upon the kitchen table. Her fingers curled around it and she hurled it at him. "Go away!" she commanded him.

He ducked, ably avoiding the coffee cup.

"Go away?" he repeated. "How very rude, Mrs. Michaelson! When I have waited all these months to return? I lay awake nights dreaming for a chance to come back to your side. What a fool I was, Callie! And still, I suppose I did not learn."

He stepped into the kitchen, swept his hat from his head, and sent it flying onto the kitchen table. "Well, I have come back, angel. And I'm very anxious to pick up right where I left off. Let's see, where was that? Your bedroom, I believe. Ah, that's right. Your bed. And let's see, just how were we situated?"

"Get out of my house!" Callie snapped.

"Not on your life," he promised. He smiled again, a bitter, self-mocking curl. "Not, madam, on your life!"

He strode toward her, and a sizzling fear suddenly swept through her. He wouldn't really hurt her, she assured herself. He'd never really hurt her. Not Daniel.

He'd threaten, he'd taunt, but he'd never really hurt her. . . .

But she couldn't let him touch her. She couldn't want him again. She couldn't fall again!

"Don't!" she warned.

"This is one invasion of the North that is going to be successful," he warned her, his tone bringing shivers down her spine. He smiled, relentlessly coming toward her, his eyes ruthless as they fixed upon hers.

Callie knocked a chair into his path. He barely noticed.

"Don't, damn you! You have to listen to me—" she began.

"Listen to you!" he exclaimed. She heard the sound of his fury explode in his voice. "Callie, time is precious! I have not come to talk this night. I listened to you once before."

"Daniel, don't come any nearer. You must—"

"I must finish what you started, Callie. Then maybe I can sleep again at night."

He reached for her arm and the fire in his eyes seemed to sizzle through the length of her. She didn't know him anymore. Or had she ever really known him? In his eyes she could see the effect of his days in the prison camp and even the days beyond. She had not imagined that he might be so ruthless. She still did not know how far he could go.

"Daniel, stop!" she hissed. She jerked free of his hold upon her arm, turned, and ran.

He was on her heels, not racing, just following her. Relentlessly.

She stopped and found a vase and tossed it his way. He ducked again, and the vase crashed against a wall. She tore through the parlor, looking for more missiles. A shoe went flying his way, a book, a newspaper. Nothing halted his stride.

She reached the stairs, and he was there behind her.

She started to race up them and realized her mistake. He was behind her. She reached the landing. When she paused to catch her breath, his fingers entwined in her hair, and she was wrenched back and swept into his arms. Struggling wildly, beating her fists against his chest, she met his eyes. For a moment she was still, breathing hard, her breasts heaving with her exertion.

"Let's finish what we started, shall we, angel?"

"Let me go!" Callie demanded. Tears stung her eyes. He was alive; he held her again. So many days and nights of dreams and memories had passed her by. If only he could be made to understand, if only she could see his smile, hear his laughter once again.

If only he could believe her.

But he would never understand, and there was nothing left for her but the violence and the fury in his eyes.

"Let you go?" he repeated, his tone bitter. "Once I tried to walk away. To honor both North and South, and everything that we both held sacred. But you raced after me, angel. You could not bear to have me leave. You wanted me to stay here. Remember, Mrs. Michaelson? Here."

He walked again, carrying her into her room. A second later she found herself falling, cast down with very little care or tenderness onto the bed. She struggled to rise, her heart beating furiously. She wanted to fight him with a vengeance, and she hated the excitement that was snaking its way into her limbs.

Did it matter? Did anything matter when he was alive, when he had returned? When she could reach out her arms and hold him once again. When the night could sweep them into fields of ecstasy where there was no North and no South and where the sounds of roaring cannons and rifle fire could not intrude. Sweet, magical places where there was no black powder to singe the air, no pain of death, no anguish of defeat.

No! She could not hold him, she could give nothing

to him, take nothing from him, for he sought not love, but vengeance. He had sworn once that he would never hurt her, and she had to believe in that vow, for in his present ruthless mood, she had no way to fight him.

"Don't!" she commanded. "Don't even think—"

But he was suddenly straddled over her, stripping off his mustard gauntlets to catch her wrists where she pressed against him.

"Just what am I thinking, Callie?" he demanded.

She lay silent, watching his eyes. There was no mercy within them. Hard and brilliantly blue, they impaled her where she lay upon the pillow. She had no choice but to fight him, and fight him with equal fervor.

"I don't know. What are you thinking?" she asked, gritting her teeth.

"Ah, if the Yanks but had you in the field!" he murmured. "Maybe you are recalling the last time we met. It was right here. I'll never forget, because I loved this room from the first time I saw it. I loved the dark wood of the furniture, and the soft white of the curtains and the bed. And I loved the way that you looked here. I'll never forget your hair. It was like a sunset spread across the pillow. Sweet and fragrant, and so enticing. Newly washed, like silk. I can't forget your eyes. I can go on, Callie. There's so much that I never forgot. I remembered you in camp, and I remembered you every moment that I planned and plotted an escape. I thought of your mouth, Callie. It's a beautiful mouth. I thought of the way that you kissed me. I thought of your lovely neck, and the beauty of your breasts. I thought of the feel of your flesh, and the movement of your hips. Over and over and over again. I remembered wanting you like I'd never wanted anything or anyone before in my life. Of feeling more alive than ever before just because I breathed in the scent of you as I lay against your breast. And when you touched me, I think I came closer to believing I had died and gone to heaven than I've ever done upon a battlefield. Damn you! I was in love with you. In the midst of chaos, I was at peace. I believed in you, and dear God, when I lay here with you, I even believed in life again. What a fool I was!"

"Daniel—" Callie said, desperate to explain.

"No! Don't!" he said coldly. His fingers shook as they grasped her wrists. She felt the terrible tension in his limbs as his thighs tightened around her. Her heartbeat lifted and soared further. "Don't!" he insisted again. "Don't tell me anything. Don't give me any protestations of innocence. I'll tell you what I've thought over all these months. I've thought that you were a spy, and that you deserved the fate of a spy. I thought about choking the life out of you." He released her wrists. His knuckles moved slowly up and down the column of her throat. She didn't move. She didn't dare breathe. In fascination, in dread, she listened as he continued to speak. "But I could never do it," he said quietly. "I could never wind my fingers around that long white neck. I could never do anything to mar that beauty. Then I thought that you should be hanged, or that you should be shot. Through long dark nights, Callie, I thought about all of these things. . . . But do you know what I thought about most of all?"

His face had lowered against hers. Taut, bitter, hard. She should have fought him then. Fought him while she was nearly free.

But she did not. She stared at him and at the eyes that held hers so fiercely and passionately. "What?" she whispered.

"I thought about being here with you. I thought about this bed. I thought about your naked flesh, and I thought about your smile when it seemed that you poured yourself upon me, heart, soul, and body. I thought about the way that your eyes could turn silver. I thought that all I wanted was to be back here."

His fingers moved suddenly upon the lace of her bodice. And still Callie didn't move. Not until he spoke again.

"I wondered what it would be like to have you when I hated you every bit as much as I had once loved you," he said softly.

At last, too late, she came to life. She tried to strike his face, but he caught her wrist. "Hate me, then, you fool!" she told him heatedly. "Give me no chance, no leave, no grace, no mercy—"

"Were I to give you more mercy, I might as well shoot myself, madam!" he swore.

"You self-righteous bastard!" she charged him. "Hate me and I will despise you. You were the enemy! You are the enemy! This is Union soil! God damn you for expecting more from me," Callie swore. Enraged beyond all reason, she managed in a fierce and violent burst of energy to twist away from beneath him.

He moved like lightning, dragging her back down. Gasping, struggling wildly, she fought him, until her breath left her, until she was caught and spent. She stared hatefully up into his eyes again.

Her situation was worse, for now the length of him lay against her, and all the fever and the fury and the heat that had burned and built so long within him seemed to encompass her.

"Here we are, Callie. You'll not leave me tonight. And you'll not betray me," he whispered fiercely.

"And you'll not have me!"

"I will."

"It would be—rape!" she spat out.

"I doubt it."

"Oh, you flatter yourself!"

"I've waited long and cold and furious nights, Callie. I will have you."

"You won't!" she cried to him. "You won't hurt me, you won't force me. You won't, because you promised! You won't, because of who you are. I know it, I know you—"

"Damn you, Callie! You don't know me. You never knew me!"

But she did. She knew the sound of his voice, and she knew the twist of his jaw. She knew the way he stood, and she even knew the way he thought. She knew the searing blue light in his eyes, and she knew both the tempest and the tenderness that could rule the man.

And she knew the raw passion that guided him now.

His mouth descended upon hers. His lips were hard and forceful. She could not twist or turn to avoid or deter him for his fingers threaded through her hair, holding her head still to his assault. She clamped down to fight him in any way that she could. She hammered her fists against his back, but he ignored her blows, and eventually they began to slow, and finally to stop. He robbed her of breath, and of reason, and of her fury. Her defenses were weak, and her enemy in gray was powerful. Even more powerful was the enemy of time, and that of loneliness, and even that of love. For there was more than determination in his kiss. Perhaps there was even more than passion.

Her lips parted to his as the thrust of his tongue demanded. Searing hot, liquid, demanding, seductive, he played upon her senses, tasted her mouth, the deep recesses, the curve of her lip. Touched and demanded that she give in turn, and seemed to reach within her, more and more deeply, fierce and volatile.

Her fingers ceased to press against him. She no longer tried to push away. She hadn't the power.

"Callie!"

She heard the whisper of her voice, fierce, passionate, spoken with anger, and spoken with anguish.

"Damn, I'll not let you sway me!" he cried out furiously. His eyes were fire as they touched hers. His fingers bit brutally into her arms.

At that moment, she did not know him. She didn't know if he would have her in anger and hatred, or if he would cry out an oath and jump from her side. She didn't know, and then it didn't matter.

Because there was suddenly another loud, fierce cry that came to fill the room. It wasn't a Rebel yell, nor was it any Yankee call.

It was a high, trembling, furious, and extremely demanding cry. And as it was ignored, it grew to new, hysterical heights.

The sound of that cry stopped Daniel flat, stopped him as Callie could have never done herself.

He sat back upon his haunches, his eyes narrowed sharply upon her. "What in God's name . . . ?"

Her breath caught. She strove for calm. She shimmied from beneath him and he made no effort to stop her. "It's—it's Jared," she said.

He was still staring at her blankly. Like a man trying to understand code when the code was plain English.

"That's a baby," he said.

"Yes! It's a baby!" she agreed. She managed to leap from the bed at last. She hurried down the hall to the nursery, throwing open the door.

Jared had kicked off his coverings. His hands and feet were flying furiously. His little mouth was open wide, and he was screaming with a demanding will.

Callie swept him quickly up into her arms.

Daniel stood in the doorway, having come behind her. He stared at her with amazement etched across his features. She realized that he wasn't looking at her at all, he was looking at Jared.

He strode across the room.

Instinctively, Callie held the child close to her breast, cradling him there. But Daniel ignored her protective hold and reached for Jared with a dogged determination. "Give him to me, Callie," Daniel warned.

Lest she hurt Jared, she had to let him go. Daniel meant to see him, and see him he would.

Daniel, ignoring Jared's squalling and the flailing of his tiny fists and feet, walked over to the flickering lamplight that filtered in from the hallway. Callie swallowed hard, feeling shaky as she watched him scrutinize the baby clad in his white cotton shirt and diaper. He stared from Jared's furiously puckered face to his perfect little feet. Daniel held the infant well, his hand and arm secure beneath Jared as he touched the long wild tuft of ebony dark hair upon Jared's head. Then Daniel's eyes—those distinct blue eyes, mirrored in the tiny face of the child—fell upon her again.

"It's my baby!" he exclaimed harshly.

She wanted to speak, but her mouth had gone dry. Then it didn't seem to matter to Daniel. He didn't need her to answer him.

He turned and started out the doorway.

With her baby. His baby. Their baby.

He couldn't—he wouldn't!—be leaving with Jared, she thought. Jared was just an infant. Daniel couldn't begin to care for him. Even he wouldn't be so cruel.

But his footsteps were retreating down the stairway.

"Daniel!" She found her voice and a frantic energy, at last. She raced after him, and this time it was she who accosted him at the foot of the stairs. "What are you doing? Give him to me! Daniel, he's crying because he's hungry. You can't take him from me! Daniel, please! What do you think you're doing?"

Daniel stood stone still, staring at her. "He's my son."

She didn't know what to do, and she blundered, frightened of his behavior. "You can't begin to know that—"

"The hell I can't. What a fool you are to try to deny it," he said softly, coldly.

"Daniel, give him back!"

"He doesn't belong here. He belongs at Cameron Hall," Daniel said stubbornly.

Callie's mouth dropped. "You can't take him! He's barely two months old. You can't care for him. Daniel, please!" Tears sprang to her eyes. She caught hold of his elbow and held on hard. "Daniel, he needs me. He's crying because he's hungry. You have to give him back to me."

A slow smile curved his mouth despite the baby's hungry screaming. "You didn't even intend to tell me about him, did you, Callie?"

She shook her head, the tears now brimming in her eyes. "Yes, I intended to tell you!"

"When the hell did you intend to tell me?" he bellowed.

"You didn't give me a chance. You came in here condemning me—"

"You knew that I'd come back. Maybe you didn't," he corrected himself bitterly. "Maybe you thought that I'd rot and die in that camp!"

"Damn you, Daniel, you can't kidnap my son!"

"My son. And he'll have my name," Daniel said. To her amazement, he started walking by her.

"You can't care for him!" she cried out. Of all the things that he might have done to her, she had never imagined this.

He stopped and turned back with a smile. "Oh, but I can, Callie. I can find a mammy to care for him easily enough. Within the hour."

"You wouldn't!" she breathed.

"He's a Cameron, Callie, and he's going south tonight."

"You can't take him away from me! He's mine!"

"And mine. Created under very bitter circumstances. He's coming home, and that's that."

"This is his home!"

"No, his home is south, upon the James."

No matter what had passed between them, no matter how bitterly he might have learned to hate her after the months that lay between them, she still could not believe it when he stepped past her again.

"I'll call the law!" she cried out.

"There is no law anymore, Callie," he wearily said to her over his shoulder. "Just war."

She followed him to the door. Jared was crying with an ever greater vengeance, furious that his meal was being denied him. The tears she had tried to hold back burst from Callie's eyes, and streamed down her face. "No! You cannot take him from me!" she thundered, and she slammed against him, beating her fists against his back.

He spun on her, his blue eyes fierce, furious, ruthlessly cold.

"Then you'd best be prepared to travel south, too, Callie. Because that's where he's going!"

She stepped back, stunned once again.

"What?"

"My son is going south. If you want to be with him, you can prepare to ride with me. I'll give you ten minutes to decide. Then we're moving. Who knows, Meade just may decide to chase Lee's army this time, though it seems poor Uncle Abe can't find himself a general to come after Lee. But I'm not waiting. So if you're coming, get ready."

South!

She couldn't travel to Virginia. Her heart had been set long ago, at the beginning of the war.

No . . .

She couldn't travel south because she was against slavery, but more than that, because she had under-

stood President Lincoln's war from the beginning. The
first shots hadn't been fired because of emancipation.
The war had begun because the southern states had
believed they could secede, that states' rights were su-
preme. Now the war was about so much more.

She couldn't go to Virginia because of Daniel Cameron. Because he was convinced she had betrayed him.
Because he was determined to be her enemy with a far
greater hostility than any northern general had ever
felt for Bobby Lee.

She reached out her arms to him. "Daniel, give me
the baby. Just let me feed him." He stared at her in an
icy silence. She gritted her teeth. "Please!"

Daniel hesitated no longer. His frigid blue stare still
pierced her condemningly, but he brought the baby to
her. Jared was suddenly in her arms, warm, trembling,
precious, still screaming. Callie shook, knowing that
the baby meant more to her than anything in the
world.

More than war. Far more than pride or glory.

"Ten minutes, Callie," Daniel said. "I'll be waiting
on this step. For Jared, and you, if you choose to come.
But Jared is coming with me."

"But we're enemies!"

"Bitter enemies," he agreed politely.

"I could betray you again, moving through this territory."

"You'll never have the chance again," he promised
softly.

She met his startling blue gaze and then turned and
fled up the steps with Jared. She ran into her room, her
heart beating. She kissed her son's forehead, and dis-
tractedly pulled upon the strings of her bodice, freeing
her breast for the baby to nurse. She touched his cheek
with her knuckles, and he rooted for a moment before
latching onto her to suckle strongly.

Love, enormous waves of it, came rushing through

her. She rested her cheek upon her baby's head. She would never let Daniel take him from her.

No matter what had been. No matter how bitter Daniel might still be.

No matter what it was she had to face as a Yank in the South.

She closed her eyes. Daniel was wrong. Their son had been conceived in love.

Not even a year had passed since she had first seen Daniel Cameron.

So little time . . .

But oh, what a tempest that time had been!

She closed her eyes and remembered. . . .

1

Enemy Territory

One

Once Daniel fell, the reality and the dreams began to blend together.

They had come riding in with glory, a cavalry unit with extraordinary horsemanship, all of them handsome astride their fabulous mounts, swords gleaming in the late summer sun, their plumed hats flying like the banners of long-ago knights. Ah, but that's what they were, the last of the cavaliers, fighting for honor, for glory, for love, for the intangible essence that embodied a people. . . .

No, that was what they had been. The love was there still, as were the dreams of honor. He had been fighting far too long to believe any longer in the glory of war. And seen too close, he and his horsemen were not so splendid. Their uniforms were torn and tattered, their boots were worn, their faces were gaunt and haggard. Yes, they rode with their steel swords glistening in the morning sun, and when they let out with their Rebel cries, they were both fierce and beautiful, and awesome to behold. Riders of destiny, riders of death.

He had not lost his horse while engaged in battle.

Not while locking swords with men in blue with faces he dared not look upon too closely.

It was the cannonball exploding just at his heels that had unhorsed him. For a few, brief, shimmering moments that seemed to waver between life and death, he had known what it was like to fly. It had all been so painless.

But then he had come crashing down, and the earth had embraced him ferociously. It was then that the pain came, searing and shooting through his temples even as the fragrant grass of the rich Maryland farmland teased his flesh. Then had come a sudden, stark darkness.

And then the dreams.

One moment, he could hear the horrible whistle of the cannons, could see the fires bursting against the beautiful blue of the summer sky. He could hear and feel the pounding of the horses' hooves, the clang of steel, and the horrible cries of men. Then it was all gone, as if a clean, clear breeze had come to sweep it away.

The James River. He could feel the breeze that came off the James, that sweet coolness, touching his cheek. He could hear the drone of bees. He was lying in the grass on the slope of the lawn at home, at Cameron Hall, staring at the blue sky above, watching as white clouds idly puffed by. He could hear singing, down by the smokehouse. Something soft, and sing song, a spiritual. A deep, low male voice rumbled, and beautiful female voices chorused around it. He didn't need to open his eyes to see the smokehouse, or the hall, or the endless slope of green lawn where he lay that stretched all the way down to the river, and the river docks and the ships that came to take the crops to market. Nor did he need to open his eyes to see the garden, bursting with bright red summer roses that wove enchantingly down the path from the wide, porticoed back porch of the hall. He knew it all, like he knew his own hand. It was home, and he loved it.

But he needed to get up. He could hear Christa's laughter. She would be coming up the slope with Jesse to get him. Pa would have sent them to bring him in for dinner. Jesse would be teasing her, and Christa would be laughing. They'd both be ready to taunt him for his daydreaming. Christa, still just a little girl, was so accomplished in the house. And Jesse always knew what he wanted. An appointment to West Point, a few years in a good medical school, and an assignment in the West. While he . . .

"Daydreaming, Daniel?" Jesse asked. His brother sat down beside him on one side, while his sister, her bright blue eyes as shimmering as the sky, sat on his other side.

"Nothing wrong with daydreaming, Jess."

"No, nothing wrong at all," Jesse said. He was the most serious of their family, and he always had been. He was the peacemaker, calm, decisive, and as stubborn as they came. There weren't all that many years between them and so they had always been the best of friends. They might fight, but let anyone else ever make a critical comment about either of the Cameron boys and the other brother would leap to his defense, willing to take on any fight. And no one had best ever find fault with Miss Christa, for both boys—though they might torment her endlessly at home—would instantly be ready for battle.

"Dreaming about what?" Christa demanded. She laughed, and the sound was like all the others that Daniel heard, the ripple of the river, the whisper of the breeze. It was a sound that belonged to the languorous days of summer, to childhood.

"Horses, I daresay," Jesse volunteered for him, and pulled his hat low over his head. The eldest of the threesome, he was always quick to speak his mind.

Daniel grinned. "Maybe. Christa is going to be the most beautiful and accomplished young lady in the country, you're going to be the greatest doctor since Hippocrates, and me, well, I guess I'm going to be a horse master."

"The best darned horse master this side of the Mississippi," Jesse promised him.

Daniel leapt to his feet, swinging an imaginary sword. "The best horseman, the best swordsman. I'll be just like one of King Arthur's knights!"

"And save damsels in distress!" Christa laughed, clapping.

"What?" Daniel demanded.

"Damsels. Fair maidens in distress. Well, it's what all the best knights are supposed to do."

"They're supposed to fight dragons."

"Or Indians," Jesse observed wryly.

"Everyone know that you have to save the damsels from the Indians and dragons!" Christa insisted.

"Woah!" Jesse, always the voice of reason, warned them. "Give him time, Christa. Damsels tend to be interested in knights before knights tend to be interested in damsels. He'll get there. But right now, there's supper on the table. Honey-smoked ham and sweet potatoes and new peas and fresh-squeezed lemonade."

A shell burst in the sky. Jesse's memory disappeared. Christa's laughter dissolved into the shriek and whistle of a cannonball as it flew through the air.

He was no longer lying on the cool green grass of home. He was in the farmlands of Maryland. The grass was no longer green, it was churning to mud beneath him as horses pranced and dug up the earth, and men fell and spilled their blood upon it.

He had learned about saving damsels. He'd never really met a dragon, but he'd had his day with the Indians in the West.

And he'd met enemies he'd never imagined. His own countrymen. Yankees. Men he'd gone to school with. Men with whom he'd fought in the West.

His own brother . . .

How much better it would have been, had there been dragons!

He was bleeding himself, he knew. Not a new wound, but an old one, ripped open as he had flown through the air.

He couldn't feel the pain but suddenly felt the spatter of mud against his cheek.

He wondered if he was dying.

He tried to turn. If they'd been able to take him, his men would never have left him here. Unless they had been convinced that he was dead.

He couldn't continue to lie here. He was injured and bleeding. Eventually, surely, someone would come to this patch of earth again. Either the Yanks, or the Rebs. Battle could rage here again.

But he knew he could just as easily die here before anyone ventured near enough to help him. And it was just as likely that Yanks might come upon him as Rebs.

He blinked, moving carefully, looking about himself.

There was a house in the distance.

It wasn't Cameron Hall. It was a whitewashed farmhouse, and there were planters of summer flowers on the front porch. An old swing hung from a big oak.

The flowers had been mown down in a hail of bullets. The white paint was pockmarked with rifle fire.

Distantly now, he could still hear the cries of warfare, the crack of steel against steel.

His company had moved on. The battle had changed terrain. Dead men lay around him. Men in blue and men in gray.

He tried to raise himself and crawl toward the house.

The effort was too much for his remaining strength. The house began to fade. Blackness descended swiftly upon him once again. Let it come! he thought. Let it bring me back to the sweet grass by the river. . . .

When he opened his eyes again he thought that he was dreaming. He thought he had died, and somehow made it to heaven, for the creature above him could not be any part of hell.

She was beautiful. As beautiful as his dreams of the river, as beautiful as a clear summer sky. Her eyes were a clear, level gray and her hair was a rich, dark, abundant auburn. It framed delicate, beautifully chiseled features, a face shaped like a heart, full, delineated, rose dark lips, a fine straight nose, and high, striking cheekbones. She was bending over him. He could almost reach out and touch her. He breathed in the sweet scent of her, as fragrant and soft as roses.

Just as he could feel and reach and touch the slope of grass back home, hear the river, be brushed by the breeze! he thought in dismay. He was seeing things again.

But no, she was real. Perhaps an angel, but real nonetheless, for she reached out and touched him. Her fingers gently moved over his face like the coolest, softest breeze of spring.

She lowered herself down beside him. He wanted to keep staring at her, but he couldn't. He hadn't the strength to keep his lashes raised.

He felt her fingers moving around his head. And still her touch was so gentle. She cradled his head in her lap.

"You are breathing!" she whispered. He tried to open his eyes. Tried to see the wide, compassionate, dove-gray beauty of her eyes.

He could see her! His lashes were raised just a slit, but he could see her against the gray powder that sat in the air like an acrid mist. Her voice was low and soft and like a melody when she spoke.

Perhaps he was dying. Even when his eyes closed

again, he could see her face, that radiant sunset burst of her hair.

"Alive?" she demanded.

"Yes." He tried to form the word. No sound came from his parched lips.

"Ma'am! Ma'am!" Someone was calling to her. "The shells are coming down again! This battle isn't anywhere near over. Get inside!"

"But, sir! This man—"

"He's a dead Reb, lady! A dead Reb officer, probably responsible for more'n half the dead Yanks lying around him. Why, he's practically a murderer! Get inside!"

A Yank! He needed the Yank to believe he was dead. Maybe he was so close to death it didn't matter. He couldn't keep his eyes open.

He thought that he saw those dove-gray eyes once again. Exotic, really beautiful, slightly tilted at the corners. That face . . . ivory, with a delicate blush upon the cheeks. Those lips . . .

"Ma'am—why it's you. Callie! Callie Michaelson! God in heaven, Callie, get yourself into the house."

"Eric!" Callie gasped. "My Lord, I hadn't expected to see a soldier I knew. This man—"

"This man is a dead Reb!"

The Yankee infantryman standing above him spit out of the side of his mouth, aiming for Daniel's feet. He hit the ground instead.

Ass! So that's why you fellows can't win this war, you can't even aim spittle! Daniel thought.

And you'd spit on a dead man, soldier! Pray God, sir, that I never rise to meet you in battle!

"Callie, my God, I'd never forgive myself if something happened to you. Gregory would be tossing in his grave. Now please, get in the house and quit wasting good time on a bad Reb! Jesu, Callie, I can't believe that you're even touching that man!"

But she was. He managed to raise his lashes. Her
eyes met his. Those beautiful, entrancing gray eyes
touched by silver, and those dark sunset lashes. Her
hair was a halo of radiant dark fire. . . .

She jumped up, and his head cracked back down on
the ground. Hard. The world went very dark. He
fought to remain conscious.

He reached out for her in desperation.

Her delicate, black-shoed foot struck his fingers as
she left him.

His angel of mercy was gone.

She had remained until she'd been reminded he was
a Reb! he thought bitterly.

Perhaps it was for the best. A Yankee company was
moving over the lawn now, and he did not want it to be
known that he lived. If there was one fate he wanted to
avoid, it was that of prisoner of war.

Best to let the Yanks think he was dead.

She was gone, and then the Yanks moving across the
lawn were gone. The light before him seemed to be
fading for real. He was losing consciousness again.

Perhaps it was a great kindness, for the shells began
to burst once again. Riders came. Horses' hooves just
missed him as they trod over the mud and the grass.
There was no slackening in the fire. There were no
moments of peace when each side came hastily for
their wounded.

The dead could always wait.

He saw a flash in the sky, and then he saw nothing
more. Not for a long, long time.

When he opened his eyes again, the world was
nearly silent.

Incongruously, he heard the chirping of a bird.

He was alive. And he could move. He clenched and
unclenched his fingers. He stretched out his legs. He
closed his eyes and rested once again.

He was stronger than he had been before. He could swallow, he could open and move his eyes easily. His fingers followed every direction his mind gave them. His feet moved when he commanded them.

He closed his eyes and breathed deeply.

He was desperately thirsty. He opened his eyes again. His head still pounded, but the pounding was lessening. He tried to rise, and did so. He rubbed his neck, and moved slowly and carefully.

Sitting up, he looked around. The ground was littered with men. Men in blue and men in gray.

He looked toward the house. He had to reach it.

The battle was over, and he did not know who had won. Maybe neither side had seen a clear victory. But his men were gone. They would have returned for him, or for his body, if they could have done so.

That meant only one thing. They had to be retreating. He would have to get through Yankee lines to return to them.

He pressed his temples together hard for one long moment then managed to make it to his feet.

As he staggered, it seemed that he was alone in the world.

Alone in the world of the dead, he thought wearily.

He looked to the house, then remembered the woman. The one with the amazing gray and silver eyes and the flow of hair like a deep rich sunset.

He wasn't alone.

His Yankee angel was in there somewhere, very near. The sweet little beauty who had cradled him so tenderly until she had been reminded that he was the enemy.

Pretty soon, Yankee patrols would be around to search for their wounded and to gather their dead.

And capture any stray Rebs for their notorious prison camps.

His fingers clenched into fists. He wasn't going to any Yankee prison camp.

He looked back to the house, and his lips slowly curved into a smile, wistful, bitter—determined.

"Well, angel," he whispered softly, "it seems that we are about to meet!"

Slowly, silently—very carefully—he made his way toward the battered and bullet-riddled farmhouse. He kept low as he approached the porch. She might well have a loaded shotgun in there, and from the snatches of conversation he had heard, she was definitely on the side of the blue.

He'd best go in by the back. He'd need to take her by surprise, and to have her understand that he very much intended to stay alive.

He touched his head and winced. Had it hurt this badly before she cracked it down on the ground? And then kicked him?

She'd looked like such an angel. He'd been sure that he'd died and gone on to the hereafter.

He smiled wryly. His angel was going to keep him from the certain promise of hell!

Two

The last drumbeat had sounded. The shrill call of the bugle had ceased to blare. The battle was over.

It was over, all but for the acrid smell of powder and smoke in the air, all but for the wages of war left strewn across the once green and fertile and peaceful farmland.

For two days Callie Michaelson had sat down in her basement and listened to the horrible sounds of war. Once before she had heard the curious sound of silence, and she had ventured out, but there had only been a lull in the fighting, a shifting of the troops, and as she had been ordered, she had hurried back inside.

How strange it had been to discover that the officer concerned for her was Eric Dabney! He came from a small town about twenty miles northeast of her. He had stood up for Gregory at their wedding, and the two of them had always been close friends. She had lost track of him since the war. He'd gone to military school as a very young man, and with Lincoln's call to arms, he'd won himself a commission in the cavalry.

Union cavalry had died here, she thought pityingly. Just as Confederate cavalry had died. And the only thing she had been able to do was to wait down in the basement.

There had been nothing she could do for the men beyond her door. The men in blue, or the men in gray.

Not once had it come again. That sound that was even more horrible, the sound of silence.

But now, the battle was over. The ravages of war would be all that were left behind.

When she emerged from her basement at last, she was first aware that the black powder from the guns and cannons still hung upon the air, thick and heavy.

When she walked through her parlor and out on the porch, an anguish like nothing she had ever felt before came rushing around her heart. There were so, so many dead.

The powder stung her eyes as she looked around her yard. Standing there, she felt a chill sweep her, for she seemed such a strange being in the midst of the carnage. She was dressed in a soft blue day gown with a fine lace bodice and high neckline. Her petticoats, a snowy white that showed when she walked, seemed incongruous against the blood and mud in the yard. Even her hair, so fiery with its auburn highlights, seemed too bright for this late afternoon.

There, before her, hanging from the old oak, the big whitewashed swing miraculously remained. As if some spirit touched it, it drifted back and forth in the gray mist.

The oak itself, to which the swing was tied, was riddled with bullets.

Callie stepped from the porch. Her gray eyes were almost silver with the glistening of tears that covered them as she looked at the lawn, heavily laden with soldiers. She was horrified. She lifted her skirts and then swung around. It seemed that something had grabbed her hem.

And so it had. There lay a hand, upturned. And the hand was that of a very young Confederate soldier. His eyes remained open.

Atop him, as if caught in a last embrace, lay another soldier.

This one in blue.

Both so very, very young. Perhaps at peace, at last, entwined in blood and death.

Where was the soldier she had held so briefly before? she wondered, gazing around the yard. She knew that she had touched life, something warm and vibrant in this field of cold damnation. And it had seemed so important that something, someone, survive the carnage. Trembling suddenly, she remembered his face. It had been a striking one despite the smudges of mud and black powder on it. Ebony dark, thick, arched brows, and lines clean and stubbornly strong. In death, his very strength and masculinity had held a haunting and gallant beauty.

Perhaps the handsome cavalry officer lay beneath his fallen enemy, just like the two young soldiers near her feet.

"Oh, God!" Callie whispered. Shaking, aware that more than the powder was bringing tears to her eyes, she sank low upon the balls of her feet and tenderly closed the eyes of both soldiers. She fought for some words, to mouth a prayer. She felt numb.

She straightened and tried to look out across the mist of powder and the coming dusk.

Where once the fields had been covered with near sky-high stalks of corn, they now were cleared, the corn literally mown down by bullets and cannonballs and canisters.

Everywhere she looked, all over the beautiful, rolling countryside, there lay the lost. The strength and beauty of two nations—their youth. Their fine young men, their dreamers, their builders. All lost . . .

The sound of hoofbeats brought her swirling around again, her heart seeming to leap to her throat. Out of the mist emerged a horseman. Who had taken the battle? Who was coming now?

The horseman wore blue. Behind him rode others.

The man saluted her. "Captain Trent Johnston, Army of the Potomac, miss. Are you all right?"

She nodded. Was she all right? Could anyone stand in the midst of all this carnage and be all right? "I'm— I'm all right, Captain."

"Is there anyone else in the house?" he asked her.

She shook her head. "I live alone. Well, I've three brothers. They're all in the West."

"Union army?" Johnston asked her sharply.

Callie felt a wry curl come to her lip. Maybe it was natural. A lot of soldiers had little faith in the loyalty of Marylanders. There was tremendous southern sympathy here. There had been riots in Baltimore when Lincoln had come through on the way to his inauguration. But she resented her loyalty being questioned when she had just spent two days hiding in her basement, and when both her father and her husband lay in the family plot down by the creek.

"Yes, Captain. My brothers are with the Union. They asked to join up with companies fighting out West. They didn't want to fight our immediate neighbors to the south here."

The captain's eyes narrowed. He rose slightly on his horse, his heels low in his stirrups, and called out a command. "Jenkins, Seward, take a look at the men on the ground here. See if we've any Billy Blue survivors."

Two men dismounted and quickly looked to the fallen men.

Callie stared at Trent Johnston. He wasn't an old man. But time—or the war—had etched deep lines of bitterness into his face. His eyes were a faded color. Maybe they had been blue once. Now they were the weary shade of the powdery mist.

"Did the Union take the battle?" she asked.

Johnston looked down at her. "Yes, miss. From what I hear, both sides have been trying to claim the victory. But General Robert E. Lee has taken his men and pulled back, so I daresay the Union has taken the battle. Though what we've taken, I'm not so sure myself," he said softly. "Jesu, I have never seen so many dead."

He looked over to the two privates he had ordered down. They were still stepping around the men strewn across her yard, studying them carefully. Callie felt her nails curl into her palms.

Good Lord, she could not look at them so closely. She didn't want to see the saber wounds and the great holes caused by the minnie balls and the destruction wrought by the cannons and canisters.

There were no living men in her yard. Not one of them had moved. Flies created a constant hum beneath the warm September sky, and that was the only evidence of life.

"See if those Yank boys are breathing, men," Captain Johnston said.

Callie looked at the captain and then gazed upon the devastation on her lawn. "What if there had been a survivor in gray?" she asked softly.

One of the men on the lawn, either Jenkins or Seward, answered her gravely. "Why miss, we'd take care of him, too, right as rain, don't you fret none about that." His voice lowered, and she was certain he didn't want his hard-nosed captain hearing him. "I got kinfolk myself on the other side," he told her. He looked to the captain. "We would take care of a Reb, right, Captain?"

"Oh, indeed, we would," the captain said. He gazed hard at Callie once again. "Are you sure your loyalties are with the North, miss?"

"Yes. My loyalty is to the North," Callie said flatly, her teeth grating. But no one could stand here and see these men, these young men, enemies in life, so pathetically entwined in death, and not feel a certain pity for the other side.

"Sir!" Callie said, remembering Eric. "An officer I know went through here in the midst of the battle. Captain Eric Dabney. Have you seen him? Has he—survived?"

Johnston shook his head. "Not as yet, I haven't, ma'am. But I'm sure that I will by nightfall. I'll be glad to express your concern."

"Thank you."

The captain tipped his hat. "We'll be back with a burial detail shortly, miss. Seward, Jenkins, mount up."

With another nod to her, the captain turned his mount. Dirt churned as his company did an about-face, and he rode into the gray mist of the now quiet battlefield.

Callie closed her eyes. She suddenly felt very alone, standing on her lawn surrounded by the dead. Her fingers wound tightly into her skirts, and she fought the overwhelming feeling of horror and devastation sweeping through her. They would come for these poor fellows. They would be buried somewhere near by, she was certain, and probably en masse.

And somewhere, far, far away, a sweetheart, a mother, a lover, a friend, someone would weep for their fallen soldier. And say a prayer, and erect a stone in memory, and bring flowers to that stone.

Just as she brought flowers to the stone that had been erected out back next to her mother's grave. Gregory's body had been returned to her in a coffin. She had awaited it at the railway station, cold, numb, and clad in black. But her father had fallen at Shiloh, far, far away, and all that she had received had been the letter from his captain. "Dear Mrs. Michaelson. It is my great misfortune to have to inform you . . ."

She had been lucky, she understood now. Officers no

longer had the time to write to loved ones of their fallen men. Widows now discovered their status by reading their husband's names aloud from the lists posted in the nearest town, or reprinted in the newspapers.

It was no good to stand on the lawn. No good to feel the air on her cheeks, to feel the coming of the darkness, the whisper of the night. For these fallen men around her would never again feel the soft caress of a breeze, or the endlessly sweet nectar of the first soft kiss of the night.

She turned, anxious not to see the faces of the men as she hurried past them.

The house, she realized, was riddled with bullets. Her front windowpanes were shattered. There was even a small cannonball lodged in the stone base of the left corner of the porch.

This was one battle Callie would never be able to forget.

She stepped back into the parlor. Her feet crunched over broken glass.

It was beginning to grow very dark and shadowy within the house, and she was anxious to light the gas lamps.

She started to move, but then her hand flew to her mouth and she tried desperately to swallow down a gasp. Fear, vivid and wild, came sweeping through her. She fought a growing sense of panic, biting down hard upon her knuckles.

She wasn't alone.

There was someone in her house. Someone who had come through the rear door, and into the kitchen.

From the parlor through the hallway, and to the door frame that led into the kitchen she could see him standing there. He was very tall, and his height was emphasized by the plumed hat he wore at a rakish angle over his brow. She could see little of his features, for the shadows of dusk hid them.

But she could see his uniform, and it was gray. Gray trousers, rimmed in gold. Knee-high black boots. A gray frock coat, also trimmed in the same gold. He was southern cavalry, she thought quickly.

The southerners had pulled out. That's what Captain Trent Johnston had said.

So what did this southerner want with her? She'd heard tales of what happened to lone women when men of an invading army came their way.

Don't panic, she warned herself.

But his mind was moving in the same direction, and his warning came down upon her like a hammer.

"Don't!" he rasped out sharply, before she had found the breath to scream.

She had to scream, she had to move. Quickly. Captain Johnston still had to be close by.

Callie spun around, ready to exit her house as swiftly as the wind. But even as her hand fell upon the door-knob the southern cavalryman fell upon her.

Her scream escaped her then, as his hand touched her arm, ripping her away from the door. "Stop it, damn you, ma'am, I am not spending the rest of the war in a prison camp!"

The voice was deep, rich, almost musical in its drawl. But it was also touched with an arrogant authority, a harshness, even a ruthlessness.

And his face . . .

He was the soldier she had touched! The one she could have sworn had lived.

He stared at her with eyes as sharp as steel blades beneath those imperious, high-arched, and deadly dark brows.

"No!" Callie screamed, finding breath at last. Her fingers clawed at the fingers that held her arm. She touched something warm and sticky. Blood.

She looked up into his eyes.

They were deep blue, nearly cobalt. They stared at her evenly and with a dangerous and determined warning.

"Let me go!" she demanded. Oh, Lord. She was a competent woman, she assured herself. She was not easily intimidated. She had lived here all alone since the war had begun.

She had never been so frightened before in all her life. This soldier looked at her as if he had some personal vengeance in mind.

"Let me go!" Her voice was starting to rise again. He was very tall, even allowing for the heels of his boots. He towered over her, and his frock coat emphasized the breadth of his shoulders. His jet dark brows framed his eyes, and hiked up high as he watched her. His mouth was set in a firm line within his square and unyielding chin.

"Miss, don't—"

"No!"

She wrenched free and made for the door again. "Captain Johnston!"

The cry rose high on her lips.

"Don't! Dammit, I do not want to hurt you!" He swung her around and planted his hands firmly on either side of her head against the door as his arms formed steel bands around her. She opened her mouth. One of his hands moved to clamp down hard over it.

She was forced to stare into those endlessly blue eyes. His face, she realized, was a strikingly handsome one. His features were cleanly sculpted, very well defined.

"Listen to me, ma'am. I do not want to . . ."

He broke off. He took a deep breath. Callie realized that he was struggling to remain standing.

"I do not want to . . ."

He blinked, ink black lashes falling over his cheeks.

A wild bravado filled Callie along with her realization
that he was barely standing. She thrust away his hand
and pushed against his chest with all of her might. "Let
go of me, Reb!" she demanded.

He fell to his knees.

And then he keeled over.

He lay flat on her floor by the door. For several seconds, she stared down at him. She prodded him with
her toe to see if he would move. He did not.

Was he dead?

She wanted to swing open the door and shout for
Captain Johnston, but she was certain that the horseman was long gone by now. And this Reb was no
longer any danger to her.

Gingerly she bent down, trying to decide if he was
dead or alive.

His hat had fallen aside, and she saw that he had a
full head of near ebony hair, rich and waving just below his nape. He was handsome, and more, she
thought, a sudden wave of pity sweeping over her. He
had gained something more than beauty in his years.
There was character to his face, something in the set of
his jaw, in the fine lines etched about his eyes and his
mouth.

He is the enemy, she told herself.

She saw a lock of damp, matted hair at his temple.
She smoothed it back and saw that he had been grazed
there by a bullet.

He was also bleeding from his side. There was no rip
or tear in his uniform, but a crimson stain was appear-
ing over the gray wool of his frock coat. She rose and
hurried into the kitchen, soaked a towel with cool water from the pump, and hurried back out to the parlor.
She bathed his forehead and determined that the
wound was not bad. He might live.

She lay her hand upon his chest and waited, and then
nearly jumped when she felt the beating of his heart.

The blood staining his frock coat and shirt at his side disturbed her. She moved his coat back and then pulled away his shirt, gingerly pulling the tail from his breeches. A small pang struck her, and for the first time she didn't think of him as being the enemy. His belly was taut, his chest was tightly muscled, his flesh was handsomely bronzed. His skin was very hot to her touch. Yank or Reb, this was what war brought, the loss of such men, so handsome, so gallant, so beautiful, and in their prime.

Not so gallant! she thought with a sniff.

She brought her towel up to bathe away the blood at his side.

It was an old wound, she discovered. A slash above the hip, probably from a saber or a bayonet. It had reopened, and he lay bleeding from it.

She pressed against the towel. The flow of blood seemed to stop.

"You're going to live, Reb," she said aloud. "Maybe," she murmured. She wasn't convinced that Captain Johnston wanted any Rebs to live.

And both sets of soldiers, from the North and from the South, dreaded the horror of the prison camps.

Well, it wasn't her problem. Her house was decimated. Not far from where the soldier lay were the shattered panes of her windows. This soldier had invaded her very home. She couldn't care what happened to him after Captain Johnston took him away.

She bit her lip, curious. He wore the insignia of a Confederate colonel of the cavalry. Southern uniforms were often very haphazard—she'd heard that many of the great southern generals still wore their old U.S. Army breeches with jackets and shirts of their own design. But this cavalryman was well dressed in gray with yellow cavalry trim. He came from money, she thought.

There was a small leather wallet attached to the

band of his scabbard. Certain that his eyes were still closed and that he remained unconscious, Callie delved into it. Hurriedly, she looked through the packet of papers she discovered within. There were a number of letters and an old pass. She glanced over the pass quickly. It had been issued to a Colonel Daniel Cameron, Army of Northern Virginia, by General J.E.B. Stuart.

Cameron. Daniel Cameron. So that was his name. She shivered, suddenly wishing that she did not know it.

The enemy should remain nameless, she thought. It made it easier to hate. But the enemy should have remained faceless too.

She had seen all those faces out on her lawn. Young faces, looking to heaven.

Stop, she commanded herself. This was war.

She thought she heard horses coming once again and relief filled her. She stuffed the papers quickly back into the wallet. All that she had to do was call Captain Johnston, and this enemy could be off her hands. She started to move, and discovered that she could not.

She looked down. Blood-stained fingers curled around the hem of her skirts. And sky-blue eyes, very much alive with a startling threat, were upon her.

He was very much alive.

She forgot that she had been feeling magnanimous toward her enemy as a swift new fear filled her. "Let go of me!" she commanded sharply.

Those blue eyes seared right through her. A lopsided grin touched his lips.

"Not on your life, angel. Not on your life," he promised her.

Three

The riders weren't coming to the house, she realized. Already, the sounds of their hoofbeats were fading.

To reach the Yankee horsemen, Callie would have to move quickly. She had to escape the Reb who had so menacingly come back to consciousness at exactly the wrong time.

"No!" she shrieked. She jerked firmly at her skirt, tearing herself away. She ran to the door. She nearly had it flung open when an arm snaked out from behind her and a hand encircled her waist.

An arm covered in gray. A hand reddened by blood.

Instantly, a scream tore from her throat. "Stop it!" he commanded fiercely. He swung her around. She tried to strike him again, growing more and more frantic. She jerked away from his arms and pounded against his chest.

But this time his arms encircled her, and they came crashing down on the floor together, rolling over. To her great consternation, when they came to a halt, he was on top, straddling her. She struck out wildly at him, her panic growing. Grimly, he caught her wrists. "Ma'am, I am trying damned hard not to hurt you. Can't I get through that thick Yankee skull of yours!

What were you doing? Picking a man's pockets before
he was quite cold?"

Her eyes narrowed. There was a tone of dead reck-
oning in his voice. He didn't want to hurt her, but he
would do so if he had to.

"I was trying to help you—"

"Oh, just like you were helping me when you
dropped my head out there and left me to die? I can
see where the enemy stands with you!"

"I thought you were dead!"

"You realized that I was a Rebel!"

"You are the enemy!" she snapped out. "One of
those fine, gallant cavaliers, fighting for your life of
chivalry, right? Is this a sampling of your fine Southern
gallantry?" she demanded.

"Darlin', I'll tell you, there's lots more chivalry
you're receiving right now than I'm in the mood to
give. It was one hell of a battle. I was down and
wounded to begin with, and you, my dear, most courteous and proper Yank, made it all the worse with that
kick in the head!"

"I did not kick you in the head!" she protested.

"You did! Right after you dropped me flat, bleeding
and in torment, on the ground! And to think that I
thought you were an angel!"

The sharpness of his stare seemed to go beyond her
for a moment, and he winced. She didn't think it was
his own pain he was feeling. She could see from the
anguish in his eyes that he thought of the rows upon
rows of dead in her yard.

But now his eyes were gleaming down upon her
again. "I'm not going to pass out again," he warned
her, his tone grating.

"Well, I am going to scream!" she threatened in
turn, and she opened her mouth to do so.

He was so damned quick. His hand landed over her
mouth again.

It was then that she heard a knocking on the door.

Her eyes widened as she stared up at the southerner. She was definitely victorious.

"Miss! It's Captain Johnston. We're out here to pick up our men!"

Callie squirmed furiously. She tried to sink her teeth into the Reb's fingers.

To her amazement, he suddenly pulled a knife from a sheath at his ankle and brought the razor-sharp edge to her throat. "Don't scream," he hissed at her.

He wouldn't do it. She was damned convinced that he wouldn't do it.

She didn't scream.

He was suddenly up, and pulling her to her feet. She still didn't scream. He still had his knife out.

He swung her around and prodded her to the door. She felt the point of the knife right at the small of her back. "Tell him fine. Tell him that you know that he's there, and thank him."

Callie stood very still.

"Tell him!"

"Go ahead! Stab me!" she hissed back at him.

His fingers suddenly threaded through her hair. "Don't tempt me!" he said.

He opened the door, standing behind her in the shadows, but keeping the blade of the knife against her all the while.

Captain Johnston stood on her porch. She opened her mouth. She meant to tell him there was a Reb in her house. She didn't give a damn about the knife. She wasn't afraid of the Reb, she assured herself.

She was never really sure why she didn't turn him in right then and there. Maybe it was Captain Johnston. She was so certain that to him the only good Reb was a dead one.

What did she care? Her husband lay dead and now long buried in the yard. Her father lay dead in a mass grave with hundreds of other Yankee soldiers. And he had fallen to a man like this one. . . .

"Yes, Captain Johnston," she said gravely. She didn't allow her eyes to flicker downward. She didn't want to see the Confederate or the Union dead.

"We should be out of here soon enough, ma'am. Can my men do anything for you?"

The knife jabbed closer against her flesh. "No, Captain, I just . . . I just want to be left alone."

The captain nodded. "You see any soldiers around here, you call for me. Someone will be around. I don't want to lose any strays. There just might be a wounded man or two separated from his company. I'll be close. Just down in the valley by the little offshoot of the Antietam stream."

"Yes, thank you so much," Callie said.

Johnston turned away. Callie almost called after him.

The door closed with a slam. Arms came around her, and she found herself sliding down to the floor with the Reb on her side.

"That wasn't bad," he told her.

"That was damned good, Colonel," she said icily. "If you stick that knife at me again, I will scream until the sun comes up."

"Lady, you do tempt fate!" he warned her roughly.

"What choice have I, cast into the company of so fine and chivalrous a cavalier!"

He gritted his teeth and exhaled. "I have to rejoin Stuart!" he told her.

"Well, you may just have to bleed to death first, Colonel," she said sweetly.

"Will I?"

Feet suddenly came tramping up the porch. He drew her near again, his hand clamped tightly over her mouth. She could barely breathe. She struggled. It made no difference. He was built like Atlas. He might be dying here in her living room, but his arm muscles were still in very fine shape.

It seemed forever that he held her. A strange eternity, for she'd never been closer to any man, never held so intimately, so tautly, for this length of time, even by Gregory. She had never sought more desperately to escape, and she had never been so securely held. After a time, she closed her eyes. The darkness continued to arrive. She could still hear the tramping of feet. Then it seemed that they slowly faded.

She was almost passing out, or almost sleeping. Perhaps she had been nearly asphyxiated, she wasn't quite sure. But when the pounding came on the door a second time, he startled her until she nearly jumped out of her skin.

He was still beside her. He pulled her along with him to her feet.

Slowly, slowly, he eased his hand from her mouth. He turned her toward the door, and opened it.

Johnston was there again.

"We're through here, ma'am."

She looked outside. The bodies were gone. All of them. She felt as if she would fall for a minute.

All the poor young men . . .

"Miss? Are you all right?"

She nodded. Her mouth was very dry. She swallowed. Johnston wasn't such a bad man. Not if you were on his side.

"Yes. I, er . . . Thank you, Captain."

"Take care, then. If you need help with anything—"

"No, no, thank you. I don't need any help."

"Oh! I'm sorry, I forgot to tell you, miss. Captain Dabney did survive the day. He took a gash to his arm, but not a serious one, the surgeon says. Captain Dabney sends his regards, and his concern, but I took the liberty of informing him that you were very well."

"Thank you. I am so relieved for Captain Dabney!"

Johnston saluted, then turned away. She watched him as he walked to his horse. He mounted it, signaled with his hand, and shouted out an order. His company —the group of horsemen and the wagons that now accompanied him—began to move. Callie stared after him.

A slow smile curved her lip. The Reb hadn't held the knife on her at all, not once during the entire exchange.

The door suddenly closed. She was careful to let her self-mocking smile fade as she met the Reb's stark blue gaze again.

"Good," Cameron muttered. "You did well."

"That's because you have such a way with women, Colonel," Callie told him sweetly.

"And you ma'am, are pure sweetness and light!" He grinned slowly. He mocked her in return, but he was surprisingly, wickedly handsome.

"Colonel—"

"Who is Captain Dabney?" he demanded.

Her brows shot up. "A friend, Colonel," she said icily.

"A friend, or lover?"

Stunned, she felt her hand go flying through the air without the least bit of thought. He caught her hand before it could connect with his cheek, but it was no stay for her amazement and fury. "War or no war, sir, how dare you come up with a question—"

"Because I have to know if this Captain Dabney is going to come stepping into this house at any given moment!" he told her.

"You'll just have to wonder, won't you?" she said heatedly.

He smiled. "Ma'am, you are a Yank to match any Rebel I've known in all my born days. Ah, but with outrage like that, you're probably innocent."

"Innocent!" Callie exclaimed. She wanted to kick

him. "Mark my words! I will assuredly be as dangerous as any man you might meet on a battlefield! And Colonel, I'd be much obliged if you'd step outside the door before closing it again," she said.

"I can't rightly do that, ma'am," he said, sweeping down to pick up his hat and set it upon his head. He seemed affectionately attached to that hat.

"Why?"

"I'm bleeding."

"Is that supposed to mean something to me?" she demanded, suddenly furious. "Men bled and died all over my property—"

"You must excuse us for dying. We don't do it on purpose," he interrupted dryly.

Callie ignored his sarcasm. "You insult me, you invade my property—"

"I invade it!" he snapped back. "Lady, if you think this is something, you should see Virginia! Your armies have ripped it to shreds. There are miles and miles where nothing grows anymore, where there isn't a horse or a cow to be seen, where the children are half-starved! And you're going to tell me about invasions!"

She stepped away from the pain and the passion in his eyes.

"I lied for you, Colonel. I kept you from a prison camp. Now you can go on to kill dozens more Union soldiers. You could even kill my kin."

He leaned against the door, suddenly very weary again. "I could kill my own kin," he said softly. Then his eyes shot open again. "I'm very sorry, but you are going to help me. I am not going to bleed to death on your property!"

He suddenly gripped her hand and dragged her along with him into the kitchen. At the sink he began to pump water. Callie gritted her teeth, but she reached for a clean towel and soaked it, and when she had done so, she pressed it against the wound on his side. "Hold this!" she snapped.

He did so, and she dragged a chair over by the sink and stood on it and delved into a cupboard above it. She found some clean linens and brought them down, and began to rip them. "Lift your shirt!" she commanded him, and he did so.

Once again, she was uneasy at the closeness between them as she wound the linen around his bronzed torso. "It seems that whoever sewed you up didn't do a complete job. And they slander our Yankee surgeons!" she muttered.

His fingers were suddenly digging into her arm, drawing her eyes to his as she gasped at the jolt of pain.

"A Yankee surgeon sewed me up, Miss Stars and Stripes. And a damned good one. He just wasn't expecting me to be riding quite so hard so fast. He did the best damned job he could for me."

Startled, Callie stared up at him. "Why, you're kind to our side, Colonel. Why should a Yank do the best damned job for you?"

"Because he's my brother," he said impatiently. "Are you done?"

"Your brother?" Callie said, startled.

"My brother," he snapped flatly in return. He didn't intend to be questioned about his words—or his family.

Perhaps she shouldn't have been so surprised. Her own brothers had asked to fight on the western front, just so that they wouldn't be expected to shoot their neighbors or friends from Virginia. Maryland itself was a state with totally divided loyalties.

"Are you done?" He nearly bellowed the words this time.

Callie jerked away from him. "You're—bound up the best that I can do for you. Now will you please leave?"

He pulled down his shirt and tucked it into his

breeches, wincing slightly. He strode out to the parlor, his boots crunching over the glass. In the darkness, he opened the door and stared out over the fields. He stood there for the longest time, and she wondered what horrors of war he relived as he waited.

He finally closed the door and turned around, striding back toward her.

She moved away, but he didn't intend to touch her, it seemed. He strode in and pulled out a chair at the big oak table and sat. "Have you got anything to eat in here?" he asked her.

She didn't know why she suddenly felt so nervous in his presence. She wasn't afraid anymore. Despite his threats, she didn't believe that he would have really hurt her, no matter what she had done. Perhaps his chivalry was not the spoken kind. It had been in his eyes when he had looked out on the battlefield.

She wasn't afraid of him but she was becoming increasingly more aware of him as a man. Not as an enemy, not as a Reb. Just as a man. Aware of his height, his scent, his voice. His nearness. Even the way he sat with his long, booted legs stretched before him.

"Look, I've done everything that I can for you—"

"Right. There's nothing like a good kick in the head. You definitely owe me for that!"

"I did not kick you in the head!"

"I do beg to differ, darlin'. I felt it, that tender touch of your delicate foot!"

"I certainly didn't intend to."

"Then you would be merciful to your enemy, eh?"

"I've been damned merciful!"

He tilted back his hat. He watched her with heavy-lidded, curious eyes.

"But I am the enemy?"

She gripped the back of a kitchen chair. How dare he sit there in his gray uniform with his gaunt and haggard face and say such a thing to her.

"Yes! Yes, you are the enemy! And I don't owe you a damned thing! I've done far more for you than I should have done in all good conscience!"

"Why did you lie for me?" he asked curiously, his voice almost soft. A voice that seemed to reach out and touch her, moving like a warm breath along her spine.

"I don't know what you're talking about. You had a knife—"

"And you knew damned well that I'd never use it. I never even threatened you with it the last time."

"What difference does it make?" Callie asked impatiently. "Can't you just be grateful—and leave?"

He pulled the brim of his hat down very low, and it was a while before he answered her. "I'm starving. I haven't eaten or slept in hours and hours. And your Yankee patrols are going to be all over the place tonight."

Callie stood by the sink for a moment. She pursed her lips and reached over the sink for a match and lit a lamp to set on the table. She started down to the cellar, and he called her back sharply.

"Where are you going?"

"For food, Reb, if that's what it will take to make you leave."

She walked down the steps and found a large wedge of cheese and a smoked ham. She walked back up the steps and jumped when she discovered him waiting for her at the top.

"If I were going to turn you in," she told him, "I would have done so when Captain Johnston was here, Colonel Cameron."

One of his ink-dark brows shot up. "You know my name? Oh, of course! You discovered it when you were picking my pockets."

"I wasn't picking your pockets."

"Oh?" His brows arched high. "What were you looking for?"

She flushed despite the fact that she had every right to be furious with him for invading her house. "I thought you were dead," she said coolly. "I thought it might be provident to know your name."

"Oh," he murmured. He stepped aside, letting her pass. She set the cheese and ham on the table and was startled when he brushed past her. She didn't have a chance to give him a plate, she didn't even have a chance to cut him a piece of the cheese. He broke off a wedge of it, and wolfed it down.

"My, my, but they do teach good manners down in Virginia!" she said dryly. "He speaks with such eloquence and dines with such gentlemanly care!"

The gaze he cast her might have frozen fire. She determined to ignore it. She set a plate before him, and sliced the ham. "Colonel Cameron, I even have bread if you think you could wait—"

"No, I can't wait, but I'll have the bread too," he told her.

The loaf was much more than a day old, but Cameron didn't seem to notice as she set it on the table and he broke off a piece. An unlikely streak of pity swept through her. She had the feeling that the bread was probably amazingly fresh to this soldier, and that neither he nor his men had eaten much in a long, long time. He was right about one thing. So much of the war was taking place in the Shenandoah Valley and in the Virginia farmlands. It seemed that the North couldn't come up with the generals to best those in the South, but in time, it seemed, the South would be starved out.

It was war, Callie reminded herself. And it was probably one of the reasons that Lee had determined to bring the battle north for a change.

But while Southern soldiers endured endless days on small rations, they still managed to tear apart Northern soldiers. She owed this man no pity.

"What can I get you to drink, Colonel?" she asked with an edge to her voice.

"Whiskey? And coffee. Both would be wonderful."

"Of course."

She went to the cupboard and set a bottle of whiskey before him. "I'm sure you don't need a glass," she said. She lit the stove and measured out the coffee. When she was done, she discovered him staring at her. She discovered, too, that the plate he had ignored had been filled with food. For her. He pushed it across the table to her.

"Sit down." He thrust out a chair for her with his foot. "I'm sure you can't have eaten much."

She sat, staring at him. But she didn't touch the food.

"What's wrong? Can't you eat with a Reb?"

She shook her head. "I just can't eat yet," she said softly. The sarcasm was gone. They were both thinking about the battle.

He shoved the whiskey bottle across the table to her. "Take a swig. It will help you to forget. It's helped me a hell of a lot of times."

She started to shake her head again, but he said, "Take a swallow. A long swallow."

To her surprise, she did so. The whiskey burned. She choked, coughed, and swallowed again. The heat warmed her. And she did feel better.

She felt his eyes on her. They were fascinating eyes. They seemed as cold as ice, as hot as blue fire. They studied her as if they saw so very much of her.

"I think . . . I think the coffee is ready," she murmured. She stood up, found cups, and poured them both coffee. She sat down and set the mugs down, too. He topped off both of the cups with a measure of the whiskey.

"Relax, Miss . . . ?"

"What difference does my name make?"

"What difference does it make whether you tell me or not?" he countered.

"Callie. Callie Michaelson."

"Relax, Miss Michaelson."

"It's Mrs. Michaelson. And it is rather difficult to relax with the enemy in one's kitchen."

"Is it?"

"Yes."

"I'll be leaving before dawn. But then, of course, we do have the evening before us. And I need to get some sleep. Tell me, where is Mr. Michaelson?"

"Out in the yard," Callie said flatly. But if she expected to see some sign of fear or alarm in his eyes, she was disappointed.

"Dead and buried?" he asked.

"Yes."

"Where did he fall?"

"In a skirmish in Tennessee."

"When?"

"A little over a year ago."

"Well, Mrs. Michaelson, I was never in Tennessee, so I didn't kill your husband."

"I didn't suspect that you had."

"Ah. You simply hate all Rebel soldiers."

Callie swallowed down a gulp of her coffee and leapt to her feet. "I don't hate anyone. But you are the enemy. You just can't stay here any longer."

"I have to."

She turned around and strode out to the parlor. She heard him drink the last of his coffee and set down the cup. Then he followed her out. "You weren't thinking of leaving, were you, Miss Michaelson?"

"Frankly, yes. Since you're not."

"You can't go."

"Why?"

"I won't let you."

"But I haven't turned you in—"

"And that doesn't mean that you won't. I'm sorry. I'm really sorry. But I can't let you go."

She swore in exasperation. His dark brows shot up and he laughed. His face was really nice then. The enemy had charm.

But then he leaned against the wall by the broken windows and the once elegant parlor drapes. "What language for such a refined and sophisticated northern lass! And a beautiful one. Even more beautiful when you're swearing away in such a ladylike manner!"

There was a statuette on the table. A little statuette of Pan. Callie picked it up and hurled it at him.

It didn't matter much. Everything else in the house was ruined.

Her enemy ducked and laughed again.

"You really will be gone in the morning, Reb," she warned him. "Or I'll shoot you myself!"

"Will you?" he murmured, appraising her with interest. "Actually, you won't need to shoot me. If what you were out in the yard doing was helping me, you could just help me a little more, right into the grave. Would you really shoot me?"

"Yes! Oh, will you please leave then!"

"Oh, yes, I'll be leaving in the morning. I promise. And you'll be coming with me."

"What?"

Blue eyes, razor sharp, commanded hers. "You'll be coming with me, Mrs. Callie Michaelson. You're going to get me through the lines, and back to Virginia."

"You are insane! That is the last thing that I'm going to do! You had a nice meal, and you'll get a good night's sleep. I'll be damned if I'm going to be here when you wake up—"

"And I'll be damned if you're not!" he replied. With a sudden swift jerk he brought down the golden tassel and pull for the drapes. Before she knew it, the decorative rope was flung around her waist, and he was pulling her against him.

"What the hell do you think you're doing, Colonel?" Callie demanded, struggling fiercely.

It was all to no avail. She was swept up into his arms, and he was striding across the room to the stairway. "Going to bed. For that good night's sleep. And like it or not, Mrs. Michaelson, you'll be sleeping right beside me." Those blue eyes met hers once again. "Right beside me. You do owe me, Mrs. Michaelson. That's the way I see it, my angel."

"No, damn you, you Rebel bastard!" Callie swore. She tried to strike him. He held her closer.

He carried her up the stairs, heedless of her flailing arms.

"Yankee," he murmured softly to her, "it's going to be one hell of a night."

"Rebel bas—" Callie began.

But his arms slammed down hard on hers, and his eyes seemed to sear their blue fire into hers once more.

"One hell of a night!" he interrupted her. "I can promise you that!"

Four

The darkness at the top of the stairs seemed engulfing to Callie, but it didn't daunt her wayward cavalier in the least. He paused on the top landing for a moment, then headed for the closest doorway. Callie, breathless, exhausted, feeling the scrape of the wool of his uniform against her cheek, wondered desperately where he was finding his strength as they burst through the doorway into one of the bedrooms.

"What would your General Lee have to say?" she taunted. Lee might have been a Rebel commander, but he was equally famous in the North. He had been with the Union army when there had been no Confederacy, and Lincoln had once asked him to lead the Federal troops. But Lee's loyalties had been to his state, and when Virginia had seceded from the Union, Robert E. Lee had gone along with her. He was a man still known for his gallantry, for his ethics, and for his code of honor. Taunting this man about him was surely as damaging a blow as any she might throw with her fist.

"You just might have the opportunity to ask him, Mrs. Michaelson," Daniel Cameron replied, his deep drawl strangely intimate in the darkness.

A ripple of unease went sweeping through her. She should have been more frightened, she told herself. An enemy soldier was bearing her into a bedroom. It was darkly disturbing to realize that what swept through her was just as much a sense of excitement as it was fear. She wanted to do battle with this man. She didn't know if she wanted him to suffer for all that he was causing her, or if she had lived alone for so long that she was thrilled at the very thought of battle.

"Is this one your bedroom?" he asked suddenly.

She tensed. "What difference does it make?"

"None. I just want you to be comfortable."

"Comfortable?" Callie demanded. "How comfortable can I be, Colonel, caught in this vise against my will? And sure to suffer worse!"

His laughter suddenly rang out in the darkness, and she wondered if she had spoken too dramatically. In a second she was no longer held in any vise, he had set her down upon the bed. He may not have done so tenderly, but neither was he careless in his handling of her. He must have carried a matchbox, for in a moment there was a flare of light, and he saw the lamp upon her dresser and lit it. Hoisted quickly up on her elbows, Callie stared at him as he surveyed the room. He took in the fine white eyelet draperies on the windows, the braid rug on the hardwood floors, the polished mahogany dresser and wardrobe and washstand, and finally, the bed, with its beautifully carved headboard and footboard and white knit spread. It was her room, a warm, welcoming room, with imported tiles surrounding the hearth, and warm woolen blankets laid over the two rockers that sat right before the fireplace. Curiously, no bullets had strayed here. The soft eyelet drapes wafted lightly in the night breeze, untouched. She wondered if the Reb colonel thought about that fact as he surveyed the room, but his sharp blue eyes gave away none of his thoughts.

With the lamp lit, Callie could see the pallor in his handsome features. How was he still standing?

He started to unbuckle his scabbard, still surveying the room. Again, unease came sweeping through her system. What did he intend? She swallowed hard, and determined that she would fight to her very last breath for her honor.

He cast his scabbard and sword onto the side chair and sat for a moment. Then his gaze came down hard on her once again.

She gritted her teeth. Well, he was welcome to stay here. She would not do so.

She leapt up, praying that she might be granted speed and endurance while the weight of his injuries fell upon him at last.

But even as she sprinted for the door, he was up, and she went flying straight into his arms.

She cast back her head, and their eyes met. There was a certain amount of humor in his.

"You're not going anywhere, Yank. Sorry," he told her.

"Let me go. You've no right to hold me here at all."

"I have to hold you here."

"You're supposed to be gallant and fighting for the honor of the South! It's your duty—"

"I consider living through this one of my duties, too, Mrs. Michaelson. So you just might—"

"You can't stay here. In my room! With—me!"

His brows shot up suddenly. His hands on her shoulders were warm and firm. She felt his nearness with the length of her body. He smiled. Slowly. A handsome, lazy, compelling smile. Long ago, at some distant ball, while the whippoorwills trilled and the moss hung low over old trees, that smile must have melted many a heart.

Now it also held a little bit of bitterness, and even, perhaps, a shade of wistfulness. Here was a hardened soldier, an enemy long in the field, probably a veteran of nearly every battle in the eastern theater of this war.

He was amused. "Why, Mrs. Michaelson, just what are you afraid of? Me?"

"Certainly not. You are merely a very rude—and I might add muddy—Rebel soldier. I'm not afraid of you a single bit."

"Why not? Is there a Yankee in the wardrobe, waiting to protect you?"

She didn't know if he was taunting her, or if he was really suspicious of her.

"Perhaps there is a Yankee in the wardrobe," she returned swiftly. "Perhaps you should leave me be and run as swiftly as you can!"

"Hmm . . . Let's see, it's Captain Eric Dabney I need to fear, right?"

"Yes, you should be running just as fast as you can."

He started to laugh. "Ah. Captain Dabney has been biding his time in a wardrobe all these hours. He doesn't mind a Rebel dining with you, but now that you feel truly threatened by a member of the Confederacy, he's going to come jumping out."

"He just might."

Cameron ran his knuckles over her cheek, so softly that the touch might have been just the warmth of a nearby whisper. But she felt the warmth come sweeping into her, felt it spiral and curl and flow up and down the length of her spine.

"A damsel in distress," he murmured.

"Pardon?"

"Nothing," he said, then he smiled again, meeting her eyes. "If I'd been in your wardrobe, Mrs. Michaelson, I'd have been out of it long ago. I'd have had a sword to the throat of any man who came within inches of you. I don't think that Captain Dabney is hereabouts. And I do think that you're afraid of me."

"Well, I'm not!" But she was! Not so much of his violence, though there was violence in him. What she feared was the tenderness of his touch.

"Not a bit?" he taunted.

She tried to pull away.

"Not even a little bit?" he repeated. He laughed softly.

Her chin lifted, and her eyes met his. Her body was flush with his so that she could feel the beat of his heart.

And he could feel the frantic pulse of hers.

"Callie Michaelson, there is a pulse fluttering along your throat like wildfire. You've had it right from the beginning. Once upon a time I was taught manners. My mother was gracious and sweet, and she taught the three of us all about the feelings of others. And yet that seems so very long ago now. War does strange things to people. Did you know that?"

His hold upon her was tight. She felt panic creeping into her despite her sure conviction that he would never hurt her.

"Afraid yet?" he demanded, his eyes ablaze.

To her amazement, her passion and courage held out. "I'll never be afraid of the likes of you, you gray-bellied hooligan!" she swore.

His laughter rang out pleasantly. Before she knew it, he had turned her around by the shoulders. "Don't worry, Mrs. Michaelson. There is no reason for you to be afraid. I have absolutely no evil designs upon you."

She swung around again to face him. "I didn't think that you—"

"Oh yes, you did! And now you're indignant that I don't."

"I most certainly am not—"

"Oh yes, you are. Well, calm down. It isn't that you aren't beautiful. And I am assuredly entranced, and I imagine, once you set your mind upon it, you could seduce a saint."

"How dare you—" Callie began furiously. But he

was still laughing, and very quick to interrupt her. "I'm merely trying to set your mind at ease!"

"The hell you are!" She swore, her hands on her hips.

Her language only served to amuse him further. "Mrs. Michaelson, they should have you on the field. You certainly do not retreat!"

"I don't retreat, and I don't lose, and I never, never surrender—" she began.

Before she could go further, a soft cry escaped her as his hands fell upon her shoulders again. This time he swung her around in a no-nonsense fashion and gave her a good prod. She went flying back down upon her bed, and quickly rolled to face him, ever wary once again.

"I don't want to hurt you or frighten you."

"Really?" Callie retorted sarcastically, her eyes narrowing.

"Really." He bent low over her, his arms like bars on either side of her as he braced himself over her. "Not that I wouldn't want you!" he whispered, and the sound was serious and deep and husky, one that seemed to sink into her body and leave her both hot and shivery. He spoke again, and this time he sounded exhausted. "I have to get some sleep. And you are a Yank, and I can't trust you. You're going to stay with me."

He pushed away from her. Her eyes widened with alarm because he had his belt off and was approaching her with it.

She opened her mouth to scream, amazed, thinking that he meant to beat her with it. But before she could even whisper, he was straddled over her, his finger pressed against her lip.

"Mrs. Michaelson, believe it or not, there is some sense of honor nesting in this Rebel bosom, and believe it or not, I've no real desire to cause you stress or pain. But I have to sleep, and I can't let you go roaming around on your own while I'm at it. Understand?"

She stared at him, still wary, uncertain whether to move or not. "Do you understand?" He asked the question in a softer tone.

She nodded, certain that if she didn't do so, he'd find a way of pressing his point.

"Good," he said softly. To her dismay, he looped the belt over her arm and then around his own. He looked down at her for a long, stern moment of warning.

Then he pitched forward, falling over her and coming to rest at her side.

For several moments, Callie lay perfectly still, feeling the beating of his heart and the frantic clamor of her own. Seconds passed, minutes. He didn't move, and neither did she.

He had passed out cold.

What tremendous strength of will he must have to taunt her so coolly, when he was so very close to total collapse!

For one frantic moment Callie was afraid that he had died. That she was tied in bed to a dead man. But then she felt his heartbeat again, felt the rise and fall of his chest where he lay beside her.

She closed her eyes, inhaling and exhaling slowly. She should have prayed for his death, for it seemed to be the only way that she would find her own escape. He was the enemy. Perhaps he had never been in Tennessee, perhaps he hadn't fought at Shiloh. He should have remained one of the nameless, faceless soldiers in gray who was her enemy.

She didn't want him to die in her house, she told herself. But if he had passed out again she needed to be quick and free herself from him. There still had to be Union soldiers in the near vicinity. This battlefield that had encompassed her home had been so littered

with the dead and dying that it would surely take days
to clear the bodies.

The thought made her ill, and she closed her eyes
tightly. But even with her eyes closed, she kept reliving
the horror of all that she had seen in her yard. She
opened her eyes again, and turned carefully to view the
Rebel face she was coming to know so well.

He was very pale, and his face was damp. He was
probably far more seriously injured than he cared to
admit and she could judge. If he was sent on to a prison
camp, he most assuredly would die.

She couldn't allow that to be her problem, she told
herself sternly. She had given her loyalty to the Union,
and before God she knew herself right to have done so.
She had not been influenced by her father, or her
brothers, or even her own husband. All around her, in
the state of Maryland, men had split on all the questions about the war. In the beginning it had been a
question of states' rights—but that question had been
there mainly because of slavery. Maryland was filled
with slave owners.

Maryland had troops fighting with the South, and
troops fighting with the North. The state had not seceded from the Union, but there was probably no
other place where it was more likely for a father to face
a son down the length of his rifle, or for a brother to
come front to front with a brother.

She had weighed and judged all that she heard, listening to her father, her brothers, and her husband. In
the end, she had concluded that they were one nation,
and that the Union must be preserved. Though many
of her neighbors owned slaves, she had asked Gregory
to free the five hands that he had owned, and Gregory
had obliged her. It was simply wrong to own a man, to
keep him in bondage, to whip him, to abuse him, to
strip him of his dignity. Though many slaves were well
cared for—just as their master's pet hounds and finest

horses were well cared for—Callie knew of few slaves
who had been left with their pride and dignity intact.

She had made up her own mind about the war.
Luckily, she had been in agreement with those closest
to her. That meant that the Rebel lying beside her was
indeed the enemy. And the war was far from over. The
Rebels had battered the Union forces time and time
again.

Rebel soldiers had brought about destruction. Just
as they had destroyed her father and Gregory.

She twisted with discomfort and with a raw edge of
anguish, thinking of her husband. Even now, she dared
not dwell upon his death too long.

Colonel Daniel Cameron. She bit her lip, and she
tried to pull her arm closer to herself. She needed to
slip her arm free of the loop he had fashioned from his
belt. She grit her teeth. She gently pulled at the loop he
had made, and then more aggressively. She couldn't
budge the knot.

She swore out loud. It didn't matter. Colonel Cameron wasn't moving.

Near tears, she continued to tug at the leather. The
more she worked at it, the tighter it became.

She tried to slide the loop down her arm. Again, her
efforts only served to bind her more tightly.

"You son of a bitch!" she swore out loud to him.

She could have sworn that even in his unconscious
state he smiled at her distress.

But his eyes remained closed, and his breathing became more ragged.

She sat up, tugging upon his arm and the loop of the
belt that tied him to her. The leather was tied from his
wrist to hers, with perhaps fifteen inches between
them. He had tied the knots so tightly she could not
budge them. She fought urgently with the leather,
breaking her nails. Tears of frustration stung her eyes.

He had known what he was doing. He was the most adept man with a knot she had ever met.

Worn, desolate, she flung herself back against the bed. The lamp was burning low. The night had become cool, and there was no fire burning in the hearth. She lay still, her teeth grating, her mind working furiously.

She remembered his sword.

She sat up. It lay against one of the rockers by the hearth. If she could just reach it, she could sever the leather that bound them together.

She lay flat and reached for the chair, her arm outstretched. She could just touch the chair with the tip of her fingers. She bit into her lip, and tugged upon her captor. Nothing. She paused, breathing hard. She tugged again. It seemed that he moved, just a hair. But she came closer to the sword hilt too.

. Silently, she began to pray, and in seconds, she was victorious. Her fingers curled around the hilt of his blade. She was startled by the weight of it, bearing down on her free arm, but she grit her teeth, determined. Suddenly, the blade came free from his scabbard, with such a force that she could not control it. It seemed to fly through the air, and then it struck down upon the braid rug beneath her bed with an incredible force and a snap that sounded like a sure hit by cannon fire.

She tried to lift it, and twist it again, and even as she did so, a startled cry escaped her.

The sound had awakened her weary Reb. Pale, drawn, tense—and seeming to breathe smoke rings of fury—he stared at her. With amazing speed and agility he reached over her, and snatched the sword from her grasp with an ease born of familiarity and skill. He was so angry that she cried out again, certain that he meant to let the blade fall upon her, slicing her in two.

He tossed the sword aside, and his staring eyes were

as hard and cold and striking as the blade. "You meant
to kill me!" he whispered.

"No!"

"Ah, you did not mean to kick me, but your foot
connected fiercely with my head! And you did not
mean to slay me—rather, my sword jumped into your
hand!"

"I meant to free myself from you!" she cried.

"One way or the other," he suggested harshly.

"I want to be free!"

"Well, you can't! Not tonight!" With a jerk, he
brought her hurtling back against him. She lay dead
still and furious, dismayed that he believed with no
uncertainty that she had meant to kill him if she could.

"Please, Mrs. Michaelson!" The whisper touched
her ear. "Please, just go to sleep. Things will look better for both of us in the morning."

A startled gasp escaped her as she was pulled more
closely against him. She was turned, and his arm came
around her, a gray band against the very thought of
movement.

A gray-clad leg fell over her own. She caught her
breath. She could feel his hand, just below her breast.
She could feel the length of him pressed against the
length of her back and limbs.

She did not move again. She barely dared to breathe.

In time, she did as he had commanded. She slept.

Heat encompassed him.

It was summer, and they were lying on the slope
above the river once again, Jesse, Christa, and him. He
could feel the sun, and he should have felt the ever soft
breeze that came in off the river, no matter how hot
and humid the day came to be. But the breeze
wouldn't come.

He knew why. The cannons were exploding. They
were exploding all around him.

Suddenly, he and Jesse were alone, riding away from Harpers Ferry. They were both in blue, and coming away from the assault on the fire-engine house where old John Brown had holed up with his few surviving raiders. He could hear John Brown, shouting around them, again and again.

". . . blood, this land shall be purged by blood . . ."

He looked from his brother's wary face down to his hands, where they lay idly upon the pommel of his saddle.

His hands were covered in blood.

It seemed that more bombs exploded. He was back at Cameron Hall, and he was standing by the cemetery. Clasping Jesse. There were no words that passed between them. The rift that had driven apart the country had also driven them apart.

His brother was riding north.

Skyrockets seemed to burst and soar.

He heard crying. Christa crying, Kiernan crying. Jesse was going away.

The skyrockets were soaring over Fort Sumter. It was April 1861. The war had begun.

He tossed and turned.

He was riding hard. He always rode hard, for he was part of General James Ewell Brown "Jeb" Stuart's fantastic cavalry. They could ride circles around almost any army. They could move endless miles in unbelievable time. They saw action again and again and again, scouting, circling, carrying information vital to Jackson and Lee.

He shouldn't have been back with his troops. He'd been wounded when Union General McClellan had made his abortive attack on the peninsula, and it had only been because he had been found by his own brother that he had avoided a prison camp. Jesse had sewn him up, and Jesse had carried him home.

In his restless sleep, Daniel twisted and turned again. Hot, it was so hot. He was back at Cameron Hall again, looking out over the James. He heard the cry of a child, and smiled. War brought death, and war brought life. Jesse's son had been born, a strapping baby boy. So tiny. The baby's little fingers had barely managed to curl around his own.

Jesse had had precious little time with his child. McClellan's troops had retreated, and it was imperative that Jesse leave behind him the Rebel-held land where he had been born.

Once again the brothers had said good-bye, and Daniel had been summoned back to duty.

With General Thomas "Stonewall" Jackson, he had been part of the army Lee had split in half for this daring invasion north. They had captured the town of Harpers Ferry—now being called "West Virginia"—and the thousands of Federal troops that had been holding it. Then, with no sleep and precious little food, they had ridden hard to meet up with Lee in this tiny town of Sharpsburg, Maryland. Under special assignment to Lee, he had seen much of the battle. Too much of the battle. He had seen the area they were already calling "Bloody Lane"—the deep trench along the farmlands where the Rebels had dug in. Where they had held so fiercely until the line had been broken and the Federal forces had rained down upon them with shot. Where bodies were piled upon bodies that were piled upon bodies.

He tossed and turned. He looked up. She was there. His angel. The beautiful angel with the fantastic dove-gray eyes and wealth of deep flaming auburn hair.

She leaned over him. She smelled so sweetly. Like the summer rose. She should have belonged to the past. To the beautiful, lazy days along the river. To the great, porticoed back porch of Cameron Hall. She should have been dressed in muslins and hooped petticoats, and she should have sat upon the wicker swing. Breezes, soft and sweet, should have played over her hair. He could see her, a great straw hat shading her eyes, swinging, white gloves upon her hands. An angel, she would turn to him. Her laughter would be music, as beautiful as her wide gray eyes, framed by the black sweep of her lashes.

Yes, she was there. Home, where the river whispered its faint harmony, where the green grasses met with blue sky and green water. Where Cameron Hall stood with its grace and welcoming beauty. Where the oaks were covered in moss. She was there, running through the trees. He heard her laughter, soft, clear, delicate, like the sound of the wind chimes in March. Against an oak she paused, looking back, her laughter escaping her once again. It was contagious, and he laughed in turn, and ran after her once again. Upon the slope, above the river, where dreams were woven, he caught her at last, and laughing together, they rolled in the sweet scent of the rain-washed lawn while the river drifted lazily by. He stared into her eyes. So intriguing a gray, rimmed with deep dark blue. He touched her cheek and held his angel.

Angel! Yes, an avenging angel who wielded a sword.

Visions began to collide. The river no longer whispered. He felt the heat, the terrible heat. But she was still there.

She was speaking to him. He tried very hard to understand her.

". . . you must help me. You have to try to help me get free of this belt. Colonel, if I don't cool you down, you'll die. Don't you understand me?"

Cameron Hall faded clear away. He was drenched. He was hot, he was shivering. Lamplight flickered against the handsomely decorated room. He lay upon a white bedspread, and it was no angel, but his gray-eyed Yankee vixen who leaned over him.

It only appeared that those dove-gray eyes were filled with compassion. She had meant to slay him once. He was nearly at her mercy now. He could almost taste death, it seemed that close.

"Colonel, listen to me!" she pleaded with him.

"Can't!" he whispered.

"Please! I don't want you dying on me!"

He almost smiled. Her voice. So soft. So musical. It should have been an angel's voice.

"You'll turn me in." His words must have been very low, for she leaned against him to try to catch them.

"Colonel, you have to have some faith in me! Help me with this! I must cool you down. I swear to you, I'll not leave you like this—"

He fought for strength. He managed to wind his fingers around her arm. His eyes met hers.

"Honor," he interrupted her.

"What?"

"On your honor?"

"What?" she repeated. "Oh!" she breathed. She hesitated a moment. His eyes started to flicker closed. He was losing consciousness again.

"On my honor, Colonel! I'll not leave you. Set me free, and I'll not leave you."

"Unless I die," he commanded her.

"Don't—"

"Unless I die!" he repeated.

"Fine! On my honor, I'll stay with you. Unless you die," she said.

His fingers were shaking. He could scarcely raise his hand, scarcely control it. He found the loop on his wrist. For a moment, he fumbled. He didn't have the strength. He caught the leather with his teeth. He pulled with his last strength. She was free.

She was up in a flash. His last thought was that she had lied, that she had deserted him as soon as physically possible.

It didn't matter. The room spun and faded.

Cannons exploded. He was in the midst of a fire. Fire was all around him, engulfing him. . . .

It seemed to be much, much later that he first felt the coolness of the cloth against him.

He savored that coolness.

It touched his forehead, and moved over his shoulders. He no longer shook, but lay there, weak, disoriented. At first, all he knew was that sensation of coolness. Had he died at last, and gone to heaven? After all, how many times could he taunt death?

Was this a Yank prison? Did they heal him now, just to make his stay more wretched, until he could succumb to some other evil?

This was so tender, so gentle a touch.

He opened his eyes. They widened still further. She was still with him. Mrs. Callie Michaelson. His shirt was gone, he lay on his back, and she moved a cool, water-drenched cloth over and over his naked chest. She continued to do so for several long minutes before her eyes met his. She jumped, suddenly aware that he had been watching her.

"You're still here," he tried to say. The words were little more than a croak.

"I gave you my word of honor that I would remain," she said. Her hand had stopped moving. It lay upon the cloth just over his heart.

He willed himself to find some strength. His fingers curled around her wrist. "You'd keep your word to a Reb?" he asked her softly.

"My word, sir, is a vow—no matter to whom it is given."

He smiled slowly. "Well, then, I thank you, Mrs. Michaelson. You've probably saved my life."

She stood up, gently tugging her wrist from his grasp.

Regretfully, still curious as he surveyed her fascinating eyes, he released her.

"Not probably, Reb," she told him. "I've most certainly saved your life. You were burning up. But it seems that your fever has abated. Let me get you some water to drink. I've barely managed to get a few glasses into you. Then I'll get you something to eat, and when darkness falls again, you can go."

She poured him a large glass of water from the pitcher at his bedside. Daniel sipped it at first. Then it suddenly seemed to be the most delicious thing that he had ever tasted. He swallowed down the whole of it in a matter of seconds. God, it was good.

She took the glass from him.

"Now, Colonel, you can rest, and I'll get you some soup. But I warn you, I do feel that my word to you has been fulfilled. You are the enemy. And I want you gone."

So battle was thus reengaged, he thought. Indeed, it was so, for there was a silver light in her eyes, shimmering, beautiful—and certainly something to reckon with.

He frowned suddenly, catching her wrist once more. He stared at her, a demand in his eyes. "You said, 'when darkness comes again'?"

"Yes, Colonel, you've come in and out of consciousness for nearly forty-eight hours now."

Two days! He had lost two full days.

She had stayed with him. She had not gone for the Yankee troops, and there must have been many Yankee troops in the vicinity.

Because of her word?

Once he had awakened to the certainty that she was trying to cut him down with his sword. But now she was still here with him. Because of her, he had survived another battle. But now she had warned him that he was her enemy.

"I have to get up," he said and started to throw the sheets back.

"No!" she exclaimed. "Colonel, wait!" For a few fleeting seconds her eyes seemed wide, alarmed. She stepped back demurely, her rich lashes falling over her eyes, but her manner entirely calm and regal. "You might not want to do that, sir."

"Why not?"

"Because you're buck naked beneath that sheet."

Stunned into momentary silence, Daniel stared at her blankly.

She sighed with impatience. "Colonel, I had to soak you in the coldest water I could find. I needed to cool down the length of your body for any hope of fighting the fever."

"So you—stripped me?"

"Don't sound so outraged, Colonel." Her words were slow and cool, and she lifted a delicate brow to a high and imperious angle. "I told you. I had no choice."

"What have you done with my uniform?"

"Your uniform was full of mud and blood." She smiled. "I burned it. My apologies. It really wasn't at all salvageable."

"It wasn't salvageable?"

"No more so than your lost cause, Colonel Cameron."

"Lost cause, ma'am? Why, it still seems to me that we Rebs are riding circles around you Yanks."

"You will not be victorious."

"I, ma'am, will be," he promised her.

"Then I must thank goodness, Colonel Cameron, that the war will not depend on one man alone."

Mrs. Callie Michaelson could be one very demure and confident woman, Daniel thought. He didn't know if he was outraged or not.

He smiled slowly, not knowing if he wanted to taunt

her, or throw his arms around her and drag her down
with him and show her all of the very real dangers of
stripping down a man who had been at war as long as
he had.

He'd never do such a thing. His sense of honor
wasn't really half as tarnished as she seemed to think.

Actually, he wasn't sure that he had the energy left
to drag her down beside him.

"Are you all right, Colonel?" she inquired. She
knew she had the upper hand at the moment, and that
he knew it. Those beautiful gray eyes were awfully
smug.

"I'm just fine, Mrs. Michaelson. If anything, I'm surprised that a gentlewoman such as yourself would show
such mercy as to strip down a Rebel soldier. I am
amazed. How alarming it must have been for you!
Such danger you cast yourself into!"

Her lashes swept her cheeks again, but he failed to
draw a blush.

"Colonel, it seems to me that beneath the fabric, be
it blue or gray, men do seem to be very much alike. I
found nothing alarming about the act at all, and my
dear Colonel, I must say, I hardly found you . . . dangerous."

With that she spun around and started toward the
stairs.

Daniel's smile deepened. He closed his eyes. He had
lost two full days. He didn't know what was happening,
and he didn't know where he needed to get to rejoin
his men or Stuart.

For the first time since the war had begun, he decided that he had to allow himself a certain period of
convalescence. He had to get through the lines to get
home. The cavalry would be awaiting him somewhere
in Virginia.

But for the moment, he determined there was something else equally important.

He wanted Mrs. Callie Michaelson to know that he could be dangerous when he chose. Damned dangerous.

He rose, pulling the sheet with him and wrapping it around his waist. He paused for several minutes, finding the strength to stand. Life and energy slowly eased back into his limbs. He flexed his fingers and then his arms. He became certain that, weak as he was, he was not going to keel over with his first step.

With the white tail of sheet following him like a bridal train, he left the room and walked carefully down the stairs.

It was time to confront his enemy angel once again.

So there was no difference between men, was there?

She wanted battle? Well, battle was thus engaged.

She was about to discover that, indeed, there were very real differences between men.

Five

Callie wasn't at all sure she had managed to appear calm and completely unruffled in front of her uninvited guest. By the time she reached the kitchen, her palms were very damp and her heart seemed to be thundering at a thousand pulses a minute. She nearly splashed the stew she had been cooking all over her fingers when she went to stir the large pot over the stove.

She was so much more comfortable with him when he was unconscious!

No, God forgive her, she hadn't just been comfortable. She had actually enjoyed caring for him.

It hadn't been easy at first. He had been on fire, his flesh simply burning, and she had been powerless, bound as she was to him. No matter how he had kicked and thrashed and turned, no matter how hotly he had burned, he had maintained a fierce strength. She hadn't been able to free herself from the binds he had created between them and she hadn't been able to get through to him. Alone in the darkness she had imagined his dying, and herself bound to him day after day while his body decayed.

But she had known it had been more than the fear of being tied to a dead man that had so frightened her. She didn't want him to die. Cocky, arrogant Rebel that

he might be, he had put something of challenge and
vitality back into her own life.

And he was, in his masculine way, beautiful.

That was what she had enjoyed.

She'd not thought this at all at first. Once she had
convinced him to free her, she had cut away his clothing because of the mud and the blood that matted his
chest and his abdomen. And then she had been so busy
soaking his flesh that she had paid it little heed. Tire-
lessly, she had run up and down the steps, fetching
more and more water from the pump. She had opened
all of the windows to cool the room, and then she had
soaked him again and again.

It had been well into the day when she had known
that she had succeeded, that he was going to live. He
didn't open his eyes, he didn't speak—he gave her very
little sign of life. But the awful heat began to cool, and
his flesh was no longer so horribly dry to the touch. He
breathed more easily. The fever was gone. He slept a
sweeter sleep.

It was then that she dared to look at the man she had
tended so long. From the handsome features that had
so intrigued her from the beginning to the broad planes
of his shoulders. His well-muscled torso and arms were
taut and cleanly defined, making his skin smooth to her
stroke now that the fever had broken. There was a wild
profusion of dark hair upon his chest, hair as ebony as
that upon his head, its course of growth just as defined
as his muscle tone, swirling across his breast, than narrowing down to a fine little whorl at his navel. That fine
lean line continued to his groin, where the wild nest of
darkness flared deep again. Against it lay that part of
him that brought a wildness to her heart, for even as he
slept his maleness seemed to have a life of its own,
veins pulsing vibrantly, his natural endowment both in-
timidating and tempting despite his restful state. She
was absolutely shocked to find herself so fascinated to

touch him, and very glad then of his sleep, for she must
have blushed a thousand shades of purple. Indeed, she
had turned him over so as not to find such a fascination
with his anatomy, but then she had discovered herself
admiring his back and, worse, his buttocks. From head
to toe he was excellently muscled, so taut, so trim, so
sleek and beautiful, like an exceptionally fine wild animal.

He wasn't a wild animal, she reminded herself. He
was worse. He was a Rebel soldier.

But while he lay there unconscious, she needn't
think of what he was, she told herself, or why she had
worked so strenuously to save him. The breeze shifted,
fall had come. Though the day was gentle and cool
enough, she was suddenly made aware of the scent of
death that still hung heavy upon the air so near the
battlefield.

She closed the window and pulled the sheets up to
his waist. She closed her eyes, holding her breath while
memories assailed her. Once upon a time, not so very
long ago, she had been in love. And she had been
loved in turn. They had both been so young, at first
exchanging shy, hesitant kisses in the fields, then ex-
ploring those kisses more deeply in the dark of the
barn. They'd been very. proper, of course, never
dreaming of discovering any more of one another until
their wedding night, but then that night had come, and
love itself had led the way. Their first night had been
awkward, but their love had let them laugh, and in the
days and nights that followed, they had learned that
their laughter was but an added boon. Callie had
learned to cherish her young husband's kisses, to thrill
to his touch, to awaken in his arms.

But Gregory Michaelson now lay out back, his
young limbs decimated by war, his soul surely risen,
but his body nothing more than food for the ever triumphant worms. When he had come home to her in a

military-issue coffin, she had been cold. Her heart had been colder than death itself, she was convinced. She would never love again, she swore it.

And she had never felt tempted to love again. No matter what soldiers came passing through, no matter what friend her brothers brought by so quickly on their few days of grace from the army, she had never known the slightest whisper of warmth to come to her heart.

Her heart had not warmed now, she assured herself.

But something else had.

Since she had first seen his face, she had found it attractive. From the first time his startling blue eyes had fallen upon hers, she had felt faint stirrings within herself. She had never felt fear that had been greater than her sense of excitement around him.

She had known, from somewhere deep within her soul, that she could not bear him to die. Not because she feared being bound to a dead man, but because it was him.

And now, in caring for him, she discovered herself ever more attracted to him. She wanted to forget the war. She wanted to go back and pretend that it had never come. She wanted him to be Gregory, and she wanted to lie down beside him and feel the warmth of his body stealing into hers, know the sweet rush of excitement that could sweep away all sense and reason.

Shivering, she stared into the pot of bubbling stew. The war had come. It was very real. The young blond Maryland farmer she had loved and married was buried in the yard, and she was a widow. A respectable, moral widow. She should be shamed by the very thoughts filling her head. Shamed by the beat of her heart. By the nervousness that shivered through her, by the recklessness that haunted all of her being.

He would leave tonight.

"That smells wonderful."

She jumped, spinning around. He had followed her

down the stairs and stood lounging comfortably in the doorway.

He was wearing her sheet. It was stark white against the sleek bronze of his torso. His nakedness had been imposing enough while he slept. Now the taut ripples of muscle against his lean belly seemed downright decadent.

"What do you think you're doing?" she demanded. She wanted to be righteously angry. Her voice was faltering.

He lifted his hands innocently. "What do you mean?"

"Colonel Cameron," she said with soft dignity, her eyes narrowing warningly upon his, "you come from a good home. I do believe, sir, that you come from a landed home, that you probably went to the best schools, and that you were raised to be a gentleman. So what are you doing in my kitchen in a sheet?"

"Well now, Mrs. Michaelson," he taunted, blue eyes flashing, "should I have dropped the sheet?"

"This from a man who lives and walks due to my mercy," she retorted.

He shrugged, walking across the kitchen, coming uncomfortably close to stir the stew and inhale its sweet aroma. "Mrs. Michaelson, from your comments, I assumed that you found me no more threatening in any state of dress or undress than you would find a toddling lad of two. And besides, you've burned my uniform. A grave injustice, I daresay, but as you've just reminded me, I must be grateful for your mercy. So what would you have me wear?"

"I'd have you back in bed, resting, gathering your strength, so as to leave this evening," she told him.

He smiled and went to sweep his hat from his head, then realized that he was no longer in dress of any kind. "Ah, well, the uniform can be replaced. I was quite fond of the hat. Was it necessary to burn it too?"

"Quite," Callie said.

"A pity."

"I think not. There are breeches and shirts in the wardrobe in my room. The fit may not be perfect, but I'm sure you'll manage."

"Union uniforms?" he asked her.

She shrugged. "I'm not sure, to tell you the truth," she said.

"I'm not escaping in a Union uniform, Mrs. Michaelson."

"I'm sure that you wore blue at some point, Colonel. You mentioned that your brother was a Yankee surgeon, so I find it quite possible that you were both in the military before secession and this war of rebellion came about. It'll not hurt you to wear blue once again."

"I prefer the sheet, thank you."

He stood by the pot on the stove, so intimately close to her that she felt the urge to scream. She fought for control, determined that he'd never best her. Perhaps that was part of the excitement. He made her determined to win. He challenged her on so many different levels.

She smiled sweetly, turning to stir the stew and managing to take a step farther away from him. "You plan to run through the Yankee lines in a sheet, Colonel?"

"Better a sheet than a Yankee uniform, Mrs. Michaelson." He took the ladle from her fingers, dipped it into the stew, and tasted it. His eyes came instantly back to hers, and he arched a brow, a slow smile curling his lip. "It's wonderful, Mrs. Michaelson. Really, Providence must have had mercy to have left me here, upon your doorstep."

"Providence was just wonderful," Callie muttered, snatching the ladle back from him. "Would you please go and put something on?"

He was quiet, watching her. She could feel his eyes

just like she could feel the heat of a flame when a candle was too close.

"Truly, Callie, I cannot wear a Yankee uniform. I am not a spy, and would not be caught and hanged as one, unless I were, indeed, involved in some necessary subterfuge. I don't relish the thought of dying in battle, but in the line of one's duty, it is, at the least, an honorable way to perish. I'd not hang unless such a death could, in truth, do justice to my cause."

"Oh!" Callie murmured. She hadn't been thinking. It was true. If Yankee troops caught him in his own uniform, they would call him a prisoner of war. And he might waste away in a prison camp, but unless he came upon them with his sword swinging or his guns blazing, they'd not hang him. Spies were dealt with harshly in this war. Why, in Washington, they'd even imprisoned Mrs. Rose Greenhow, a lady who had once been considered a belle of the capital's society. There were many suggestions that even she might be executed, although Callie tried to convince herself that the poor lady would not come to such an end.

"Callie, surely you did not offer me so much mercy so very tenderly, only that I should be well when I was hanged?"

"I was never tender," she informed him.

"So, you did intend that I should be hanged."

"No, sir, I did not," she said irritably. She waved the ladle at him, taking a step forward, determined that he should retreat. "Colonel—"

He took the ladle back from her. "Really, Mrs. Michaelson, I have been attacked by swords and cannons and guns, but I am weary still, and haven't the heart to defend myself from a soup ladle!"

In exasperation she grated out a soft oath. "Colonel, surely your mama would be quite horrified to see her son in a young woman's kitchen garbed in nothing but her sheet!"

"My mother, ma'am, was a sage and careful lady and would surely have been as matter-of-fact as you yourself have been. She would be grateful that you had saved my life, however, and I'm quite convinced that she wouldn't even ask why I found it necessary to be clad in nothing but a sheet."

"Colonel, I am about to throw you out in that sheet!" she warned him.

"Cast me naked to the wolves, eh?"

"You forget, I am a Yankee. Those are but the wolves I run with myself."

"No," he said softly, "I do not forget."

A curious shiver swept through her as he said the words and as his gaze met hers with a startling blue sizzle. Since she was hardly a danger to him at the moment, she didn't understand the strange dread that filled her, almost like a premonition.

She took another step away from him. "Well," she murmured, "I cannot bring back your uniform. I did burn it. You'll have to find something. There should be enough civilian clothing to choose from." She stared him up and down. "My husband was not, perhaps, so tall, but . . ." She paused, then shrugged. "My father's breeches might well fit you. And my brother's shirts are in a trunk just down the hallway."

"I take it that I am not invited to dinner unless I am decently clad?" he said. His voice was light, a tone that teased. Were he not naked, he might easily have had the manner of the Virginia gentleman he surely once had been. The effect upon her was both sweeping and alarming, for she smiled quickly, wishing he were not capable of being quite so charming.

"You most certainly are not," she assured him.

He bowed to her in a courtly gesture. "Then I will return as decently clad as I can manage."

He turned with his sheet trailing. She watched him

for a moment, then sank her teeth into her lower lip, fighting the sudden temptation to cry.

War had changed everything. It had stolen everything from her. And now it had brought the enemy to her doorstep, and even robbed her of the luxury of hating him.

She turned back to the stew, impatient with herself. While he was gone, she set the table. She had had precious little time to do much about the house while she had tended him over the last hours, but she had managed to pick up the kitchen and sweep up all the glass that had littered the living room. She wondered if she hadn't become obsessive, or partly crazed, for it seemed to her now that it was almost ridiculously important to behave as if life and the passing days were just as normal as any others.

Of course, the days weren't normal at all. Union soldiers had passed by this afternoon, still trying to collect all of the dead from the battlefield. A sergeant to whom she had nervously offered a dipper of cold water that afternoon had been near parchment-white when he had stumbled onto the porch. Before realizing that he was speaking to a young lady—and that manners dictated he take grave care to make his words delicate —he had told her about a trench the Rebels had been holding, and how, at the end, a New York regiment had broken their hold on it, and shot down the Rebs until they were piled two and three deep in death.

The gulley was now called "Blood Alley."

Fifty thousand men had perished in the one battle. More blood had been spilled here in one day than in any other battle of the war thus far.

No, life was not normal today. Not while soldiers still prowled fields where the corn had been mown down to the ground by bullets, and the blood of two great armies was still damp upon the ground.

Not normal at all. Out of twenty chickens, three re-

mained out by the barn. Two of her goats were dead,
three had just disappeared. For some miraculous reason, her horse had been spared both injury and theft,
but her milk cow was long, long gone, along with numerous sacks of wheat. The garden had been trampled
down to nearly nothing. Indeed, war had changed everything.

But there were certain things that she could do, she
determined, and so she set the table as if she were
sitting down to any meal with her family. She lit candles on the table and used the good English dishes and
her mother's fine silver, and the Irish white linen table-
cloth and napkins. She dug deep into the cellar to find
a bottle of vintage wine, and she was just pouring it
into her best crystal wine glasses when Colonel Daniel
Cameron, C.S.A., made his appearance downstairs
once again.

He had chosen one of her father's simple cotton
work shirts and a pair of blue denim breeches. He'd
found his boots, and they came up to his kneecaps. The
whole ensemble should have given him the appearance
of a farm boy, but instead he had the look of a pirate
about him, dashing and dangerous, and intriguing.

"Will this do, Mrs. Michaelson?" he asked politely.

"Yes, quite," she told him. She indicated the table,
untying the apron she had been wearing about her
waist. "Do sit down, Colonel."

"Why, I thank you, Mrs. Michaelson," he told her.
But he drew out a chair and stood behind it, politely
waiting. Callie dished the stew into a server and
brought it to the table. Once she had set it down, she
allowed Daniel Cameron to seat her.

He did not seat himself immediately, but picked up
the wine she had chosen. "Ah, how nice, Mrs. Michaelson. A French burgundy, 1855." With practiced ease,
he uncorked the bottle, casually inhaled the scent of
the cork, and expertly poured out the wine into their

glasses. He lifted his to hers, tasted the wine carefully, and grinned. "An excellent vintage, Mrs. Michaelson. I must say, the hospitality here in the North is far more than this Rebel ever dared hope."

The smile that had just begun to curve Callie's lips faded. "Must you keep reminding me that you are the enemy?" she asked him irritably.

He grinned and took his seat at last. "Perhaps I should eat before I do so again, since this stew promises to offer an even sweeter treat for the senses than that given by the wine."

Callie stared at him gravely across the table. "You do have a gift with words, Colonel."

"Only when I mean what I say, Mrs. Michaelson. May I?" He reached for her plate, and spooned a fair portion of the stew into it. He set it down before her, then helped himself. He tasted a bite of the meat, then another. He was famished, she saw. He went through half the food on his plate before suddenly pausing, having realized that she had yet to touch her fork.

"Excuse me. I'm afraid that my manners have become atrocious as of late."

Callie shook her head. He'd had nothing but water in almost two days. She thought lamely for something to say. "My mother, sir, raised three sons, and she'd have been delighted to see any man who had been so ill enjoy a meal with such gusto."

She was startled to realize that his free hand had moved across the table, and that his fingers had fallen over her own. Warm, intimate. His touch sent a quiver tearing raggedly down her spine. "Callie, should all Yankees have your way, war might well have been averted."

The touch of his fingers, the sensual feel of his eyes upon her, were suddenly too much. She snatched her fingers back quickly.

"There you go again. You are the enemy. If you cannot remember that fact for a meal, then you really should eat alone."

He hesitated, then shook his head. "It's dangerous ever to forget the enemy," he told her.

"Meaning?"

He shrugged. "Did you know, Mrs. Michaelson, that soldiers trade? Time and again, my Rebel troops have been encamped on one side of a stream, with Federal troops encamped on the other. And all night they send little boats of tobacco and coffee back and forth, and sometimes they get to be darned good friends. Sometimes we're close enough to see their faces."

His voice was harsh, his words were bitter. Callie shook her head again.

"There, sir, goes a touch of humanity within this insanity we have set upon. Why should it disturb you?"

"I'll tell you why it should disturb me, Mrs. Michaelson. One of my young privates became very friendly with a boy from Illinois one night. And then he met his newfound friend on the field of battle the next day."

"And?"

"And he hesitated to pull the trigger. His newfound friend did not. My private died, Mrs. Michaelson."

Callie kept her chin high. Her lashes swept over her cheeks. "Colonel, you are not going to meet me on the battlefield, ever. Therefore, you need not worry about my status as an enemy."

"Ah—" he began, but then he fell silent, tense and still—listening. For a moment, Callie did not know what he heard. The sound of horses' hooves pounding against the earth came to her ears. Someone was riding up to the front door.

He was instantly on his feet, vibrant, filled with tension and with readiness for battle. She was suddenly very afraid for him, because she knew then that no one would ever take him easily, he would always fight until the very end.

"Don't you dare draw a knife on me again!" Callie warned him as he started to reach for her. Despite her words, he was quickly around the table, his fingers creating a vise about her arm as she stood. "Callie—"

"Let go of me!"

"I can't—"

"I've already kept silent about you for two days. I didn't mention a word about you when the soldier came by today."

"What?"

A certain tension gripped her as he shook her arm. "Soldiers have been crawling all over the place, Colonel. If I were going to turn you in, I would have done so by now."

Slowly, cautiously, he released her arm. Callie walked through the kitchen and the parlor, going to the front door. She threw it open and gasped. She wasn't startled to see a Yankee soldier at her door, but she was surprised to know the officer who came this time.

It was Eric Dabney, Gregory's friend.

"Eric!" she said.

"Callie!"

Disconcerted to say the least, Callie stared at the Union cavalry captain standing on her porch. He was a young man, in his early twenties, of medium height and build with warm brown eyes and a head full of thick brown hair. He had a sweeping mustache and well-manicured beard. He was an attractive man, Callie thought, but he'd often amused her because of his vanity. She wondered, upon occasion, just how he managed to get in much soldiering, because he was very proud of his mustache and beard, and Gregory had told her once that he spent hours grooming his facial hair.

But he was concerned for her, she knew. She should be grateful to see him on her porch.

As it was, she couldn't think of anyone she'd less rather see at the moment.

"Callie!" he repeated.

"Eric!" she said and fell silent.

He was certainly expecting more. She had to ask him in.

"Callie, I had to make sure for myself that you were all right. What with Gregory . . . gone." he said. He cleared his throat. "I have time for a cup of coffee."

"Oh, of course, you'll have to come in!" she spoke loudly. She hoped her Rebel guest heard her. She had no choice. She had to ask Eric in. She could tell he was already suspicious. She should have hugged him and told him how glad she was that he had survived the battle. She shouldn't have left an old friend on the porch.

What was she doing? There was an enemy in her house. She should tell Eric that this minute.

No. She had made up her mind long ago—maybe right from the beginning—that she was going to shelter this particular Rebel, wrong as it might be.

Besides, she wasn't sure that Eric alone would be any match for this Rebel, even if Daniel Cameron was wounded. There was a quality of strength about Daniel. He had grown very lean and hard. Callie was convinced that he was very adept with any weapon he might choose to use. He wouldn't have survived this far if he were not.

The only way to best him would be when he was completely down.

For Eric's sake, she needed to take grave care.

"I was worried through the whole battle," Eric said as he took a step closer to her. "As soon as I saw you outside in the lull, I was worried sick. I imagined us losing this ground, I was horrified about the Rebs coming in here and finding you. A woman alone . . . ." He touched her chin, and then he drew her against him in a warm hug. "Callie, if anything had happened to you . . ."

She wondered if she was being watched. They were standing in the doorway. She wondered why she should care if her uninvited Rebel guest saw her being hugged by another man.

They were enemies, but Daniel owed her for her silence, and for the care that she had given him.

Still, the thought of his watching her now with Eric made her uneasy.

She broke away, taking Eric's hands and holding them, but creating some distance between them.

"I'm fine, Eric. And I thank God that you came through this horror alive."

"I thank the Lord too," he murmured. "But I mean to come out of this war all right. And I mean to come back here, Callie, for you."

"Eric, I promise, you mustn't worry about me!" She assured him as lightly as she could.

"Callie, it's my beholden duty to worry about you," he said. He patted her hand and started walking into the house. Her heart began to hammer again. What would happen when they reached the kitchen? How would she explain two plates, two wine glasses?

And the Rebel soldier at the table?

"Gregory was more than my friend," Eric explained to her as they walked through the house. "He was as close as a brother. And, of course, there's more."

She barely heard his words, she was so worried about what they were going to find at the table.

They reached the kitchen, and she dared to breathe easily again. She wasn't going to have to explain anything. Daniel had disappeared along with his plate and wine glass.

"Callie, I care about you. Deeply."

"What!"

Eric had swung around suddenly. She was nearly trapped against the entryway leading to the kitchen.

His eyes were dark and earnest. His voice had a waver in it.

"I know that this isn't particularly the time—"

"You're right, Eric, this is not the time!" she exclaimed. Where was her wandering Rebel? Watching the scene?

Eric moved closer. He reached out to stroke her cheek, his emotion naked in his face.

Oh, Lord!

"Callie, Gregory hasn't been gone long, but in this wretched and war-weary world, it has been time enough. We both loved him. Who better to care for you, to love you, in his absence? Callie, don't—"

"Eric!"

"What?"

"I—I can't talk about this now. I . . . coffee! Eric, sit down, let me give you a cup of coffee." She pressed her hands against his chest and quickly hurried by him. She took coffee from the stove, poured him a cup, and set it across from her dinner plate. "I have stew—"

"I've eaten, thank you."

"Army rations. Have something."

He shook his head and sat where she had set down his coffee cup. It was the same seat that Daniel had so recently vacated. "Callie, I came to see you."

She breathed in deeply and sat down. "I appreciate that, Eric, and I'm fine. Thank you."

He reached across the table, and his fingers curled over hers.

"Callie—"

She pulled her hand back. "Eric." She lowered her lashes, growing desperate for a way to make him stop without being entirely cruel. She even forgot that Daniel Cameron might still be moving stealthily about her house. "Eric, listen to me, please. It's simply too soon.

I can't even think about anyone but Gregory. Please understand." She raised her eyes to his and smiled as sweetly as she could, giving a promise for a future that could never be. "Give me time. I'll pray for you; you will come back."

Eric swallowed down his coffee in a gulp, his eyes never leaving hers.

He set the empty cup back down on the table. Callie gazed at it.

The coffee had been hot. She hoped that his throat was scalded all the way down to his gullet.

Eric stood up, drawing her along with him. "Just think about me, angel. Please, just think about me. Callie—Callie, I will love you until my dying day!"

Startled, she blinked. She wanted to give him something to go away with, some sign of affection. She had never realized that he felt this kind of emotion for her, and she had never given any thought to her feelings for him. He had been Gregory's friend. She had loved her husband. His friends were her friends.

And if war had never come, no man would be acting this way. She would have still been clad in black, shielded from the passions and emotions of others.

Eric would face bullets and swords and bombs in battle. He could easily die before another month was over.

She brought a smile to her lips. "Eric, I care for you. You know that. For the moment, my heart lies out back with my husband," she said softly.

"Tell me that I can come back," he urged her.

"Eric, I will be praying that you are able to come back," she said. She meant that he must make it back through all the battles.

That wasn't what he heard at all.

His eyes lit up, and a smug, triumphant smile went sailing across his features.

His mustache fairly twitched.

Callie sighed, ready to correct him, but then decided against it. Who knew what tomorrow would bring.

He drew her fingers to his lips, kissing the tips. "Then, Callie, I bid you good-bye. 'Till this cruel war is over!' " He quoted from the song that grew more popular daily.

Callie nodded. "Good-bye, Eric. Take care."

She walked with him through the parlor again and stood in the doorway while he moved past her.

He suddenly pulled her into his arms and kissed her.

It was probably a passionate kiss. On his part. It was merely a surprise to Callie. She pressed against him. He made no effort to be daring, he did not try to part her lips, but seemed happy enough to hold her. Just as suddenly as he had touched her, he released her. In the doorway, he saluted her sharply. He whispered her name, turned, and left her, hurrying down the pathway to his waiting mount.

"Oh, Jesu!" Callie whispered aloud. She closed the door and leaned against it, not knowing whether to laugh or to cry.

She rushed back into the kitchen. "Daniel?" she called his name, not whispering, but not speaking loudly, either. There was no answer.

She hurried back into the parlor. "Daniel?"

Again, there was no answer. She picked up her skirts and came running up the stairway. She hurried into her bedroom. The door was already open and she burst through the doorway.

"Daniel?"

He didn't answer. She sat down at the foot of her bed, then fell flat against it.

"Oh, thank the Lord! The Reb's gone south!"

But then the bedroom door, thrown against the wall, suddenly squeaked and started to swing. Callie leapt up to her knees, staring at the patch of wall now displayed.

There stood Daniel Cameron, grinning. "No, angel, not on your life." He walked toward her, his eyes alive with wicked flames of amusement. "He's going to love you until his dying day?"

"Oh, will you please shut up!" she snapped. "How incredibly rude. You were listening to every word."

"I wouldn't have missed it," he assured her. He stood over her, then reached down for both of her hands. He pulled her up so that she stood right before him. He stood so close their bodies touched.

" 'When this cruel war is over . . .' " he murmured.

"I'm warning you, quit!" Callie threatened.

His smile broadened. The searing flames in his eyes seemed to catch hold of her heart. His face lowered, and the flames came closer.

And burned more hotly. All through her. Warming, searing her limbs. Sweeping along her breasts, her hips, invading her thighs. Taking root deep, deep within her.

"Don't wait for him, angel. Not unless he can do better than that."

"Better than that? Just what should he be doing, Colonel Cameron?" she demanded.

"I'll show you," Daniel whispered.

It seemed that the flames within her sizzled and soared, and then leaped to become an inferno.

His arms closed tightly around her, and his was a passion Callie couldn't begin to deny.

Six

Perhaps because he had taken her so very suddenly, Callie stiffened. And then, for the very same reason, she felt herself meld against him.

He knew, it seemed, just how to hold her. Just how to sweep the length of her against the length of him. He held her tightly, warmly, securely.

In his arms, she felt the quicksilver fanning of a heat that was deep and undeniable, seeping through her limbs, to her breasts, to her hips. She felt the thunder of her heart, nearly suffocating her, yet combining with the still stronger pulse of his.

There was the startling comfort of feeling that she belonged in his embrace. There was the strength of his arms when she had been alone for so very long.

She felt the touch of his eyes. So searing a blue. In that sweeping gaze, she felt anew the fire, the burning, the instantaneous warmth created by this man. All of this she experienced in seconds as he brought her against him, stared at her, touched her. He smiled slowly, lowered his head to hers, and kissed her.

Then came an entire new burst of sensation as she tasted his lips, felt the pressure of them against her own. He kissed her as if he had intended on kissing her for a long, long time. Kissed her as if he savored the

very breath that came from her lips, as if he had desired just that touch with every bit of longing within
him. She could not deny him, not when he held her so
tightly and securely in his arms. He demanded her acquiescence, but he knew how to kiss, how to take, how
to give.

He flooded her senses as he molded his mouth to
hers, slowly parting her lips with a sure thrust of his
tongue that entered more and more deeply into her
mouth. It was just a kiss. But perhaps that was its true
magic. He made her think of so much more. Made her
long for more. The sinuous, undeniable stroke of his
tongue brought with it a sweet ravishment of the whole
of her mouth.

His mouth lifted from hers, leaving a breath of air
between them. She reached up to him, and he kissed
her again, open-mouthed, hungry, drawing her more
swiftly and more deeply into his intimate swirl of desire.

A trembling began within her as she felt his fingers,
gentle and determined upon her cheek. She felt the
length of him against her and knew the growing pulse
of his desire.

He felt good, and he smelled wondrous. She'd never
felt such a burst of passion within herself, not even
with Gregory.

Gregory!

The memory of her husband burst into the bubble of
longing and sensation that had seized such sure hold of
her, eclipsing everything else. Gregory! She had never
imagined wanting another man until this Rebel had
happened upon her. Why, in Eric's arms just moments
ago she had felt nothing except for discomfort and the
longing to escape.

She wanted this man, she cared for him. She loved
the contours of his face and the light in his eyes and the
sound of his voice. She had found him so very beautiful

naked, and when naked, a man wasn't in blue, nor was he in gray or tattered Rebel butternut.

No! she told herself fiercely. This man wore gray, naked or clad. His cause was in his heart, and she could not strip it from him.

And she was a widow, betraying her own heart.

"No, please, no!"

She managed to twist from his touch at last. He had not forced her. He had held her, so firmly. He had demanded from her, so sensually. But he had not forced her.

His mouth lifted from hers. His gaze met hers. His arms remained loosely around her, and he waited for her to speak.

She shook her head, horrified by the hot sheen of tears that glistened in her eyes. "No! Please, I can't. I won't. I . . ." Words eluded her. Explanations eluded her. "You have to leave!" she choked out.

Her lashes fell, hiding the anguish in her eyes. She pushed against the arms that held her. He tensed for one moment. "Callie . . ."

"Please!" She pushed harder against him. And then she was free.

She backed away from him. "You have to leave!"

She turned and fled from the room, racing out the door and down the stairs. But not even that distance took her far enough away from him. She burst out the front door, closed it behind her, and leaned against it, breathing deeply of the night air.

What was she thinking? Her father was dead, her best friend, husband, and lover was dead, and all at Rebel hands. So many dead, her own home made into a battlefield. And none of it mattered a single bit when this man touched her.

Bless the night! The darkness closed around her, and the coolness seemed to steal away some of the dreadful heat that assailed her. He would leave tonight, and she would forget.

She closed her eyes. He was wounded. A horse soldier without a horse.

But his fever had broken, and the wound that had caused him the difficulty was an old one. Perhaps he was weak, but even weak, he was a formidable enemy. He was not far from Virginia. He would go now, she knew, because deny it or not, he was one of those southern cavaliers.

A sound in the night suddenly startled Callie. Her eyes flew open. She didn't see anything to mar the stillness of the night. She closed her eyes again and listened. She could hear horses' hooves. There were a number of them. She stiffened.

Slowly, she relaxed. The riders were not coming to the house. She heard someone call out an order. The words were clear, but distant.

"Captain! We'll form an encampment next mile south, by the old orchard. There will be two sentries per company, sir!"

"As you say, sir!" came a brisk reply.

The slow hoofbeats of walking horses continued to sound. The troops were moving on.

Thank God. No one else was coming to her house.

But they would be close! There in the woods and the farmlands and fields. So very easy to stumble upon.

"No!" she whispered out loud, her hand flying to her mouth. Tears stung her eyes once again.

She swirled around, swinging open her door again and flying into the house.

He was in the parlor, buckling on his scabbard. As she entered the house, his sword came free of its protective sheath. Those startling blue eyes pierced into her, as sharp and vibrant as any blade.

She backed against the door, catching her breath, staring at the glistening silver of the sword.

"Jesu, Callie!" he muttered irritably, sheathing his sword once again with a practiced movement. Hands on his hips, he stared at her, slowly smiling. "Callie, I've been tempted to do a few things, but running you through with this sword has not been one of them," he said more lightly. Still she didn't speak, but remained with her back against the door.

"Callie, I'm leaving," he said very softly.

She shook her head strenuously. "You—you can't."

His eyes narrowed. "Why can't I?"

"Because there are Yankee camps all around us tonight."

He shrugged. "I can move around the countryside very well," he said quietly.

"No man can move well enough to escape the number of men out there now."

He smiled slowly. "You don't want me captured?"

"You're still injured, you fool."

His smile remained in place. "But I'm much, much better now."

She stiffened. Damn him. She was worried for his life. She squared her shoulders, and lifted her chin imperceptibly.

"Had you allowed yourself to heal properly the first time, Colonel, it's doubtful that wound at your side would have reopened and caused you that awful fever. If you're all fired determined to go out there tonight, be my guest. It's likely they'll shoot you down in the darkness. If not, it's likely they'll take you prisoner."

"And you know enough about Yankee prisons to assume that I'll die there?" he inquired.

She stiffened. Both sides complained about prison conditions. They were bad in the North, she knew, from a number of articles and editorials she had read on the subject. Despite the war, and despite anything that Daniel might believe, there were those in the

North who were appalled by the way that prisoners of war were treated.

Conditions in the South were far worse. Callie was convinced it was not done on purpose. Half of the southern fighting men were shoeless. Their uniforms were tattered, nearly threadbare. They fought on meager rations. They were half-starved themselves. Under those conditions, what could they spare for their imprisoned enemies?

Abraham Lincoln had been dealt many a defeat at the hands of the talented southern generals, but he understood his war. He had superior numbers. When his men died, they could be replaced. And they could be fed. The northern blockade was slowly but surely taking its toll upon the South. The war that tore up the farmlands was taking its toll upon the South. If they couldn't feed their own, how could they be expected to feed others?

But horror stories of the way that Union men starved in the South reached the North. And for every humanitarian who worked for better conditions, there was a bitter person who demanded that southern prisoners should not be coddled. There were widows and orphans who hated any man in gray. And for every respectable and decent jailor, there might also be a warped and angry commander, grown cold and heedless of human life. No one, northerner or southerner, wanted to face a prison camp.

Callie clenched her teeth. What should it matter to her what happened to this damned Reb.

She stepped coolly away from the door.

"You may stay, Colonel, if you so desire. And sir, you may leave, if you so desire."

She was alarmed by the rueful curve that came slowly, wistfully, to his lip. She was further dismayed by the quickening beat of her heart.

There was nowhere to go when he walked slowly

toward her, then stopped just before her. He touched her chin briefly with the back of his knuckle.

"I can't stay, Callie. Because if I do, I can't give you any guarantees or promises."

Pursing her lips, she determined not to wrench away from him. "You may stay, Colonel. Because I am the one who can give the guarantees."

He arched a brow, and she thought that the curve of his smile was definitely wicked now. "Callie—"

She pushed his hand aside and walked past him. He turned to lean against the door, watching her wander over by the hearth as she spoke. "You have recovered very nicely, Colonel. Many men—most men—would surely have died from the type of wound you suffered. And if not then, they'd have surely died from the fever. You have done miraculously well. But how far would you test fate, sir?" she demanded, swirling around to face him again.

"I keep going, Mrs. Michaelson, because I must," he told her.

"What you need to do, Colonel, is go home. Rest. Heal properly."

"I cannot do that."

"And why not?"

"Because," he said simply, "I am irreplaceable."

"Sir—"

"We haven't the manpower," he said, and to Callie, he at last sounded weary of the war. "I must always go back. I should be back now."

"You are weak. And if you die you'll not go back," she stated flatly.

"True," he agreed.

Callie's eyes suddenly came alight. "Your brother!"

"What?" he demanded darkly, a frown quickly descending upon his face.

"I can go out! I can see what I can do about finding your brother. Perhaps—"

"No!"

"But if he's a Union surgeon—"

"No, damn you! I am well and fine enough. Jesu, I'll not have Jesse risking anything again! Do you understand me?"

She had seldom seem him so furious, even with all that raged between them. Irrationally, she felt the heat of tears burning at the back of her eyes again. She was doing her best to help the enemy, and the damned enemy wasn't cooperating in the least.

Let him go! she told herself. Let him go out, let the Union take him!

She turned away from him, determined that he would not see the emotion in her eyes. "Do whatever you choose to do, Colonel. I cannot be bothered with it any longer."

"Ah. You've ceased to care whether I am caught or not!"

She spun around once again. "At this moment, Colonel, I'd set the shackles around your wrists myself!"

He smiled. A cold, set smile. "Madam, that is something that you could never manage to do. I think you know damned well that—weak as I may be—I'm still far more than a match for one or two or maybe even three of your Yankees. And I think, Mrs. Michaelson, that one of the reasons you were so careful to rid this house of your dashing Yankee captain—the one who is going to love you until he dies"— The last was added in a curious tone, and Callie wasn't sure if it was a bitter one or one of amusement. But then his voice hardened as he continued—"is because you knew damned well that he might not be any match for me."

"You are extremely arrogant," Callie informed him. "You should just be grateful that I didn't call the whole Union army down upon you."

"The whole Union army isn't around anymore."

"Enough of it is."

"You were afraid for your friend," he insisted.

"I didn't care to have the inside of my house as well as the outside littered with bodies!" she returned sharply.

"Ah, a true tender heart!" he said, laughing.

"He might have slain you on the spot!" Callie stated.

"He might have. But I doubt it."

"My, my, sir, but you are pleased with your own prowess."

"I haven't been pleased with anything in a long, long, time, Mrs. Michaelson. And I've been out there for a very long time. There are few battles that I've missed. And even when I've fallen, I've brought down countless men before doing so." His eyes looked old and weary, his face drawn. "I'm not pleased at all, Mrs. Michaelson, I'm sickened. But I'm a survivor, and an officer, and I'm needed. And I'm good with a sword. It's very unlikely that I could be taken by one man. And you know it. You saved your friend's life by not mentioning the fact that you were harboring a Rebel."

"You are not just arrogant, you are insufferable," Callie muttered. She determined that she couldn't stand there any longer, and that it was one thing for him to guess that she hadn't wanted him to clash with Eric, and quite another to know it for certain. "Do what you will!" she told him. "Although, who knows? Perhaps I should tremble for the entire Union once you are loose upon it!"

She swung around a final time, heading back for the kitchen.

She didn't reach it. She felt his hand on her shoulder, spinning her around.

"Do you want me to go or don't you?" he demanded, his eyes dark, nearly cobalt, his features tense.

She jerked free from him. "Yes. No. No, I don't! I'm

sick of the death and the pain. And God help me, I do not want your death on my conscience!''

"And what of those I may kill later?" he demanded.

She inhaled sharply, staring at him, stricken with the thought. God in heaven, who had invented this horrible thing called war?

"Better a Rebel soldier now, not scores of Yankees later, eh?" he asked softly.

Callie swallowed tightly as she continued to meet his steel-blue gaze. "Do what you will, Colonel," she repeated.

He shook his head. "No, I want to please you, Callie," he persisted.

"What?"

Dismayed, she tried to pull free from him. Damn him! He was too close again. She could feel the things she had felt when he had kissed her. She breathed in the scent of him, the clean scent of the soap she had bathed him with, the deeper, more subtle scent that was his alone, and part of the things that made him the man he was.

She didn't want to see his face so closely, see the fine set of his cheeks, the molding of his jaw. She didn't want to grow attached to this man. And she certainly didn't want to be held in his arms again, to feel the startling, overwhelming sense of desire that had risen within her. And most of all, she didn't want to feel as if she could fall in love with him, as if loving was something that could come all too easily, as if it might be something that had already begun.

"What are you talking about?" she demanded harshly.

"I want it to be your call, Callie. You tell me to stay, or you tell me to go. Thousands of men are dead, from both sides. Thousands more are going to die before it's over. Tens of thousands."

"Would you stop that!" she cried out, horrified. She

backed farther away, afraid of the stubborn set to his chin.

He came toward her again, and she should have run from his touch but she did not. He cupped her chin and lifted it so that her eyes were caught in the charisma and determination of his.

"The call will be yours."

She didn't want him standing there. So painfully close again. So close that she wanted to forget everything.

Again, she jerked away—and retreated. "I don't want you to die," she said simply.

"Because I'm in your house?"

"Because I know your face."

"More than my face," he reminded her ruefully.

"Oh!" She let out an oath of impatience, curling her fingers into her palms. "Because you're no longer a stranger. You're not just a number." He still stared at her, waiting. "All right! Because I care for you!" she admitted, but when he would have walked toward her again, she set a hand into the air, stopping him. "I don't want you to die, but I don't want you near me. Do you understand?"

His smile was slow, bittersweet. "Yes, I think that I understand," he told her.

To her amazement, he walked by her. She was still for a minute, then she heard a clattering in the kitchen.

He was picking up the dishes that remained on the table. He ignored her when she stood in the doorway, bringing things to the counter and to the water pump to rinse them.

She watched him for a moment. "Did you—manage to eat anything?" she asked him.

"Yes, thank you. I ate just fine," he told her. He shrugged, glancing her way. "I took my stew upstairs. Remind me. The dish is still on the floor."

He seemed adept enough at picking up. Callie

leaned against the door frame, watching him. "You're quite useful, so it appears," she told him.

He glanced her way, arching a brow.

"Well, you do come from a big home, right? A plantation. And I'll bet you grew up with lots of slaves—"

"Excuse me," he interrupted her, setting down the plate that he had just rinsed and putting his hands on his hips to face her. "I'm the younger son. Jesse—my Yankee brother—is the one who owns them. Or owned them," he corrected himself.

"You don't have slaves on your plantation anymore?"

"It's Jesse's plantation, the main house, anyway. But yes, they're still there. Most of them. They just aren't slaves any longer."

"Jesse freed them?"

"We freed them. The three of us. My brother, my sister, and I. In June. Jesse was home for a spell, and considering that he's a Yank himself and damned unwelcome in Virginia at the moment, it seemed the time to settle some family business. We knew then that the war wasn't going to be over in a few more weeks, or months even. We needed some things settled, what with Jesse going one way, and me going another. But don't go applauding us, Mrs. Michaelson. We didn't do anything spectacular. We freed our people because we could afford to do so. We can pay them. The good majority of them chose to stay on. God knows what will happen by the end of the war. I'm going to worry about some of them then."

"Why is that?"

"Why is that?" he repeated. He smiled. "Well, now, I don't take anything away from your Mr. Lincoln. Oddly enough, I rather admire the man. Maybe slavery —and the South's determination to cling to that institution—is why we got so fired up over states' rights to begin with. But Lincoln didn't go to war to strip the

South of her slaves. Lincoln wound up fighting a war to preserve the Union. Maybe the outcome of this war will be hundreds and thousands of freed slaves. Then what? Will they all be welcome in the North? Welcome in New York City along with the thousands of immigrants that seem determined to flood these shores? I don't know. I do know that my people—whether they are owned or free—have work. And they have food. They have roofs over their heads. Not many of them live in the plantation house. But human life, black or white, has always been respected in my house. I just hope their lives will be worthwhile in the North, once this thing is over."

"Any price is worth freedom," Callie said.

"Well, now, maybe that's true, Mrs. Michaelson. I don't rightly know. Hunger can be a pretty fierce enemy."

Callie shook her head. "You said that you admire Lincoln. There's right, and there's wrong, he said. And it's wrong to own another person!"

Daniel Cameron lowered his eyes. She could see the small, secret smile that curved his lip. "Is that what he said, Mrs. Michaelson?"

"Well, more or less! Really, Colonel—"

"Callie," he said, raising his eyes to hers, "I'm not making fun of you. I'm admiring your passion! God alive, Callie, I wish it could be so simple for me! Many men have decried slavery. Thomas Jefferson wanted to abolish slavery when he was writing the Declaration of Independence! And he owned slaves! But it's not that easy. There's an entire economy based on slavery. There are men who insist that even the Bible condones slavery. Callie, I'm not God, I don't know!"

"So you're a Rebel!"

"I'm a Virginian. And Virginia chose to secede from the Union."

"But your brother—"

"My brother followed his conscience, Callie. I followed mine."

"So he is your enemy."

"He is my brother, and I love him."

"But you fight him!"

"Jesu, what is this!" Daniel exploded, throwing his hands into the air. "I didn't start this war! Sometimes, I don't even give a damn, except that it might be over. There are days when my only real hope is that Cameron Hall survives both armies, that it will be there for me to see when at long last that day comes that I can really go home. But a man has to be what he is, and do what his heart dictates to him! Virginia seceded, and my oath, my allegiance, is to my state! I'm a cavalry officer, and I serve the cavalry. I serve Robert E. Lee, a man of ethics, grace, and honor, and in return, I serve with all the ethics, grace, and honor I may possess in turn. I cannot walk away from the war because I am tired of it. I am what I am, Callie. A Rebel. Your enemy!" He exhaled a long breath, watching her where she remained silent and wide-eyed, in the doorway. "Oh, hell!" he muttered. Tense as a jackal, he spun around and strode across the kitchen to one of the shelves. There was a whiskey bottle upon it, and he grabbed it by the neck and walked angrily toward Callie.

There was such a leashed passion to his stride and taut features that Callie jumped back, unnerved by the way he seemed to be bearing down upon her. But long before he reached her, he paused, his mouth twisted into a bitter facsimile of a smile.

"I've no intention of harming you—or touching you, Mrs. Michaelson. But if the countryside is that packed with Yanks, then I will accept your gracious hospitality for the night. And since I dare not come near you, I'm going to go and lock myself in a room. And since I don't want to lie awake all night wondering just where you are and what you're doing, I'm taking the whiskey bottle. What a companion it will make!" He paused in the doorway and bowed very low to her.

He walked through the parlor and started up the stairs, the whiskey bottle tucked under his arm.

A moment later, Callie nearly jumped a mile as she heard the ferocious slamming of a door.

Indeed, it seemed that her Rebel was here for the night.

Seven

It seemed to Daniel that he spent the majority of the night leaning by the window, staring out at the darkness.

He felt surprisingly well—almost too damned well. Because of that, he had decided not to remain in his hostess' bedroom, but had come down the hall to the second bedroom.

This room was every bit as impeccably neat as the first, but furnished with more of a masculine flair. There was a bed with a polished oak frame, a heavy desk, a large wardrobe, and a seaman's chest at the foot of the bed. He had come here before to find the clothing he was wearing, but he hadn't thought much about the room's occupant. Did it belong to one of Callie's brothers? Or had it been the private domain of her father?

Sitting on the windowsill in the darkness, Daniel took another long swig from the whiskey bottle. There was a beautiful painting of a horse that hung over the desk, and sitting on top of the desk was a fine antique compass. There was a Revolutionary War sword hung on the wall, a trophy passed down from generations before. There was a deck of cards in the bottom drawer at the base of the wardrobe—he knew that because the cards were just beneath the breeches he had borrowed. It seemed those cards had been kept there discreetly. Somebody was a bit of a gambler.

He'd probably like the fellow who was supposed to be sleeping here. They both had a passion for horses. And Daniel liked to gamble just as much as the next man. They shared an appreciation for the past, and . . .

They probably shared a passion for Mrs. Callie Michaelson.

Daniel swore softly and swallowed more of the whiskey. What was it that was so damned entrancing about her? She was a beauty, but he'd known many beauties, he'd admired them, and he'd even loved one or two. This was different. Seeing her was different, listening to her was different. Touching her was different.

What was it that made him want her so badly? The war, he tried to tell himself. The days and nights of nothing but dirty water and hardtack. The endless riding, the company of soldiers.

No.

Had he spent the last months in a whirl of socials, he would still have felt such emotion for this woman. She was unique. There was wisdom in her eyes. After all, she had been a married woman. But there was innocence in them too. There was something beneath the beauty of her lips, the silk of her flesh. Something that smoldered, something electric, something so alluring and seductive that being near her was nearly more than he could stand.

"Damn! So what am I doing here?" he murmured aloud. He looked out on the darkness beyond the house. He should have moved on. He was restless, and he needed to be back. He needed to find out just how many men had been lost by Antietam Creek, and he needed badly to let Jeb Stuart know that he was alive.

His friends and superiors might well be mourning his loss this very moment.

But he couldn't allow himself to be killed, either. He'd be no damned good to anyone that way.

He flexed and unflexed his hand, then stood and looked out the window again. He really shouldn't let his guard down. How the hell did he know what really went on in her heart? She might care for him, but she might also have signaled that Yankee captain somehow. She hadn't wanted them to clash in her house because Daniel would have been forced to slay her friend. But maybe she had given him some message, some clue.

They could be surrounding the house right now.

No, he determined dryly. She hadn't given the man a message. She'd been too busy trying to dissuade him from his sudden turn of passion.

"I will love you till the day I die!" Daniel said out loud. He lifted the whiskey bottle. "Yes, Mrs. Michaelson, I can well understand the poor man's anguish. I pity my enemy, ma'am. And I pity your poor young husband, facing death, and knowing that he left you behind, angel," he murmured.

He looked outside again. No one was coming for him tonight. He needed to get some sleep.

She'd done a fine job binding his wound. When he stripped off his borrowed shirt, he looked carefully at the gash on his lower abdomen and side. The bleeding had completely stopped. It looked no worse than it had when he had entered into battle.

His head no longer ached, and his fever, he knew, was completely gone.

"Jesse, she's damned near as good as you are!" he murmured, speaking to the whiskey bottle he'd set on the desk. "And she's much, much prettier."

She wanted him gone.

She wanted him.

He stalked across the room, running his fingers through his hair.

That was the rub. She cared about him, she wanted him. There was all that sweet and wonderful and simmering passion within her, just waiting for him. Yes, for him. He'd watched her with the Yank. And he'd listened to her. She hadn't offered the Yank anything at all.

Life and love didn't work that way, Daniel knew. She didn't *want* to feel an attraction to him, she just did. When she came close, he sure as hell felt the depth of that attraction.

Damn. It was going to be a long, long night.

He stripped back the calico covering and white cotton sheet from the bed and lay down. He stared at the ceiling and reminded himself that he'd just recovered from a severe fever.

But he felt good. Really good. Strong. Ready to be up and about. To walk, to run . . .

To make love.

He groaned, rolled over, and pulled the pillow on top of his head. It could be so easy. They could both forget who they were and give in to temptation. Had he forgotten? She was a widow, but a respectable one. She should never have been kissed the way that he had kissed her. There were ways to act with a young woman, and ways not to act.

War made a mockery of propriety.

She had asked him not to touch her.

And so he would not.

Sleep. The Yankees are not coming tonight. She's given you back your life, your health. She's sheltered you from the enemy. She's fed you, and given you clothing. And she's cared for you.

He leapt up and went back to the dresser for the whiskey bottle. He swallowed a big draught, then fell back on the bed.

Colonel, you will sleep, he told himself. That's an order.

But he didn't sleep. Lying awake, he thought of home. Kiernan, Jesse's wife, was there now, with her new baby. His nephew. Daniel at last smiled, thinking of the big, lusty fellow with a fine temper to match any Cameron who had come before him.

His smile faded. That's where the future lay. With their children. What would the South be now, after this ravishment had gone on even longer? What world would they inherit?

He reached out in the darkness, almost as if he could touch some intangible beauty that might soon be gone. A very special world had been his. His, and Jesse's, and Christa's. Cameron Hall had provided everything for them. All of those lazy days by the river. All of the dreams that they wove and dreamt beneath blue skies and powdery white clouds, beneath the shade of moss growing thick on old trees. Maybe it had been a world of privilege, and maybe the privilege was about to be lost. He wouldn't mind that so much, he thought. Since the war he had become extremely self-sufficient, as there was little other way to be. But if they were to lose Cameron Hall, he was not sure he could ever learn to live with the loss.

Cameron Hall, or Christa—or Jesse. His brother, his enemy.

Daniel had understood when Jesse had kept his loyalty to the Union. Maybe because he knew his brother better than anyone else in the world. The first Cameron to come to America had left behind vast estates and wealth. He had turned his back on those riches and built in a wilderness. More than a century later, Daniel's great-grandfather had set his cap with the struggling new colonies, despite the fact that he had been an English lord. Win or lose, they had always been taught that a man had to follow his heart and the dictates of his soul.

The way that Daniel saw it, Jesse's soul had just told him to go the wrong way. But he understood. And he would never have asked Jesse to go against those dictates.

It had been hard to watch him walk away the first time, back in '61, right after Virginia had made its decision to leave the Union. He was the oldest son, the inheritor. Still, he had walked away.

They had not met in person again until McClellan had waged his peninsula campaign early in the summer.

Then it had become necessary for Daniel to find Jesse because he had to tell his brother that Kiernan was expecting his baby. Kiernan, who was as passionately southern as Jesse was determinedly pro-Union.

A smile crept slowly onto Daniel's face then. He'd been badly wounded in the battle that day. Jesse had found him and had risked a hell of a lot to bring him home to Cameron Hall, along with Kiernan, who had been trying to reach her own home. And Jesse's Yank friends had turned blind eyes toward Daniel, and a whole troop of Rebs had pretended not to see Jesse along the way.

Kiernan had married Jesse, and the baby had been born, and Daniel had healed up nicely in a few days. In that time they had almost brought back the magic. They had all played with the baby on the grass, they had lain back and listened to the river, and they had felt the heat of summer and the soft breeze of the night.

And then Jesse had ridden out again. A number of Yanks might have been dispensable, but not Jesse. He was a doctor, a good one. No army in this war could afford the absence of a good doctor and crack surgeon.

They'd stood by the old cemetery, surrounded by

their long-gone ancestors, and in silence they had embraced once again. The silence had been broken by the sounds of Kiernan's sobs. She had discovered that she loved Jesse far more than any cause.

Kiernan was at Cameron Hall now, along with Christa, the baby, and Kiernan's young in-laws from her first marriage. The slaves had been freed, but most had remained. There was nowhere that they really wanted to go. So right now, it was still possible to dream of home.

He rolled over, wishing that his thoughts would cease to haunt him, that he might sleep.

But no thoughts of others could keep his thoughts from the one Yankee who now shared this house with him. If Kiernan had married Jesse in the midst of the conflict still raging, then all was possible.

It could be possible for him to touch his angel once again. She of the dove-gray eyes and dark-fire hair and swift, elusive tenderness. She was so near him. Just down the hall.

She had asked him not to touch her.

Asked him after he had already touched her once, felt the fever in her body, felt the shape of her, sensed the longing, known the taste of her lips.

He flung himself up, swearing loudly and violently. One more swig of whiskey. Hell, no, maybe the whole bottle. He had to do something. He was a wounded soldier, needed back in action. He had to sleep, to heal.

He glanced at his sword across the room and took another pull from the near-empty bottle. At long last, he slept.

The sound of something heavy falling awoke him from a deep, deep sleep. He jumped up, startled, instantly on the alert.

He was no longer drunk though he did feel slightly

hung over. The more awake he became, the more his head hammered.

He stood shirtless and barefoot, clad only in his borrowed breeches, listening. The sound didn't come again. He narrowed his eyes, realizing that it had come from the bedroom to his left down the hallway.

Callie's room.

He reached for his hip, accustomed as he was to wearing his Colts and sword even as he slept. He didn't know what had happened to his guns, and his sword lay in its scabbard across the room. Silent on his bare feet, he strode across the room, sliding his cavalry sword from its scabbard. Still moving in silence, he slowly twisted the knob on his door and began to move down the hallway.

The door to Callie's room was closed. He was certain the sound had come from there. He clenched his teeth tightly together, hesitated just a moment, then twisted the knob, and thrust the door open in a single, fluid movement.

A startled "Oh!" greeted his arrival. He stood in her doorway, his sword at the ready, the tension in him rippling the muscles in his naked chest. His hair was in rakish disarray over his forehead from the night he had spent tossing and turning.

There was no enemy within the room to meet him, just Callie herself.

She was not ready to welcome him at all. Her eyes, enormous in the white heart of her face, flashed out a silver dismay. Deep auburn wisps of hair escaped a knot she had fashioned at the back of her head to trail damply about her cheeks and forehead. Her flesh, too, was damp, touched with little buttons of water.

She sat in a hip bath, her knees drawn halfway to her chest, the wooden tub itself barely blocking the length of her body from his view.

It was the most extraordinary torment. There was so

much that he could see. The long ivory column of her throat. No woman had ever possessed a throat so beautifully long, so slim, so elegant. He could see the slope of her shoulders and the hollows of her collarbones. Lovely hollows, shadowed, dark, seducing, demanding a kiss or a caress. Beneath the shadows, he could just see the rise of her breasts. Full, fascinating, taunting.

He had to walk away. Fast.

But just then she nervously moistened her lips with the tip of her tongue. He didn't know if it was the wetness of her lips, or the glimpse of her tongue, but every bit of his control vanished, swept away in the mist that rose from her bath. He didn't move. He remained transfixed, his eyes upon her lips.

"What—what are you doing?" she managed to demand in a whisper.

He had to wet his own lips to talk. He couldn't quite draw his eyes to hers.

"I heard something."

"I dropped a kettle," she said defensively. Still, he didn't move. His gaze was slipping. Her mouth was fascinating, but so was her throat. And the lush hint of the fullness of her breasts.

He dragged his gaze back up to hers.

"I thought that the house was under attack," he said.

A smile flashed quickly across her features. "So I see. You were ready to defend yourself. So, Colonel, would you skewer me through?" Her voice was still almost a whisper. Husky, throaty. A voice that titillated, that sent hot spirals curving into his groin. If he hadn't felt the raw surge of desire searing into his body already, the sound of that voice alone would have brought him to attention like a bolt of steel. "What with your sword so raised, Colonel . . ." The hush of her voice trailed away all together. Her smile faded and a flush infused her cheeks as she realized the double meaning of her words. Indeed, both his "swords" were well raised and certainly at the ready.

"Cause you injury, madam? Never," he said gallantly. But had he really been gallant, he would have turned at that moment. But his feet were lead, and he could not leave. He remained, watching her.

"You are interrupting my bath!"

"I came rushing to your defense."

"I am in no danger."

"I could not know that."

"I take that back!" she cried. "I am in grave danger now."

Indeed, she was. "The danger, Mrs. Michaelson, was in choosing to bathe, I'm afraid," he murmured regretfully.

"Oh, damn!" she swore softly. "Damn! I could have bathed in the kitchen, but with you here, I did not! I dragged the tub and the buckets up the stairs, and . . . and . . ." She paused, staring at him. "And here you are, invading my privacy." She was really beautiful with her eyes flashing so. He'd never seen a color closer to true silver. Shimmering, haunting. So elusive, so seductive.

"I didn't mean to invade your privacy. Only—"

"Defend me, indeed," she murmured.

"I should leave now," he said.

"Yes, you must."

But he didn't leave.

Watching him there, Callie knew that there had been no conviction in her voice. Leave, yes! Walk away, she thought. But the words would not come. She had watched his eyes. She had felt their blue fire move over her. Felt them touch her own eyes, felt them slip lower. And where his eyes touched her, she felt a sweet fever, as if that mere touch could warm and excite her flesh. As if some exotic caress covered her shoulders, and skimmed her throat. She felt the desire, and feeling that raw passion deep within him ignited some essence within her own soul.

It was so wrong. She was a widow. She had loved her husband. She honored his memory. She never should have had a man in her house. She never should have allowed a man's eyes to touch her in this way.

But sweet visions of the past had faded away. All sense of propriety seemed to slip through her fingers like the water that she bathed in.

From the moment that she had seen him, she had felt a fascination with his face. From the moment that she had touched him, she had felt a growing affection for him as a man. From the moment he had first touched her, she had felt the overwhelming stirrings of desire that came now to haunt her heart and limbs and soul with a vengeance.

Tell him to go! she commanded herself.

But she could not.

She stared into his eyes, and then her own vision slipped. She was staring at his chest. At the sleek muscle there, so taut now, rippling with his every breath. At the dark whorls of hair that grew there. She wanted to touch that whorl, feel it spring beneath her fingers. He was so bronze. He had probably tanned in the rivers where he bathed while camped with his men. He had gained that muscle from wielding his sword, she tried to tell herself. But reminders of war meant nothing. Enemy or no, she liked the man she had come to know. Watching him now, she wondered if even that mattered.

She wanted him. Wanted him to come closer. And touch her.

"You have to go." She managed to speak the words. That was not at all the message in her eyes.

"I know," he said. But neither was that the message in his movement, for he had lowered his cavalry sword and was walking toward her.

Closer, closer, until he stood over her.

And then he smiled. Ruefully. Sensually. His fingers wound around the rim of the tub.

"I like my women to want me badly," he drawled softly, his blue gaze burning into hers.

"Ah, but I don't want you at all, Colonel," she told him smoothly. What a lie. In all of her life she had never wanted anything so badly as she wanted this man now. Her lips were dry again, despite the steam that rose from the bath. She could feel the swell of her breasts, the hardening of her nipples. And dear Lord, what she could feel between her thighs . . .

His smile had deepened. "I like my women to want me very badly, Callie. I like them just as hungry as they can get. I like my women—"

She crossed her arms over her traitorous breasts and raised her chin in a taunting challenge. "Ah, but Colonel, I am not one of your 'women.' I am the enemy, remember?"

"Indeed, Callie. But what a way to do battle!" he murmured.

"We cannot do battle."

"On the contrary, Mrs. Michaelson. I'm afraid that we must." He lowered himself down on his haunches, his eyes on a level with hers. "You are one Yankee to best me beyond a doubt, Mrs. Michaelson, for I could not leave this room were I threatened with Hell's damnation itself! To think!" he added softly, ruefully, "I mocked that poor fool last night, Callie, when I, myself, will want you now until I die."

He could not know what he did to her, how he made her feel, how deeply, how desperately she wanted him in turn. But how could she dare touch him, stroke his shoulder, taste the salt upon his flesh, lie naked beside him. . . .

Flashes of desire, like melting stars in the sky, caught fire and danced all through her.

"Callie!"

Her name on his lips was a caress. He stood above her once again, and still he had not touched her.

"Think!" she charged herself to say once again. "I am the enemy! Vile, fearsome—"

"Never, never vile!"

She drew her knees more tightly against her body. Sensations tore madly through her as he walked behind her slowly. To have him here, so close, where she could not see him! To know that soon he would touch her and then . . . She felt the blood begin to race through her body like wildfire and a raw, searing excitement bring shivers to soar up and down the length of her spine.

"Really. You have to go," she whispered. She was barely able to create sound. The words were a breath on the air.

He knelt down behind her. "I know," he said. But he made no attempt to leave. "Really. I have to go. Dear God, Callie, we both know that I cannot!"

Just when she thought she would scream with the waiting, with the anguish, with the denial, with the desire, she felt his lips at the back of her neck. Felt his kiss cover her flesh. Felt a searing, sensual heat that was so sudden and so startling and so welcome that it sent a burning ripping through her.

"Oh!" The softness of her cry escaped her. She nearly slipped beneath the water, but he was there. Lifting her up, pulling her into his arms. She fell against him. The water from her body formed rivulets that snaked along his. Her breasts were crushed against the dark hairs that had so fascinated her before, and now brought such a new rush of sensation to fill her. He held her still for one breathless moment, held her against him, feeling the mist-laden heat that fused between them. His hand stroked the side of her face. He cupped her jaw. And he kissed her. Kissed her again and again.

Deep, wet, hungry kisses rained down upon her. Kisses that raped and ravished. Kisses so tender that she strained and ached to have more. Kisses that again plundered and excited, kisses that left her both weak and hungry. As hungry as he might ever have desired her to be.

Her arms wound around his neck and he lifted her high from the tub. Water sluiced over both of them, and neither of them seemed to notice. He stretched her out on her bed, freeing her hair from its wound knot as he did so, and splaying it over the white covering on the bed. He watched his handiwork as he surveyed the dark fire and sable strands, then his gaze met hers.

He found her eyes full of wonder.

Once again, he kissed her. This kiss was soft and slow and achingly tender. Everything wild and raw and urgent was held tightly back, and his mouth very slowly caressed her. Liquid and effusive, his lips moved over hers, his tongue tasted them, his teeth grazed them.

She felt the movement of his hand upon the length of her, his fingers grazing over her thigh and her hip, her ribs, her breast. His knuckles grazed the lower side of her mound, then his hand cupped around it. She realized that he was no longer kissing her, his eyes were on her once again. His gaze lowered, focusing on her breast, and on a tiny bead of water on the hardened red peak. Once again, his gaze touched hers. His head lowered against her body and the tip of his tongue touched the droplet of water, and moved erotically over the very crest of her nipple. His mouth closed over that taut bud and the dusky rose areole, and began to tease and taste and savor, to suckle and caress.

She cried out at the strength of the sensations that

seized a tight hold of her. Her fingers curled into his hair, and she heard herself calling out his name.

Deep within her body began a pulse, an urgency unlike anything she had ever experienced. She felt the power of his body over hers with every inch of flesh, with all of the searing fire now burning swiftly through her limbs. Her fingers moved in his hair, stroked down his neck, then down over his back. She stroked hard muscle, alive and vibrant. Flesh and muscle she had touched before, to cool, to heal.

And now she touched him, adding to the heat, adding to the fire.

When his gaze met hers again, she knew she was even adding to the healing.

"Should all the armies fall," he said softly, "I do not think that I could regret this invasion of the North."

She wet her lips, about to reply. He did not need one. He lowered himself against her again, just touching her lips with his. His mouth brushed briefly over her throat, against the hollow of her collarbone. His tongue teased the flesh at the valley of her breasts.

He inched himself lower, creating a searing liquid line of heat, slowly, surely, down her midriff, between her ribs to her navel. She wanted to cry out, she wanted to move. She wanted to fight the very force of the sensations he evoked. She could not. She lay still, feeling the tremors rock her body again and again.

His tongue moved leisurely upon her abdomen. Caressing, stroking, tasting. She tried to say his name again. The words would not come. She set her fingers once more into the rich mat of his ebony hair. She did not desist him in his purpose.

His kiss swept to her hip, and back to her navel. Fire, shooting, golden streaks of it, seemed to spring forth from the deepest, darkest, most intimate recesses of her desire as she felt the movement of his lips and the searing wet stroke of his tongue. He couldn't be intending to kiss her there . . .

Anticipation swept through her along with the protest that bubbled to her lips but went unspoken. Surely a flush covered the length of her body. The expectation was the sweetest agony. It was too intimate, too deep, too close to her soul. . . .

He shifted. He kissed all of her flesh, the sweep of her stomach, the top of her thighs. He moved all along them. He came everywhere but there.

And then he was gone. She was cold and bereft, and she was in anguish! How she needed him, wanted him. Her body moved, as fluid as water, seeking his touch in a subtle undulation. It was the sweetest ecstasy of wanting, it was sensation so strong that it was anguish.

What did he now intend? She didn't dare meet his eyes. The intimacy had gone too deep.

He lowered himself against her body, stroking her leg. His kiss fell upon the back of her kneecap.

And then that hot and molten trail of steaming moisture began to move up the length of her inner thigh once again. Higher and higher now until she trembled and writhed and waited.

She cried out, the breath escaping her, the very life seeming to escape her as he at last ceased to circle the velvet petals of her deepest desire and treasure them with his liquid caress. The world itself spun with the leisurely, supple movement of his intimate kiss. But it was swift, so swift, for the sweet, spiraling soaring was barely upon her before it burst into blackness, then came crashing down upon her in wave after wave of shimmering crystal, wracking her body with quivers. Words began to escape her then; if not words, then sounds. What she had done, what she had permitted—what she had felt!—came rushing in on her senses. Again she felt that the whole of her body must have blushed a vibrant red, and she was wholeheartedly eager not to have to meet his eyes.

"Oh, no!" she whispered, but soft laughter greeted her, words that she barely heard in her sudden and swift desire to hide away.

His eyes were above hers, deep cobalt blue, so hot and demanding still, so very alive with their startling blue fire. In his arms, she was reassured. In his arms, she realized that he wanted everything. His mouth found hers even when she would have twisted away. His lips parted hers, his tongue plunged and plundered past her teeth, capturing her own.

Just as his body at long last captured hers.

Ecstasy had come so swiftly before. It could not come again. But he intended that it should, and those startling eyes pierced and held hers as he began to move. He entered deeply into her. More and more of him became a part of her, until she thought that she would shriek, for he could go no further, she could give no more. But he could, and he would.

And she could, she discovered, give endlessly.

His eyes remained upon hers as he began to move. She gasped softly, realizing that she was moving again herself, undulating, writhing, grasping again for the elusive wonder. His eyes closed and he clasped her tightly into his arms, and a sound choked from her as he gave a total free rein to the strength of the desire he had restrained so patiently, so very long.

And then it was as if a storm swept through her, wild, reckless, violent, encompassing everything within its pass. The thunder and the size and power of him seemed to rock her to her extremities, seize her in tempest. She clung to him, her arms around him, holding tight. And he lifted her higher and closer, whispering to her, until her legs were also locked around his back, until tears of pleasure and pain stung the back of her eyes.

Until the world, and all the stars within it, suddenly exploded.

Night descended, eclipsing the room, eclipsing life itself. She wondered if she had died. She knew vaguely that she had not.

She opened her eyes slowly. She was indeed alive. A silver sheen of perspiration moistened her body, and her body remained entwined with his. A hot flush covered her cheeks as she felt him, still inside her, still filling her with the searing sweet nectar of his climax. His body lay limp, though his thigh was still cast over hers, his arms still about her. The desperate tension was gone.

He slept, pray God, he slept. With her passion spent, she suddenly realized just exactly what she had done.

She had made love with a stranger.

No, no, not a stranger!

She had made love with her enemy.

A choked cry caught in her throat and hot tears of shame nearly fell then from her eyes. She had betrayed everything that she had been taught, and she had truly betrayed the love she had once known.

But she had wanted him. She had seen the male glory of his nakedness, and she had felt his kiss, and she had known that she wanted him.

Wanting him was one thing. Having him was another.

She cared for him. More deeply than she could ever dare admit!

He moved his forefinger tenderly over her lip. She looked at him to discover the warmth of his eyes upon her and compassion etched deeply into the cobalt of his eyes. She shivered. Even while lying here ashamed of herself, she wanted him again.

She liked his face. Liked the character there, and the honesty, and yes, the honor, and both the tempest and the peace.

He appeared very much at peace at the moment. But he did not appear smug, or triumphant, rather, it seemed that his features were touched by concern.

Daniel *was* concerned. Now that the ragged fires that had threatened to incinerate his very soul had been somewhat quenched, he was worried about the very object of those desires.

She had given him so very much. She had surrendered herself to his every lead. Yet even while he had lain there, spent, amazed by the climax of desire when he was not an inexperienced boy, she had begun to withdraw.

He couldn't let her withdraw from him. Ever. Not now that he had felt the silken fire of her hair flow over his fingers when he held her. Not now that he had feasted upon the beauty of her nakedness, tasted the sweetness therein, known her, loved her. He was amazed still by the natural and fluid movement of her body, by all that she had brought forth in him. She was so alluring looking up at him with her dark lashes shielding those silver and gray eyes. Her lips, parted and moist and slightly open with the whisper of her desire, had sent him into new realms of need and pleasure, into a world he was suddenly certain he had never quite been before.

He held her when she would have turned away. "Callie, I am ever more entranced. Yet *you* look now as if you had truly come from battle."

Her eyes, soft gray now, flickered shut, then met his again. "A battle lost," she whispered.

"No, angel. A battle won. By North and by South."

She still seemed distressed, and he understood. It was one thing in this world for a man to want a woman. But in that same social world, her wanting him would be condemned, time and time again. Prim and proper madams would whisper, and all would swear that their daughter would never be so bold or promiscuous. Be she rich or be she poor, a woman should be chaste, so society claimed.

Daniel had decided long ago that society could be damned. What needs and emotions lurked in the hearts and minds of men and women could not be dictated by society. There were other reasons for Callie to have regrets now, when the flames cooled between them.

He was the enemy. One of the enemy who had taken her husband.

A husband she had loved.

Daniel wished that there were something he could say to convince her that there had been something special and unique between them. That no intimate action could be condemned when two people had been so strongly attracted to one another, when emotions had come so swiftly, when need had been so deep. There was nothing at all wrong because he loved her, he thought with a growing amazement.

He loved the gravity and emotion in her eyes, and he loved the way that they could fall upon him. The way that she spoke would remain in his memory forever, the softness of her voice, the beautiful tone of it. During long lonely nights ahead, he would dream of the perfection of her face, and he would remember both the thrill and the tenderness of her fingers upon him. He would remember, too, the steadfastness of her heart, her loyalty to her cause, right or wrong. He would remember the way that she had loved him, and he would know that, yes, he loved her.

Perhaps he couldn't tell her such a thing. Not now. She mourned a husband and lived in the midst of a battlefield. Perhaps all that he could do was hold her and let that be enough.

"I surrendered everything!" she said suddenly, fiercely.

He cupped her cheek and met her gaze, and smiled with all his tenderness.

"No, angel. I surrendered everything."

He felt her trembling and hesitated to speak again. Her eyes widened with a sudden gratitude, then suddenly she pushed away from him, sitting up. Her gaze met his, a sizzling, shimmering silver. She lifted back a long, wild wayward skein of her deep flame hair, sending it sliding down the length of her back as she straddled over his hips and leaned closely over him.

"Want to fight again?" she whispered softly.

He grinned, knowing that she was going to be all right with her decision to lie with him.

Her head lowered, her lips touched his chest, the tip of her tongue seemed to singe it.

"Fire away, Yank," he told her, caressing her neck, cradling her head against him. "Fire away!" he repeated, and he wound his arms around her, sweeping her beneath him, as all the fires that had just begun to cool found a new and wild ignition with her touch.

The whole world could be damned, Daniel thought. Even as he lost himself within the musky sweet scent and taste and feel of her, he dimly marveled at the very idea.

He was falling in love.

With a Yank . . .

It was a strange war.

And a strange, strange battle.

Eight

"We call him 'Beauty.' Of course, we try very hard for the rank and file not to hear such terms. After all, we are military men. But Beauty he became, and so Beauty sticks."

"Is he really so handsome a man, then, so beautiful?" Callie asked, laughing.

It was night again. They had spent the day like newlyweds until dusk had fallen, and then Callie remembered the few animals that remained on the farm. Feeling more than a little guilty toward the poor creatures, she had enlisted Daniel's help to feed them.

It was interesting to watch him—not because she had discovered it was hard to take her eyes off him—but because he was so at ease with everything she asked of him. He knew what he was doing, whether measuring grain for Hal, her one remaining horse, or strewing out the grain for the chickens. Of course, a plantation was just a big farm—a very big farm—she reminded herself, but Daniel had been born and bred a child of privilege, of the southern aristocracy, and she had never imagined he would have such ease with manual labor.

Not that he had given her a chance to talk about it. Still barefoot, in her father's breeches and open plaid flannel shirt, he might have been the image of any farm boy. Against the setting sun, atop the gate of the barn-yard door, his legs dangling, he seemed so very young. The lines had eased from his eyes while he chewed upon a blade of hay and entertained her with stories about some of the more infamous southern commanders.

"Is he really beautiful?" Daniel repeated, then laughed. They were talking about Stuart—General James Ewell Brown Stuart, "Jeb," as he was known. He was Daniel's immediate superior, but it didn't sound to Callie like Daniel gave that matter much thought at all. He called Stuart "Old Beauty."

Daniel shrugged, the light of laughter still in his eyes. "Beautiful, well, let's see. He is certainly gallant. And he loves to dress. He is flamboyant, he is courageous, and to Flora, I imagine, he is beautiful."

"Flora?"

"His wife," Daniel said with a grin. "But beautiful? The name was given him at West Point. I fear it was given him as a joke, for apparently, his classmates found his features not beautiful in the least."

"And what do you think?"

"Well, he is my superior officer."

"And you do not sound respectful enough."

"Well, I have known him forever, so it seems," Daniel admitted. "He's older than I by a few years." He was quiet for a minute. "He and Jesse were in the same class, but we were all Virginians, and were all assigned to the West together." He shrugged again, as if he didn't want to dwell upon the past any longer. "Beauty and I are friends, we are both avid horsemen, and we work very well together. In truth, I am very respectful, for I know of no cavalry commander more talented, dashing, or bold."

"Here, here!" Callie applauded, smiling. Then her smile faded, and she swirled about in the dust to cast more seed to the chickens. Dear God, how strange. He was speaking about the men who were grinding countless companies of the Union army into constant bloody defeats. The way that he spoke, she found herself smiling far too frequently, and anxious to meet such a man as Beauty Stuart.

"There was an occasion when the Federals under Pope managed to take Stuart's magnificent cape and his plumed hat," Daniel told her, his eyes twinkling.

"And?"

"And so we had to go after Pope—and get back his cape and hat."

"I don't believe you."

"It's true, and we succeeded nicely, thank you. You see," he advised her, his tone grave, his eyes alight, "we are entirely bold and dashing and daring, and there's nothing that can stop the southern cavalry."

It was often proving all too true, Callie thought. Northern horsemen had a difficult time keeping up with their southern counterparts. Too many of the South's men were like Daniel, born and bred to ride and hunt and master the slopes and hills and valleys and forests of their region.

"We are Lee's eyes and ears—" Daniel began, but he broke off, looking into the darkness of the night.

"What is it?" Callie asked him.

"Nothing," he said after a moment. He shrugged. "I thought I heard something." He stared at Callie again. "Cavalry was all-important in the battle here. Lee's orders for the campaign were discovered by the Federals, and it was our scouting and riding around the Federals that brought back that information."

"Lee's orders were found by the Union?" Callie said. One point for their side. How unusual.

Daniel nodded, watching her. "Special Order Number 191," he said. "It advised a number of Lee's key generals that he was splitting the army, that Jackson

would be taking Harpers Ferry. Someone was careless.
There were seven copies of the order. One was found
by Federal men in the grass at one of the campsites we
had abandoned near Frederick, Maryland. It was
wrapped around three cigars, can you imagine? It was
an incredible gift to the Union—and a blow to us. But
McClellan moved too slowly. Jackson managed to take
Harpers Ferry, and to meet us here to do battle. And
Lee was forewarned that McClellan knew about the
order because we looped around to get the information."

"You didn't win the battle," Callie reminded him.

"Do you know that for a fact?"

Callie shrugged. "Union soldiers are keeping you
here," she said softly.

"I wonder. I wonder if it is Union soldiers keeping
me here," he murmured softly. He tore his eyes from
hers, looking out over the night that settled around
them. "Perhaps we didn't win. Maybe we didn't take
the territory. But I don't think that the Union won
either."

Callie didn't want to remember the aftermath of the
battle. The bodies had been taken away from her lawn.
More selfishly, she didn't want to give up the night, or
this very strange time between her and this Rebel. He
was anxious to leave, she knew. Now that she was anxious that he stay, he was feeling the hard pull to return
to duty. She was very afraid for him to go. He wasn't
strong enough yet, she had convinced herself. And the
countryside was crawling with Union troops.

He wouldn't allow himself to be taken. Not easily.
He'd die to escape, or he'd bring down more men to
whom she should owe her loyalty and concern.

She smiled at him, dispelling the desolation that had
intruded between them.

"So the southern cavalry can all ride," Callie said.
"Watch it. The northern boys just might catch up."

"But we ride very well," he assured her with a grin.
"So might they."

"We ride exceptionally well."

"And you also excel in your humility," she said.

"The prim and proper Mrs. Michaelson, returned to
me at last!" he teased.

Callie threw out a handful of seed to the chickens,
which hurriedly pecked away at the offering. "I am
very prim and proper, and you must keep that in
mind," she told him. She didn't dare look at him to see
the warmth of the smile that curved his lip. Perhaps she
had been prim and proper once. But he had changed
her. Irrevocably. He knew her more intimately than
any man alive . . . or dead. He had demanded so
many things from her, and he had given back so many.
He had robbed her of old emotions, and given her new
ecstasy—and anguish. She didn't dare dwell too closely
upon it. She was falling in love with her enemy, and in
this war, that was a very frightening thought.

She turned back to face him and met his gaze. He
was looking at her with that blue fire kindled within his
eyes once again. A fire that caught deep within her just
because he glanced her way. A fire that evoked sweet
longings and seemed to touch down upon her flesh
with a dance of sweet little flames.

A fire from which she needed some distance.

"Let's hear more about these famous—infamous!—
men in gray," she told him. "What about Lee? Is he
really so great as they say?"

Daniel grinned. "There is no man greater." He slid
down from the gate, leaning against it. "Imagine, Callie. He had a beautiful home in Arlington. It still sits
there, high upon a ridge, looking over the Potomac,
right in Washington, D.C. And it wasn't just his home,
it was his wife's home. And she is—"

"Martha Washington's great-granddaughter, and the
step great-grandchild of George Washington," Callie

interrupted softly. Daniel looked at her with an arched brow. "So I've heard," Callie said. "Your General Lee is a legend here, just as he is in the South. Many people believe that the war would be over now if we had had him leading some of our troops. They say that he is a brilliant commander, and an extremely fine man."

Daniel smiled ruefully. "It's quite true; he is both of those things. And sometimes, when the war seems to drag on and on and I'm thinking of home with every breath I take, I think about Master Lee, as we sometimes call him, and his wife, Mary, and that beautiful home of theirs."

"And what of Mary Lee?" Callie murmured.

A slow, wry curl worked its way into Daniel's lip as he looked down at Callie. "Mary Lee loves her husband very much. And trusts in his decisions."

"It is her home that is lost," Callie said. "He is off riding around the countryside."

"Skedaddling Yanks," Daniel said lazily. She cast him a most condemning gaze and he laughed softly.

He leapt down from the barn gate and came toward her. "He's very, very good at it."

"Is he?" Callie said.

Daniel nodded. "Yes. All Rebs are. Look. All I'm doing is walking very slowly toward you. And you're already trying to skedaddle."

Her heart was thudding already. Yes, she was backing away from him. She just couldn't feel this warm, lusty wonder every time he looked at her. It was wrong, and she had created a fool's paradise. She had to learn to walk and talk and keep her distance from him, to regain her sense of propriety, dear God, to regain her morals!

But all that he had to do was beckon, and she felt the heat come simmering through her.

"I'm not trying to skedaddle," she assured him.

"Then stand still."

"But I'm not ready to surrender!" she said quickly. He was still coming. She dropped the bucket of chicken feed and veered around toward the paddock fence, making sure she kept her eyes on him all the while.

"How futile to battle when the war is already lost!" he told her.

"No, sir! The war is not lost. Battle after battle may be won, but that does not mean that the war is lost!"

"The enemy can be worn down."

"Not a determined enemy."

He paused for just a moment, his head cocked, a crooked smile playing into the corners of his mouth. "Have you ever made love in the hay, Mrs. Michaelson?"

Her mouth dropped, although she didn't know why anything that he should say or do should surprise her anymore.

He didn't wait for her answer, but came toward her again with his long, relentless stride. A sound escaped her as he came too close, and she made a beeline past him, slipping behind the barn gate and using it for a barrier between them.

"Colonel, things have happened very quickly here," she told him, "and I think that a measure of constraint—"

"The moment is constraining me to sheer distraction, Mrs. Michaelson," he said pleasantly enough. But then his hand touched the rim of the gate and suddenly he was leaping up and over it, and facing her.

"Daniel Cameron—"

"You never, never made love in the hay?"

She pushed away from the gate, backing away from him once again. "Well, it's hardly the proper thing to do—"

"Callie, Callie, Callie, making love is not supposed

to be a 'proper' thing at all. And the scent of the hay is so delicious—"

"And it surely sticks into your flesh and tangles in your hair!"

He laughed, his blue eyes sparkling and alive, even in the darkness. "Come here, woman!" he commanded. He reached for her hand, pulling her to him.

She felt as if she were melting inside. Was this love? So quickly, so easily? Or was this the effect of war?

"You behave, Reb!" she informed him regally, and she jerked free from his hold, only to fall backward with her effort—and wind up right where he wanted her, in a pile of hay.

In seconds he had fallen down beside her, his arm about her, lifting a handful of straw to breathe in its scent. "It's wonderful, it's fresh, it's clean—"

"And one should be careful of cow manure!" Callie interrupted.

But his laughter rang softly around her, husky, seductive. She needed to protest, they were moving too quickly, he was the enemy.

He touched her lips with his own. She was well dressed for seduction in the hay, wearing nothing at all but a simple blue cotton day dress with a button-up bodice and full flaring skirt.

One by one, her buttons were coming open. In the darkness, she felt the stroke of his hand moving up the hem of her skirt.

Her bodice fell open, her breasts spilled free. Her skirt was shoved to her hips, and she felt the swift, sudden, and breathtaking weight of his body come boldly atop hers. His fingers stroked between her thighs, touching, probing, as he kissed her.

His lips moved from hers. He buried his face between her breasts just as he thrust his shaft deeply, firmly within her.

She gasped, and breathed in the hay. The scent was

sweet and titillating, just as the feel of the earth around
her and the raw scent of the man atop her combined to
bring within her an explosion of wild and reckless passion.

He was not so tender a lover as he had been before.
When he touched her, surrounded as he was by earth
and night air, it was with a wild and reckless need that
boldly mingled with the scent of the dirt and the hay.
He did not tease or cajole, but his lips lay claim to a
response, with no protest allowed her.

His body moved with the same hard passion, not
tempting or eliciting a response but, rather, provoking
one. Yet all that he did was what she craved. She did
feel the hay against her naked flesh, and she did feel
her body pressed low and lower into the earth. The
scent of his body and the scent of her own then mingled with all those other earth scents, and as he moved
so boldly between her thighs, she felt again a starting,
wild thunder of passion seize hold of her. In seconds it
seemed that the desires that sang so within her blood
and coursed through her limbs were appeased with a
swift and startling volatility. Hot honey filled the very
center of her. She saw blackness and then light. She did
not know if the cries she heard were sounds she emit-
ted, or part of the words he whispered tensely to her,
or if the searing nectar had spilled from herself, or
from him. She only knew that she lay spent on the hay
when he was done, exhausted, and still drifting in distant fields of beauty.

They were silent and it was long minutes later when
she again felt the prick of the hay against her flesh. She
smiled, and he was suddenly over her, wickedly grinning. "Mrs. Michaelson. There is hay in your hair!"

"Oh, you wretched Rebel!" she cried, laughing, and
shoved at his chest. He did not intend to let her go, and
so she laughed as they rolled over in the hay together.
She managed to elude him, but just as she did so, she

reached the edge of the hay, and shrieked as she went teetering over the two-foot pile to the ground below. His head instantly appeared above her. Tousled, blue eyes alight with laughter, he stared down at her. "There you go, Mrs. Michaelson! See what happens to wayward Yanks? I daresay—"

His voice suddenly broke off and his laughter faded. He reached down a hand to her, and his voice was suddenly grave. "Callie, give me your hand. Come back up."

He didn't want her to look to her side—she knew it instantly.

But like Lot's wife, she couldn't help doing so. She turned to her left, to stare at a spot where there were just a few feet between the hay pile and the rear wall of the barn.

It was dark in the barn. Shadows were intensified and increased because of the one lamp that illuminated everything from the spot where it hung near the door. There was a moon out, but its glow was pale and did little to illuminate the corners of the barn.

Still, she could see the man and see his face, with horror. A terrible scream rose in her throat. It choked there, and the sound that came from her was simply one of horror.

He leaned against the barn wall, his hand over his abdomen. His eyes remained open, his mouth was in an O, as if he were still surprised by his own untimely end. He was a young soldier boy, a sad, pathetic figure in deep, dark, haunting blue.

"Callie!"

She couldn't seem to move on her own. Strong arms enveloped her, and in seconds she was swept up and held tightly.

Daniel sat on the hay with her upon his lap, cradling her head against his chest, murmuring assurances. She couldn't even hear his words.

She had seen so many dead men. She hadn't thought that the sight of another could do this to her.

Perhaps that was it. There had been too many before. None of them had been like this poor soldier. Alone. He had crawled here, into her barn, to die. He didn't stink yet, so he hadn't been dead that long. He had holed up here, weak, afraid, dying. She had come and gone the last three days, feeding the animals, and she had never seen him. He had just lain there. . . .

They had just lain in the hay, half-naked, entwined, whispering, crying out. And all the while the poor young soldier's sightless eyes had been open upon them.

"Oh, God!" she whimpered against Daniel's chest, and she was shaking again.

"Callie, it's all right. It's all over for him. He's at peace. Callie, look at me, will you."

She tried to stare at him. She tried to focus on him. Tears swam in her eyes and guilt riddled her.

She had spent those days tending to an enemy soldier, wanting an enemy soldier, making love with an enemy soldier. And this boy had been out here, dying.

She jumped up, pulling her bodice together. "Oh, my Lord, how could we—"

"Callie, stop it!" He was instantly on his feet, calmly belting his breeches.

She shook her head, feeling wild, as if she wanted to run and run until she made it all disappear—the hatred, the war, the guilt, the love. "No, Daniel." She backed away from him, but his hands were quickly on her shoulders, shaking her lightly. "Callie, we've done nothing wrong. It's not wrong to live, to survive! You cannot feel guilty for living!"

"I do not feel guilty for living!" she protested. "I feel guilty for—"

"For loving?" he inquired softly. She stiffened, trying to escape him, but he drew her to him, holding her very close. "Callie, we did not take his life—"

She jerked free again. "But you might have! You might have shot him down. And I might have allowed him to die by neglect!"

"Callie, I didn't shoot him. I fell in your front yard. And nothing that you did or didn't do could have saved him."

"How do you know?"

"He was gut shot, Callie."

"He didn't die quickly. He just lay there—"

"Unconscious, Callie," he assured her, advancing toward her.

"No!" she shrieked. "No! You are the enemy. Don't touch me, don't touch me—"

But he did touch her. He took her into his arms again, and she beat furiously against his back until her energy drained from her. Tears fell down her cheeks once again.

He didn't say anything else to her, he just held her. He smoothed back her hair, and rocked her. In time she felt the tremors that had seized her begin to fade. She sniffled raggedly, and then she felt the simple edge of exhaustion come over her.

She was dimly aware that he rose, and that he would take her back to the house. She stopped him.

"Daniel, we can't just leave him."

"You're right. We can't just leave him," he agreed. He set her down upon the hay, and cupped her chin, lifting her face so that he could meet her eyes. "Are you all right?"

She nodded. She wasn't all right at all. One moment she was freezing, and the next she was numb. She felt as if all the agony of the war had descended down upon her, and then it was as if she couldn't feel anything at all.

But she nodded again, trying to assure him.

He left her sitting on the hay. She heard him moving about the barn, looking for a shovel.

It seemed forever that he was gone. She waited on the hay, and then she remembered that she was alone in the barn with the young soldier with the dead eyes that still seemed to watch her. She leapt up and started to run out of the barn.

Daniel was just coming back in. He caught her shoulders. "I dug the grave in your family plot. You may want to send his things home; I'll collect them for you. Maybe his family will want to send for his body later too. But for tonight . . . tonight, we'll just lay him to rest."

She nodded, not realizing that she was clinging to him.

"Callie, I have to get him," Daniel reminded her softly.

"Oh!" She released him and walked on out to the small family cemetery. There were monuments to her mother and her father, and to Gregory. Farther back were the stones for her grandparents, and for her aunt Sarah, who had died as a child of six. There, by Gregory's grave, was a gaping new hole.

A moment later, Daniel reappeared. He had wrapped the soldier in an old horse blanket, but carried him as gently as if he were alive.

He just as gently set the body into the grave he had dug.

Watching him, Callie felt the cold close around her heart again. This poor boy, so far from home! None to mourn him, none to say a prayer.

But she was wrong. Daniel repacked the earth over the grave, and when he was done, he drew a cross in the dirt. And to her surprise, he began to speak.

"Dear Lord, this is Private Benjamin Gest, an artillery man. Brave, loyal, true, he gave his all for his cause. Into your hands, we commend his keeping.

Ashes to ashes, dust to dust, earth to earth. Father, look gently down upon him, for he was just a boy. Be with his loved ones, God, and give them strength."

He stepped back from the grave, his hands dirty but folded, his chest still naked and streaked with dirt and sweat. His head bowed low, he was silent for several long seconds, and then he looked to Callie again.

She felt tears rising once more. She didn't want to shed them.

"Thank you," she said.

"It is the least that any man deserves."

"You knew his name."

"I went through his haversack. It's in the barn, with his personal effects. There's a letter in there for his mother. You might want to make sure that she gets it."

Callie nodded.

"Callie, go in. Go to bed," he told her.

"What are you doing?"

He shrugged awkwardly. "I'm covered in dirt. I'm going to clean up."

She felt the same herself, but she was suddenly so exhausted, she didn't know if she could stand much longer. He wanted her to go in. She didn't know where he meant to clean up, but she didn't ask. He obviously wanted to be alone.

She walked woodenly back to the house and up the stairs. In her room she discovered that she was desperate to wash up too. She poured out water and scrubbed her face and her throat and her arms and her breasts. She dug into her wardrobe and crawled into a white nightgown.

She caught sight of her reflection in the swivel mirror in the corner of the room. The gown seemed mockingly virginal.

She closed her eyes, and turned away, and crawled into her bed. But once she was there, she couldn't sleep. She lay awake, staring up at the ceiling and wait-ing.

She had assumed that he would come to her. But time passed, and Daniel did not come. A slow aching began to build inside her.

She got up and opened the door. She could hear him in the parlor below. Hurrying down the steps, she saw him before the fireplace, staring into the flames of a blaze he had just built against the chill of the late night. His arm rested against the hearth, his head against his arm.

"Daniel?" she said softly.

He looked up at her. Blue eyes meeting hers. She felt a special warmth grip hold of her heart. There was something very noble in the structure of his face, in the weary slope of his broad shoulders.

"You should sleep," he told her.

"I don't want to sleep alone," she said.

He smiled, understanding exactly the need that she couldn't quite voice aloud. He came up the stairs and lifted her into his arms.

He brought her back into her room and laid her down, then stretched out beside her. He took her gently into his arms, and smoothed out her hair.

She managed to close her eyes and to sleep.

All through the night she was warm and safe and protected from all the demons of war that had come to haunt her. Even in her sleep, she knew that he held her.

He might have been her enemy.

But she had never been kept more safely.

Nine

Callie slept late the next morning, and when she awoke she was alone. The bed beside her still retained a little warmth. She ran her hand over the sheets and then closed her eyes.

She had liked sleeping beside him. Feeling his arms, warm and strong, wrapped about her. Turning to rest her head against his chest. Feeling the even tremor of his breathing.

When he was gone, she would be bereft. It would be worse than it had been when she learned Gregory had died. She had learned to stand alone, and now she was going to have to learn that bitter lesson all over again.

He couldn't go, not yet. He was well enough to help with the animals, or in the house. He was certainly well enough to make love. But he was not yet recovered enough to make the dangerous and difficult trip through enemy lines. He had to see that.

But he wouldn't, she knew. It was time he made his move, whatever came of it. A feeling of dread settled over her.

Maybe she would still have tonight.

She slipped out of bed and walked over to her window and looked down into the paddock in front of the barn at the back of the house. He was out there, fixing a broken hinge on the gate. He moved as if he would lower his hat against the rising sun, and then he seemed to realize that he no longer wore his magnificent hat. She smiled, and bit lightly into her lower lip, wondering if she hadn't gotten just a bit carried away when she'd burned his hat.

After all, Beauty Stuart had ridden after General Pope's army just to retrieve his hat and cape. Daniel Cameron must have been very attached to his hat.

He looked up suddenly, as if he sensed that she was there. He waved to her. "Good morning."

"Good morning."

"The gate is all right now." He looked around and shrugged. "I replaced a few rails in the fencing for you, but there's not too much that I can do about all the bullet holes."

She looked down at him and lifted her shoulders in a small shrug. "No, not now," she said. "Would you like breakfast?"

"The coffee is already on," he told her. "I'll be right in," he added.

Callie stepped away from the window and moved back into her room. He was leaving. He was trying to repay her in some way for what she had done for him.

She dressed quickly, simply, in a muted blue plaid cotton that buttoned to her throat. The day might well be warm, but she welcomed the long sleeves on the dress, anything that might put some distance between them and give her the dignity she would need to let him go.

When she was dressed, she surveyed the length of her hair, thick and curling over her shoulders and down her back. She picked up her brush and worked through it vigorously, then twisted it into a severe knot, which she secured with pins. She was determined on a look of staid respectability.

He had not been here very long. Not quite a week.

Why did it feel as if he had changed her whole life, as if things could never be the same again?

She heard the back door close, and she hurried down the stairs. He was in the kitchen, sipping a cup of coffee, ready to hand her one when she walked in. His eyes rode over her. Blue, endlessly blue. She thought that there was anguish in them, and despite herself, she was glad of it. He had torn her world in two. He hadn't made her question her own loyalties or her beliefs, but he had forced her to see the face of the enemy, and she realized all too painfully that they were one people. And that it was possible to love and agonize despite their differences.

"Callie—"

"You're leaving today," she said softly.

"Tonight."

She nodded, sipping her coffee.

"Last night, when we found that boy . . ." He paused, shrugging. "Callie, they'll have reported me as missing by now. I don't want that kind of news getting back to Virginia. My sister and my sister-in-law would be devastated."

"And your brother?"

"It might take longer for the news to reach Jesse," Daniel said. He cocked his head, reflecting. "And then again, the news might already have reached Jesse."

"That's right," Callie murmured. "He and Beauty went to school together."

Daniel smiled. "That's right," he said softly. "Callie, I can't let them mourn for me, or go through the anguish of wondering."

"I know," she said.

"I've tried to—to do what I can around here."

"You don't owe me anything."

"Other than my life," he said lightly. He set his mug down, walking toward her. In seconds, he undid all that she had done to keep her facade of composure. He pulled the pins from her hair, letting them fall to the ground. The knot unwound into a wild mass. He lifted her hair from her back and spread it out over her shoulders, watching his handiwork as it streamed down her back. "What I do has nothing to do with owing you, Yank," he said very softly. "It has everything to do with not wanting to leave you."

She still needed to keep her distance. She stood still, not protesting his touch, but not giving in to it either. "Duty calls. I understand."

"My God, do you?" He demanded, suddenly fierce, his voice trembling. His hands locked around her shoulders and he shook her so that her head fell slightly back. She raised her eyes to his, cool still, as if she calmly awaited his words. She was anything but calm, her heart racing, her blood seeming to seethe and boil.

"You can't possibly understand. I would give everything to forget the war and stay here with you. I'm sick to death of dead men, of blood, of heroes in tattered jackets and bare feet. I'm weary of camp fires, and orders, and trying to learn new and better ways to kill my enemy. I would give everything . . ."

His anger suddenly faded as she stared silently into his eyes. He shook his head. "I have to go back. I am fighting for something. I can't explain it to you. I'm fighting for the river. I'm fighting for the bricks and pillars of my home. I'm fighting for those hot days in summer when you can hear the chanting from the fields and quarters. For the rustle of silk, for the soft tone of a drawl. Maybe I'm fighting for a dying empire, I don't know. What I do know is that it's my empire, and right or wrong, I must defend it to the last."

She felt that she could move at last. She reached up and stroked his cheek. His lips came down upon hers, nearly brutal in all that he demanded. When he raised his head at last, she was shaking. Her lips were swollen from his passion.

Her heart was lost, her resolve shattered.

"You cannot go until nightfall," she whispered.

His eyes touched hers with their fire, and he swept her up into his arms. Callie reached up, winding her arms around his neck, meeting his gaze. He started for the stairway.

She rested her head against his chest. "I knew that you had to go. But I could not let you go. Not without being with you one last time."

"I could not go without having you one last night," he whispered huskily.

He started up the stairs, his arms tight around her. But even as his long-legged gait brought them upward, they were both startled from the intimacy of their private world by a hard knocking upon the door.

Daniel stiffened instantly. Panic swept quickly through Callie, then she managed to control it. "Let me down, quickly, Daniel."

To her amazement, he did so. She raced up the stairs herself, with him fast behind her. From the hallway window, she looked down, but the eaves over the house shielded their visitor.

The knocking sounded again. Tense, Callie held still. She could hear Daniel moving away from her now, walking toward her brother Joshua's room.

She knew that he was going for his sword.

"Frau Michaelson!"

She heard the deep, slightly accented voice and she let out a quick sigh of relief. Daniel was back in the hallway, watching her, his sword hilt held tightly in his hand.

"Who is it?" he demanded.

"It's all right," she said quickly.

"Who is it?" his voice was tense.

"It's just Rudy Weiss—"

"And who is 'just' Rudy Weiss?"

She hated his tone when it became so imperious. She hated him when he became so cold.

"He is my neighbor. A Dunkard."

"A Dunkard."

"He's one of the German Baptist Brethren who worship in the little white church that must have been in the middle of your battlefield," Callie said quickly.

"That could make him an ardent Yank or a southern sympathizer. Which is he, Callie?"

"He's neither!" Callie replied irritably. She lifted her hands with aggravation. "There isn't even a steeple on their church, these people believe in such a simple lifestyle. They want no part of the war, they don't want to hurt anyone. They lead very strict, religious lives. I'm not even sure that Rudy approves of me, but he is a caring man, and he knows that I am alone. He has come to see to my welfare, nothing more."

"Frau Michaelson?"

They heard the voice again, rising, concerned.

Callie spun around, heedless of Daniel's staring at her. She hurried down the stairs and opened the door.

Rudy Weiss, white-haired, white-bearded, a man who looked as if could have been close to one hundred years old, but still tall and agile and very dignified, awaited her with anxiety in his powder-blue eyes. But once she had opened the door, he smiled.

"So, you are well. I was getting very worried. The place, it was loaded with soldiers, jah?"

"Yes, Herr Weiss. There were many soldiers."

"You were not hurt?"

"No, no, I wasn't hurt at all."

"And none of the soldiers have disturbed you? If you are worried, we will take care that you are not alone."

"No, no, thank you," Callie said quickly, then she

asked anxiously, "Your wife, your family, were any of them injured?"

"Nein, nein, we are well," he said. He continued to stand on her porch, then said worriedly, "There is a friend staying with you, then?"

Callie froze, staring at him. He lifted a hand, palm up, and explained. "Karl, my oldest son, saw a man feeding your chickens."

Callie exhaled, "Oh." She didn't know what to say. It didn't matter. She didn't have to say anything. She hadn't realized that Daniel had followed her down the stairs until he stood by her, offering his hand to Rudy. "Daniel Cameron, Mr. Weiss. Yes, I am a friend of Callie's."

Rudy nodded gravely, surveying Daniel. "Well then, perhaps you can stay on a bit longer, Herr Cameron." As Daniel frowned he continued, "There is a bit of news. Grave excitement in the North."

"The war . . . ?" Callie said.

"The war—it goes on," Rudy said. He slipped a newspaper from his pocket, handing it to Callie. "I do not usually bother with the affairs of others," he said to Daniel. "Mein frau insisted this might be important for Callie, for she lives here alone."

"What is it?" Callie said, for Daniel was taking the paper from her and scanning it quickly.

"President Lincoln has issued a . . . a preliminary e-man-ci-pa-tion pro-cla-ma-tion," Rudy Weiss said, speaking very carefully, and very slowly.

"Emancipation proclamation?" Callie repeated, trying to take the paper from Daniel. He wouldn't allow her to do so. He was avidly reading every word in the article.

"By God, he's gone and done it!" Daniel exclaimed.

"It frees the slaves," Rudy said.

Daniel swung around, laughing hollowly as he stared at Callie. "No, no, not exactly. It frees the slaves—in the states that are in rebellion! It frees the slaves in the South, not in the North, not in the border states! This is rich, really rich. Oh, God! Do you know what this means!''

Callie wasn't sure that she did know what it meant, not the way that Daniel seemed to understand it. He released the paper to her at last and sank down into one of the upholstered chairs in the parlor, staring straight ahead at nothing.

Callie looked back to Rudy Weiss, who remained on her porch.

"Your friend, Herr Cameron, understands," Rudy said softly. "The slaves are freed as of January third, next year. The slaves in those 'states in rebellion.' Herr Cameron knows. The southern men will not consider any proclamation of Lincoln's as law in their Confederacy. But the slaves will want to be free. They will begin to escape. Many of them will be hungry, and they will come north, looking for food, looking for jobs, looking for ways to be free. Many may become desperate. That is why mein frau is so anxious for you, Callie. She says that you must take care if these people come this way. Myself, I told her that you must take care with the soldiers too. Some men are good, and some men are evil, no matter what the coloring of their skin or their clothing."

Callie nodded, moistening her lips nervously. Daniel was watching Rudy, and Rudy, his old eyes very bright, was watching Daniel. Daniel rose and walked back to the doorway. "You take care, too, Herr Cameron," Rudy said quietly.

"I will. Thank you," Daniel said.

Rudy knew damned well that Daniel was a Reb soldier, Callie thought. And he didn't care. If he was a friend, he was a friend. And a friend who needed to be warned, it seemed, for Rudy turned then to leave, saying over his shoulder, "There's still a troop of soldiers camped just south of us, in a cornfield. They seem to be watching the roads." He stopped, and looked up at the sky. Then he looked back to Callie and Daniel. He wrinkled up his nose, then shook his head sadly. "There is still the stink of death about us; the creek still seems to run red with blood. It is a sad thing, this war. A very sad thing."

He left them, walking down the walk, then out and across the road and into the field that faced Callie's house.

Daniel watched until he was gone, then his fingers suddenly crumpled over the newspaper. "This is rich. Damnation, but this is rich! Your Mr. Lincoln is no fool, Callie." He threw the paper across the room with a sudden fury that brought Callie's eyes to his, wide with amazement.

"You told me that you'd already freed your own slaves!" She exclaimed. "If the South doesn't recognize Lincoln's authority, what difference does any proclamation make?"

Daniel turned his fury on her, swirling around with his teeth clenched. "I'll tell you what difference! Slaves will be escaping by the dozens, hundreds—maybe even thousands! And some of them will be dangerous. But that's not the crux of it. Don't you see what Lincoln has done?"

Startled and hurt that he could direct his fury so wrathfully upon her, she retorted with a sarcastic and passionate anger of her own. "Yes! Yes, I do! He's freed a lot of people who were in bondage! I see exactly what he's done!"

"He's done more for his war effort than any general he's ever had!" Daniel snapped back. "Don't you see? Europe will never recognize the Confederacy now. And England! England who takes our cotton by the balefuls but looks down her regal nose at our 'institutions'—she will side now with Lincoln, surely. There will be no help for us anywhere. My God, but I have always said that he is a painfully smart man!"

Callie felt a fluttering in her heart as she grasped the things that Daniel was saying. The Confederacy had hoped for supplies, for funding, from Europe. The Confederacy had been desperate for recognition. And perhaps the Reb government had almost achieved it.

But Lincoln had circumvented that. The English despised slavery. And Lincoln was no longer fighting a war just to preserve a Union. He had created a noble cause, a cause for humanity. The war had taken on another dimension. Passion everywhere would truly be aroused.

Daniel was laughing. "You'll note, Callie, that slaves in Maryland are not freed. President Lincoln would not dare test the loyalty of his border states any further. Oh, it is rich, I say. It is a death knell!"

He stared at her as if she had sounded that knell herself. She felt as if her breath were leaving her. He was challenging her, accusing her—awaiting some response from her.

"What would you have me say!" she cried out. "I do not believe in slavery. If Lincoln can bring the South to her knees and end this war with such a proclamation, then I must be glad!"

He exploded with an oath, his fingers clenching into fists at his side. "Do you know what he will do eventually in Maryland, Callie? He will see that the slaves are freed here, but it will be with some type of compensation for the owners."

"So he is not a stupid man!"

"No, he is not a stupid man at all!" Daniel spat out. "It is only to us—" He broke off, and she didn't miss the handsome but bitter twist that curved his lip. "I keep forgetting," he said softly. "There is no 'us.' You are 'them,' or 'they'—the enemy. And to think—I had almost forgotten!"

"Yes!" she cried passionately. "I am the enemy! And you should not forget it! You told me once that no man should ever forget his enemy. Your private died for hesitating before he could shoot a friend. Don't forget your own lessons, Colonel!" she reminded him. She gasped, backing away as he took a sudden, menacing stride toward her. "Oh!"

He stopped, his features taut, his shoulders and his body ramrod stiff. "Damn you!" he grated out. He turned about, straight as steel, and started for the stairs. He paused, his back to her. "Enemies, madam, until the day that we die. I will be out of your house as hastily as I can manage!"

Callie stared after him, furious, shaking. As he disappeared past the upstairs landing, she felt her anger begin to fade.

He was going to leave her when he was still so furious. They might never talk again. So much for love! So much for the hunger, the need, and all the passion that had flared between them. So much for his whispers that he could not leave without having her again.

Then damn him, her pride cried out. Let him go! If he wished to see her as the enemy, then so be it! She would not apologize if her side—after defeat and humiliation and death—was finally beginning to see signs of hope. She would not say that she was sorry for her beliefs when she knew in her heart that she was right.

Daniel knew, too, that slavery was wrong. No man, black or white, should be owned, body and soul, by another. He had freed his own slaves. He was angry because Lincoln wasn't just a 'long drink of water' as political opponents had labeled him. The backwoods lawyer from Illinois might prove to be one of the greatest men of their time. Daniel saw it, and he was angry because of it.

Alone upstairs, Daniel plucked a pillow from the

bed and hurtled it across the room. It felt so good that he picked up the next pillow and threw it too.

He sank down at the foot of the bed, running his fingers through his hair.

Damn Callie! Damn her.

No. Damn Lincoln. And damn the war.

If Callie had been born in the South, she might be on a different side. She had never lied to him. She had never pretended to be a southern sympathizer. She hadn't even tried to fight him. She had simply refused to back down.

He frowned suddenly, thinking he heard something from outside. He rose and looked out the window. It must have been Callie. If he wouldn't leave her house, then maybe she was planning on leaving it herself.

He shouldn't be so distracted, he thought vaguely. On the battlefield, it would be deadly to lose oneself so completely to emotion.

He was going to leave now, he decided. He rose and reached for his scabbard and buckled it around his hip. He pulled on his boots and clenched his teeth against the sudden onslaught of pain that assailed him.

He was in love with her. With the beauty in her dove-gray eyes, with the fire in hair, and in her voice. With the passion of her heart.

The past half hour had proven them enemies. He had no right to stay longer. He was needed at home. And he had probably just cost them any chance of a tender good-bye with his irrational display of temper.

Walk away, he told himself. Make it easy on both of us, and walk away!

But as he started down the stairs he knew that he could not just walk away.

She waited in the parlor, her fingers wound into her palms, her palms held tautly at her sides, for what seemed like forever. Daniel didn't reappear. Tears stung her eyes. She refused to shed them.

He was angry, she realized, because he was losing his grasp upon his world. He was fighting with all of his heart and with all of his strength. He could ride, and he could wage battle, and he could best his enemy. But it wasn't enough. He couldn't be brave enough, he couldn't be daring enough, and he couldn't be loyal enough. The numbers were against him.

She knew then that she understood him, maybe better than he did himself. If she knew Daniel—and dear Lord, yes, she had come to know him—he would realize it all soon enough.

He had to go. He had to go back to his damnable dying cause, because if he didn't, he'd never be able to live with himself. But he'd never, never admit—not even now—that his precious Confederacy might really lose the war.

She moistened her lips and fought the tears that stung her eyes. She turned on her heels and walked through the house to the kitchen, and then out the door to the back. She walked down the steps, not knowing exactly where she was going, except that she was leaving the house—and Daniel—behind her.

But she did have a direction in mind, she discovered. Her footsteps took her past the barn, and far out back to the little family graveyard. She plucked a wildflower from a thicket and dropped it atop the new mound of dirt over the Yankee soldier they had buried just the night before. She stared down at the tombstones that honored her father and Gregory, and she felt as if a rain of tears suddenly fell upon her soul. How many? How many would have to perish in this awful contest? What price this honor that all the fool men of her acquaintance seemed so desperate to shed their blood for?

She sat down atop the grass that had grown over her

husband's grave and closed her eyes, remembering. It seemed as if they had loved and laughed in another world. He had not died very long ago, but it seemed like forever since she had seen him. He had held her, laughing, in his arms. The war would be over in just a few weeks, he had told her, and he would be back. He had seemed invincible then with blond hair curling over his collar and his blue-green eyes solemn with both his cause and his duty. But he had been so certain. All that they had to do was give the surly Rebs a good lickin', and they'd come marching home.

Instead she'd met his body in the railway station, a lonely figure clad in black, awaiting a coffin.

She'd been so much younger before that day.

She started, hearing something by the house. She shaded her eyes and looked toward it. There was no one.

Sighing, she moved her fingers over her husband's tombstone. It was then that she heard a soft voice, Daniel's voice, coming to her gently from across the graveyard.

" 'He is dead and gone, lady,

He is dead and gone;

At his head a grass-green turf,

At his heels a stone.' "

Callie stood, dusting off her hands on her skirt, touched by the sad, haunting quality in Daniel's voice.

He seemed so far away, so distant from her. His temper had faded. Just as he had seemed to mourn the life of the boy who had died in the barn, he seemed to mourn her husband's life too.

"I'm sorry, Callie."

But she wasn't sure if he was apologizing for their argument, or if he was saying he was sorry Gregory had died.

He was ready to leave, she saw. His scabbard was buckled over his hips, and his fine cavalry sword with its menacing edge was situated in that scabbard. He was still in her father's breeches and cotton shirt, but he was clad in his high black boots once again, and curiously, he looked every inch the soldier. His ebony dark hair fell low on his brow, but his eyes were unobscured, and they were filled with a breath-stealing tenderness as they fell upon her.

"Shakespeare," she murmured softly.

"*Hamlet*," he agreed.

"Ophelia's words," she said.

"Yes."

She tried to smile. "You read fairly well, for a Rebel."

His smile deepened. "Yes."

She stared at him, over Gregory's grave, as the breeze rose between them, lifting her hem, playing a bit of havoc with the stray tendrils of her hair. The sky was blue, the day was pleasantly cool, the sun touched down upon them over a cloudless sky.

The scent of death was gone. There seemed to be just a hint of wildflowers on the air.

It was a beautiful day. Such a beautiful day to say good-bye.

She wanted to say his name, but no sound would come. A ragged little sound escaped her, and he stepped across Gregory's grave and took her into his arms.

His kiss was long and deep. It was filled with tenderness and with anguish, and it seemed that it lasted forever. When he raised his lips from hers, it seemed that it had lasted not at all.

He stared into her eyes as endless seconds ticked by. He was waiting for her to speak, but words would not come.

Maybe there were no words that could be said. He had to go. They both knew it.

Maybe he would return.

And maybe he would not.

He touched her cheek with his knuckles.

"Once I mocked a man for words that I heard him whisper to you. No more. For Callie, I, too, will love you until my dying day!" he told her quietly.

She tried to blink away the sheen of moisture in her eyes. Despite his words, he was building a wall between them, holding himself from her.

"And still I remain your enemy!" she cried softly.

"And I, yours," he reminded her.

"It isn't dark yet," she said stiffly.

"No, it isn't dark. Damn you, Callie, I can't wait for the dark. Lord in heaven, I'm trying hard for just a bit of nobility here. . . ." He pulled her close against his heart. She stiffened. No, she could not beg him to stay, she had to let him go! She could not plead, or seduce, for he was right, they had to part. God! Give her strength, give her pride!

"Ah, Callie!" he murmured.

He released her, then turned around and began to walk.

He skirted around the house, and she stared after him, unable to believe that he had really left so easily. Yes, he had to go. But not yet, oh not yet! They had to be together, they had to have their last moment.

She had to tell him.

Damn strength, and damn pride.

She had to tell him that she loved him.

"Daniel!"

She cried out his name and started to race after him. He was already around the house, starting out across the field, she thought.

"Daniel!"

She raced around the back porch and had nearly turned around the back corner of the house when suddenly fingers wound tightly around her arm, jerking her back.

She spun around astounded, gasping.

Her eyes widened with horror and alarm and she opened her mouth to call out a warning.

She came flying forward, jerked hard against her assailant. She choked and gasped, trying anew to scream, but she was swirled around and a hand clamped down hard on her mouth.

Her cry became a silent scream of anguish.

A whisper, furious, harsh, touched her ear.

"So you've been harboring the enemy right to your bosom, Callie Michaelson. And right over Gregory's grave! Traitor, witch!"

He paused, so furious that words failed him. "Whore! Well, you're going to pay for it, lady. Because you're going to get your lover back here for me, Callie, and you're going to render him vulnerable and harmless, or else you're going to watch him die!"

Ten

"Eric!"

Callie tried to fight his hold upon her. He held her tight, his fingers trembling with emotion. He didn't intend to let her go. She looked around wildly, trying to understand how he had managed to arrive at the house, with neither she nor Daniel aware of his presence.

She realized that he had probably come upon them very easily. He had probably ridden near and heard the argument ensuing in the house. Daniel was usually so wary. But he had not been so careful after Rudy Weiss had appeared and after he had read about Lincoln's emancipating the slaves. Neither had paid heed to anything around them once they had begun to argue. They had allowed Eric the perfect opportunity to approach the house.

And he wasn't alone, she saw quickly. Three of his men were flattened against the wall of the house.

Eric and his men had only had to dismount and leave their horses down the slope. Then all they'd had to do was slip around the house while she was out and Daniel was upstairs.

Why hadn't they attacked him already, she wondered? Chills sped over her spine. Why hadn't they just drawn their swords or attempted to shoot him down?

She opened her mouth to scream out a warning again, but was jerked back hard against Eric.

"Don't do it, Callie. I don't want to have to try to shoot him down."

"Why not?" she demanded, fighting his hold.

"Because I want him alive."

"So why haven't you taken him?"

Eric hesitated. She heard the grinding of his teeth. "Because he's carrying that sword of his."

"There are four of you."

Eric's lashes fell over his eyes, and when his gaze fell upon her fully again, it was bitter. "I guess maybe you didn't know just who you were entertaining, Callie. That's Daniel Cameron."

"I know his name."

"I'll just bet. I'll bet you know lots more about the man too."

She didn't want to flush or falter, but she felt the warm red coloring suffusing her cheeks despite her best efforts. Eric's fingers tightened over her arms like a vise. She bit down hard on her teeth to keep from crying out with the pain.

Meeting his eyes, she realized that he hated her. As much as he might have once coveted her, he hated her now. It wasn't because Daniel was a Confederate, she thought. It was because she had turned Eric down, and because she hadn't been able to stay away from Daniel.

She lifted her chin. For every second that they spoke, Daniel gained some advantage. But Eric knew that. A ragged fear swept over her. Seconds were ticking by quickly now. What did he want of her?

"Get him back here," Eric commanded, his eyes on hers.

She shook her head. "I can't get him back. He's gone. You saw the way that he left."

"Yes, I saw every poignant moment of it—you wretched little whore," he added softly.

She broke free from him, her fury stronger than his hold. She struck him, swiftly and hard. His face reddened where her fingers had touched it, and she heard the quick intake of breath by one of his men.

His fingers stretched out, entwining into her hair so tightly that she cried out, but softly. Daniel wouldn't have heard it. He would already be moving across the field by now.

Eric's taut grip upon her hair pulled her close to him, and his heated whisper touched her ear. "You're going to go get him right now, Callie. You're going to say something, anything. You will convince him that he can't leave until dark. You can promise him—" He hesitated, then lowered his voice even further to tell her exactly what she could promise. Shocked, Callie tried to whirl upon him and hurt him, but she could not. His grip upon her hair was too tight to allow her any movement.

"Bastard!" she hissed at him. "And to think that you were Gregory's friend—"

"To think that you were his wife!" Eric retorted.

"But it would have been fine if I had chosen you, is that it?"

"Captain," a young soldier interrupted, "Colonel Cameron is nearly across the cornfield yonder."

"Go get him. Bring him back here. To your room."

"Why the hell should I do it?"

"Because if you don't, I will kill him. I'll keep my distance from his sword, and I'll shoot him."

Callie swallowed hard. Eric meant it.

"You're afraid of him!" she murmured, "You're afraid of his sword. Four of you, and you're afraid to do battle with one Confederate—"

"Not a Confederate, ma'am," interrupted the young soldier who had spoken before. He cleared his throat nervously, looking at Eric. "Just that particular Confederate. We really don't want to hurt him, ma'am. We want to capture him. If we can capture him, he won't have to die."

"And he will die, Callie, if you don't go out there and get him," Eric said.

She wrenched free from his hold. To her surprise, he let her go. His eyes continued to condemn her as he watched her.

"What if I do manage to get him, and bring him back?" Callie demanded. "He'll still be wearing his sword."

"I'm sure you won't have any trouble getting that scabbard off him, will you, Callie? I don't think that you'll have any difficulty getting anything off him. How convenient for me."

"I never knew that you could be so despicable, Eric," she said icily.

"And I never knew that you could be such a hussy, but that's rather beside the fact, Callie. This is war."

"There's been enough death! Just let him go!"

"You're trying to kill time, Callie. Don't waste too much of it. If he's goes too far, I'll risk any number of my best sharpshooters to take him down. He's not just the enemy, Callie. He's one of the most dangerous."

She still couldn't move. They were going to try to kill Daniel, and because he had been so concerned with her, they had slipped past all his defenses.

If she didn't go after Daniel, they would kill him. They wouldn't give him a chance at all, because they did not dare do so. They would shoot him down, there in the field, and his blood would run with the blood of all the countless others who had perished there.

"If he's so dangerous, let him go!" she pleaded.

Eric's eyes narrowed on hers. His mustache quivered

with the wry quirk of his mouth. "Bringing him in could give me the promotion of my career, Mrs. Michaelson. Damn you! Do you know how many Yanks he's brought down? Or maybe it just doesn't matter to you anymore. Maybe your father doesn't matter, maybe your husband has ceased to matter!"

"My husband is dead and buried. And nothing will bring him back!"

"Then realize this. You've got three seconds, and if you don't go racing across the field, I'll kill him. I'll have that field so alive with bullets that not even a blade of grass will survive. Do you understand?"

"Let me go," she told Eric coldly.

He released her instantly. "Run, Mrs. Michaelson," Eric hissed to her. "Run quickly, before he is too far gone!"

She backed away, staring at Eric. She would never forgive him for what he was forcing her to do. Because Daniel would never forgive her. She couldn't allow that to matter. As Eric had commanded her, she ran.

He had moved quickly and carefully.

There wasn't much left standing tall in the region—full cornfields had been mown down to stubble by the barrage of canister and bullets that had clashed over the gentle slopes of the region. Still, he had found a patch of still-standing corn in which to move. It would have been much better if he had waited until dark to leave. But if he had stayed, he would have wanted to say good-bye properly.

No, it would have surely been improperly. It would have been in a way that she could not forget him. No matter how long the war raged, no matter what came between them. No matter who else entered her life, she would not be able to love again, because she would feel that imprint, that brand. And then he would come back.

What a fool. He could not guarantee that he would come back. It was a wretched, bloodly, horrible war, and no man could guarantee his life. And when it was over, what would there be to offer her? A devastated landscape? Good God, no, Cameron Hall could never fall, he could not believe that it could fall. And still, when the last shots had been fired, would they be any the less enemies? One side would win, and one side would lose. What would there be for the victor and the vanquished?

He paused in the midst of the field of corn, closing his eyes, fighting the wave of pain that assailed him. He was in love with her. More deeply in love than he had ever imagined being. The feeling was supposed to be beautiful. It was wretched. It made him want to go back, just for an hour. Just long enough to hold her, really hold her, once again.

Memories for all the lonely nights to come.

Why had he left just now? Because the hours of waiting might have become more and more painful?

"Daniel!"

The call was faint at first. It might have come from deep within his heart or mind. But then he heard her calling him again, the sound louder, even frantic.

He frowned and started moving quickly back through the tall corn stalks. Green leaves rippled as he passed through the plants.

"Daniel?"

"Callie?"

He still couldn't see her. He began to run through the corn.

He heard his name called again, closely. He paused.

"Callie, I'm here!"

She stepped into the path, perhaps twenty feet away from him.

She stared at him, her hair wild and flowing down her back, touched by the sun and radiant. Her eyes were wide, dark in the distance, large and imploring, so beautiful and seductive.

Her breasts heaved with the exertion of her movement, and electricity seemed to sizzle in the air all around her, as if lightning had rent the sky.

"Daniel!" His name was a whisper on her tongue, ardent, soft, and still impassioned.

And then she was running through the corn again, trying to reach him.

He spoke her name again. It was a whisper on the air, as soft as the breeze. He ran, too, until he reached her, the stalks of corn waving just above their heads, the green leaves softly wafting, the smell of the earth and autumn as sweet as an aphrodisiac.

He lifted her into his arms and he spun beneath the sun with her. As he came around she sank slowly down against his body.

"Daniel, don't go!" she whispered.

"I have to go."

"Not now."

"Callie, we're only making this worse."

"No! No!"

She rose upon her toes, cupping his neck with her hand, reaching to kiss him. Her lips trembled, her kiss was sweet and ardent and impassioned. He tasted her tension and her hunger and, he thought, even the salt of her tears.

He broke away and stared into her eyes. They were luminescent, silver, wide.

"I have to go," he repeated.

"When it's dark. Daniel, when it's dark. Please, come back with me."

His heart shuddered and slammed against his chest. He had to move on.

But how much better in the darkness. How much better to leave when their own peace had been found, when he could move through these fields without daylight giving him away.

She lowered herself against him, her eyes upon him. He could feel the sure pressure of her breasts against his chest. And so softly as to be almost imperceptible, he felt the pressure of her hips. He closed his eyes. He wanted her one more time. With her hair spread out across the whiteness of the pillows, a deep dark flame to ignite a blaze between them.

"Callie!" He buried his head against her neck. "Dear Lord, but I should go!"

She pulled away and looked at him. By heaven above, he had never seen such a dark and seductive hue in such a beautiful set of eyes.

"Daniel, don't leave me. Yet. Come back now. Give me the hours until darkness falls. Daniel, for the love of God, come back with me!"

Her tone was urgent. Her fingers curled around his.

"Until darkness, Callie," he said. "It's all that I have."

She stared him straight in the eyes, her lashes barely flickering. "It is all that I need," she whispered.

She turned, her fingers still entwined with his. They started walking back toward the house.

They reached the road and the open lawn before Callie's house. Daniel paused, and Callie released his hand, stepping out into the road. She spun about, looking.

The rays of the sun seemed to touch every highlight in her hair. Her skirt spun about her along with the radiant fire waves of her hair. She seemed to move in slow motion, as though she had been captured here for all time. He would hold tight to this vision for an eternity.

She faced him again, reaching out to him.

"It's all right. Come."

He stepped forward. Without question, he stepped forward, trusting her.

They hurried across the lawn and into her house. When they had stepped through the door, he caught hold of her arm and pulled her back into his embrace. He kissed her, holding her close. His fingers ran through her hair. His open lips parted from hers and reclaimed them, his tongue running over that rose circle, his mouth finding the sweetness of hers once again.

She seemed strangely stiff in his arms. He raised his head, looking into her eyes.

"Callie, truly I'm sorry. For all that I said before. For my anger against you. I'm sorry."

She shook her head. "It—it doesn't matter."

"It does. I can taste it in your kiss."

She shook her head, and she suddenly seemed pained. "No . . ."

"Then come back here!" he urged her softly. Again, he kissed her, putting into this embrace all of his passion, his need, the sweetness of all the desire that had raged between them. His fingers moved over her cheek, his arms pulled her close.

Suddenly, it seemed that she was stiff again. Confused, he lifted his head and met her eyes. They were more silver than he had ever seen them, filled with her tears.

"Callie, I shouldn't have come back—"

"No! I needed you back."

"But—"

"Not here, Daniel. Not by the door. And not—not with your sword between us."

She was everything soft and feminine. There was a trembling in her voice, and a trembling in her fingers. She was so very beautiful.

"Callie . . ." he murmured. He kissed her temple, and he kissed the pulse at her throat. His fingers played upon the button at the neckline of her dress. She shied

back from him, her cheeks suffused with a soft rose
color. Her lashes fell over her eyes, and it was almost
as if she feared they had an audience in their intimacy.

He laughed softly. "Callie—"

"Come with me, Daniel," she whispered. She looked
up at him, and her eyes were deep pools of entreaty, of
sweet silver seduction.

"Anywhere you wish to lead," he told her. His arms
came around her, sweeping her up and off the floor
into his embrace. She laced her fingers around his
neck, those soulful pools of silver and gray staying
fixed with his. He could not tear his gaze from hers.

They reached her room. She moistened her lips as he
moved through the open door with her.

She pushed against his length, sliding to set her feet
upon the floor. She placed her palms against his chest
and offered him a quick and breathless kiss, then
stepped back.

Puzzled, he reached for her. She smiled, shyly, ruefully.

"The sword, Daniel!" she murmured. She stepped
forward, her fingers shaking wildly while she unbuck-
led his heavy scabbard from about his hips.

The weight of the weapon in the scabbard was more
than she had been expecting. He took it from her,
holding it while he watched her. She smiled, moistening her lips again. She stepped back, then twirled
around and walked toward her bed. The bed with its
beautiful white sheets and spread.

She stood by the bed, noting the narrowing of his
eyes as he stared at her. She crawled atop it and lay
back.

Her hair was spread across that elegant white, a fire,
a flame, as endlessly seductive and appealing as he had
dared to dream.

Her gaze met his. Radiant, shivering. She touched
the rose of her lips with the tip of her tongue.

"Daniel, get rid of the sword, please." She moved her fingers over the spread, invitingly. She leaned up on an elbow. "Please, get rid of the sword. Come to me."

Circe had never sung so seductively upon the sea.

He was in love with this Circe.

He set his sword down on one of the chairs by the cold hearth, and walked to the foot of the bed. He paused, then unhooked the single button at the throat of his shirt and pulled it over his head.

He smiled at her and mouthed the words, "Angel, I love you."

He started to stretch down beside her.

He had scarcely begun to move when he heard the quick flurry of footsteps behind him. Instantly on the alert, he tried to swing around.

A fist caught him in the jaw.

The world seemed a blur, but it was a whir of blue he recognized well. Yankee soldiers! The room was crawling with them.

Far more startling than the pain that stung his jaw was the gut-wrenching agony that streaked through him.

Callie.

She had betrayed him. She had brought them here. She had seduced him like any fool, and God damn her to a million hells, he had fallen.

"Bitch!" he snarled. The blue clad arm with the fist attached was swinging again.

"Hell, no!" Daniel raged.

Then a sound filled the room. Callie, leaping from the bed to lean flat and miserable against the wall, nearly screamed with pure terror. She clasped her hands over her ears, aware that the sound had come from Daniel, and that it was the ear-piercing warning known as a Rebel yell.

Every man in the room blanched at the sound of it,
just as surely as she did herself.

Shirtless, his naked shoulders and chest shimmering
sleekly with his every movement, Daniel almost
seemed to dance with an agile ease about the room.
Eric's three subordinates fell atop Daniel one by one,
and one by one, he fought them off with his fists. A
slug to one man's jaw, a kick to the next man's groin.
Then his fists flew again, and the sickening sound of
those fists against human flesh filled the room.

"Rebel, be damned!" Callie heard Eric growl, stepping into the fray.

She heard a thud again, and Eric came rolling out of
the huddle of the fight, clenching his bleeding jaw with
his hand.

He drew his pistol.

"No!" Callie shrieked.

But no one was listening to her. Daniel's opponents
at last managed a well-coordinated attack, one of them
slamming a pistol on the back of his head just as he
turned to face the two others. Gritting his teeth and
holding the back of his head, he fell to his knees.

Before he could rise, Eric was behind him, the shining rod of his revolver set against the base of Daniel's
skull.

Everyone in the room heard the cock of the trigger.

"Don't make a move, Reb," Eric warned. "Not a
move."

Callie waited, praying.

She saw Daniel's eyes close, saw his teeth grate
down harder. He opened his eyes again.

They were a different blue from any color she had
seen before. Suddenly they fixed upon her.

They were the cold blue of hatred.

He was still as one of Eric's men carefully grasped
his wrists and drew them back. Callie winced, trying
not to jump as she heard the snap of steel.

They had set slave shackles around his wrists.

Eric caught hold of his shoulder, pulling Daniel to his feet. He was a tall man. Callie hadn't realized just how tall until she saw him rising an inch or so over Eric and his Federals.

Eric spoke to him, gloating. "How do you like the feel of them shackles, boy? It's just what you folks do to your people down there. Kind of puts a crimp on things, eh, boy?"

Daniel suddenly spun, and his feet moved in a flash. Shackled in steel, he was still a dangerous man.

His feet hit Eric dead in his middle. Stumbling backward and turning white, Eric clutched his wounded body and swore.

Freed for the moment, Daniel took the opportunity to stalk Callie. His long strides brought him quickly across the room until he was standing just an inch from her. She could see the sheen of sweat on his chest, feel the exertion of his rapid breathing. Feel the cold ice-fire of his eyes upon her.

She felt the blood drain from her face. A trembling like a palsy swept through her.

"Daniel—" she tried to whisper.

"This steel won't hold me forever, Callie. No chains and no bars can ever do that. And I'll be back. I promise you that. I'll be back for you."

"Shut up, Reb!" Eric called to him suddenly. "She was just a good Yank, turning you in. It was a damned good job, Callie."

She wanted to scream. A pulse ticked violently against Daniel's throat, and she knew that he believed the very worst, that she had planned on turning him in for a long time. It was your fool life I was trying to save! she wanted to scream. But there couldn't be any explanations, not here, not now. Not with Eric and three of his badly battered Union soldiers looking on.

She moistened her lips. She saw the mocking sneer that curled his mouth.

"Daniel, I didn't—" she began at last.

"Poor Yank!" Eric said. "She's a pretty piece, isn't she, southern boy? We have our weapons here in the North too. And she's a deadly one, isn't she, boy?"

He didn't turn. "It's Colonel Cameron, Captain, not boy," he said flatly. He smiled at Callie. A smile so cold that chills began to sweep furiously through her once again.

"I'll be back, Callie. And when I come for you, there won't be anywhere for you to hide. Believe me. I'll be back. It's a promise."

"That's enough!" Eric cried out sharply. "Take him, Corporal Smithers."

Smithers didn't move quickly enough. Daniel turned around, still smiling. They were all still afraid of his booted feet.

Callie flattened herself against the wall because Daniel was turning back to her. She could breathe in the scent of him, feel the slow, sure pounding of his heart.

And feel his eyes once again.

Eric brought the butt of his revolver down hard upon Daniel's head. Without a whimper, without a sigh, her passionate Rebel fell at last, black lashes closing over the blue hatred in his eyes.

2

Captive Hearts

Eleven

October, 1862

It was still daylight when the wagon carrying Daniel to Old Capitol Prison in Washington, D.C., stopped before the building.

Daniel was able to see it clearly. There were no shadows of darkness to take away any of the squalor of the sight before him.

Dark, dank, decaying walls greeted him. A miasma hung over the place. High plank walls surrounded it, and iron bars covered the windows.

It was a building he knew well enough, as any frequent visitor to the capital would have. Before the war, Daniel had certainly been in Washington often enough.

He had always loved the city. It had been planned and built with the purpose of being the capitol of a country. The vistas down the long mall were exquisite, the government buildings were handsome, and the wide streets and rich boulevards were inviting. In spring the river kept the scent of flowers fresh and clean, and in the fall, no place could be more beautiful.

But even here, a man could find the results of ill treatment and abandonment. At no place could that be seen more clearly than at Old Capitol Prison.

When the Capitol had been destroyed during the War of 1812, a brick building had been constructed for the temporary use of the government on 1st Street. Then the Congress had moved back to their permanent quarters, and the building, simply called "Old Capitol" the last time that Daniel had seen it, had begun to deteriorate.

It had been deteriorating ever since, Daniel thought wearily.

Someone prodded him in the back. "We're here, Colonel. Your new home in the North," his Yankee driver said with a snigger. "Get on up and out of there, now."

It wasn't easy for Daniel to do. His feet and wrists were still shackled. In fact, he'd lain on his side in the jouncing wagon so long that all of his body felt bruised and knotted and stiff, and trying to arise at all was difficult.

It had seemed like an endless journey from the Yankee encampment where he had first awakened to find himself so trussed. He'd been in pain from the first, aware that he'd been kicked and beaten by his captors even after he'd lost consciousness. His ribs were sore, his old wound was oozing a trickle of blood.

He hadn't been bothered by much at the encampment. He'd seen enough soldiers, though, all coming around to peek in the tent where he'd been taken as if he were some kind of circus animal. They all wanted to see Danny Cameron, the horse soldier with the rapier sword, brought down at last. Some of them jeered. Some of them asked how it felt to be trussed up like a pig for gutting. Some of them just stared gravely. One soldier said that it just wasn't any way to treat a man, any man.

A Union major had agreed, and before Daniel knew it, the onlookers were driven away, and he had been brought a chair to sit on and a blanket. None of it really mattered to him at the time because he was still living in a haze of pain. But the major seemed a fine enough fellow, determined that Daniel be given good, clean water and a decent meal. His own troops were eating well enough, it seemed.

Not even the major seemed to feel safe enough around him to see that his shackles were removed. It wasn't until Daniel told the young private assigned to look after him that he couldn't possibly eat the meal— or take care of any other human necessities—with his hands shackled that they were undone. The nervous private faced him with a rifle aimed at him all the while he ate and attended to other necessities. Then the irons were put back on him.

The major also demanded that his prisoner be treated with respect. They'd all been brothers once, and God willing, they'd all be brothers again. It seemed that this major knew Jesse, and was appalled that any West Point graduate should be treated so shabbily.

"Beauty himself chose to ride for his homeland," the major said wearily. "I'd not even have you cuffed so, sir, were I certain that you could not escape."

"Sir, it would be my duty to Beauty himself to escape at any possible opening," Daniel told him honestly.

He wondered about his damned honesty because the stinking irons remained. Night had come and he'd been left to sleep in his shackles, but had spent most of the night awake, cramped, bruised, and in pain.

He hadn't minded the pain, he'd rather welcomed it. It had kept him from thinking.

Thinking was dangerous. Every time he dared to think, a blind red fury settled over him.

He'd been such a fool. Half the Yank army hadn't been able to drag him down, but that little flame-haired witch with the silver eyes had only to crook her finger to do so.

Lying in agony, he'd seen it all, over and over again, every word that passed between them, his wanting to walk away, her beckoning him back.

The fury that raged in him was so strong, he wasn't sure he cared who actually won the war anymore.

Just as long as he could go back. For her.

He wasn't sure what he wanted to do to her. He just wanted it to last long. And to be unendurably agonizing. He felt his fingers jerk, and he thought that he wanted to wind them around her neck.

Too smooth. Too easy.

What then?

An ancient English torture maybe. Like the rack.

Not vicious enough . . .

Morning had come. His temper hadn't eased a wit.

Another day passed with the major being a decent enough fellow. Daniel hadn't known the man before the war, but apparently his reputation in the West before the start of the war had circulated through the night.

Maybe some of the Union soldiers hated him more for having resigned when Virginia seceded.

But for the most part, he thought that the men understood. Little things began to appear for him. A really beautiful red apple. A small flask of Irish whiskey.

That night, he played cards with the major, and it was then that he learned he'd be moved to Old Capitol in the morning.

"I'll see to it that your brother knows where you are, safe and alive and out of action," the major assured him.

Daniel winced. Jesse would start moving heaven and earth, and get in bad with his own side, to get Daniel out. Especially if he was worried about the wound. Jesse never stopped being a doctor.

"Thank you just the same, Major. Jesse's got his own war to fight, and he's busy somewhere patching up men. I don't want him informed."

"He'll find out soon enough."

"I reckon. But give it till then. I'm a big boy, and I chose my own side." He was quiet for a moment. "And I made my own fool mistakes," he added. He smiled to the major, just to assure him there were no hard feelings.

"I'd like to let you go, Colonel Cameron. But I can't. You're just too damned important. Maybe they'll exchange you. They're still trying to swap a private for a private, a sergeant for a sergeant—a colonel for a colonel. Sixty privates for a general. But I hear that our side is starting to say we've got to quit exchanging. Every time we put one of you Rebs back in the field, you just start killing Yanks all over again."

"It is a war," Daniel said politely.

"To our great sorrow, Colonel, yes. To our great sorrow." He sighed, and rubbed his whiskered chin. "I can't even make you more comfortable. If your wrists are free, I've got to keep the shackles on your ankles. They tell me you fight like a son of a gun. Where did you learn to fight like that?"

Daniel grinned. "Why, Major, I learned how to fight back home."

"Your pa bring in a professional to teach you?"

"No, sir. Jesse was bigger, and we'd disagree now and then, so I had to get tougher."

The major laughed. He shared the Irish whiskey with Daniel.

But the major wasn't there when the soldiers came to load Daniel into the wagon. These soldiers weren't interested in respecting their enemy in any way, shape, or form.

The driver who had prodded him shouted out an order.

"Move it, Colonel!"

Hands grasped hard upon his shoulders, wrenching him up to his feet. He was shoved hard from the open back of the wagon.

There was no way to gain his balance, not with both arms and legs shackled as they were.

He sprawled down into the dirt road, striking hard. Gritting his teeth, he stumbled up to his feet.

There was a handsomely uniformed Union lieutenant colonel hurrying toward him. The uniform didn't bear a single speck of dust, and the officer didn't look as if he was many months past his twenty-first birthday.

"That will be enough, soldier!" he said. The soldier snickered beneath his breath, but saluted. "Yes sir, whatever you say, sir!"

"Colonel Daniel Cameron, you are now a prisoner of war, here at Old Capitol. Be a model prisoner, sir, and we will strive to see that your stay isn't too painful."

"He means he'll try to keep you alive, Colonel!" someone shouted from one of the barred windows.

"Yeah, yeah, yeah," the soldier who had brought him said. He caught Daniel's shoulder. "Let's move him in, sir. He's a dangerous one."

It was obvious that a number of the guards considered him to be a "dangerous one." There was little chance of his harming any of them, what with the numbers they had on their side. Guards encircled the walled structure, and guards seemed to be in abundance within it. But though his hands were freed, they shoved him roughly into the large room with its heavy doors, trying to keep a distance from him.

And there he met a ragged band of Confederates.

They stood, gaunt and disheveled, some with bone-thin faces, some with fraying blankets around their

shoulders. They wore all manner of uniform, a few
with the colorful remnants of Louisiana Zouave baggy
trousers, some in plain old washed-out breeches; some
in proper militia uniform, and some in the butternut
and gray of the regular army.

They watched as he was thrust in among them.
Thrust so hard that he stumbled again, and fell to his
knees. Squaring his shoulders, he rose painfully. His
bare feet were bruised and bleeding. He'd been given a
shirt, but it was torn and tattered now too. His hair was
matted, his face was covered with the dust from the
street where he had fallen before.

He might have been dressed in scarlet robes.

All around him, cheers rose up. Then a Rebel yell
sounded, nearly shattering the prison walls.

"Colonel Cameron, sir!" his name rang out; he was
saluted again and again, one by one.

The Yankee guard at the door swore softly. "I'm
getting the hell out of this one!" he muttered.

The heavy door clanked shut. Daniel looked around
him, greeting his countrymen as they greeted him.

"Your feet look bad, sir, cut up and swollen," said
one young private with snow-blond hair and corn-
flower-blue eyes. He came up, setting down a pair of
boots. "I've got kinfolk in D.C., and I got an extra pair
of shoes, sir. I'd be beholden if'n you'd wear these."

"Thank you, son," Daniel said.

Another soldier stood before him. "My wife just
knitted me a pair of socks, and the pair she sent before
ain't hardly got a hole in them, sir."

Daniel smiled. Someone else brought him a blanket,
and then someone brought him a thin little cigarillo,
the likes of which he hadn't tasted in a long time. He
thanked them all. He told them what he knew about
the battle of Sharpsburg, and he laughed when they
told him tales about his own exploits in the saddle.

"Well, are they true, sir?"

"It's like anything, Billy Boudain," he told the young man who had given him the boots. "Some is true, and some is the storyteller's relish for the story." He winced. Sitting against the cold stone wall had aggravated a crick in his neck.

"Colonel, there's a nice thick thatch of hay over yonder for you. Wish we could do more. Some of us have money and kinfolk near, and we can bribe a tiny bit of luxury, but not much."

Daniel stood, stretching. He inhaled on the cigarillo, enjoying the fine taste of the tobacco. He grinned at the young soldier again, unaware that the bitter curl of his mouth was extremely chilling.

"Don't worry about it, soldier. Don't worry on it a bit. I don't intend to stay long. Not long at all." He crushed out the cigarillo. "I've got business elsewhere," he said softly.

The ice-blue fury in his eyes belied the very softness of his words.

"You—you sound determined, sir," Billy said.

"Oh, I am. Nothing will stop me from getting out of here." He realized that his words had brought about a hush in the room, that the men were all staring at him, with maybe just a little bit of fear themselves.

"I thank you all," he said more softly, and he offered them a rueful grin. "I thank you very much. I am weary, though. Good night, men."

The pile of hay wasn't much. It didn't matter. He was surrounded by his own again.

He fell into it, and curiously enough, slept like a babe.

Fall was coming to the Maryland countryside. The leaves on the trees were just beginning to show the beauty of wild red and yellow and flaming orange.

Dusks were cool, with a cleansing breeze.

Callie sat out on her porch after a long day, anxious

to feel that breeze. No matter how fresh or gentle it came to be, no matter how cooling, or how cleansing, it never seemed to blow away the feelings that had settled over her. She tried to tell herself again and again that she had done the only thing possible. It didn't help her. Daniel's voice still came to her in the night. His promise, spoken so bitterly, so hatefully.

"I'll be back. . . ."

But he would not be for a long while. They had taken him over to Old Capitol Prison in Washington, and he was a prisoner that the guards would watch well and warily. Eric had assured her so.

She shivered, remembering the end of the night once Daniel had been knocked out.

They had shackled his ankles just as they had shackled his hands. One of the officers had stolen his boots.

Eric's men had carried him off, and Eric had stayed behind.

She would never forget that night. The anguish of what had happened to Daniel and what had come after.

Eric had cornered her against the wall. She remembered him caging her in, his palms flat on the wall on either side of her face. She remembered the bitterness in his voice when he told her that all that he wanted was what she so blithely gave the enemy.

She remembered the awful choking horror of wondering if he would go through with the violence that he threatened.

She never knew what gave her strength. She smiled sweetly at him and slipped his revolver from his pocket as he moved in closer. When he would have pressed his lips to hers, she aimed the revolver right at his gut.

She warned him that she knew how to pull a trigger, and that she would do it without blinking.

He believed her. He'd stepped back so quickly it was comical. He'd scowled and sworn. Callie had told him to get out of the house or she'd be out riding hard to find his superior officer to let him know just what his cavalry captains were doing in the field.

Eric had left, swearing his own form of vengeance against her.

She had then sunk down in her corner against the wall, and cried. Eventually, she'd fallen asleep.

In the morning she'd realized that she had to go on. Daniel had not been in her life so very long.

But the time before he had stepped into it no longer seemed to matter.

The day after Daniel's capture, a different soldier had come by. Callie had kept Eric's fine revolver. She had six shots to use if she needed them.

But the man hadn't come by to threaten her. She was amazed to discover he had come to replenish some of the livestock that had been taken from her. There were now two pigs in back, two horses, two cows, the goat, and scores of chickens. The animals gave her plenty to do, as did the effort to restore her garden, although with winter coming on there was not much she could do.

There was definitely going to be a shortage of corn in the area.

She was glad of work, any work, for it helped to keep her mind off Daniel, and both the anguish and the splendor that had so briefly been hers.

She tried to tell herself that it was all for the best. Daniel was too daring, too talented, too able. If he fought on, he was sure to get himself killed. He was an expert with his sword, he was probably an amazing sharpshooter, and he could fight bare-handed with a vengeance. But no man alive was immune to bullets, and with his determination to lead his men straight into every fray, it seemed only a matter of time.

He was safe in prison.

But as she sat on the porch that dusk, watching the

swing wave gently in the breeze, she knew that he would never see it that way. He dreaded prisons. Callie couldn't believe that Old Capitol Prison could be as bad as they said. It was right in Washington, D.C. There were any number of good citizens in Washington who despised the war, and who would demand fair treatment for the prisoners. After all, weren't the northerners fighting this war to prove that they were all one Union?

It didn't matter. Just remembering the look in Daniel's eyes made her shiver.

She closed her eyes, determined to forget. She had to get over everything that had happened, and get on with her life.

She still had a little unfinished business, she reminded herself sadly, and she stood, and walked back into the house. On one of the big plush parlor chairs lay the bedroll belonging to the young Union soldier who had crawled into her barn to die. She had to get those belongings back to his family.

She turned the bedroll, trying to compose in her mind a message to send to his family. "Your son died instantly, painlessly. He died a hero's death. . . ."

The truth. He died in terror and agony, lingering away in my barn.

No, she didn't have to write the truth. No one knew the truth about the soldier's death except for herself.

And Daniel.

Swearing softly, she started to untie the bedroll. If there were tobacco or pipes or playing cards within it, she would get rid of them. She was convinced that if a boy was big enough to go into battle and die, no one should care if he wanted a bit of tobacco or had taken to a fun game of cards on a quiet night. But mothers still looked for honor in their sons, and boys, she knew, still longed to please their mothers. So if this boy's mother had to receive the sad news of her son's death,

Callie was going to see to it that she was spared all possible extra pain.

The minute she undid the bedroll the first thing to flutter out was the boy's letter. It had obviously been signed in quite a rush, and he had never had a chance to find an envelope for it, or a way to post it back home. He'd probably just finished up before he heard the bugle's blare calling him to battle.

Callie bit her lip and absently set her free hand against the small of her back. She stretched and wandered back out to the porch, sinking down on the steps to feel the night breeze while she read the letter.

Dear Mother,

Just a letter to tell you that I am well, and feeling fine. I wanted to write, because we're ready to go into battle. Some soldiers found an important order given out by the Confederate General Lee, and there's all kinds of excitement going on. Seems like we'll meet up with the Rebel forces real soon, and real big.

Well, Mother, I've just got to say that it won't be easy. Seems like it was just a week or so ago that we were down in Virginia—so close we could see Richmond—and just across the river from some of those Rebs. Ritchie Tyree—you know Ritchie, Mother, he grew up down the road by the dairy farm—he had some kinfolk over on the other side, cousins he was right close to, and so I promised him that I'd sneak across the river with him. I know that it wasn't right to go against my orders, but no one really ordered me not to go across the river. If a man doesn't owe his friends, then we can't have much of a country to fight for, right? Anyhow, that's the way I saw it, and I did weigh the decision real careful, just like you and Pa taught me to do. Ritchie and I slipped across the river that night, and we met his cousins Zachary, Tybalt, and Joseph. We sat around in the dark, gnawing on jerky we'd brought over, us having much more in the way of vittles than the Rebs. We talked about old times, and who had died, and who had been married, and it was a right nice night. We came back across the river, and we slipped into our tents, and no one was the wiser, so I was glad of the chance to embrace my enemy.

The only thing is, I started wondering in the morning just why those boys were my enemies. We knew a lot of the same folks, we spoke the same language, and Ritchie and Tybalt even look close enough alike to be near twins. We laughed just alike. And Mother, I tell you, we pray to the same God every night, we pray mighty hard, both of us praying to live, and both of us praying to win.

Well, Mother, I don't mean to burden you with my thoughts. I may question this war, but I swore my oath to my country, and I know my duty, and I will serve.

How is Sarah? Give my love to her. I write to her often, but I've so little time now, and I must write these words to you. God willing, I will come home, and Sarah will be waiting. And we'll wed, Mother, and though you've already lost Pa and Billy, I'll be the teacher in the old schoolhouse just like I've always wanted with Sarah there at my side and all manner of little ones belonging to me and Sarah to people up your life again.

It's going to be a big one, though. A mighty big battle. If God wills that I not return, Mother, remember me to Sarah. Tell her that I loved her, that she was often in my dreams. Know that I was ever your obedient son, and that I'd never bring dishonor upon you. If God so wills that I fade away, hold me with you in your heart.

There goes the bugle, Mother, calling me to war.

*God keep you, for you are ever the greatest lady.
Your loving son . . .*

                                              Benjamin

The letter fluttered to Callie's lap. She hadn't realized that she was crying until the first of her tears splattered down on the paper.

Quickly, almost frantically, she blotted the tear with her skirt.

The boy's mother was going to receive this letter.

She started suddenly, realizing that she had become so involved with the letter that when hoofbeats had sounded, and were now coming closer, she had paid them little heed.

She leapt up, wondering if she should hurry inside for the revolver.

But the approaching rider had already arrived at the front of her lawn.

Her heart began to beat hard as she slipped back into the shadows of the porch. The rider hadn't seen her, and he certainly hadn't come furtively. He dismounted from his horse and walked across the lawn to the well. Callie couldn't see his face. His uniform was a regulation blue. His hat was plumed, cockaded at the brim with a large feather. She watched him for some moments, trying to read his insignias. He looked like cavalry, but some of the insignias on his shoulders were different from any she had seen before.

She must have made a move that made him aware of her presence, for he turned quickly, staring at the porch. She was in the light from the house; he was in the shadow. She still couldn't see his face.

"Good evening!" he called out. He had a low, cultured voice, but it still carried a touch of a drawl. "Please excuse me. I've just stopped for water, if I may. And I'd like to ask you a few questions, if you don't mind. I've not come to hurt anyone." He paused.

Callie knew he had to be reflecting his position. Maryland was a border state in every sense of the word. There were "Maryland" troops fighting for the North and for the South. Even a lone Union soldier took a chance riding here.

"May I?"

He had lifted the dipper from the bucket of water that swung into the well.

Callie stepped out from behind the post, still holding on to it for moral support.

"Yes, of course. Any man is welcome to water," she said.

"Thank you kindly."

He sank the dipper into the water, and then drank from it deeply. Callie exhaled, realizing that she had grown so wary because of Eric, and walked the few steps down to the lawn.

This soldier could be a godsend to her. If he didn't mind waiting just a minute, she could quickly compose her note to the dead boy's mother and send his things on to her. Perhaps the poor lady did not want to learn that her son was dead, maybe she wanted to live on hope, knowing only that her son was missing.

No, there was nothing worse than the wondering, Callie determined. She needed to turn this letter over to this soldier, along with her own words of condolence. That is, if she felt that she could trust him.

He had just finished drinking, and he seemed to know that she had come down the steps.

"I'm looking for a man," he said, his back still facing her. "He disappeared somewhere around here in the recent battle."

The soldier turned around, and Callie stepped back, gasping. For a moment she felt as if she were going to faint.

His face was so familiar in the shadows it might have been Daniel.

His appearance so stunned her that she froze, unable to speak or to move.

He had the same very blue eyes and near-ebony hair. The handsome structure of his face was similar and yet different. This man was just a little bit older. He was perhaps a bit heavier in the shoulders and across the chest. There were a few more lines about his eyes; his face was fuller.

"Ma'am? Are you all right? I assure you, I pose no danger to you. I've recently discovered that my brother didn't return to his troops. If he didn't return to them, well, I know my brother, you see," he said huskily, and Callie thought, yes, he knows Daniel well. Nothing on heaven or earth would have kept Daniel from returning, unless he had been killed—or captured.

She still couldn't quite speak, and so her visitor continued. "I guess I should explain. This man isn't a Union soldier, but a Rebel. No one saw him killed, and he was rather well known, so I'm hoping that he is alive. He might have been injured. He shouldn't have been fighting to begin with. It's a strange story, ma'am, but his commander is an old friend of mine, and word just got through a number of the lines that he hasn't been seen or heard from since the battle. Have you seen anyone, or heard tell of any missing soldier, trying to move toward the South, perhaps?"

"I . . ." she paused, moistening her lips. She fought desperately for composure, determined to remain calm.

He strode across the yard to her quickly, hope filling his eyes. He gripped her shoulders, and when he touched her, she at long last felt a warmth dispel the chill that had assailed her.

"Have you seen him? Please, help me! Tell me anything that you can, I am so desperate!"

Her heart beating wildly, she stepped back. She blinked, then she found her composure.

"You met my brother!" he said urgently.

She smiled. "Oh, yes, we met," she said with irony. She extended her hand. "You must be Jesse."

"God, yes, I'm Jesse! And Daniel—"

"Is alive," she said.

"Thank God! Thank God in heaven! Where is he now? Has he headed back? Jesu, our lines are thick around here!"

She shook her head. "He isn't headed south."

"Then?"

"Daniel is safer than he has been in a long, long time," she said softly.

"I beg your pardon?"

"He fell here," she said, keeping the cloak of composure about her the best she could. "During the battle, he fell here, not far from where you're standing. He was deathly ill one night, but he roused himself quickly enough." She hesitated, forcing herself to breathe regularly, even as she stared into these blue eyes that were so very familiar. "Perhaps you should come in. I have coffee."

He watched her for a moment, obviously aware that there was quite a story behind her words.

"Yes, thank you, I'd like very much to come in. But if you're certain that Daniel isn't headed for home, where is he now, Miss . . ."

"Mrs. Michaelson, Callie Michaelson. Daniel is in Old Capitol Prison in Washington."

"What?"

"He's where he's really safe."

Jesse Cameron tilted his head. "Maybe, and then maybe not. You don't know my brother all that well, ma'am."

Oh, sir, you don't know the half of it! Callie almost cried. But his words made her uneasy. "What do you mean by that, sir?"

"I'll be happy to explain. And then, if you don't

mind, I'd like to hear whatever else you can tell me about my brother. Coffee sounds right fine, Mrs. Michaelson."

Callie turned around quickly, heading up the steps. Jesse Cameron was right behind her.

Dear God, just exactly what was she going to tell him?

And what did he mean by saying that maybe Daniel was safe, and then maybe he wasn't?

"Do come in, sir," she told Jesse. He was right behind her by the door and she knew that she needed to go on with her story.

She lowered her lashes, and then she raised them. "Come into the kitchen, sir. I'll put the coffee on." Damn these Camerons, she thought. Those blue eyes were so intently on hers.

Twelve

Mrs. Callie Michaelson was an incredible and fascinating woman, Jesse determined, sitting down to a cup of coffee at her kitchen table.

The coffee was the best he'd had in some time, even though he was lucky enough these days to spend time now and then where the shortages were few. There was cream for it, a taste he'd gotten away from on the battlefield, but which, here in this warm and welcoming place, tasted delicious.

Watching his hostess, he wanted to go home.

She was beautiful. She had a soft, cool reserve about her that, joined with her gracefulness, added mystery to that beauty. The kitchen table reminded him of home; she reminded him of Kiernan, his wife, and suddenly the desire to be back where he really belonged was so strong he could scarcely stand it.

But he couldn't go home.

He would take this time to search for his brother. Sometimes, there were ways around the war. Beauty Stuart had gotten word through to him that Daniel hadn't returned after Sharpsburg.

His heart heavy with dread, he had come to the battlefield. He had asked every Union man left he could find about the burial places of the fallen Rebs, but he'd gotten no word on Daniel at all until he had met this woman.

A fair estimate of the body count was in. More blood had been spilled in one day at Sharpsburg than at any other battle. Looking for Daniel could have been a never-ending task.

Friends had tried to dissuade him from the search, shaking their heads sadly.

But he had believed that Daniel was alive, that he would know, somehow, if his brother had died.

So he had strayed by this little farmhouse, and this beautiful woman was calmly telling him about his brother.

When the coffee was poured, she sat, her hands folded in her lap, her lashes slightly downcast over her eyes.

"The best that I could see, sir, there was quite a skirmish going on here. Cavalry first, then infantry. At first, I believe the Rebels held the area, but then they were frightfully outnumbered and your brother's men were cut off. There was a lull in the fighting when I found him first, but an officer came by and told me Daniel was dead, and that the firing was about to start again."

She paused, her lashes rising. Her eyes were large, a fascinating, provocative gray. She was dressed rather primly, in blue cotton edged with white lace that buttoned to her throat. She wore a petticoat, but no hoop, and she should have appeared very much the demure young farm woman.

Her coloring, her radiance, were extraordinary. Her hair was a glory, a deep, dark red, and free as it was tonight, it cascaded like a river of haunting splendor. Her manners were correct, everything about her was correct, but there was still something deeper about her, something beneath the prim exterior, the soft, cultured voice. Tension radiated from her despite her demure calm. Were he not so in love with his own wife, he would probably be fantasizing about this woman. As it was, he thought wryly, the less he told Kiernan about Mrs. Michaelson, the better.

"Was Daniel seriously injured?" Jesse asked her.

She shook her head. That blaze of hair shimmered over her shoulders. "No, I don't think so. He was knocked unconscious. He must have received a good wallop upon the head. But that was not what made him so ill. He had an old injury, and it must have reopened with his exertion. I have nursed before, but I'm afraid that my experience has not been extensive. I knew that he had a very serious fever, and I worked to keep him as cool as possible. He pulled out of it, and he seemed fine."

Watching her, Jesse nodded. She had cared for Daniel, she had kept him alive.

But he couldn't help it. He was curious.

"You did not turn him over to any of the Yankee patrols?" he said.

She shrugged. "There were enough dead men all around me," she said softly.

Jesse sat back in his chair, a wry twist touching his lip. "I've heard my fellow physicians and myself maligned greatly by the Rebs—and sometimes with just cause. But I've met an endless array of very good men in this war too. Yankee surgeons who fight as energetically for any man in gray as they would for those in blue."

"But sir, I did not know what manner of man I might be turning your brother over to," she said. "I knew he had a brother who was a Yankee doctor, but I'd have had no way of finding you. And besides . . ."

Her voice trailed away. Her lashes fell, sweeping her cheeks.

"Yes?"

"Well, I was his prisoner in my own home for a

while," she tried to say lightly. "Once I knew how ill he had become, I swore that I'd not turn him in if he'd only release me. I gave my word, you see."

No, he didn't see. Jesse leaned over the table toward her.

"But he's in Old Capitol now?"

He thought that a slight flame made its way into her cheeks. Her gaze suddenly flew up to meet his. "Sir, I don't know if you're aware of it or not, but your brother has a rather deadly reputation among your soldiers. I was put into the uncomfortable position of watching them take him—*or watching them murder him,*" she said. Her eyes dropped again. The edge of a desperate tone entered into her voice. "They wanted him alive. They thought that bringing him in could mean a promotion. I'm sure that they kept him alive."

"Who took him in? Did you know the men?"

"Er . . . well, yes, one of them," she said, waving a hand vaguely. "A Captain Eric Dabney. Do you know him?"

Jesse frowned. Yes, he had heard of the man. He knew a lot about the cavalry troops fighting in the eastern campaigns because he had been cavalry himself until the Union had begun to build a separate medical corp. Captain Eric Dabney. An interesting man. He was known for being cautious with his troops. It was rather difficult to imagine him tackling Daniel.

Not if he had help. Lots of it.

Callie Michaelson looked at him with worry in her eyes. "You do think that . . . he made it to Old Capitol?"

Jesse nodded, watching her. She was very anxious.

And why not? He had learned in the many "hospitals" where he had worked to patch men up that the war hadn't changed a thing. Men were still men, some with honor, some without. Despite the fact that his wife Kiernan remained a Confederate, he had seen her be as tender to any young Yank as she might be to an injured Reb.

"I was so torn," Callie murmured suddenly, and that liquid gray gaze was on him again, beautiful, shimmering its special silver. "I—I truly had no choice in the matter. But when he was taken, I told myself that it had to be for the best. Because he's safe now. Or, at least he should be." Her voice was growing anxious again. "You're a colonel, too, are you not, Doctor Cameron? That's an impressive rank. If you were to stop by the prison, if you were to make sure that the people there knew he was your brother, maybe they'd be careful not to let anything happen to him. And if he's locked up, he won't be able to lead any more raids. He won't come charging into battle. They were so afraid of his sword. He's just so determined—" She saw the curious light in his gaze and quit speaking, then flushed again. "Am I wrong? Maybe he'll be safer."

"Maybe," Jesse said. He didn't tell her that he knew Daniel well and that Daniel would never stay in prison. He'd be looking at every single possible avenue of escape, and if a means was there, Daniel would find it.

Her eyes lowered again, and Jesse almost grinned. Leave it to Daniel. Daniel would never have fallen on the farm grounds of an old woman or a graybeard. No, Daniel would manage to fall here. With this beautiful, exotic woman. He was good with horses, good with swords, damned good with reconnaissance—and good with women.

He started suddenly, realizing then what the tension in her was all about.

She had done more than care for Daniel through a fever. Things had gone much farther between these two.

He sipped his coffee, anxious that she not see what he had discerned in her eyes. She was something, this

Mrs. Callie Michaelson. Elegant, reserved, and so composed and well mannered.

It must have been interesting, Daniel, he thought.

He finished his coffee and set the cup on her table. "Don't worry, Mrs. Michaelson, I do intend to go by and see my brother. And the conditions under which he's being kept." He arched a brow at her. "You are on our side, correct?"

"Which is 'our' side?" she asked him dryly.

He grinned. "Well, I was talking about the North. But my home is in the South, as you must know. It is a bitter feeling, Mrs. Michaelson, not to be able to go home."

"I can well imagine, sir."

He shrugged. "I live for the day when it will be over. When I can ride back and see the house sitting on the river. . . ." He shrugged again. "Sorry, Mrs. Michaelson. I have a wife and a son back there."

"In Virginia?"

"Yes. A very old plantation. The cornerstone was laid in the mid-sixteen hundreds. It's very gracious and very beautiful, and sometimes I just pray that the house survives the war."

"It must be quite a place," Callie murmured.

Jesse watched her smooth her fingers over her skirt.

"Once upon a time it was a very rich estate. Fields lie fallow now—not enough people to work them. Daniel was the one who looked over the estate. He knew how to keep up the house, and he knew what to plant, and what not to plant, and where to sell, and when to hold. It will not be such a rich place once we return." He paused. "If we are ever able to return. I don't know, Callie. Some people say that you can never go home again. What do you think?"

"I think that you can always go home," she said softly. She looked up at him and tried to appear very casual once again. "Your wife and child are there, so far from the world you're living in?"

"Well, my boy is not very old. There is no place else where he could have been born, except for Cameron Hall. And Kiernan . . ." He smiled. "She's quite a Rebel. It's an interesting dilemma, isn't it? Well, I've taken enough of your time, as apparently my brother has also done. I'll leave you, but I promise I'll write once I've seen Daniel."

"Yes, will you please?"

He nodded. "I'd promise to try to come by, but the war being what it is, it's hard to make such promises. I will write, though."

"Thank you." Her eyes were downcast again. She was the perfect lady. She might not realize it, clad as she was in simple cotton, but Callie Michaelson was every inch a lady.

He hoped that Daniel realized it.

He hurried down her path to his horse, Goliath. Coming to the porch, she called him back.

"Doctor Cameron?"

"Yes?"

"There was a boy who died in my barn. A Union boy. He's—he's buried out back, with my family. But I have his effects, a letter for his mother, his bedroll, a few other things. I'd like to write a little note myself. Would you mind waiting just a minute and taking them for me?"

He shook his head. "Not at all."

She swirled around and slipped back into the house. She returned with the soldier's things, handing him a letter. Again, there was that anxious look to her eyes. "Would you read the note I've written, sir, and see if it will help?"

Jesse quickly scanned her words.

Dear Madam,

I am heartily sorry to inform you of your son's death, here before my home outside of Sharpsburg. Please know that he knew no suffering, that his death wus instant. And know, too, that he died a hero, protecting the men around him even as he fell. We honored him when we buried him, and he rests by my husband's grave, and near a headstone to my father. May God be with you.

Callie Michaelson

Jesse glanced at her. "Is it the truth?"

She shook her head. "No."

"It's a beautiful note. I'll see that it reaches the proper party."

He took her hand. He was about to shake it, but he squeezed it instead.

"Good-bye, Mrs. Michaelson. Take care of yourself."

"God go with you, sir. God go with you."

He saluted to her and rode away. Turning back, he saw that she was still standing there, tall, beautiful, both proud and ethereal in the moonlight.

Daniel, you son of a gun, he thought. Now if I could just be sure that they could keep you in prison until the war ends!

He doubted it. He wondered if he'd even return soon enough to find Daniel in Old Capitol Prison if he rode straight through tonight.

He quickened his pace.

It was exactly what he was going to do.

Prison was sometimes an interesting place to be, Daniel thought. He leaned back on his straw, lazily chewing on a piece of it.

But his eyes were moving. Not that there was much to see right now. Four of the men were engaged in a game of cards, gambling little bits of tobacco and flasks of whiskey. Some were just sitting back, as he was himself. Old Rufus MacKenzie, the one real graybeard in their midst, was reading his Bible. They were all grouped together, twenty-four men, in the one big room. They had themselves one "necessary" pot built against the wall, and the stench could get pretty bad. Billy Boudain told him that you forgot about the smell after a while.

There were no cots, just beds of straw and whatever else the men could lump together. It wasn't so bad. It was just bleak. As bleak as the decaying color of the walls, as bleak as the cry of the rats that became daring and loud at night.

At least, he thought wryly, he was in the company of friends.

And he watched. Daniel watched everything. Over the past few days, he had watched all that took place. He'd watched the coming and going of food and supplies, and he'd watched the way that the prison worked.

The guards, most of them, were easy to bribe. Captain Harrison Farrow from Tupelo, Mississippi, had a sister married to someone in the Yank Congress, and she saw to it that he received all manner of goodies from home, from baked pies to blankets and extremely fine cigars. Some of the fellows didn't do so well. Private Davie Smith, a small-time farm boy from the Shenandoah Valley, didn't know a soul in the North. But like Daniel, he had been shoeless. Prison had a way of drawing out the best and the worst in men. Captain Farrow couldn't acquire enough from his sister to keep them all in the lap of luxury, but he had been careful to get Private Smith a pair of shoes. And Private Smith was one good-looking Southern lad who liked to flirt with the girls through the window bars as the young ladies passed by.

Every once in a while, Private Davie Smith managed to get one of those giggling young ladies—young ladies who's mamas would have them strung up if they knew their girls were fraternizing with the enemy—to give him an important piece of information.

It was through Private Smith that Daniel learned a lot. The Rebel troops—who had done such a daring and spectacular job of taking the Union garrison—had abandoned Harpers Ferry. Jackson was moving back into the valley again. Lincoln's Emancipation Proclamation was stirring up public sentiment just the way Daniel had assumed it would.

The Yankees were feeling mighty proud of themselves at the moment. They were claiming Sharpsburg a victory.

But so was the South.

Hell, anyone who had been there would just call it a disaster, Daniel thought, but he never said it aloud. He was the ranking officer among the prisoners, and it was up to him to watch out for morale.

As long as he stayed.

There were ways out of here. He had watched the supply wagons come and go, and he had watched the coffins come and go, and reflected on that as a means to escape.

A lot of coffins came and went. Daniel didn't think their warders were exceptionally cruel—except for one or two of the men. When those guards jeered the prisoners, the Rebs jeered them right back, usually asking what able-bodied men were doing watching over tattered and injured Rebs. "Afraid to be out on the battlefield, eh, Yanks?" they taunted back.

The food wasn't so bad. At least, it wasn't any worse than what Daniel was accustomed to eating in the field. A few more years, and he'd be able to convince himself that worms were the best part of meat and that "hardtack" was just that—so hard that the challenge for a man was not in managing to eat enough, but in managing to keep his teeth.

Old Capitol Prison was survivable, he determined, because he meant to survive. Every night, when he felt the cold dankness of the surrounding walls, when he heard his fellow prisoners hacking away with the coughs they acquired here, he thought about Callie.

He thought about her when he felt his straw crawling with all the bugs that were alive and thriving in it, and he thought about her every time one of the coffins came and went.

I will get out, he promised himself. But he meant to be careful. He didn't mean to get caught again, he didn't want to do anything rash or stupid. If he were caught again up here in plain breeches and white cotton shirt, he just might be considered a spy. If he was caught, he would likely soon be a dead man.

As he idly chewed his grass, he watched Billy Boudain and handsome young Davie Smith at the window. Billy was favoring his right arm, Daniel noted with a frown. He couldn't see anything wrong with it, since Billy was wearing a gray coat with red artillery trim.

"Hey, Billy!" he called, sitting up straight on the straw and beckoning to the young man. "Come here."

Billy crawled down from his post at the window, eyeing Daniel apprehensively.

"What is it, Colonel?"

"What's the matter with your arm?"

Billy shook his head. "Just a little piece of shrapnel I picked up at Sharpsburg, Colonel Cameron."

He said it lightly, as if the injury were nothing. "Let me see it," Daniel said.

"Colonel, it ain't nothing at all."

"Billy, that's an order. Take off your jacket and roll up your sleeve. Let me see your shrapnel."

Bland-faced, Billy did so. He tried damned hard not

to wince when the jacket fell over his arm as he removed it. He kept trying not to wince as he rolled up the dingy white cotton sleeve of his shirt.

Daniel bit his lip so as not to cry out when he saw the wound. Billy was doing one hell of a job not to make a sound.

The wound was not just a little shrapnel scratch. Daniel was certain that something—some piece of metal or grapeshot—remained in the wound. All around it, the flesh was turning unnatural colors. It was mottled and oozing.

With a sinking heart, Daniel thought that Billy was going to lose his arm. If he wanted to live, he was going to have to lose it soon.

"Hell, boy!" Daniel muttered softly. "We can't just ignore this one!"

"We got to ignore this one, Colonel," Captain Farrow said, stepping up beside Billy.

"Ain't nothin' else we can do," Davie said.

Daniel shook his head. "Something has to be done, Billy," he told the boy bluntly. "You're going to die if you don't let them take off your arm."

Billy blanched, looking to Harrison Farrow for help. Farrow shifted from one foot to another. "Colonel, I imagine that Billy would just as soon die right here as under the knife with one of them Yankee sawbones."

Daniel looked back and forth between the two, then glanced at Davie. Davie looked away.

"They're not all murderers," Daniel said. He paused, looking at faces that politely hid their disbelief. "Billy, isn't your life worth a chance?"

No one answered. Apparently, they didn't think that Billy had any chance.

"Billy—" he began.

"Colonel, there ain't no hope that I could keep the arm?" Billy said.

Daniel hesitated. He wasn't the doctor, Jesse was.

But he'd been around Jesse enough, and he'd been around enough maimed limbs. Maybe it could be saved, but he only knew one man who could do it, and that man wasn't around.

"I don't think so," he told Billy frankly.

Billy looked a little white around the gills. "Maybe I oughta just die a whole man then, sir."

"Damn it, Billy! You don't want to die! Hell, you're just a kid—"

"Then this war is being fought by a bunch of kids," Captain Farrow interrupted softly. Daniel stared at him. "Meaning no disrespect, sir."

"None taken," Daniel said. "But Billy, we've got to call the Yanks in on that arm."

"Ain't no way I'm going off with the Yanks—"

"Yes, there is. You'll go, because I'll go with you."

"What if they say no?" Billy demanded.

Daniel shook his head. "They aren't going to say no. Not unless they're planning on putting a gun right to my head."

"What the hell you mean by that, Colonel?"

"As it happens, I have a brother who happens to be a Union sawbones. He'll know soon enough where I am, and he'll have to come here. Every man jack out there knows it. So as far as playing fair with me, they're in a bit of a knot."

"You've got a brother who's a Yankee sawbones?" Billy said incredulously.

Daniel smiled slowly. "Yeah."

"And you're still speaking to him?" Billy said.

"Yeah," Daniel repeated. He lifted his shoulders. "He's my brother."

Billy still looked dubious. "That lieutenant colonel fellow in charge of the place when I came in didn't seem so bad," Daniel said.

"You mean Lieutenant Colonel Wadsworth P. Dodson," Captain Farrow said with a broad grin. "Our boy colonel."

"He does look a little wet behind the ears," Daniel agreed. "But sometimes that's good. Sometimes a young man is a good man. He hasn't had time to find out just how worthless it is to be good sometimes."

Farrow shrugged. The little group looked from one to another. "Billy, I'm going to call for him," Daniel said. "That arm is bad. You can't wait any longer."

At last, Billy nodded, biting down hard on his lower lip.

"But if you call, will they come?" Farrow demanded.

"You just have to be nice to them," Daniel assured him. He stood up and went to the door with its small barred window. "I need some help in here. This is Colonel Daniel Cameron, and I want a meeting with Colonel Dodson."

"Ah, take a nap in there!" one of the guards called out.

"I want Dodson!" Daniel demanded.

The guard came to the door. "I told you—"

Daniel slipped a hand through the bars, catching the man's collar and jerking him hard and flat against the bars. He twisted on the fabric, and the guard's face began to turn a mottled red. "I said, I want Dodson. Please. And if I don't get him, soldier, you'd best hope we never meet outside these walls!"

Daniel smiled complacently as he allowed the guard to break free from his grasp.

"See? You just have to be nice."

The guards eyes appeared between the bars. "I'll bring him along just as soon as I can. You stay quiet in there while you're waiting."

"Quiet as a church mouse," Daniel agreed pleasantly.

It wasn't long before Dodson appeared. Daniel noted with a certain amusement and a certain respect that the young man wasn't afraid of him—or the others. He walked right into their dank prison room, into the midst of his enemies. Dodson had treated them all well enough. He had nothing to fear.

Other men in the prison systems, North and South, might not feel so safe.

Dodson might have gotten his military rank and appointment at his young age because of who he knew, but he was sincere in his determination to be a fair warden.

"What is it that I can do for you, Colonel?"

"One of my men has a severe injury. He needs to see a doctor. I don't doubt Yankee physicians myself, but my young friend is afraid of them. I want to accompany Billy here to see a doc."

One of the guards snickered outside.

Young Dodson peered anxiously at Billy. "We ask every morning in the prison yard if any of the men needs to see a doctor."

"Colonel Dodson, we both know that there have been rumors out—on both sides—that the physicians claim they can kill more of the enemy than the generals in the field. But Billy is going to die if something isn't done about that arm. It's my order that he do something. And I want your guarantee that I can be with him to assure that he's going to be all right."

"This is highly irregular—" began one of the guards in the hallway. But Daniel fixed a cool blue gaze on him, and his voice died away.

Dodson watched Daniel. He looked to his guards. "Irregular or not, I can't see any harm in it."

"Cameron is trying to escape!" a guard said.

Dodson looked at Daniel. "Are you trying to escape, sir?"

Was he trying to escape? Hell, yes, he'd spent days watching for a way to escape. But this wasn't it. Not with Billy as a possible sacrifice.

"Sir, you have my word of honor that I will not escape when I'm in Private Boudain's company."

"A Reb word of honor—" the same guard began.

"The colonel's word is enough for me," Dodson said flatly. He looked to two of the guards, the one Daniel had threatened, and the older man who had been making the bitter comments.

"Palacio, Cheswick, you'll accompany these men to the hospital. Tell Captain Renard that I've given Colonel Cameron permission to sit in and"—he paused, looking at Daniel—"assist in whatever surgery is necessary. Is there anything else, Colonel?"

Daniel shook his head and smiled broadly to Dodson. "No. That about covers it. Thank you, Lieutenant Colonel Dodson."

Dodson nodded and left the room. Daniel slipped his hand beneath Billy's elbow. "Come on. Let's go."

"Hey, Billy, it's going to be all right!" Captain Farrow called out.

"Yeah, it's going to be just fine!" Davie agreed. "The girls will be waiting, Billy!"

"For a one-armed man?" Billy asked.

"Sure!" Davie said with a grin. "They like to be tender and sympathetic."

A sound started in the prison room. Low, and then growing. Billy was being sent off with a Rebel yell.

"Stop that caterwauling!" the guard Dodson had called Cheswick yelled. The sound just increased. Muttering beneath his breath, Cheswick led the way and Palacio followed behind.

They were brought to an anteroom and told to wait. Dr. Renard, a staid man with iron-gray hair and a rigid countenance, appeared shortly.

"Let me see the arm," he told Billy.

Billy looked at Daniel, and Daniel nodded. Billy showed the doctor his arm. Renard didn't even blink. "Yes, it will have to come off. You're going to be a lucky young man if the poison isn't already moving through your system." Renard looked at Daniel. "I hear, Colonel, that you want to clutter up my surgery. You've assisted before, I assume."

"Often enough," Daniel told him. He was certain that Renard knew Jesse.

Renard looked at Billy. "You're not going to suffer as you might have on the battlefield, soldier. I've got morphine, and a syringe to inject it with. Colonel, you're still going to have to hold him tight. Are we understood?"

Daniel nodded. They walked in to Renard's surgery. There was an operating table in the center and Billy was set up on it and given the morphine. His eyes met Daniel's all the while. The look in them was so trusting that Daniel was surprised to feel a chill sweep along his spine. This had to work out.

He smiled encouragingly. Billy's eyes began to close, and Renard began to assemble his instruments.

Renard took out a sponge to soak up the blood. Daniel's eyes narrowed. There were traces of his last patient's blood on that sponge.

"Wait a minute, Doctor Renard," Daniel said.

"What is it?"

"You can't use that sponge on Billy."

"And why not, Colonel? It's the same type sponge I use on every man, Yank or Rebel."

"I'm not accusing you of being prejudiced against a Reb, Doc," Daniel said. "But you can't use that sponge." Renard was still staring at him blankly. Daniel sighed, gritting his teeth. He didn't want to aggravate Renard, but he didn't want Billy dying in the next couple of weeks either.

"You need linen, sir," Daniel said. "Clean linen. And a new square for each man."

"So you think you're a doctor now, eh, Colonel? Well, I tell you, I spent my years in medical school—"

"Sir, I'm not questioning that. I imagine that this is fairly new. My brother told me he'd learned from a Rebel surgeon that the survival rate was much higher when clean linen was used every time."

"Well, Colonel, I'm not a Rebel surgeon!"

"But, Doctor Renard—"

"And I'm operating my way!"

"Then you're not operating on Billy!"

"This boy is going to die if I don't!"

"I'll let him die whole."

Determined, Daniel reached for Billy, ready to lift him over his shoulder.

"Put that man down, Colonel!" Renard demanded.

When Daniel failed to oblige him, Renard suddenly called out. "Guards! Get in here!"

Palacio and Cheswick were quickly inside the operating room. Daniel swiftly laid Billy back down. Cheswick came for Daniel first. Daniel ducked and swung, and flattened the man in a second. Palacio intended to be more careful. He circled around Daniel, looking to Renard. "Better get help!"

But two other guards were already rushing in. "He's trying to escape!" someone shouted.

Daniel barely heard him. Men were coming at him one after the other and he had to move like lightning to keep up with them. He watched his space carefully, managing to get a wall to his back so that he could put all his defense efforts forward. A fist connected with his jaw. He tasted blood, but he fought the sensation of dizziness. He kicked, and he swung, and he managed to avoid further blows while connecting his own fist nicely with the guts and chins of a number of his opponents. He was good, he reckoned, but he'd have been taken by now if the soldiers hadn't been so cautious.

"Get him!" someone called.

"You get him!" came the reply.

Suddenly, in the midst of the melee, a gunshot ex-

ploded. The room went still. Daniel, tasting blood on
his lip, leaned back against the wall.

Two men were coming into the surgery. The first was
Lieutenant Colonel Dodson.

The second man stood in shadow for a minute. Then
the light touched his face.

It was Jesse.

Daniel closed his eyes, leaning back.

"What the hell is going on here?" Dodson demanded.

"He was trying to escape!" Cheswick excused himself.

"Renard needed us!" Palacio said.

"Were you trying to escape, Colonel?" Dodson
asked.

"No, sir, I wasn't," Daniel said. He crossed his arms
over his chest and tried not to grin. "Hello, Jesse."

Jesse, grinning, leaned against the doorway. "Hello,
Daniel. In trouble again, I take it. Were you trying to
escape?"

It was good to see Jesse. It had been several months
since he had seen his brother. He never knew when
they parted if he would ever see him again. Blue eyes
so like his own met his. Jesse was aging with the war.
Tiny lines of gray entwined with his ebony hair at his
temples. Those were new. But his brother looked good.
Damned good. It was almost worth having been taken
prisoner to see him again.

"I gave Dodson my word that I wouldn't try to escape," Daniel said.

Jesse, the ranking officer among the Yanks, shrugged
and looked to Dodson. "If he gave you his word, Colonel, then he was not trying to escape."

"Then what was going on?" Dodson asked.

Jesse looked back to Daniel. "What was going on?"

"Doctor Renard wanted to operate with a sponge. I
asked him to use clean linen."

Jesse looked at Renard. "Since it seems to mean so much to the Rebs, couldn't you possibly oblige them, sir?"

Jesse was so pleasant. There was just the slightest edge of steel to his voice.

And Renard heard it. He answered just as pleasantly, with just a bit of an audible grate to his teeth.

"Perhaps, Colonel Cameron, you'd like to take on this particular operation yourself, since you are with us."

Jesse glanced to Daniel and cocked his head. "Why, Doctor Renard, thank you. I'd very much like to take this one on."

"Is that all right with you, Colonel?" Dodson asked.

Daniel grinned. "Yes, sir, it is." Billy didn't know just how lucky he was, Daniel thought.

Thank God. Jesse was here.

Thirteen

"Davie's been here a long, long time. Why, he was here all the time they kept Mrs. Rose Greenhow here." The last words slushed together, but Billy didn't seem to mind or even notice. "She was quite a lady, Davie said. The Yanks brought her here because of the Allan Pinkerton fellow. He suspected her of spying for the South, and of course, that's exactly what she was doing. She's the one that got the message to our General Beauregard about the Yankee troop movements before the first battle at Manassas. 'Course, Pinkerton's a damned fool, always telling the Yanks that we have twice as many men as we do. But he brought Mrs. Greenhow here, separated her from her daughter, and threatened to kill her, so Davie told me. She was incredible throughout her long ordeal, sir. The men here were gracious and supportive, giving her their full respect. I hear now she's in the South, far away from harm's touch."

Billy rambled on and on.

"Jeff Davis has sent her over to Europe to see what support she could drum up for us over there," Daniel told Billy with a touch of amusement. The operation was long over, but Jesse had warned that there would still be pain, and Billy was hugging a flask of whiskey as if it were a long-lost brother.

"Now, that cute little hussy, Belle Boyd—the one spilling all the information to old Stonewall—she kind of comes and goes here all the time. All the time, so it seems."

"Billy, she ain't no hussy!" Davie called over. He was seated against the wall. They'd all been listening to Billy ramble on for some time. Mostly, they just let him talk. Every once in a while, one of his comments brought a rise out of someone.

"Davie's in love with her!" Billy said, and he started laughing. "Davie's in love with Belle!"

"Colonel, make him stop that, won't you?" Davie demanded. "Order him to quit. Belle Boyd is a beautiful young woman, and a heroine to the Confederacy."

Daniel grinned, leaving Billy's side at last to rise and stretch. "He's got so much drugs and alcohol in him right now that about the only thing I could order him to do and expect a response on would be to smile."

Billy was smiling right then. A crooked smile that had reached his red-rimmed eyes. "She's a heroine all right, Colonel. A heroine with two of the biggest, ripest, juiciest tomato—"

"Colonel, make him stop!" Davie pleaded.

"—like cheeks I've ever seen. She's got the cutest little round face."

"Well, there's a little more respect," Davie said.

"And what a great pair of breasts!" Billy sighed.

"Colonel!"

Daniel laughed. "I don't think he means any disrespect with that one either, Davie. We all salute our sisters of the South, eh, gentlemen?"

A cheer rose up, and as it did so, Daniel had to fight to keep his own smile in place. To the women, yes, dear Lord, to the women. Of the North and South. Rose Greenhow had made fools of many men. She had been more valuable to the Confederacy than many a practiced general. Belle Boyd had proven herself a priceless gem to Stonewall Jackson. There were more.

But the North was not to be undone, Daniel thought bitterly. Maybe Callie Michaelson hadn't turned the tide of any battle, but she had surely done him in. Maybe she would move on to bigger things now.

He almost groaned aloud. It wasn't so much that she had betrayed him. It was that he had been such a damned fool to have fallen for her every step of the way.

But I'll get back! He promised himself.

"Someone's coming, Colonel," Captain Farrow warned. Daniel left Billy's side, walking across the room. He could already hear the key twisting in the lock. The door opened, and Jesse stepped inside.

Every southerner there stood. They stared at him for a minute.

Jesse saluted the group. They saluted in return. "Colonel Cameron and Colonel Cameron. Blue and gray. Don't that just beat all!" Captain Farrow murmured.

"If anybody else has got health complaints," Daniel advised quickly, "now's the time to voice them."

Davie Smith took a step forward. "I ain't got no health complaints, Doctor," he told Jesse. "But you saved Billy's arm, and we're all beholden to you."

"You don't need to be beholden to me," Jesse said. "I'm a doctor, and I took an oath. I drained his arm of all the poison and I pulled out the lead. But if he doesn't take real good care of it now, infection will set back in, and he'll be right back where he started. It's up to you all now. Make him keep dry and clean. I won't be around later to see to him." Jesse turned to his brother. "How's my patient doing?" he asked Daniel.

"Drunk as a skunk."

Jesse grinned and walked over to where Billy was lying on a pallet of straw. Billy smiled broadly for him. "Hello, Doc!"

"Hello, Billy. How are you feeling?"

"Like I could whomp the whole Yank army," Billy admitted, still with his grin in place.

"Well, I think that you'd better lay low on that for a little while," Jesse advised.

"Maybe. Till I sober up, at least."

Jesse unwrapped the bandaging, looked the arm over carefully, and then rewrapped his handiwork with a gentle touch. Billy watched him all the while.

"What are you doing on the wrong side, Doc?" he asked.

Jesse paused just a second, then went on wrapping Billy's arm. "Son, I'm not so sure there is a 'right' side or a 'wrong' side. There's just a point of view here." Finished with his task, he stood and saluted Billy. "Whatever, I hope to see you when this war is over."

"Yes, sir!" Billy saluted in return.

Jesse walked back to Daniel.

"You're leaving," Daniel said.

Jesse nodded. "I have to. You know that."

"Yes, I do."

"Come with me. I've permission to have a few minutes alone with you."

Daniel's brows arched high. "They don't think I'm too dangerous to be out with you?"

"I'm allowed to talk to you in an empty room across the hall." He knocked against the door, then saluted the entire room of men again.

"Colonel Cameron!" They said en masse, saluting him once again.

Daniel was surprised to see the faintest hint of a flush touch his brother's cheeks. "Watch it, fellows," he said gruffly. "They'll be in here accusing me of all manner of things. Gentlemen, take care."

With that, he slipped through the door that a guard had opened for him. It was a new man, Daniel noticed. A big one. He had to be almost as tall as old Abe Lincoln himself. He towered over Jesse and Daniel and they were both a very tall six feet two inches.

And he was built like a gorilla, with a flat, stupid face.

"He can fight like a lion, so they say," Jesse advised Daniel wryly.

"So he's in honor of me, huh?"

"I imagine. I was told to warn you."

Daniel grinned as they slipped into the room across the hall. It was very much like the room where he and the others were kept, but it was very small. He imagined that it was where the female prisoners were kept when they were housed at Old Capitol.

For a moment he and Jesse stood staring at one another. They'd seen each other in surgery, and they'd worked together over Billy's arm. Daniel was long accustomed to helping his brother when they'd both been regular cavalry out in the West. But there had been guards in attendance this time, and after the surgery was finished, Daniel had accompanied Billy back to their room. Jesse had suggested that Billy be isolated in a hospital bed, but Daniel felt certain that Billy would much rather be among his own people. At any rate, they'd never really had a moment to say anything personal, and standing here, they both started to grin. They embraced, holding tightly for a moment, then stepped back.

"Jess, it's good to see you. Damned good to see you. You came in the nick of time. Did the colonel reach you about my whereabouts?" Daniel asked.

Jesse shook his head, watching his brother curiously. "Nope. A certain young lady told me where to find you."

Daniel stiffened just like a poker. His words fell

from his lips like cubes of ice. "So you met the little bitch."

"Brother, what a way to refer to the lady! She speaks so highly of you!"

"Yeah, I'll just bet," Daniel said. "Did she mention how I happen to be in here?"

"She more or less mentioned that she felt responsible."

"Oh, yes. She was responsible. I'm just curious. Did she mention just exactly what she did?"

"Why don't you tell me?"

"Let's suffice it to say that she used every last power known to women."

Jesse grinned suddenly. "She seduced you. And you fell for it."

Daniel felt a tightening rip through his muscles. A pulse that he could feel beat against his throat. "If you weren't my brother—"

"But I am your brother, and I told all the powers that be here that I'd be safe in your company. Who knows—maybe I can beat the tar out of you."

"And maybe you can't," Daniel warned.

But Jesse was still laughing. "Jesu, Daniel. She was glad because she thought that you were safe. Hell, it's drafty, the walls are dank, there are rats, but you're probably eating better than half of the Confederacy. I'd be just as glad if they managed to keep you in here for the rest of the war."

"They won't, Jess, you know that," Daniel said softly.

"God in heaven, Daniel, be careful! You push things too far, and they'll hang you, and there won't be a thing in the world that I can do about it!"

"Jesse, don't worry about me. I will be careful. I'm always careful. Damn you, you can't take on the whole weight of the war and the weight of worrying about me too!" Daniel told him.

"I'm not taking on the whole damned war, Daniel."

Daniel smiled ruefully. It was all so hard for him; it had to be harder for Jesse. "Jess, it's me you've got to quit worrying about."

"Do you ever stop worrying?" Jesse demanded.

No, he didn't. Daniel tried again.

"You know that I'm good, and you know that I'm careful."

"You know, she was right, your Mrs. Michaelson. You are better off in prison, Daniel."

"She isn't my Mrs. Michaelson. Is that what she told you?"

"Oh, I think she's yours, all right. And yes, I think that, more or less, she told me something like that. She was very impressive. She's got to be one of the most beautiful women I've ever seen—"

"Then there's your wife," Daniel reminded him politely.

"Yes, of course. Kiernan is extraordinary. But this Callie shines—"

"Just like a beacon," Daniel agreed. "Until you're right betwixt her teeth and she clamps down hard."

"What was that you were betwixt?" Jesse asked.

"Damn it, Jesse, I—"

"Seriously, she is fascinating, Daniel. When I leave here, I am going to try very hard to ride by and tell her that you're safely locked up. And that if we're both lucky, they'll keep you locked up—and alive—until the war is over."

Daniel slowly crossed his arms over his chest. Goddamn, if it wasn't so easy to see her in his mind's eye all the time. If she didn't haunt his dreams. If he didn't see those eyes with their captivating silver luminescence! Hear her voice, the whisper of her pleading.

And if he didn't remember what it was like to make love to her. To stroke the silk and softness of her flesh, drown within the flaming bounty of her hair.

Not again. She'd never seduce him again. Never.

But the dead-set determination could not erase the dreams. He clenched his hands. Yes, he was going back one day. They could finish what they had started. He could strangle her. Hang her up by her toes. Take a horsewhip to her. No, have her drawn and quartered . . .

Touch her . . .

"If you go by, Jess," Daniel said softly, "just remind her that I'm coming back for her. It may take some time. But I'll be back."

Jesse had never seen Daniel so heated with emotion. Not in all the years he had known his brother. His fingers wound into fists that still trembled while he spoke.

"Daniel, you can't hate her for being on the other side!"

"I don't hate her for being on the other side."

"Daniel, think about it. Things could work out. You have to remember how Kiernan hated me. I did everything that I could for the longest time—"

"Well," Daniel interrupted politely, "you could have changed sides."

"Other than changing sides," Jesse said dryly, "and she still hated me. But if you could just realize that *we're* not at war with each other—"

"That's just it, Jesse. We never want to realize it, you or I. But we are at war with each other. And I am—thoroughly and completely—at war with Mrs. Michaelson."

Jesse started to speak, then changed his mind. "Well, I've got to head out of here. Take care of your friend. And if you should get out and get home, give my love to Kiernan and to our sister and to my baby."

"Sure, Jess. And if for some reason you get there before I do, you do the same."

"Right."

"And Jesse."

"Yes?"

"Thank you for Billy. I'm grateful that I've got a Yank doc for a brother."

"I took an oath, and it's just like your word when you give it. I have to save life—any life—when I can."

"I know, Jesse. Hey, God go with you, brother."

"You too, Daniel."

They hesitated, still awkward with these partings. They embraced tightly for a moment and drew away. And then Jesse was gone.

Daniel stared up at the ceiling, fighting the wave of painful emotions that washed over him. But within a matter of seconds, the gorilla guard returned to escort him back to his prison room with the others.

Billy was sleeping. Or Billy was passed out in an alcoholic stupor. Daniel sank down on the floor by Billy's straw bed and closed his eyes wearily.

"Colonel Cameron!"

Captain Farrow was beside him, his eyes alive with excitement as he rubbed his stubbled cheek.

"What is it, Captain?"

"Something of grave interest, sir."

What could have happened in the ten or fifteen minutes he was out with Jesse?

"Well?" Daniel said.

Farrow sank down beside him and plucked at a stray blade of straw.

"Billy's Aunt Priscilla made an appearance."

"So Billy had a visitor, huh? Before or after he passed out?"

"No, sir, he was plumb out when she arrived. But you've got to meet Aunt Prissy. She's some girl."

"Sir, I don't—"

Farrow's voice lowered to something that couldn't even be called a whisper. "We've got a plan, sir. Seems Beauty knows where you are and he wants you out.

'Aunt Prissy' ain't really Billy's relative at all. She's a friend to us here.''

"And?" Daniel said, feeling his heart slam against his chest.

"Well, sir, we think we've got a plan to get you and a few others out. General Stuart wants you back. Are you game, sir?"

Daniel grinned, leaned back, and closed his eyes tightly with gratitude.

"Sir?" Farrow repeated.

"Oh, yes, Captain! I'm game. You'll know just how game. Tell me about this plan!"

Luckily, Jesse had been ordered to report to Frederick, Maryland. It was close enough for him to take the time to ride back by the farmhouse where he had first seen Callie Michaelson.

It was midafternoon when he rode by.

He found her on the front porch of her house. Curiously, she didn't seem to hear him as he approached. Even more curious, she was just sitting there, barefoot, in a very plain gingham dress with a high collar. Very proper for the time of day, he thought with a slow nostalgic smile. It had been a very long time since he had lost his mother, but he could still remember the things she was so determined to teach his sister, Christa. "Never, never show bosom during the day, darling. Only after five may a lady wear a dress that is at all revealing, and then, of course, in the most fastidious taste!"

"Mother, I haven't got a bosom," Christa would reply. "Therefore, I can't show it at any time."

"Oh, but darling, you will have one, you will!"

"Yes, and Daniel and Jesse will grow hair on their chests. Maybe!" Christa would tease.

And their mother would sigh, and roll her eyes, and then she would laugh and swear that she was raising a family of ruffians who were just playing at being gentry. Maybe that was true, but his mother could be the first "ruffian" among them because upon occasion, she would lose her austere dignity and slip off her shoes and go running through the grass with the rest of them. They had all adored her. To this day, Jesse was convinced that his father had died soon after she succumbed to pneumonia because no matter how he loved his children, he simply could not bear life without her.

Maybe death was easier for them now. He wondered vaguely if they could look down from heaven and see that he and Daniel were on opposite sides.

They would understand, he thought. They were the ones who had taught their children about conscience and dignity and moral duty and . . .

Honor.

He smiled slightly as he approached Callie. Yes, his mother might well approve of her. Her collar was high, her feet were bare.

"Mrs. Michaelson." He called her name softly. He was nearly upon her at the steps to the broad porch and she still hadn't noticed him, despite the fact that her eyes were wide open. She seemed so lost and vulnerable and waiflike.

She gazed at him. Her eyes widened and a look of panic flashed through her eyes. She leapt to her feet nervously, almost like a child who had been caught with something that she wanted to hide.

"Colonel! Colonel Cameron!" she gasped.

He frowned, dismounting from his horse. "I'm sorry, Mrs. Michaelson, I didn't mean to frighten you."

"I'm not frightened."

She was lying. No, she wasn't, Jesse determined. She was very startled, but she wasn't frightened. She had been seriously caught off guard. By him—in particular. He wondered why.

"I didn't think that I could come back, but as it is, I

have to report to Frederick. I thought that I'd stop by instead of writing. I wanted to let you know that, yes, Daniel is in Old Capitol Prison. He's well, and with any luck, he'll stay there."

"Thank you. Thank you very much." She still seemed unreasonably nervous, but her appreciation and concern showed in the beautiful gray of her eyes.

"It's nothing, really."

She regained her composure. She regained it so completely that he had to wonder if he hadn't imagined the lost look in her eyes just seconds before. Her voice became soft and very gracious. Her eyes were downcast. Her bare feet were hidden by the sway of her simple skirt.

"You've come out of your way for me, Colonel Cameron, and I appreciate it very much. Come in, please. Let me make you something to eat before you travel on."

"It's not necessary—"

"But it is. Please, Colonel Cameron. I'd very much like to have you here."

"All right then," Jesse said. "Thank you, Mrs. Michaelson." He hesitated on the step, watching her. What a miraculous change she had made. He suddenly felt like grinning.

So here was the woman to bring down Daniel at last. It was intriguing. It was amusing. It could be wonderful.

If they could just get through the war.

"There's just one thing, Mrs. Michaelson."

"What's that?"

"My name is Jesse."

"Callie, sir."

He smiled and walked up her steps.

She paused. "Did you mention that we had met? Did he say anything?"

Jesse reflected for a minute. Yes, Daniel had had his message for Callie. But Jesse wasn't going to deliver it.

"He wasn't very talkative. Do you know, a home-cooked meal does sound wonderful, Callie. Shall we?"

She turned, and he followed her into the house.

Surely, he decided, there was some little twist of evil in his soul. He couldn't wait to write to Daniel. He wanted to tell him just how gracious and beautiful Mrs. Michaelson was and what a wonderful meal he had had in her company.

He was composing the letter even as he followed her into the house.

It occurred to him that he had never seen his brother angrier than when he had been talking about Callie Michaelson. Maybe Jesse would merely be adding fuel to that fire.

Maybe Daniel and this woman would just have to fight their own battles.

And maybe, just maybe, find their peace.

"Now?" Daniel said.

Captain Farrow nodded solemnly. Daniel started to lift the vial to his lips, determined that his hand would not shake. But Billy Boudain—up and about and doing darned nicely—suddenly interrupted.

"Jesu, Colonel, is it worth it? What if the—er—what if the box don't go where it's supposed to go?"

"But it will go where it's supposed to," Daniel said wearily. All of the men were staring at him. It was night, and the prison was quiet. Every man in the room was up, tense, waiting. Daniel grinned, saluted—but then paused himself.

The drug had not been his companion's choice for his method of escape.

Daniel hadn't been able to tolerate the first method planned for him.

Aunt Priscilla had planned on acquiring a Union

Colonel's uniform with all the proper medical insignia upon it, slipping it to Daniel, and boldly walking out of the prison with her arm slipped right through his, convincing the guards that Colonel Jesse Cameron was leaving after a quick visit to see to the welfare of his brother, and his recent patient, Billy Boudain. No one had realized just how alike the Cameron brothers were —not until they had been seen there together at the prison.

Daniel had refused point-blank.

"I'm not using Jesse."

"Colonel, if you're afraid of getting caught, I imagine that you've got a justifiable concern. If you're afraid of being hanged—"

"I'm not afraid of being hanged, although I admit, it's not the way that I want to go. I want to get out of here so badly, Captain, that I can taste it. I dream of it, night and day. But I'm not using Jesse. He saved Billy's arm—and his life. And if he hadn't, I still wouldn't use him. Damn it, don't you see, it just wouldn't be right!"

"But sir—"

"What are we fighting for?" Daniel demanded.

Captain Farrow had grown quiet, and the next thing Daniel knew, he was listening to a new and wilder plot. Aunt Priscilla could get hold of a drug. Foul-tasting stuff, but it would do the trick. Daniel would appear to be dead. The Union would try to hold his body, of course. They'd want to get hold of Jesse to see what he wanted done with his brother's remains. But Aunt Priscilla would appear with a woman swearing to be Christa Cameron and between the two of them, they would demand the body.

There would be no discernable heartbeat in Daniel's body. His breathing would have become so slow that the doctor would not be able to detect it. The effects would last approximately forty-eight hours, so all that they had to do was get Daniel safely into Aunt Priscilla's hands by then.

Aunt Priscilla, Daniel reckoned, must be quite a reader. There were fine shades of Shakespeare in this wild scheme. He just hoped that the Union officers weren't quite as up on their classics.

"Well, men . . ." he murmured.

He shook his head. He capped the vial and handed it to Captain Farrow. "Put it away."

Farrow frowned.

"Billy Boudain, Davie Smith, you're both with me." He clasped Farrow's hand. "Sir, you are a fine inspiration to the men. I'll see if I can't arrange for a prisoner exchange for you once I get back to Richmond."

"But, Colonel—" Farrow said, confused.

Daniel shook his head, grinning. "I'm walking out of here tonight, Captain."

"But—"

"Watch me, sir."

He strode casually to the doorway. "Hey! You—you, the gorilla out there. Come over here. I've got to talk to you!"

He saw the big man sneer. Everybody had been warned about Daniel Cameron. But this hulk thought he was just too big to be taken.

Maybe he was. Daniel had one chance. Just one chance.

When the guard approached, he moved like lightning. He reached through the bars, caught the man's collar, and jerked him as hard against the bars as he could.

Steel struck the man's balding temples. The crack was quite audible. Heavy as lead, he started to fall.

Daniel fought to keep him up. "Davie, get the hell over here! Get the keys out of his pocket before he falls. Quick."

Davie was shaking uncontrollably. "Is he dead, Colonel?"

"No, he's not dead. He is going to have one hell of a headache. He's going to wake up as mean as a bear. So we've got to move. Fast."

Shaking, Davie managed to get the keys. Twisting, turning—and making way too much noise and taking way too long—Davie at last managed to twist open the lock on the door.

Daniel flung the door open and dragged the body of the guard into the room. He slipped the guard's revolver from its hip holster and shoved it into the waistband of his breeches.

He saluted the others. Silently, they saluted in return.

He urged Davie and Billy Boudain through the door. Even as he did so, he began to wonder at his own intelligence.

Now what the hell was he going to do? There were still monstrously high walls around Old Capitol Prison.

More than that, there were still scores of Yankee guards surrounding it.

"What now, sir?" Davie demanded.

What now, indeed? There was still an army between him and freedom.

But he could almost taste that freedom.

He could almost taste revenge.

If only he hadn't loved her so much.

It seemed very late when Jesse Cameron rode away from the farm at last.

She had been good, Callie thought. She had been cool and calm and composed when she had longed to shriek and tear her hair out. But he had been such a gentleman. So handsome.

So damned much like Daniel!

Except polite. And kind. And courteous to a fault.

Once upon a time, Daniel had been tender.

Too tender. That was why she was in this mess!

Jesse had reined in his horse. He turned back, and she waved to him. Cheerfully. He turned again, and within minutes, he was swallowed into the darkness.

"Oh, God!" she gasped aloud, and she sank down to the porch step, hugging her knees to her chest. A sob escaped her. It couldn't be true.

How long had Daniel been gone now? Over three weeks. Almost four. She picked up a stick and drew out lines for the days. She tried to convince herself that she was counting wrong.

Yes, she was counting wrong. And she was imagining that she had been queasy several mornings last week and was downright sick every morning this week.

She felt dizzy. It was a good thing she was sitting. She might have fallen. It had struck her like a ton of bricks while she had been feeding the chickens, just an hour before Jesse Cameron had come riding up.

Jesse Cameron. With blue eyes just like his brother's. That captured and imprisoned Reb who had sworn to come back for her.

"Oh, God!"

She buried her face in her hands. She had dallied with the enemy. She was going to have the enemy's baby. Her brothers might very well come home and throw her out of the house. Her neighbors would turn their backs on her. She would be ostracized by everyone. It was horrible.

She leaned back. She wondered why she didn't feel so horrible. She was a fallen woman. She closed her eyes.

She had loved him. She still loved him. She ached nightly for the way that she had been forced to betray him. Seeing his brother had reminded her of so many fine things about the man. His courage, his valor, his charm. The sound of his laughter.

The harsh sounds of his anger, she reminded herself. And those blue eyes could turn as cold as ice.

He'd had no right to condemn her. He hadn't given her the least chance to explain.

There was nothing that she could have explained at the time.

He had judged her mercilessly. She should be as furious with him as he was with her. She should hate him just as fiercely.

But after a moment, a smile curved her lip. The baby would still be part his. And maybe have those extraordinary eyes. Or the fine bone structure of his face. She might convince herself she was angry with him, she might even hate him fiercely in self-defense . . .

But still, it was difficult to mind having him as a father for a child.

Except that she was a woman alone, having a child alone.

After a while, she stood up. Though it was dark, she found herself walking around the house in the moonlight to where her father's stone stood in the graveyard.

She pressed a kiss to her fingers and set them on Gregory's tombstone, but she smiled because she did not feel the guilt she should have felt. It was her father's ghost to whom she spoke softly, in the moonlight.

"I think I want this baby, Pa. Can you understand? Oh, Pa, I've lost you, and I've lost Gregory. And I came out here and I watched all those handsome young boys die. This baby is life. In all of this misery, perhaps he can be hope. I think that you'd understand. I know that you'd love me anyway."

She sat there a while, and then she was stunned by how easily she had managed to accept what was happening.

Perhaps the way that she felt would change in the morning, she warned herself.

She wanted the baby. After all of the death, she wanted the life.

But as she walked toward the house, she paused.

The baby would be Daniel's too.

A chill settled over her.

She had loved him. He had beautiful blue eyes, he was proud and tall and valiant and all manner of good things. . . .

And he wanted to throttle her.

Daniel . . .

She'd had enough for one night. She'd have to worry about Daniel in the morning.

Thank God he was locked up in prison!

Fourteen

The hallway was silent; the door was closed behind them. Daniel moved as quietly as he could along the hallway until they came along the next set of guards.

They were seated at a table, playing cards. Real Union greenbacks and gold coins were casually laid out on the table.

There were three guards and three of them. Pretty fair odds, Daniel decided. And they weren't expecting any trouble. They were playing loudly. A whiskey bottle sat in the middle of the table. Daniel was certain Lieutenant Colonel Dodson would not be pleased to know that his men were imbibing while on duty.

He smiled, and then his smile faded. He didn't want to kill anybody. It was horrible enough to kill in battle, when an opponent was seeking his death. If this went smoothly enough, they wouldn't have to spill any blood.

He motioned to Billy, pointing to his boot, and to the man in the center, the one with his back to them. Billy was healing nicely, but Daniel still wanted to give him the advantage of complete surprise. Davie, watching Daniel's signs to Billy, quickly understood Daniel's strategy, and nodded when Daniel pointed to the guard that he would take on.

He raised his hand, then one finger, then another, and then a third. And simultaneously they moved, striding in as if they had every right to be there.

"Hey!" began the corner man, the first to see them.

It was all that he managed to say. Daniel had the guard's heavy revolver and he gave the man a good clunk on the head with it. He crashed over, just as Billy and Davie reached their victims and likewise dispatched them with good clouts to the head.

"Look at this, will you? This ole bluebelly here was sitting pat on a full house," Billy commented.

"And look at this one!" Davie exclaimed. "Why, the ace of spades is sitting up his sleeves."

"Leave it," Daniel advised. "They might wind up more interested in fighting over the card game than looking for us." He picked up the bottle of whiskey and began to liberally sprinkle it over all of their heads and the card table. He grinned at Billy and Davie. "If they don't tear into one another, Dodson will. It will buy us some time. Billy, get that Colt over there. What a handsome gun! Davie, there's another service revolver there in that Yank's holster. Slip it out and let's move on."

Although that Old Capitol was crawling with guards, they managed to move about the prison rather easily. Billy was hesitant—Daniel knew why. The Yanks weren't expecting any break like this. Not that they hadn't had a few already. But prisoners hadn't risen up en masse, and none had pulled any tricks recently. Live men sometimes went out with their dead companions in coffins, and Daniel should have been playing a dead man in a coffin by now himself. He was glad he wasn't. He'd heard tell of an infantry commander who'd gone out of a Chicago prison that way. And he'd been buried alive, just as planned. But communications had gone awry, and when they'd dug him up two weeks later, he was found glassy-eyed, his fingers shot through with the slivers he'd received trying to dig his way through the box.

Daniel, Billy, and Davie came down another hall. The exercise yard was ahead of them. It was small, and the high walls surrounded it. There were guards at the gates and guards all around the high walls.

"What now, Colonel?" Billy demanded.

They could brazen their way out with their guns, but they'd probably be gunned down in turn.

"I—" Daniel began.

But it was then that fate stepped in. Out in the street there was the sudden, deafening sound of an explosion.

Davie dropped to his knees. "Merciful heaven, what was that?"

For a moment, Daniel wasn't sure. Then he realized what had happened, and he grinned broadly. "A supply wagon exploded out there. It was probably carrying a ton of dynamite. Every man jack around will be forgetting his position and running out to see what's happened or if he can help. Let's go! Fast. Move, move, move!"

Heedless of being sighted, Daniel began to run. To the amazement of his two men, no one paid them the slightest heed. Everyone was running, racing toward the street. There were shouts of help.

The gates opened, and men in various stages of dress began to rush through them.

Daniel made it through the gate with Davie and Billie behind him. There was smoke everywhere, helping to screen their escape. But better than that, there were screams in the street and a wild mass of people in any manner of dress running in every possible direction.

Street lamps were lit, but they did little against the heavy, acrid smoke in the air.

"Close the gates!" someone shouted. But it didn't matter. Daniel and his men were out.

Billy kept running with the crowd. Daniel snatched

him up firmly by the collar. "Jesu, Billy, we're trying to get away from those men, remember?"

"Right!" Billy said.

Daniel led them down a cold, dark alley. He closed his eyes, trying to think of what to do, or where to go now. He could hear horses' hooves thundering as fire engines hurried toward the street in front of the prison. It might be a long while before they were discovered missing. And then again, it might be too soon.

Huddled in the alley, their hearts pounding in equal rhythm to the thundering hooves, Daniel tried to think. Who did he know in D.C., where could he turn for help?

"There's Aunt Priscilla's," Billy offered.

Daniel stared at him. "You know how to find her?"

"Sure. E Street. Come on."

Billy led the way. Daniel felt like a snake, slinking along the buildings, falling flat against them any time they came across citizens out in the night. But bit by bit they moved through the city, and at last they stood in the alleyway behind a fine old Federal-style house of red brick with big Greek columns. "That's it," Billy whispered. "But I think that Aunt Priscilla is entertaining."

Through the shades they could see movement. A man and a woman, entwined. No, they were dancing, Daniel decided. No, they were just entwined. Her laughter rang out, and the characters caught in shadow on the drapes disappeared. A moment later, a light appeared from one of the upstairs windows.

"What do we do now?" Davie murmured.

"We go on in. Quietly. I'm not staying in this alley."

Daniel led the way across the yard, keeping a careful eye on the upstairs window and watching the downstairs too. They reached the porch, and moved carefully along it to a window. Daniel looked in. The room was empty. He slipped on in, motioning to the two others to follow him.

They did so. Then Daniel jumped, for he heard the soft cadences of a black woman singing. He motioned the others back and hurried to the hallway door. An attractive young housekeeper was just closing off the dining room, humming away. Daniel slipped back against the wall as the girl passed by the hallway. He watched as she hurried along to a back set of steps, the servant's stairway. She disappeared up the stairway, and Daniel stepped back, sighing softly.

Maybe they were safe for a spell. Maybe not. They needed to move. At the least, they needed a plan. By morning, their disappearance would definitely be noted.

He motioned to Billy and Davie to stay behind and started silently up the main stairway. It was beautiful, with a carved mahogany banister and red velvet runners. The runners silenced his footsteps.

He stood outside in the upper hallway, listening. He could hear a woman giggling again. He tiptoed closer to an open bedroom door.

A heavyset man with an iron-gray handlebar mustache sat up in his long johns in the bed. His uniform— that of an artillery commander—lay across the footstool at the bottom of the bed.

Aunt Priscilla stood before her mirror dressed in a set of some of the most outrageous undergarments that Daniel had ever seen. Brilliant orange lace frothed in between rows of black. Black mesh stockings barely covered her legs. A fine set of breasts were well displayed, popping over the orange-and-black lace at the top of the garment.

He saw that she had passed through many more years than her body gave hint to. Her hair was red, but not a real red. It was almost as orange as the color in her garment.

"Don't you worry your little head none about what old Abe's planning on doing with his army now. He'll think of something—"

"But you know what he's thinking, Louis, and I feel so much safer here when you talk to me!" she replied. She frowned suddenly, and Daniel realized that she had met his gaze in the mirror. He had thought to withdraw quickly. He did not want to embarrass this helpmate of the Confederacy.

But he didn't embarrass her at all. She smiled at him in the mirror, and moistened her lips. Her eyes were large and brown and fine, and she winked.

"Louis, I believe that I need just a touch of sherry tonight. I've a chill. If you'll excuse me—"

"Why, Prissy, I'll get you anything that your heart desires—"

"No, no, no, Louis! You stay right there! And stay warm, darling. I'll be back in just a flash."

She slipped a flimsy wrap around her shoulders, kissed Louis on his near balding pate, and hurried out of the room, closing the door behind her.

She leaned against it breathlessly. "You're Daniel Cameron," she mouthed softly.

He nodded. She gripped his hand and urged him quickly down the hall, pressing him into another room, and closing the door.

"You're supposed to be in a coffin!" she told him.

"I didn't want to do it that way."

"It's amazing that you haven't been caught!" she exclaimed. "You fool! You should have done things my way. I'd have found you and brought you here—"

"Well, I'm right beholden for that, ma'am, but I'm here on my own now—"

"They'll be looking for you!" she exclaimed.

"Well, yes, that they will. By morning."

"I wanted to keep you for a while!" she exclaimed. Startled, Daniel took a step back. She wasn't an

unattractive woman. She was perhaps ten years his se-
nior, and in her way, she was very pretty. Her face was
round, her eyes were intelligent.

Her hair reminded him of Callie's. Hair that was real
fire, hair that he had swirled around his fingers, hair
that had covered his body like a sweep of silk.

Hair I could string her up by, he reminded himself.

"You are just like him!" Aunt Priscilla said.

"I beg your pardon?" Daniel said.

"Your brother. You're just like your brother."

"You know Jesse?"

"Oh, of course. I move in all the right circles, very
carefully. I wanted that brother of yours the moment
that I saw him, Colonel. But I heard that he'd lost his
heart to some little southern girl. Then I heard that he
had a brother in prison who was very near his double."

Her voice trailed away suggestively.

Daniel didn't know whether to be amused or of-
fended.

"I'll have to have you out of here by morning!" she
wailed.

Daniel cleared his throat. "Ma'am, have you forgotten that you've a man in another bedroom?"

"Oh, Louis!" She waved a hand in the air. "I can
dispatch him rather quickly." Her eyes opened very
wide. "I do enjoy my work, Colonel," she said. "And I
have been invaluable to the troops. General Robert E.
Lee said so himself!"

Daniel tried to envision the exceedingly dignified
Lee in the same room with this woman. He couldn't
quite drum up the sight.

"Ma'am, I imagine that your services have indeed
been invaluable," he assured her. "But please, don't
dispatch Louis on my account."

"But I've waited—"

"And I have to move on, ma'am. I've two men with
me. I want to be in Virginia by morning."

Virginia! No, he wanted to go back. To Maryland. He wanted to go back to Callie Michaelson's farmhouse, and he wanted to confront her there.

He gritted his teeth, suddenly realizing—or admitting—that he couldn't go back now. His first responsibility was freedom—for himself, and for Billy and Davie. He had to cross into the South, and he had to make his way back to Stuart's service as quickly as possible.

A time would come. Soon. There would be another campaign into the North again, he was certain. They'd have to attack the North for supplies. If they didn't attack the Yanks on their own territory, the Yanks would never see just how ugly war could be.

He would go to Virginia now.

"Colonel, you're not even paying any attention to me!" Aunt Priscilla complained.

"I'm sorry, ma'am. My mind is on my heartland!" he assured her dramatically.

She sighed, looking very peeved. "Colonel—"

He stepped forward, took her hand, and kissed it. "Alas, regrets, ma'am! But I do have to move on. And I'm sorry, but Jesse married that southern girl. I'm afraid you won't have any luck with him in the future either."

Once again, she sighed, and turned.

She could turn nicely. Everything about her seemed to move and sway.

He should have wanted her. It should have been an escapade, like some of the nights they had all spent out west long before the war.

His jaw clenched down hard. Callie. Damn her.

He wanted her. Wanted the flame of her hair, and the flame of her love. No other woman, strumpet or lady, could fire him the same way.

Damn her, he thought.

Priscilla stopped suddenly, saying over her shoulder,

"Get your men, Colonel. There's a wagon out back in the barn. Harness the horses to it. Get yourselves in it and as soon as I get that old goat Louis off to sleep, I'll be out. I may even have something for you to bring to your commander."

She swayed out of the room.

He smiled. Maybe he should be flattered that she had been interested. After all, to most Rebs, Jesse looked like Daniel, and not vice versa.

Downstairs he found Davie and Billy, and they slipped just as quietly out of the house as they had entered it. The night seemed just about dead silent now, and there was only the sliver of a moon out. They found the barn easily enough, and the wagon. It was loaded up with hay and straw. Without even speaking, they set about choosing a team of horses, and hitching them up to the wagon as quickly as possible. The three men crawled in, covering themselves up the best they could.

Moments later, a dark-clad figure hurried into the barn. Daniel was startled to see that it was Priscilla, and that she had made a drastic change. She was in black widow's weeds, with fabric to her throat and a heavy black veil over her face. Curiously, Daniel found her much more fascinating in such apparel, for her eyes now wore a look of tragedy or pain that made them a mystery, one that deserved unraveling.

But when she spoke to him she was very business-like, and the interlude upstairs might never have happened.

"They're looking for you already," she told Daniel. "I sent my maid out. They discovered you gone after that awful accident with the dynamite. Luckily, they've no idea when you made your escape, and they've no idea at all where you might have gone. I'm going to take you over the Potomac. You'll be in Virginia when I leave you, but I warn you, the Federals are holding most of the extreme northern areas. There's a ring of forts around Washington. There's a farm over the river where I go regularly to buy my eggs. I'll get you there. If we're caught, I'll deny all knowledge that you were with me. I have to. Do you understand that?"

"We understand. We won't jeopardize your disguise," Daniel assured her.

"Thank you," she said.

She was about to crawl into the wagon. Daniel tapped her on the shoulder. She turned around. "Did Louis go nighty night?" he asked very politely.

She stared at him and then smiled slowly. "Just like a babe, Colonel. Just like a babe. Let's go now, before I change my mind about getting you there."

Priscilla crawled up to drive her wagon, and Daniel sank back into the hay.

The wagon began to rock and roll.

Covered with the straw and deeply nestled into it, Daniel could see little. Light became more prevalent as they came across busier streets. In his mind's eye, he tried to plot Priscilla's course, but beneath the hay, he lost his sense of direction.

All he knew was that the journey seemed endless. He could not see Davie or Billy; he couldn't even see his own hands. Sometimes there was a lot of light, sometimes there was a little. Sometimes the road was smooth, and then it was rough, very rough.

Sometimes the wagon stopped, and he could hear Priscilla's voice as she charmed her way past the city's guards. Each time his heart seemed to cease to beat. Then it would slam against his chest when the wagon began to move again. We owe this woman our lives, he thought.

He heard the clip-clop of the horses' hooves over the bridge, and then he felt that they had veered off on a rougher road.

Then it seemed that they stopped in no time. "Colonel!" she called softly in the night.

He crawled out of the straw, with Billy and Davie following suit. The moon was out a little more brightly, but they were alone. "Follow that road, sir, and it will take you down to Fredericksburg. There are patrols in this area, so watch yourselves. And—" She paused, then handed him an envelope. "Please see that this gets to General Lee."

"I'll do that." Daniel promised her. He frowned, looking at the envelope. "Priscilla, if we are killed or taken again—"

"Then I will be hanged," she finished for him. She smiled. "Don't get killed, Colonel."

He swept her a low bow. "No, ma'am. I will not get killed."

She lifted a hand in a salute. Daniel returned it, and Billy and Davie followed his lead.

The wagon began to clip-clop away, the sound seeming to echo in the stillness of the night.

"Well, boys, we are almost home free!" Daniel said. "Shall we walk?"

"Walking seems mighty fine to me, sir!" Billy told him.

"Yessir," Davie agreed.

Daniel paused suddenly. A breeze had picked up in the night. He turned to the northwest. Maryland. He wanted to go back. For a moment the ache was so strong he could scarcely bear it. And it had nothing to do with revenge. It had everything to do with wanting to touch her.

He swallowed hard, then grinned to his men. "Well, gentlemen, this is home for me." He started walking, the others behind him.

Twice in the night they heard the sound of horses' hooves. They melted into the trees, off the road. Yankee patrols rode by.

In the morning, they found a cove and slept. By afternoon, the pangs of hunger were tearing at them. Though Davie convinced Daniel he could catch a rabbit with his bare hands, Daniel convinced Davie that they couldn't light a fire. They had to settle on some wild berries.

By night, they walked again. With careful scavenging, Billy managed to slip an apple pie off the windowsill of a small farmhouse.

Some small boy was probably going to take a licking for a crime for which he wasn't guilty, Daniel reflected. They were in Virginia, but he wasn't ready to test the loyalty of the farmers yet. One day, he'd come back and pay for the pie.

They had been on the road for four days and nights when they heard horses' hooves and jumped into the foliage for what seemed like the thousandth time. Daniel tried hard to see through the brush. His heart hammered hard.

The uniforms were gray. Peering through the bushes, Daniel frowned. They weren't just gray. They were familiar. As were some of the faces.

"We've got to keep looking," an officer said. Daniel knew the voice. "Our intelligence is certain that they'll be coming this way, down toward Fredericksburg."

"What's that?" someone demanded.

Daniel stepped out of the bushes, grinning broadly, his hands raised. They weren't just cavalry men. They were cavalry men who had been in his command at one time. "Don't shoot, my friends. I believe we're who you're looking for."

"Daniel!" someone cried. A man slipped down from his horse. It was Captain Jarvis Mulraney, a neighbor from the peninsula, a good friend under Daniel's command since the war had begun. Red-haired, freckle-faced, he looked too young to be in the war, but he was the captain of a crack group of horsemen.

Daniel embraced him.

"Thank God, you're home!" Jarvis told him, beaming. "Jesu, we thought that we'd lost you for sure back in Sharpsburg!"

"No, I'm back," Daniel said. "And yessir, thank God. I'm home."

Men were dismounting from their horses all around him, embracing him. Harry Simmons, Richard MacKenzie, Robert O'Hara. He called Billy and Davie from the bushes and introduced them all around. It almost seemed like a party, right there in the road.

Yes, he was home, he reflected.

But there had been a piece of him lost for good back in Sharpsburg.

The days seemed to pass endlessly for Callie. October rolled into November.

She went into town for supplies, and she visited there with friends, but she felt strangely isolated, as if she wasn't really a part of the community anymore.

She received letters from all three of her brothers, Joshua, Josiah, and Jeremy, and she was grateful, for all three of them were alive and in good health. It seemed forever since she had seen them. She wrote to them frequently, but she never knew just how often they actually received the letters that she wrote.

She never mentioned Daniel. She wouldn't have known what to say.

She did tell them about the battle that had been fought in her front yard, and she carefully minimized any danger to herself. She was determined to be cheerful, and she told whatever stories about the antics of their neighbors that she could embroider upon.

The letters she received in turn were too much like those of the young man who had died in their barn. They all knew that they might meet death any day and they stressed emotions and feelings. Mainly, they stressed love, and the appreciation for the quality of the lives they had already lived.

On Thanksgiving, Rudy Weiss appeared very early at her door with his wife at his side. Surprised to see them, Callie stared at the pair for a moment, then quickly invited them inside.

Helga, Rudy's wife, a tall woman with a broad, ample bosom and truly apple-red cheeks, brought in a big basket and offered it to Callie with a shy smile. "Thanksgiving. And you are alone. You should not be alone. We have brought you a goose and corn and mein own apple sauce. It is good."

"Well of course, it's good! I'm sure it's wonderful. I thank you very much."

They stayed with her, and they shared the goose, and before he would leave, Rudy wanted to know if she needed anything done that she could not handle herself. She told him that no, she was fine. She'd had the windows repaned soon after the battle by glassworkers from town, and she felt that she was really in very good shape.

All of the Sharpsburg area was slowly healing. What remained of the corn was all in. Winter was coming to cleanse the rest of the landscape.

"Thank you for coming," Callie told them at the door when they were leaving. "I know that you—I know that it is important for you to remain with your own people, and so it is doubly good of you to come to me."

Helga clicked her teeth. "We are a plain people, not a mean one!" she assured Callie. She kissed her cheek, just like a surrogate mother, and she and Rudy quietly walked down the steps.

Callie wondered whether she might spend Christmas with Rudy and Helga, but just a few days before the holiday, she saw a soldier walking down the path toward the house, leading a handsome bay horse. Something about the way that he moved drew her attention, even while he was at a distance.

She dropped the feed bucket that she had been carrying for the chickens and started to run. She ran as fast as her feet would carry her, and then she threw herself into the soldier's arms.

"Jeremy!" she cried, delighted. The youngest of her brothers had come home.

"Callie, Callie!" He held her face between his palms, staring into her eyes, then he crushed her to his chest once again. "God, it's so good to see you! I've missed you so much! And home. Callie, I can't tell you what it's like to be away from home like this!"

"But you look wonderful, Jeremy, wonderful! What a mustache! That's one of the finest mustaches I've ever seen!"

And it was. Rich, dark red, full, well-manicured, and twirling nicely.

His eyes were silver-gray. Quick to burn, quicker still to sparkle, as they did now. "You like it, huh?"

"Well, it makes you look old. Very old."

"Old enough to be a lieutenant?"

"You've been promoted! Oh, how wonderful!"

He shrugged. "Callie, we have an atrocious death rate. It's horrible to say, but sometimes the Rebs are better fighters. Not many Yanks can deny that Bull Run was a 'skedaddle.' There have been lots of battles like that. We fare better in the West than they do in the East, but not much. Callie, those Rebs are fighting for their homeland. We're marching all over it, stripping everything from it. And they're killing us right and left. Promotions come quickly in wartime."

"Jeremy, I'm proud. And I know that Pa would be proud, and glad that he made you all go to military school, even if we are farmers. But I don't care about that right now, I'm just so glad that you're home. And on leave. You are on leave, aren't you? Jeremy! You didn't desert, did you? I heard in town the other day that desertions were pouring in from both sides, that men were trying to go home for winter. You didn't just pick up and walk off, did you?"

"No, no, I'm on leave. I have until the day after Christmas, and then I'll have to start back. But Josiah couldn't come now, and neither could Joshua. They're outside Vicksburg, Mississippi, and there aren't many leaves being given there. I reckon I'll have to report there, too, once I get back. Lucky for me, this promotion gave me Christmas."

"I'm so grateful!" Callie exclaimed.

The days that passed were wonderful for her. She loved all of her brothers, but Jeremy was her favorite. They had been closest in age. They had fought in the haystacks, they had tried to tear out each other's hair.

They had banded together against their older brothers, against their parents, against anyone who would dare say something ill of the other.

It was so good to have him home. Somehow the nights were a little easier. Her sleep was still plagued with dreams, but during the day she was no longer alone.

She wanted to tell him about Daniel, but she knew that she couldn't. She wanted to tell him that he was going to be an uncle, but she couldn't do that, either. She couldn't send him back to war upset or angry or worried about her.

On Christmas morning Callie presented him with a beautiful navy blue scarf that would help keep him warm in the brutal winter weather. It was a fine, handsome piece of clothing, and his gratitude for it showed in his eyes.

"I didn't have time to be anywhere near so creative, Callie," he told her.

"Your being home is gift enough, Jeremy."

He smiled. "I said that I wasn't creative. I didn't say that I didn't have anything at all."

He presented her with a box wrapped in silver paper. She opened it to discover a beautiful cameo. She stared at her brother.

"I bought it. Legitimately."

"From?"

"A lady in Tennessee," he said softly. "She had four children and a husband dead at Shiloh. She wasn't doing well feeding the children with her Confederate paper money. She wanted Union dollars. I gave her plenty of them, I promise you."

"But you took this brooch from her—"

"Callie, she didn't want charity. I told her about you. She said that she'd be happy if you wore it."

He took the pin, and carefully set it on her bodice. He stepped back, smiling. "Callie, I promise you, I paid her much more for it than it was worth."

Callie smiled. "I'm glad."

She hugged him, then pushed him away. "We have to get into town for church, and then I've got one of the biggest chickens for the fire that you've ever seen."

"And apple pie?"

"Of course."

They sat through the Anglican service in town. Callie kept her head bowed all through the service, certain that she should be praying and begging pardon for her sins.

Up by the altar was an old crèche. The Christ child lay in a cradle of straw, tiny arms outstretched. As she watched the crèche, she felt a warmth almost overwhelming her. She closed her eyes tightly. She could almost envision the baby, feel the softness of its flesh, see the tiny fingers, hear the squalling cries. Perhaps she had been wrong, perhaps she had sinned. A war was going on. The "war of the rebellion" as Jeremy was calling it—or the "civil war" as Daniel had referred to it. No matter what was going on, there could be no evil in a precious babe, and she was convinced of it. She felt like crying, and she felt incredibly happy.

She must have been crying, because Jeremy pressed a handkerchief into her hands.

When they left the church, Callie stepped back as Jeremy was greeted by the townspeople. The men shook his hand. Women kissed his cheeks. A few of the more brazen—or lonelier—of the ladies left behind were so bold as to kiss his lips. Callie just leaned back against the church building, watching and enjoying.

They headed back home at last.

Callie thought that she had been well over the sickness. She had felt wonderful for days before Jeremy had arrived home. But right in the middle of setting the table for their meal, she suddenly felt a violent upheaval.

Jeremy, putting out the forks, looked up at her strangely. "What's the matter?"

She wanted to answer him; she couldn't. She tore out the back door and leaned over the railing, then choked and spilled out the apple and the porridge she had eaten that morning.

"My, Lord, Callie!" Jeremy cried, concerned, his hands on her shoulders. He pulled her around. He touched her forehead. "No, no, you're not feverish. Come in and lie down. I'll hitch the wagon back up and head to town for the doctor—"

"No! I don't need a doctor."

"Callie, I won't leave with you being sick like this!"

"I'm not sick, Jeremy."

"I just saw you—"

"Jeremy, it was nothing. Trust me. I'm not sick."

She didn't know when something he had learned about women suddenly dawned in his mind.

"My Lord, Callie, you're—why, you're in a family way. Oh, poor Callie, with Gregory dead these many,

many months—" He broke off, staring at her, his mouth gaping for a moment. "Callie, Gregory's been dead way too long."

She stared straight at him. She tried to feel the coolness of the breeze.

"The baby isn't Gregory's."

"Then whose baby is it? I'll find the man, Callie. He'll do right by you, I swear it."

She shook her head. "Jeremy, I don't want you finding anybody."

"It was a soldier?"

She hesitated.

"Why, those bloody bastards! Callie, you were"—he couldn't quite seem to spit out the word, and then he did—"raped?"

She shook her head again. "No."

He lifted his hands, at a loss. She'd never seen him more hurt.

"Callie, I can't help you if you won't let me."

"I don't want to be helped."

"Callie, any Union soldier would be proud to come back here—" He broke off, his eyes widening, then narrowing sharply. "My God, it wasn't a Union soldier. It was a goddamned Reb!"

"Jeremy—" She reached out a hand to him.

He backed away. "A goddamned Reb. Pa's dead, and Gregory's dead, and hell, you'll just never know how many others. You don't get to see your friends and neighbors explode daily! My God. My sister's having a Reb bastard. My own sister! Goddamned, Callie, I don't even want you in my house anymore!"

"Jeremy—"

"Don't touch me, Callie!" he snapped. He spun around and went stomping off the porch.

"Jeremy!" She tried to call him back, but he was gone. She leaned against the wall, and then she pushed away from it and made her way back into the house.

The chicken was ready. She had cranberry sauce on the table. And thick gravy, the kind Jeremy loved the most. The table was beautiful, and she'd been so very happy.

She leaned her face down upon the table, right against the linen. She was too weary and heartsick to cry.

It didn't matter. She'd fight for the baby. She'd fight Jeremy and Joshua and Josiah and the whole town.

She'd fight Daniel too.

But she'd lost her brother. There were more ways than death to lose someone, she realized. She bit her lip and closed her eyes. She couldn't cry, she couldn't. Not anymore.

Her eyes opened, for she felt soft fingers against her cheek. She opened her eyes again and her brother was there, kneeling down by her side. "I'm sorry, Callie, God forgive me, and I pray that you forgive me. I love you, Callie. I don't understand what you did, but I love you. And I'll love my nephew—or niece—I swear it. I'll be here for you."

She started crying, despite all her determination that she wouldn't do so anymore. She threw her arms around his neck, and he held her.

"Callie, I can help you still, if you let me. I can maybe find this Reb—"

"No," Callie said firmly.

"Oh Lord, he hasn't been killed already, has he?"

She shook her head. "He is, er, out of action for the moment. Jeremy, please, just leave me be. Maybe, when the war is over, if he survives it and I can find him, I'll let him know."

"Callie, damn it, he has a responsibility—"

"Please, Jeremy, please!"

He sighed. "Callie, I'm going to get the truth out of you if it takes me an eternity."

She smiled at last. "Well, I can't stop you from try-

ing. But I want this baby. And the baby is mine. Anything else is for a far distant future. All right?"

Jeremy still wouldn't agree. He stood up, and he
started to prepare their plates. He sighed. "Well, I've
made supper a bit cold here."

"I can stoke up the fire again—"

"No, the gravy's still warm. That's what's important."

She smiled at him.

"Callie?"

"Yes?"

"Merry Christmas, sister. Merry Christmas."

She jumped up, because she just had to hug him one
more time.

Fifteen

The end of 1862 proved to be an especially brutal period for Daniel.

While he had been held in Old Capitol, Jeb Stuart
had been managing another of his sweeping raids
around the Yanks, going so far as to encircle the enemy
in Pennsylvania. But by the time Daniel returned to
active duty, it was necessary for the Rebs to begin a
tight watch around the area of Fredericksburg, Virginia.

In the North, President Lincoln had given up trying
to believe in his very popular general, George McClellan. Rumor had it that Lincoln felt sending reinforcements to McClellan was like "shoveling flies across a
barn." McClellan was removed and General Burnside
was sent in to take his place.

Daniel wasn't so sure about the wisdom of such a
choice. They were calling a bridge over Antietam
Creek "Burnside's Bridge" these days because the
general had tried so long—and at such a great cost of
human life—to cross that bridge.

Burnside was a good man, though. Daniel knew him
by reputation, and knew that he was loyal to his cause.
He knew that Lincoln was totally disgusted with the
way that "Little Mac," as McClellan was known, had

hesitated time and time again when he could have moved against the Rebels.

It would remain to be seen just what Burnside would do. Because there was one certainty about the South. The Rebs might be low in manpower, and they might not have industrial strength, and Lord knew they hadn't the sheer numbers of the North, but the South could boast some of the finest generals to come along in centuries. Lee would be careful, watching Burnside. Daniel still doubted there was any way Burnside could "out-general" Lee.

Still, it seemed apparent that the new Union commander was going to be making a strike toward Richmond. The North was growing more and more desperate to take the Confederate capital.

On the fifteenth of November, they skirmished with Federal troops at Warrenton, Virginia. By the eighteenth, General Burnside and his Army of the Potomac had arrived in Falmouth, on the banks of the Rappahannock River, across from Fredericksburg. Jeb's cavalry was positioned at Warrenton Station.

It was good for Daniel to be back with his troops. He was still with Billy Boudain, having managed to get the boy transferred into his cavalry regiment. Billy had been given a promotion to sergeant and was serving as Daniel's staff assistant. Although the cavalry prepared for heavy battle, they remained the "eyes and ears" of the Confederacy, and it didn't seem to Daniel that a single night passed in which he wasn't sent out to scout Union positions.

He didn't mind. He liked falling into his cot dead exhausted every night. Sometimes the exhaustion kept him from dreaming.

But sometimes he dreamed anyway. The dreams were sweet, and the dreams were cruel. Sometimes he'd be back on the river. He'd see the rolling landscape, feel the breeze. The river air would rustle the

leaves in the trees and all around him the world would
be rich with the sweet scent of the earth.

And she would be there. Her eyes so wide and gray,
touched with shimmers of silver. She'd be whispering
and in his arms. The feel of her flesh would be warm
and velvet, the sweep of her hair like a caress of silk.
She'd come closer, closer, whispering . . .

Then, from somewhere, would come an explosion of
heavy artillery, and she would be gone.

It was war, Daniel told himself wearily. And there
was nothing to be done but fight it.

And live. Yes, live. Because he had to go back. No
matter how long it took him, he had to return to that
small farm near Sharpsburg.

Sometimes when he lay awake at night, he wondered
what he would do once he got there. It wasn't to be
soon. On the thirteenth of December, the situation
around Fredericksburg came to a head. Burnside's
force of one hundred and six thousand men attacked
the Confederates under Stonewall, a force of seventy-
two thousand.

During the battle, the Yanks were forced to attack
Marye's Heights. The slaughter was horrible.

By nightfall, it was clear the Confederates had taken
the day. For Daniel, there was little other than a hollow feeling in his heart. He'd heard that one Union
soldier had commented, "They might as well have
asked us to take Hell!"

When the fighting had ended and the generals had
conferred, a very weary "Master" Lee had said, "I
wish these people would go away and let us alone!"

Dear God, yes, Daniel thought. By midnight he'd
made his reports, he'd been to the field hospital, and
he'd braced himself against the horror to be found
there. Now his men were preparing to sleep, and he
was free from responsibility until morning. He walked
down to the river and looked out over the water.

Jesse would be busy tonight trying to put back the pieces of human beings.

Just leave us alone, he thought, remembering Lee's words. Lee had looked so weary of the war when Daniel had seen him last, delivering Aunt Priscilla's package to him. Daniel was sick to death of the killing, and there was so much more to follow. Why couldn't Lincoln just let them go? He didn't understand it.

But Jesse did. That's why he had stayed in the Union. "God in heaven, I am at war with my own brother!" He whispered aloud. He lifted his hands, suddenly remembering that he carried a package in brown wrapping. He had seen Harley Simon, a neighbor in the artillery, when he had gone through the hospital. Harley had been carrying the package with him for two months. It was a silver baby cup, a present for Jesse and Kiernan. Harley's wife had gotten it to Harley, and Harley had been carrying it in his haversack ever since, hoping he'd see Daniel soon enough. Jesse might be on the other side, but he'd always been the Simons' friends.

How could it be that they were all trying to kill one another, but they were still friends?

Daniel closed his eyes, then opened them. The moonlight glistened on the water. How many good, good friends did he have in the Union army, not to mention his brother? He didn't want to think about it. Jesse and Beauty. When the war was over, would they all be able to drink good whiskey and laugh over pranks again?

Would they survive the war? Would they be able to forgive one another?

Yes, he could forgive anyone. He had understood Jesse from the start.

Not Callie. He would never forgive her. She had betrayed him. He had fallen in love, and she had betrayed him.

And now his every moment, waking, sleeping, fighting, was consumed with her. Maybe if he could just touch her again.

Burnside retreated the next day, but Daniel was swamped with duty, being sent almost daily to observe his enemy. Christmas was approaching, and it seemed the action had somewhat quieted here in the East, although skirmishing did take place. The situation was different in the West. President Jeff Davis was furious with the happenings in New Orleans. Since the fall of that city, a Union general named Butler—"Beast" Butler, as he was being called—had been in charge. The women in the city had been so rude to the Union officers that Butler had issued a proclamation called his "Women's Order," in which he stated that any female acting rude to his officers would be considered a woman of the streets, plying her avocation, and be so duly treated in turn.

Jeff Davis wanted Butler executed on the spot if he could be captured. It was a strange turn of events, for once upon a time, when there had been only one country, Butler had been one of Jeff Davis's strongest political supporters.

Thankfully, despite strong support in the North, Butler was removed, and General Banks was sent in to take his place. Banks was far less objectionable to the citizens of New Orleans.

December wore on.

Three days before Christmas, Daniel was given ninety-six hours leave. When he heard the news, his heart began to thud with anticipation.

He was going to go to Maryland. He was going to find out just what he would do when he saw her again. He would wrestle with both the beauty and the beast that haunted his dreams, his days, and his nights.

But another Beauty got wind of his plans, that Beauty being Jeb Stuart. Beauty, dashing as ever in his flamboyant plumed hat and cape, came to visit him, carrying a bottle of a fine vintage wine and good-humored Christmas stories. As they sat there, Jeb suddenly ceased to smile and told him flatly, "You're not to travel north, Daniel. I need you too badly. You cannot risk capture now."

"I risk capture almost daily!" Daniel exploded. "How else does one encircle an enemy for intelligence?"

Stuart sighed. "Daniel, war is a danger. Bullets are dangerous! We cannot avoid either. But I'll not lose you again over something . . . unnecessary. Daniel, you've chosen not to speak about Sharpsburg, or your capture, or even your days in prison. I can't make you. But you've changed since then. Even the men have noticed it."

"I'm a damned good officer, and I never ask more of my men than I'm willing to give."

"I agree, the men would agree, and hell, yes, you must be a cat, you're so willing to lead into the fray rather than ask another man to do it. But Daniel, you can't go north now. I'll see that your leave is revoked unless you give me your word that you won't head into Maryland."

Daniel scowled. Anticipation had been so sweet. Seeing her, shaking her, touching her. It had all seemed so close he could almost taste it.

"Daniel, damn it, don't put me in a position to pull rank!" Stuart pleaded.

Daniel swallowed hard. "I've got to get back to Sharpsburg."

"I'll get you there. In '63 sometime. I swear it," Stuart promised him.

Daniel exhaled. It hurt. Almost physically. Stuart rose and stretched out his hand. "Your word, Daniel. I need you back here."

His word. His precious honor. Wasn't that what they were fighting for?

He gave Stuart his hand. Beauty turned and headed out of Daniel's field tent. He paused, his back to Daniel. "Jesse is just across the Rappahannock. Did you know that?"

"I figured he was still with the Feds, somewhere close."

"We're exchanging some prisoners right before Christmas. Anything you want to send him?"

"Yes," Daniel said quietly. "Tell him that Harley Simon sent him a gift for the baby, and tell him that I'll be taking it home to Kiernan. And send him his brother's warmest regards. Tell him that I've gone home for Christmas. And that we'll all be thinking of him."

"I'll tell him," Stuart agreed, then left the tent.

The next morning, Daniel started off.

From his position near Fredericksburg, Daniel needed the time to carefully skirt the Yanks and ride the distance, stopping overnight in Richmond, where he was able to attend an evening at the White House of the Confederacy with President and Mrs. Davis. The house, which had been donated to the city of Richmond and then to the Confederate government, was gracious and beautiful, but what made it more so, Daniel thought, was the South's first lady. Varina Davis was many years her husband's junior. Where Davis was known for being reserved and opinionated, Varina was all warmth and beauty. The cares of the Confederacy were etched in her features, but she had lost none of her warmth that Christmas season. Daniel came into the entryway with numerous other officers. He was led into the house, where all of the pocket doors had been thrown open to make one large space for all of the guests. The president and his lady were not elusive creatures, but hardworking individuals who strived to

be available to friends and associates. Daniel had never
known Jeff Davis well; still, the man was kind and concerned when they spoke. And Varina reminded him of
everything that they were fighting for. Beautiful, viva-
cious, and still regal and dignified, she moved with a
rustle of silk and a whisper of femininity. Watching her
brought a warmth to him, until her movement reminded him of Callie.

He still had far to go, and so did not tarry long in
Richmond. It was a careful day's ride out to Cameron
Hall from the capital, since he didn't know if there
might be any Union troops on the peninsula.

But coming home, he thought, when he first saw the
drive leading down a length of oaks to Cameron Hall,
was worth any care or danger. The house still stood,
and stood regally with its huge white columns and
wide, inviting porches. Seeing the house, he began to
ride hard. Even as he neared the house, the large doors
to the grand hallway were thrown open and a woman
appeared on the porch. She was dressed in deep ma-
roon velvet and her hair was darker than his own. She
cried out, and was joined in seconds by another
woman, this one blond, and dressed in deepest royal
blue. The brunet was his sister, the blonde his sister-in-
law.

"It's a soldier, Kiernan!"

"Reb or Yank, Christa?"

"Reb. It's—"

"It's Daniel!"

The two of them came flying down the stairs, running for him. Daniel felt the bitterness of the war melt
from his heart, and he leapt down from his horse and
began to run himself. Seconds later they were both in
his arms, and he was swirling with them and holding
them close. They each kissed and hugged him, and he
returned the kisses and hugs, meeting his sister's crys-

tal-blue gaze first, then Kiernan's entrancing emerald-green one.

"Oh, Daniel, you made it home for Christmas!" Christa said happily.

Kiernan was observing him more carefully. "I sent all kinds of things to you in Washington, Daniel. Jesse got a letter through that you'd been captured. But then I received another letter saying that you'd escaped before my goods ever reached you!"

He grinned. "Kiernan, you know I couldn't stay."

She shook her head, nervously biting her lower lip. "Oh, Daniel! I was almost glad! You might have survived very well up there."

He arched a brow to her. "Is my brother changing you into a Yank, Kiernan?"

She flushed, and he was sorry he had spoken. No one could be more torn than Kiernan. Her heart had been so completely for the Confederacy—and yet her love for Jesse had proven stronger than any war. She and Daniel had been friends all of their lives, good friends. But even as she greeted him now with warmth and tender concern, he knew she was wishing that another Yankee soldier was also coming home for Christmas.

"Never mind," Daniel said quickly. He slipped an arm around her shoulders and turned to his sister. "Christa! Will we be able to have a Christmas dinner?"

"Of course," Christa said, her head high, a smile still teasing her lips. "We've had no battles on the property, Daniel, nor even skirmishes. The closest difficulty has been in Williamsburg. So we've all manner of good things. I gave a number of chickens and several cows and numerous bales of hay to a group collecting for the cause the other day, but everything is running very well. Kiernan and I do quite nicely, really."

Daniel laughed. "Remember all the times Pa used to spend with Jesse and me determined we'd be very well-

educated planters? Who would have thought you'd be
the one to carry on with the family business!"

Christa grinned. "I have lots of help," she assured
him, winking at Kiernan, and the three of them walked
into the house.

It was good to be home. Jigger, the very dignified
butler of Cameron Hall, was quick to see that Daniel
was pampered during his stay. Some men had brought
slaves or servants right to the battlefield with them, but
neither Daniel nor Jesse had ever seen the right in
dragging another man along in a fight that wasn't his.
On the line, he took care of himself. Here at home, it
felt good to let Jigger take charge of his life. That
meant steaming hip baths with a brandy at his finger-
tips. Slippers ready to cushion his feet, soft cotton
shirts to slip over his head. It meant coffee with rich
heavy cream in the morning, and it meant eggs and
ham and bacon. It meant fine tobacco. Being home was
good.

Being home meant that he was even more amazed at
how well the plantation was running. Kiernan and
Christa could give him long accounts of everything that
they had done, ledgers on planting and harvesting,
sales of horses and livestock, the buying of carriages
and equipment. Except for salt and sugar, they were
almost entirely self-sufficient at Cameron Hall. They
had lots of help, of course, because life at the house
had really changed very little. Most of the slaves had
stayed on as freemen, willing to work for wages, for the
right to better their small cottages, and knowing that
they could move on if they chose. Some had left. Several of their people had gone north and then come
back, Christa told him. When he complimented her
and Kiernan again, she was quick to remind him that
Jigger ran the house, Janey had come back with
Kiernan from Montemarte, and that Taylor Mumford,
a freeman of mixed blood, ran the plantation just as he

always had. Christa wasn't alone because Kiernan was
there, Kiernan's father was nearby to advise them, and
the children, Jacob and Patricia Miller, Kiernan's sister
and brother-in-law from her first marriage, were always eager to help with the garden, or with making
soap or candles, or whatever else might be necessary.

"And of course everyone dotes on the baby!"

The baby was his nephew, John Daniel Cameron,
named for Kiernan's father and himself. Now six
months old, he was creeping about the house with a
thick thatch of raven-black hair and a pair of startling
blue eyes and a set of lungs to defy any army. The very
best part of being home, Daniel thought, was spending
time with the baby. He liked to jiggle John Daniel on
his knees after a meal while Christa, Kiernan, and Patricia amused him with the harpsichord and piano and
all manner of songs.

It was just like old times; almost like old times.
Walking with his sister by the river one morning, he
looked back at the house, and a shiver seized him. He
glanced back at Christa. She was growing older, and so
very, very beautiful with her pale skin, ebony-dark
hair, and crystal-blue eyes. There was a serenity and
maturity about her now. In a yellow day dress, she was
stunning. She was smiling at him. "What is it, Daniel?"

"I'm afraid every time I ride away."

She shook her head. "Daniel, we're safe here. The
Rebs keep clear of us because it's your home. Even
when the Yanks are on the peninsula, they stay away
because it's Jesse's home."

"Yes," he said softly. "But, Christa . . ."

"What?"

He shook his head. "It ought to be over," he said
softly. "I've seen more men die, more men maimed,
left limbless, emaciated. We fight better, but that Lincoln, he's a tenacious man. It's going to go on and on.

And it's going to get worse. I've seen what happens
when the battle actually comes to your doorstep. . . ."

He broke off. Damn. He was trying so damned hard
not to think about her—Callie. He'd given his word; he
hadn't traveled north. He'd come home.

Cameron Hall was a huge and magnificent plantation. Life here was complex, with ships still moving on
the James, with the fields still bringing in an income,
with meals an affair, with life rigorous but still played
by the codes that Kiernan and Christa had learned as
girls. And his sister and sister-in-law were still gowned
in fine materials, with deep layers of petticoats, with
hoops and stays.

While Callie survived alone. Serene, regal, she had
come from a different life. She kept the farm running
herself, in the hope that someone would come home.
She'd survived in the very midst of battle, with windowpanes shot out and cannonballs in the very eaves
of her home. Her clothing was not nearly so elegant.

Her beauty was every bit as deep.

And her mind just as cunning, for she had betrayed
him so completely. He groaned, amazed that he could
still feel the bitterness, the anger, the pain, so deeply.

"What is it, Daniel?"

"Nothing. I've just seen what happens when the battle hits home. Christa, if it comes to that, neither Yanks
nor Rebs will care about our traditions. Both armies
will be seeking food and supplies. Both will strip us
bare. Both will burn the house to the ground if necessary. I want you to remember this, Christa. As much as
we love it, this place is wood and brick. You and
Kiernan and John Daniel and the others are what matter. Guard yourselves first, always. Promise me that."

"Daniel—"

"Promise me that!"

"I promise!" she said softly. Hand in hand, they
walked back to the house together.

That night, they stayed up late, sipping cinnamon wine that Kiernan had made. The baby was put to bed, and Patricia and Jacob were encouraged to tell them all that they wanted for Christmas. Patricia wanted one of the new foals that had been born that spring, a little Arabian. Jacob wanted a sword and a uniform. "There will be time for that later," Daniel told him gruffly. The twins were sent to bed, and the three of them were left in the living room. "What do you want for Christmas?" Daniel asked Christa.

Kiernan laughed softly and answered for her. "His name is Captain Liam McCloskey. He was here on a reconnaissance ride out of Williamsburg soon after you and Jesse left last June. He's been back a few times since then. Buying grain."

"Really?" Curiously, Daniel looked at his sister. She was the shade of a tomato, but didn't deny anything. "How serious is this?"

Christa was looking at her fingers. "Well . . ."

"Well?" he said.

"Well, I believe he intends to find you when he can. He's asked me to marry him."

Marriage! Well, of course, she was all grown up now, and she was beautiful. It was such a huge step. Jesse should have been asked too. They should have done all kinds of checking up on this man, this captain. They should have known exactly where he came from and all about his family. Most of all, they should have known if he could care for Christa properly, if he could provide her all that she had grown up with.

But none of them would know, or could know. Who knew what would be left when the war was over.

I shouldn't say yes, I should meet him, Daniel thought.

But he loved Christa, and Christa was intelligent, and exuberant and beautiful and young, but she knew her own heart and he thought her a good judge of men. If she loved this captain, it was enough for him.

Daniel exhaled and then laughed. "I take it that you do want to marry him?"

"With all my heart. Daniel, have I your blessing?"

"Yes, with all my heart. I look forward to meeting this young man."

"That's all that I want for Christmas," she said softly. "What about you, Daniel?"

He couldn't say all the things on his mind. "I don't know. Let me think. Kiernan, what about you?"

She smiled. "That's easy. I just want to see Jesse."

He rose and kissed them both, and went on to bed. He stayed up half the night, looking out at the river.

Despite his lack of sleep, he rose very early. He walked out to the family graveyard where nearly two centuries of Camerons were lain to rest. For some reason, there was always peace to be had here. He walked back to the house and walked the length of the portrait gallery. Jassy and Jamie, the founders of the line, looked down upon him in their seventeenth-century finery. His great, great—he didn't know how many greats—grandparents. She'd had nothing when she had met Lord Cameron, so the legend went. Nothing but sheer guts and tenacity. Together, they had forged this place from the wilderness.

Dear God, let it stand! he thought.

But it wasn't so much a house that they had created, he thought. It was something intangible, something that had given him and Jesse the right to go their separate ways, and to love one another still. That something wouldn't live on in brick and stone and wood. It would live on in John Daniel Cameron, and Lord willing, in themselves.

He turned from the pictures and hurried down the elegant hall, rapping hard on Kiernan's door. She opened it, startled, her hair wild, her eyes wild, dressed in a white cotton nightgown with the baby on her hip.

"Daniel!"

He grinned. "You want Jesse for Christmas, eh? Well, I know where he is, and I'm going to get you to him. Get dressed, pack up, let's ride!"

She stared at him for a moment, then her face broke into a smile so beautiful he was convinced sacrificing the remaining days of his leave would be well worth this early trip back.

"Oh, Daniel!"

She kissed his cheek, then slammed the door on him, and he had to laugh. Within half an hour she had herself dressed, and Janey and the baby ready to travel.

It was difficult to say good-bye to Christa, but Christa was delighted for Kiernan.

It was difficult to ride away from home, because he wondered if he would ever come back.

They reached Richmond with little problem, and as they were there for the night, they once again attended an evening at the White House of the Confederacy. Many officer's wives were there, as were many officers, politicians, and socially prominent citizens. It was a curious war. Kiernan greeted old friends, some of whom snubbed her for being a Yankee's wife. One woman actually turned her back on her. But Varina took Kiernan's hand, mentioning that if she had time in the future, they could always use help at the hospital. Kiernan was surely experienced, having worked with such an excellent surgeon and physician.

The next morning they started out again. The roads were clear; the weather held. By late that night, they had returned to Daniel's encampment. The Yanks were right across the river.

"Welcome back, Colonel!" Billy Boudain called, seeing him approach his command tent. "What you got there, sir—oh, sorry ma'am!"

Daniel laughed. "I've got a Christmas present for my brother across the river," he said. "Billy, send out a messenger for me under a white flag. Ask the Yanks for a private rendezvous with Colonel Jesse Cameron, Medical Corp. I'll see him at the pontoon bridge."

"Yessir!"

That night at dusk Daniel rode down to the make-shift bridge the Yanks had used to cross the river. There were pickets—numerous pickets—on either side, and he was careful to call out that there was a meeting going to take place. He didn't feel like being shot by his own men, or getting Kiernan or the baby shot either. He left her in the shadow of the trees while he moved down by the water. A horseman stood on the other side.

"Jesse?"

"Daniel. I was hoping to see you. Merry Christmas, brother."

Daniel grinned. "I got a present for you, Jesse."

"You're living and breathing, Daniel. That's present enough."

Daniel shook his head. "This present is even better."

He turned back, and beckoned to Kiernan. She rode out from the trees, the baby in her arms. Slowly, she rode down to the river.

"Jesse?" Her voice, soft and feminine, touched the air.

"Kiernan! My God, Kiernan!"

She was off her horse, and running across the bridge. Jesse dismounted from Goliath and went running to greet her. Darkness fell over the moon, and they both disappeared in the shadows. Daniel heard their glad cries mingling in the night.

He smiled, and turned his horse away. He rode back to his tent, and gently refused the company of his men. He retired with a brandy bottle.

Later that night, Billy Boudain and some of the others arrived at his tent. He heard giggling, feminine giggling, and he knew they had arranged some companionship for the evening. In the pale light of muted camp fires he could see a woman's silhouette in his doorway. "Colonel, this is Betsy. She's heard a whole lot about you. She wants to wish you Merry Christmas."

Why not? Betsy was young, it seemed. Maybe even fresh at her profession. Hell, it was Christmas. It had been a long, long time.

In the shadows he could see the girl. She was small, slim, dark. Forget the world, forget the war, forget the night, he told himself.

But he could not. Visions swam before him. Visions of his own bronzed flesh entangled in silken hair that flamed like a fire run rampant. Of silver eyes that met his. Of a voice that whispered and caressed, beckoned and betrayed.

He could touch no other woman until he had found either his vengeance or his peace.

"Thanks, Billy," he said softly. "Young lady." He inclined his head to the girl. "I'm, er, well, I'm just in for the night. You all go on. Merry Christmas."

Billy was disappointed, but he had come to know Daniel, and he knew even his most polite tone of command. He bid Daniel good night and Merry Christmas.

Merry Christmas. Merry Christmas. Yes. Where are you tonight, Mrs. Callie Michaelson? Is your Christmas warm, is it full of wonder?

He did get through Christmas. And then into the new year.

And into more battles.

But even as the battles began to rage, he had no idea what 1863 would bring.

They were well into the year before he even heard of that little town in Pennsylvania called Gettysburg.

Sixteen

May 1863

"Lord God, he's down! Stonewall is down, he's been shot by his own troops!"

The agitated cry of a Reb horseman was the first that Daniel heard of the injury to Stonewall Jackson.

He was down, Daniel thought quickly, but that didn't mean that he wouldn't be up again. Men were frequently injured.

And injury frequently meant death.

He'd been in his tent, dictating his own current situation to Billy Boudain, who was proving to have a marvelous craft with letters. He was surely the finest staff assistant that Daniel had ever had.

The fighting was over for the day. Again, some of the fiercest fighting Daniel had seen. They were at Chancellorsville, and Jackson had just completed one of the most amazing feats of military agility ever accomplished.

The general had cut short a visit to his wife on the twenty-ninth of April when he heard that one hundred thirty-four thousand Federal troops—now under the Union General "Fightin" Joe Hooker—were crossing the Rappahannock on both sides of Fredericksburg. It

had been the first time he had ever seen his infant
daughter, but he had rushed back to take command.
Splitting his forces, he had sent troops against Major
General John Sedgwick's left wing, and then he had
taken the majority of his men into the wilderness near
Spotsylvania. Daniel's troops had been with him, and
they had driven the Federals back to Chancellorsville.

The next day, Jackson and Lee split the army again.
Lee and his men faced Hooker at the front; Jackson
completed his wide sweep around Hooker's flank to
attack from the rear, and on the morning of May second, they completely routed the Federals.

Now they were saying that he was down.

"Soldier!" Daniel called out, stepping forward. "It's
true? Jackson is injured?"

"Mightily, sir. He's been taken to a nearby farm."

"God help him!" Daniel murmured.

"Indeed, sir!"

And well God should be on his side, Daniel thought,
for Stonewall was a deeply religious man. A discipli-
narian, strange to many, stoic, and sworn to duty.

And necessary to Master Bobby Lee, Daniel
thought.

There was nothing that he could do for Jackson, but
all through the night, messengers rode back and forth,
reporting on the general's condition.

By the late hours of the night, his wounded arm was
amputated. He could survive still, Daniel thought, and
he couldn't help but think of Jesse. He could survive if
it could be kept from infection. If, there were so many
ifs.

And there were still the Federals to be fought. . . .

The battle continued through the third and the
fourth of May. At the end, Sedgwick and Hooker were
forced back, and the Army of the Potomac was with-
drawn. Though it was a southern victory, the Confederates also lost, and lost sorely.

On the tenth of May, General Thomas "Stonewall" Jackson died, succumbing to the pneumonia that had set in following his surgery. He died in the company of his beloved wife, and he died at peace with the God he had so worshipped. But he died a soldier still badly needed upon the battlefield.

The entire South mourned, and mourned deeply, no one more so than Robert E. Lee. Daniel had seen death hurt General Lee; he had seen the pain in the man's gray-blue eyes at the death of any soldier. He had never seen anything like the expression that now haunted that gallant gentleman with the loss of Jackson.

And still, the war went on.

Lee had made the decision to carry the war northward once again. There were very good reasons for doing this, the main one being that while the fighting went on in the South, it was the South that was being stripped of her resources. It would be far better to have the southern armies stripping the North for food and sustenance.

Also, there were many northerners wearying of the war. McClellan—Little Mac—the general Lincoln had removed from command, was now moving politically against Lincoln. He was planning to run for president of the U.S. McClellan wanted to sue for peace. If Lee could just bring the brutality and horror of warfare north, more and more northerners might begin to side with McClellan, and look forward to a negotiated peace. Then the Confederate States of America could move on separately.

On the western front, Union troops were beginning to move against Vicksburg, Mississippi. It was imperative that Vicksburg be held—the Mississippi River was one of the lifelines of the Confederacy.

The Rebels needed the war to end.

Daniel felt a growing heat begin to move in his veins.

They would soon be traveling through Maryland once again.

Beauty had promised him time. He didn't know when it would come; he just prayed that it would come soon.

Don't let her forget me, he prayed in silence to himself. Don't let her forget that I am coming. . . .

As always, the emotions knotted tightly within him.

Callie could not forget him.

And certainly not the very beautiful morning of the twenty-fifth of May.

It began as a morning much like any other for her, for she awoke very early, dressed, and hurried down to feed the animals.

She felt the first twinges in her back while she was doling out grain and hay, and the next came while she was throwing out feed to the chickens. She barely noticed the first, and the second only gave her a momentary qualm. It was really too early for the baby. He—or she—wasn't due until June. When June came she had planned on moving into town, near Doctor Jamison. He might not approve of her, but he was a good and kindly man and he'd not see anything bad happen to her or an innocent infant.

She still had so much to do. The vegetables in the garden were almost ready for jarring to see her through the winter. She was in the midst of making several little winter sacques for the baby, and she had recently gone into a frenzy of spring cleaning.

The cleaning didn't matter, the jarring didn't matter. In fact, very little seemed to matter when the third pain came streaking through her spine and around her middle like a bolt of vicious, clutching lightning.

She was in the back, by the paddock, and she staggered with the onslaught of it, reaching out for the fence. For a moment she was so startled that she didn't even think; then it slowly dawned on her that she must be having the baby.

The pain faded. It remained with her for a moment, then it disappeared so completely that she began to wonder if she hadn't imagined it.

Perhaps she had. She turned around and walked toward the well, drew up a bucket of water, and sipped a dipper full of it. She felt fine. Perfectly fine.

Still, perhaps she should lie down for a few minutes. She was here alone, with no one to care exactly what time anything got done. She very seldom received visitors from town anymore. Her condition was known, and on occasion, when she had gone in for supplies, old friends had actually turned their backs on her. It didn't matter, she had told herself, fighting back the first sting of tears. When the war ended, when her brothers returned, she would take the baby and she would leave. She'd heard marvelous stories about New York City and Washington D.C., and she dreamed of a day when she could go there.

After she had seen Daniel.

And what? Apologized for the fact that she'd sent him to a prison camp?

He was coming back for her. He'd warned her that he would.

She felt a quivering take flight inside of her and she tried to swallow her thoughts of the man. She was always trying to do that. To forget the excitement, and the love, and the fear. The color of his eyes and the slow sensual drawl of his voice.

"Stop!" she commanded herself aloud.

But it was impossible to stop thinking of a man in her current condition. When people turned away from her. When she was so heavy that she dragged herself about.

When she could feel the movement of life within her.

Damn them all, she thought. She loved the baby, loved it fiercely. A tiny creature who would need her, who would love her and trust her, who would not condemn her.

She started to walk away from the well. She felt dizzy. She should lie down.

But even as she walked toward the house, she felt a sudden onslaught of water. It was so startling, soaking her skirt and her petticoat and pantalets, seeming to come like a river. She had no experience with human birth whatsoever, but having lived on a farm her entire life, she was very much aware that she had lost her waters, and that the baby must come soon, or die.

"Oh, no!" she cried softly to the morning air. She had never felt more alone. Nor had she ever felt such fear. Women died in childbirth. Frequently. She wasn't terrified of death itself—too many people she loved dearly had already gone before her—but the idea of having her baby live with no one to find it or tend to it was terrifying.

She stood there a moment, drenched and freezing in the cool morning air. Should she try on her own to reach town? The birth could take hours, she knew that, perhaps she had time.

But even as she finally found movement and began to walk to the house, a pain was upon her again. It was so sharp and horrible that she screamed, heedless of the sound. She doubled over, shocked, stunned by the intensity of it.

This was going to go on for hours?

She grit her teeth against the pain, and then she tried to inhale and exhale with it.

She wasn't going to be able to go anywhere. She was going to have to move very quickly. She needed to sterilize a knife for the cord, she needed blankets, she . . .

She needed not to be alone!

She reproached herself furiously for not having taken into consideration the fact that the child might come early. She saw pictures of herself too weak to force out the child. Bleeding to death. Dying with no one to hear her screams, or to care for the tiny life inside of her that she loved so passionately.

Move! she commanded herself, and with the pain still tight around her, she hurried into the house and into the kitchen, seeking a knife to sever the baby's cord. Now she needed to gather fresh bedding and cloths to clean the baby and herself and tiny garments for the baby to wear.

She gripped the doorway as she left the kitchen. She was shivering like a blown leaf tossed in winter, trying to block her mind. But it was then that she saw a picture of Daniel. Laughing, casual, standing in the doorway, watching her. His smile so beautiful, his eyes so seductive. She could remember everything about him so clearly. The breadth of his shoulders, the bronze of his flesh. The feel of it, oh, the feel of it, so warm, so supple, so powerful, beneath her fingers. She could remember the way she had wanted him. Wanted so much she would willingly be damned for just one touch.

She remembered his anger, remembered his eyes.

She suddenly began to laugh. "Oh, Daniel! If you wanted revenge, here it is! No one could be more terrified than I at this moment!"

She started to laugh hard, but then once again, a pain came around her. Hard, tight, instant, growing.

She'd been to Doctor Jamison. He had looked down his spectacled nose at her, and he had been totally disapproving of her. But he had told her that the pains might come slowly, that they might last all day. That she would be near to time when the pains came very near one another. Most first births took a long time.

Of course, there were exceptions.

"Oh!" Her laughter became a scream, but she didn't

care, there was no one to hear her. She was wet and
freezing, and she didn't care about that either.

She waited for the pain to ebb, and then she pushed
away from the door. She started to walk through the
parlor, anxious to reach the stairs.

Another pain came, before the first had really faded.
Panic seized her, and then an agony unlike anything
she had ever imagined. She buckled down on the stairs,
fighting the tears that sprang to her eyes, fighting to
retain some control over the awful pain. It clutched
like rivulets, like fingers, starting at her lower back,
sweeping all around the circumference of her abdomen. She could bear it in the front; it was the agony at
her spine that was so very vicious. How much could she
stand?

Whatever came. She had no choice.

She started to rise from the stairs. It seemed that the
pain came immediately. She cried out and fell again,
and for a moment, there was blackness, the pain was so
fierce. The blackness lifted, and she ceased to care for
her own life, or for that of her child.

She just wanted someone to walk in and shoot her
and put her out of her agony.

"Dear, dear, dear!"

Dimly, she heard a voice. A gentle, soothing, female
voice. Then she heard a clucking sound, and soft, gentle arms were around her. She blinked and looked up.

Helga Weiss was there, and Rudy Weiss was right
behind her. It was Helga who held her, Helga who
spoke softly, giving her strength, giving her assurance.

"Poor child, poor child!" she clucked again. "All
alone here and soaking wet and the babe on its way.
Rudy, we must get her to bed. And into something
dry."

Callie shook her head, tears suddenly streaming
down her cheeks as she stared at the woman. "I'm going to die," she said.

Helga laughed kindly. "No, no. You are not going to die. Helga is here."

Helga tisked away as she and Rudy carried Callie up the stairs. Then Rudy was sent away, and Helga worked on her own. In minutes, Callie was in a warm gown. The pains still continued to assail her, but Helga talked her through them, and the panic that had seized her was gone. The pains remained very close together.

The closer they came, the more she wished that Helga would just shoot her instead of trying to talk to her.

No! Daniel ought to be shot. Prison wasn't good enough for him. He ought to be shot, and then she ought to be shot.

"Hold tight, it will be soon!" Helga told her.

Callie told Helga where she thought she should go.

But the kindly German woman never lost her gentleness, no matter how Callie tossed or screamed, or fought her assurances. Then, along with the pains, came a new sensation, the desperate desire to push.

"What do I do?" she begged Helga.

Helga competently looked into the situation and smiled at her, smoothing back her hair. "You push, Frau Michaelson. You push. Your little one is here."

It wasn't quite that easy. The pains remained savage, and she had to push and push and push. She thought that she passed out again, she strained so hard, but Helga was telling her that the head had been born and that they needed another shoulder, and another shoulder.

She heard the cry. Her baby's cry. Drenched in sweat and tears she cast her head back and began to laugh, and then to cry again, and the sensations seemed to overwhelm her. That cry! That pathetic little cry. It reached inside her and touched her heart, and filled her body with wonder. The tears, the laughter, both remained as she reached out to Helga. Helga, smiling like a saint, handed her the bundle of her baby, so tiny! And so, so beautiful! He was a little pinched, and very much a mess, but so beautiful. He screamed like a banshee!

It was a he!

"Helga! A little boy!"

"A son, yes. A beautiful, beautiful son."

Callie forgot all about the pain. She barely noticed as Helga cut and tied the cord, and she was heedless of all sensation as Helga reminded her that they were not done, that she must deliver the afterbirth.

Callie didn't care. She had already forgotten that she had wanted Helga to shoot her.

Her hands were on her tiny son. She was counting fingers and toes, and she was marveling at the exquisite beauty of her baby. Hers.

"Come, come now," Helga told her. "Into a new gown with you. And now, I must have the baby. You won't recognize him when I give him back. He will be so beautiful; you will see!"

Callie held him for a minute, then released him to Helga. She closed her eyes, overcome with wonder. Then, amazingly, she slept.

When she awoke, she was completely disoriented. She remembered her baby, and she bolted up, panicking.

But Helga was there, sitting in a rocker by a fire she had built against the coolness of the night. She was singing softly in German.

"May I see him?" Callie whispered.

Helga gave her one of her beautiful smiles. "He wants his mother. He has waited patiently, but now he is hungry."

Callie reached out for the baby and Helga brought him to her. He took one look at her and began to howl. Helga laughed, and Callie fumbled a little with her gown, then awkwardly tried to lead him to nurse. His mouth was so wide against such a tiny face!

But her son instinctively knew what he wanted. The wide but tiny mouth closed over her breast. The first tug that touched her as he suckled sent a new wave of emotion sweeping through her, emotion so strong that tears instantly rose to her eyes again and her heart seemed to warm there within her chest, beneath the little body. With trembling fingers she touched his head. It was covered with ink-black hair. She touched his hand, resting against her breast, and she was in awe of the perfection of the little fingers. Nothing that had come before could matter now. Nothing. People could turn their backs to her; they could damn her. None of it mattered. He mattered. This precious child. Her child.

"Jared?" She looked at Helga.

Helga shrugged. "It's a fine name. But perhaps he should be named for his father."

Callie lowered her lashes. "Jared was my father. It is a fine name."

The baby fell asleep, right against her flesh. Helga came to move him. Callie didn't want to release him. "You need something to eat," Helga told her. "You will need strength. For him."

Callie released the baby. Helga had made him a bed in one of the dresser drawers. She set him down to sleep. "I've made soup. I will bring it," Helga told her.

It struck Callie just how wonderful this woman had been to her. She reached out for Helga's hand. "Thank you. Thank you so much, Helga. You have been so good to me. And surely, in your eyes, what I have . . . done," she said lamely, "must be so very bad."

Helga smiled. "All around us there is death. Today, there is life. God has given us this beautiful life. What can be bad? You are good, Callie. You are good, and life is good. And God has let me be here." She squeezed Callie's hand. Callie smiled.

"Thank you so much!" she whispered again.

Helga hesitated. "You must find the baby's father."

"When the war is over," Callie said.

"He has a right to know about this child."

What rights did Daniel have? Callie didn't know. She felt the usual shivering seize her. All she really knew was that Daniel hated her, that he had promised to come back. She had never, never forgotten the look in his eyes.

"He's in prison," she told Helga. "When the war is over, I will find him. I promise."

She was still shivering. She had time. The war was nowhere near being over. Maybe Daniel would not care. Maybe he would not want to acknowledge the child.

Maybe he would want to strangle her, and take the child.

She moistened her lips. For the first and only time, she was grateful that the war was going on.

And that as long as the battles waged, Daniel would be safely locked away.

In the days that followed, Callie quickly regained her strength.

Helga and Rudy stayed with her nearly a week, but then she felt very well and she was anxious to get on with life in the way that she must learn to live it. It was not so difficult. Jared was demanding, but he slept frequently, and she was able to manage very well. She felt wonderful. She was so very in love with her child that she felt more exuberant than ever. She walked with a new spring to her step, and lived for the moments when she could just lie with the baby and inspect him over and over again.

By the time that he was three weeks old, his resemblance to his father was startling. It was more than the ink-black hair or the startling blue eyes. His mouth was

Daniel's, his nose was Daniel's, the set of his brow was
Daniel's. Callie often lay on the bed with the baby
sleeping beside her, seeing Jared, feeling the softness
of his breath, remembering Daniel.

She had loved him so fiercely.

But he hated her. Hated her with as much passion as
he had ever loved her. She had betrayed him. He
would never let her explain. He would never believe
that she had fought only for his life.

Every time she thought of Daniel, she began to
shiver again. It was best not to think of him.

She couldn't look at Jared and not think of him.

And then came the rumors that the southern army
was going to come north again.

Lee wanted to attack.

In Virginia, the armies were beginning to move.

On the eighth of June, Lee attended a review of Jeb
Stuart's troops at Culpepper Courthouse.

Word reached them that on the westward front, the
Yanks had reached Briarfield, Confederate President
Jefferson Davis's home. They had burned it to the
ground.

Two days later, Beauty Stuart's cavalry were able to
pursue their anger at any and all insults, for Union
cavalry met them at Brandy Station, Virginia.

The most furious clash of cavalry in all the war took
place that day.

For Daniel, commanding his troops, it was a night-
mare like none other. Horses trampled men and other
horses, guns were emptied of their shot and used as
clubs. Sabres slashed and rained down death, creating
bright red streams of death.

And through it all, the cries of the animals and the
men met and melded, and as the day progressed, Daniel could no longer ascertain whether it was a man or
beast who screamed in ragged agony at his side.

Time and again, he just missed the blade of a Yankee sword; time and again he felt a bullet whiz by his cheek so close that he could hear the rush and whisper of the displaced air.

Time and again he wondered how he could live, how he could survive the awful mechanics of the day.

But he did survive; and the battle did end. The Yankees had come on reconnaissance, and perhaps they had learned something of the southern troop movements. But it was the southerners who had held their ground.

Brandy Station was theirs. For what it was worth. Brandy Station, littered with the dead and the dying.

In the dusk he looked over the death-littered terrain and shuddered. He set his fingers before him in the coming darkness. He hadn't sustained a single scratch.

He didn't want to think of the death he had wrought himself.

A shivering seized him. This battle was over. They were no closer to a certain victory than they had been before it.

But now they were really moving north. He'd been given partial orders already about moving his troops. The North had been testing their movements—now it was his turn to test the movements of the Yanks.

Through Maryland, on up to Pennsylvania.

Again, he felt the most curious trembling sweep through him. He closed his eyes tightly. It had been a long time. A long, long time since he had stepped foot on that Maryland soil.

A few days later, Jeb gave him their orders. They were to move ahead. Lee's ultimate goal would be Harrisburg, Pennsylvania. The cavalry was to move on.

As always, the horsemen were ordered to be the eyes and ears of the South.

"I want my time in Maryland," Daniel told Jeb. The words were almost cold.

"Not on the campaign north. You'll get your time on the return south. You've got my word."

Beauty's word was as good as gold. Daniel knew that he would see her soon, and the excitement and the bitterness and the fury and the passion all churned tightly within him.

There would be fierce battles in the North.

They didn't matter. He knew that he was going to live because he had to see her again.

He didn't know at that moment that his emotions would run even more deeply when he saw her again at last.

And he had no way of knowing that there was a city called "Gettysburg" to stand in his way.

At the moment, it was nothing more than a little speck on the map.

Seventeen

As it happened, Daniel and Stuart and his cavalry arrived late for the battle.

By the time they made it, a day and a half of bloody fighting had already occurred, fields were already strewn with the dead, and a great debate over what was going wrong was already in process.

Some said it was the first major battle Lee was having to fight without his right-hand man, Stonewall. Some said that Stuart, in his attempt to make another great sweep around the Union army, had ridden too far and deprived Lee of his eyes and ears.

In their journey north, the cavalry had become involved in battle again and again. Even after the inconclusive battle at Brandy Station, there had been skirmishes at Aldie, Middleburg, and Upperville. On the twenty-second of June, Lee gave Stuart discretionary orders, permitting the cavalry to harrass the Union infantry. Stuart and his men were also to guard the army's right flank, remain in communication, and gather supplies.

They came close—very close—to the Maryland farmland where Callie lived. So damn close that he could almost reach out and touch it. So damn close that the thought of desertion touched both his heart and mind. At that, he had to convince himself she had become an obsession.

She might not even be there. Who knew? Perhaps she had turned from him to her Yank cavalry comrade, the damned Captain Dabney who had delivered the coup de grace once Callie had disarmed him.

Maybe she had married him.

It didn't matter. She could have married a hundred men, he was still going back for her. But not now. He could not give in to his desire and pursue her, even though they passed so near. His honor was at stake, he reminded himself dryly. Ah, yes, honor and ethics! Without them, what were they?

They rode very hard, and they rode very fast. On the twenty-seventh, late in the day, they crossed the Potomac. On the twenty-eighth they captured one hundred and twenty-five Federal wagons, but the capture was surely a mixed blessing, for the wagons slowed them down.

They rode all night toward Pennsylvania, slowed down by their wagons and their prisoners. Near Hood's Mill, they destroyed part of the Baltimore and Ohio railroad. At noon they rode on to Westminster, and there they were attacked by Federal cavalry.

They were victorious, repulsing the Yanks, but the Yanks, like the wagons, had cost them time. The next day they entered Hanover, Pennsylvania, and immediately, they were charged by another Union brigade. Once again, they repulsed the Federals, but only after a savage battle had been fought. When it was done, they rode on through the night, halting at Dover.

On the morning of July first, they rested and fed their mounts.

They had no idea that Lee's army, having heard nothing from Stuart, had stumbled into the battle of Gettysburg.

A message reached Stuart by late afternoon. It was

then that he and Daniel and a few other officers rode hard ahead of the brigades to report to Lee at Gettysburg.

And Lee, the careful gentleman, the ultimate officer, looked hard at Stuart and said, "Well, General Stuart, you are here at last."

But the matter went no further; there was a battle to be fought. Daniel found himself quickly thrown into communications, surveying the landscape of the area. He was assigned a young captain from Tennessee to explain the current positions and situation. His name was Guy Culver, and he was an excellent horseman. Though he'd barely graduated from the VMI before the onset of war, he had a good sense of strategy, and was quick to give Daniel a good overview in one of the command tents.

"Can you beat it, Colonel, it all began over shoes! There was this big advertisement, you see, for shoes, in Gettysburg. So we have a brigade under Heth marching down the Chambersburg Pike and they're seen by some Union cavalry. Well, the Union cavalry commander must have decided that this place held strategic importance—it does, there's nine roads go through here—and he engages his cavalry with our infantry. Before you know it, both sides are calling for reinforcements, and now, the bulk of both armies are engaged."

He spread out a map of the area, and Daniel quickly acquainted himself with the layout of the area.

He spent what was left of the day riding from one area of carnage to another. Little Round Top, Big Round Top. Culp's Hill, Cemetery Hill, the peach orchard, the wheatfield, Devil's Den. The fighting was fierce, the battles were savage. At the end of the day, the fighting came to a halt with a last abortive Confederate assault upon Culp's Hill.

After two horrible days of fighting, Lee was still determined to hold. That night he laid out his plan for a direct assault against Cemetery Ridge. General Longstreet protested, but Lee was determined. The Union Army was under Meade now, but the Union had a history of dissolving quickly under pressure, and a reputation for retreat.

Stuart and his cavalry were to attack the Union rear from the east.

But Daniel was still assigned to communications. Few men, even among Stuart's fine cavaliers, could ride as fast or as hard as Daniel, and few seemed to have quite as many lives. While Jesse had managed to keep Goliath fit and well during these two long years of war, Daniel had lost at least seven horses from beneath him.

Lee did not want to be blinded again.

By noon, a seven-hour assault upon Culp's Hill was giving the Confederates no success. Lee decided to send eleven brigades against the very center of the Union line. Stuart would come from the rear; the other men, led by General George Pickett's fresh division, would charge straight across the field upon the Union line.

It was ominous, Daniel thought. Silence pervaded the field; dear Lord, it seemed like forever. It was only an hour.

Then the cannons began to roar. For two hours, Confederate gunners sent a barrage soaring across the heavens. The sky became sickly gray. The noise was deafening. Firestorms exploded.

And then, again, silence.

After that silence came the awful sound of the Rebel yell, and with startling, near perfect precision, thirteen thousand Confederate soldiers came marching out across the field. They were awesome; they were majestic. They moved like a curse of God, and they moved with a stunning courage and devotion to God and duty and state.

They were mown down, just the same.

The Federal artillery burst upon the men, and they fell. They fell with horrible screams; they fell, men destroyed. Canisters sprayed out their death.

And still, the men charged on.

There was no help from the rear assault, Daniel discovered, for riding around the action he found Stuart and the cavalry engaged in a fierce battle and gaining no ground.

Sweeping back around with his information for Lee, Daniel found the remnants of the charging Confederates limping, crawling, staggering back to their own line.

He found Lee, the grand old gentleman, there to greet them. "It's all my fault. It's all my fault."

Pickett's Charge was over.

Indeed, Gettysburg was over.

There was nothing to do but count the losses. That night, the estimates were horrible. Nearly four thousand Rebs killed, nearly twenty thousand injured, and over five thousand missing.

Then there was the battlefield. In all that he had seen, in all that he had witnessed, Daniel had never known a sensation like standing on Seminary Ridge and looking down over the fields of devastation. Men moved among the fields of bodies. Sad bodies, twisted bodies, destroyed bodies. Young bodies, old bodies, enemies embraced again in death.

Now the medics moved among them, and again, Daniel thought of his brother, and he knew that Jesse must be out there, that he must be up to his elbows in blood. He wished that he could be with him, that he could help him. It didn't matter to him that night whether the injured were Reb or Yank. War was horrible. And it would not end.

He looked down and saw one of their own regimental physicians moving about the wounded. He started down toward him, walking first, then running. The doctor, a Captain Greeley, looked at him, startled.

"Colonel!"

"Tell me what to do. I'm a fairly decent assistant in a surgery."

"But Colonel—"

"I am at my leisure, sir, at the moment, if such a thing can exist on such a night. I am not a doctor, but I know something of medicine. God knows what lives I have taken. I wish to help save those that I might tonight."

Greeley still seemed unnerved that a cavalry colonel was offering assistance in such a way. But he shrugged, and he asked Daniel to pick up a young man he had found still breathing by a tree stump. "We've not enough stretchers. We've not enough doctors. We've not enough anything," he finished lamely.

"Then any hands will help," Daniel said, and he scooped up the private with the blood-spattered uniform.

For the next hour, he served by searching out the living. There weren't enough stretchers. He found a few of his men to help, and he knew that they had made a difference while the hours wore on. Greeley stopped him before he could make a return trip, asking him then to help in the surgery.

He had done it before. Yet nothing made it easy.

He helped hold down the men while Greeley removed limbs. He tried to talk to them; there was nothing to stem the cries. All that could help a limb so shattered was its removal.

He didn't know how many men he had assisted with when an orderly brought in a figure he knew well.

It was Billy Boudain.

"Colonel!"

Billy's handsome face was pinched and gray. He smiled nonetheless. "They let you ride in to surgery, eh?"

Daniel didn't like the look of Billy. He was too gray. He smiled in turn anyway, knowing how important the will to live could be.

"Hell, you know I have some acquaintance with what I'm doing, right, Billy?"

"That I do, sir. That I do."

"What did you do, Billy? Get too close to one of those Yankees?"

"Hell, sir, I wasn't close at all. Something exploded by me, and I just woke up a few minutes ago, it seems."

"It's going to be right as rain, won't it, Doctor Greeley?"

Greeley had peeled back Billy's cavalry shirt. His face lifted to Daniel's, and Daniel instantly saw in his eyes that there was no way at all. Daniel glanced down to Billy's chest. Bone and blood were shattered and mingled.

He almost cried out. He felt tears welling behind his eyes, stinging his lids, and he fought them, furious with himself. Officers could not cry, and Camerons never gave way, and by God, he would not be weak, especially not now, not now when Billy needed him so much.

He curled his fingers around Billy's hand. "Just hold tight and breath easy, Billy."

"I'm going to die, Colonel."

"No, Billy—"

"Don't tell me that I'm not, sir. I can feel death. It's cold. It—it doesn't hurt."

Daniel choked, then knelt down by Billy. "Billy, you can't die on me. I'm going to take you home with me to Cameron Hall. Billy, you've never seen anything quite like it. The grass is as green as emeralds and it rolls and slopes down to the river. The trees are tall and very thick, and there's always a breeze, so they sway there. And there's a porch, Billy, a broad, wide porch, and you can just sit there and feel the breeze—"

"And sip on a whiskey, eh, sir?"

"Whiskey, brandy, julep, whatever you've a mind for, Billy. We'll get back there."

Billy's fingers tightened around his. "The grass is like emeralds?"

"Just like."

Billy coughed. Blood spilled from his lips. "Pray for me, Colonel. Someday, we'll meet again. In an Eden, just like Cameron Hall."

"Billy—"

Billy's hand tightened, and then went limp. Daniel's fingers curled around him. He grated his teeth hard.

"He's gone, Colonel," Greeley said softly.

Daniel nodded.

"We need the table."

"Yes."

Daniel lifted Billy in his arms, and walked out of the surgery with him. He walked into the night, and found a tree, and sat down beneath it, still cradling Billy in his arms.

He sat so for a long time. Tall cavalry boots appeared at his side.

"A friend, Daniel?"

Stuart, worn, haggard, and weary, sat down beside him. He didn't seem to notice that his friend cradled a corpse.

"You've got to let him go, Daniel."

Daniel nodded. "He wouldn't be here if it weren't for me. I brought him out of Old Capitol."

"God decides what happens to all of us, Daniel. And God knows, I failed Lee these last days!"

"We've lost a big one," Daniel agreed.

"Armistead is dead; Pickett has sworn that he will never forgive Lee. And what can any of that matter to all the boys, Union and Confederates, who have gone on from here. Hell, Daniel, any of us can die at any time. But it's God's will, not mine, not yours."

They were both silent for a minute.

"We begin a retreat, you know." Stuart motioned to someone. A soldier walked over and saluted Daniel sharply. He reached for Billy's body.

Daniel gave it up.

"Yes," he said to Stuart.

"We're going south, through Maryland once again. We'll be a long time regrouping from this one. I'll give you your time now, if Meade doesn't follow us. If Meade does follow us, God alone knows what will happen. But if the Union does not attack, you may have the time I promised you. Do whatever it is that you're so desperate to do in Maryland. I'll give you until the end of the month. Then report back to me."

Daniel looked at Stuart.

Maryland.

Yes . . .

It was time to see her again.

Callie could see the movement of part of the armies as they headed north.

They didn't travel a path that led directly by her farm. They remained at quite a distance, and it was only with her brother Josiah's glass that she was able to see them clearly at all, and that from her bedroom window.

From the first moment she saw a gray uniform and the straggle of poorly clad men around it, she knew that the Rebels were advancing again.

Her heart seemed to leap to her throat. Rebels. Coming here, coming after her.

No. There was only one Rebel who might be coming

after her, and he could not possibly be doing so. She was so grateful. She'd heard about the huge cavalry battle in Virginia, and she'd had to sit down and hug her knees to her chest, grateful that Daniel could not have been part of it, that his name could not have appeared on the list of the dead.

Now the Rebels were heading north again. She closed her eyes, and prayed. Prayed that the battlefield would not be her front lawn again, that she wouldn't have to see the awful horror of war.

Her eyes flew open and she prayed simply that they would not come her way at all.

There were more and more deserters these days. From both armies. Some of these men could be dangerous. She hadn't only herself to worry about anymore.

She had Jared.

Fear drove her to the room she had set up as a nursery for her son. He was sleeping, but she slipped him up into her arms anyway and held him close. She'd die before she'd let anyone harm him in any way.

She squeezed him so tight that he awoke and let out a cry of protest.

"My love, my little love, I'm so sorry!" she said softly. He quieted, studying her with his wide blue eyes. He let out a little cooing sound and pursed his lips, and she laughed. Well, she had woken him up. He thought it was time to eat.

She carried him to the old rocker in his room and sat with him, rocking while he nursed. She ran her fingers over his silky ink-black hair, and when she closed her eyes, she couldn't help but think of Daniel again, and her thoughts were torn. Thank God he could not reach her. Dear God, but she had to reach him. One day.

He'd merely want to throttle her. Perhaps he wouldn't want anything to do with the baby.

Perhaps he would want the baby and nothing at all to do with her.

Her pulse beat too quickly with just the thought. Guiltily she realized she had been thinking once again it was a good thing the war raged on.

No, no, Lord, I did not mean that!

The war was horrible. Jeremy and Josiah were outside of Vicksburg, Mississippi. Jeremy had written to her about the awful battles they had fought, and how they were trying to starve out the population of Mississippi. There were those who managed to get in and out of the city, and Jeremy's letters were full of pity for the citizens who were living in caves in the hills—and dining upon rats when they were lucky enough to catch them.

No, no, God, let the war end! she prayed fervently.

She heard the sound of a wagon. A sizzle of fear ripped through her, and she jumped up, holding Jared tightly to her.

She looked down from the window and breathed a sigh of relief as she saw that the wagon below carried Rudy and Helga Weiss.

"Callie!" Rudy called to her, standing up in the wagon.

She looked out of the window. "Hello! I'm here."

"Thank the Lord!" Helga muttered.

Curiously, Callie watched as Rudy helped his wife from the wagon. She hurried down the stairs, the baby still in her arms.

She met the two of them at the back door. Helga burst in, sweeping the baby from her arms, and murmuring to him in soft German. Callie looked at Rudy, her brows lifted.

"You are all right? You haven't been disturbed?"

She shook her head. "I'm fine."

Rudy sighed and sank into a kitchen chair, mopping his brow.

"They came through our place, they did."

"Who?"

Rudy grimaced. "First a Confederate major. He left us a wad of his Confederate money, and took almost everything that moved on the property, goats, chicken, cows. Then, not long after, another soldier comes by. This one is all dressed up in a blue uniform. He lays another wad of money on the table, and cleans us out of everything that the Rebels forgot to take!"

"Oh, Rudy!" Callie murmured. She sat down across from him. "Did they take your grain and everything else too?"

"Everything."

"Well, then, you must help yourselves to what I have here."

"Nein, nein! We did not come to take from you—we came to be certain that you were all right. Our people need very little, and we look after one another."

"But I don't need all that I have. You would help me if you took some of the animals."

"Perhaps the armies will still stumble upon you," Rudy said wearily.

"Then they might as well stumble upon me with half of what I have, right?" she said cheerfully.

Rudy argued, Helga argued. But before she would allow them to leave, she had a goat tied to their wagon and a dozen chickens within it, along with several sacks of grain and numerous jars of her preserves and pickled vegetables.

A few days later, Rudy was back.

"Callie, you must be careful. Come home with me."

"Why?"

"The battle has been fought. A big, horrible battle. They say that between both sides, near fifty thousand men were killed or injured."

"Oh, my God!" Callie gasped.

"They are coming home. The Rebs are coming home. They will come limping and worn and hurt. And many will pass by here. Come home with me."

Callie shook her head. She felt an awful dread, and an awful anticipation.

Her heart was beating too hard once again.

He couldn't be among them. He was in prison. Thank God, she had really done something good. She had kept him from the horror, from the death, from the blood.

He would never see it that way.

"Callie, come with me!"

She shook her head, feeling an awful fascination. Pity filled her heart, and the startling certainty that she had to stay. She had to offer them water on their long journey homeward, if nothing more.

Perhaps there would be someone who knew him.

Someone who could tell her that he was still in Washington, that he lived, that he was well.

She shook off the awful shivers that seized her. "Rudy, I cannot come. I must stay here."

"Callie."

She didn't understand it herself. "I must stay, Rudy. I—I simply must. Maybe I can help. Maybe I can do something."

Rudy shook his head. "These men . . . these men are the enemy."

"A beaten enemy."

"This war is not over."

"I will be all right, Rudy. I need to see these men. I need to hear what has happened."

He argued with her, but she would not be budged. She simply could not fight the compulsion to stay.

Eventually, as Rudy had said, the men began to come back. Slowly. Beaten, ragged, weary.

And Callie found herself down by the well.

And it was there that she stood when Daniel Cameron rode into her life once again.

Rode in worn, weary, ragged.

And furious still!

"Angel . . ."

Interlude

DANIEL

July 4, 1863
Near Sharpsburg
Maryland

Perhaps, after the long months of waiting, of dreaming, of seeing her in his sleep, of hearing her voice even in the midst of shells, he had not believed that she could be as beautiful as he had remembered.

But she was.

Daniel watched as she offered his officer water. Watched her move, listened to the musical flow of her voice. Even as he did so, he felt his fingers curling into fists, felt a sizzling heat of fury and bitterness come sweeping through him. He had to hate her. She had used her beauty, used the softness of her voice, the fiery flow of her hair against him.

And still, she enchanted. Enchanted every man who passed her way. The word came to the lips of these men as easily as it had once come to his. Angel. God alone could have sculpted such a face. Created the color of her hair, the pools of her eyes.

This sweet creature from heaven!

And seductress born of Hell, he reminded himself, swallowing hard. Looking at her a man could forget that she had so sweetly coerced and lured him, forget the irons about his wrists, the days in prison, the cold dampness of Old Capitol, the misery, the humiliation.

By the gate, he dismounted from his horse and watched her.

Damn her. Was betrayal perhaps her business? Had other soldiers stumbled her way, had she seduced them, and seen them turned in, just as she had done with him?

God, he was weary! But no weariness could take away his fury at this moment! Had she but turned old and haggard, had she not been so unbelievably beautiful still! But there she stood. His angel. Their angel. Her dress so simple that it enhanced the perfection and loveliness of her womanhood.

Did she remember him?

Ah, but she would, he swore.

As the last of his cavalry soldiers passed by, Daniel came in to greet her by the well.

"Angel of mercy indeed. Is there, perhaps, a large quantity of arsenic in that well?"

She didn't move, but just stood there. The slight breeze lifted her hair, and in the coming night it seemed to burn with a dark fire. She seemed to gaze about him, and then her eyes fell on his, wide, gray. Did they dilate, perhaps? He felt the grinding of his teeth, the tearing emotion sweep through him. If she was afraid in the least of his revenge, she showed no sign of it. She stood like crystal, no, porcelain, still and perfect, the perfect heart of her face an ivory softly tinted rose at the cheeks, her beautiful lips as red as any long forgotten rose, her eyes, as always, silver orbs that shimmered and taunted the soul.

He smiled suddenly. She certainly wasn't going to cower. She was, as ever, ready for battle.

"Hello, angel!" he said softly.

Still she was silent, proud and silent. Yet at last he

could see the rise and fall of her breasts with the un-
even whisper of her breath; he could see a pulse at her
throat, beating there in fury. Why? he wondered. Was
it fear at last? Did his angel realize that a man cast into
hell came back by far the worse for wear?

The heat was ripping through him, tearing through
his limbs, spiraling around his chest, and tightening low
in his groin. Well, here he was at last. Standing before
her as he had dreamed so often, as he sometimes felt
he had survived to do. His fingers itched. Yes, he
wanted to strangle her.

He wanted her. He wanted her with a blind fury,
with a desperate desire. He wanted to hold her tightly
and shake her, and he wanted to feel the softness of
her flesh. He wanted to hear her cry out his name, and
he didn't give a damn if it was with anger or despair or
love or hatred. He wanted revenge, but most of all he
wanted to cool the heat that imprisoned and embraced
him, slake the thirst that lived with him day and night,
through days of battle and days in the saddle, through
rare moments of quiet, and even in the midst of the
shrill shrieks of guns and cannons and men.

"Cat got your tongue?" he asked. Damn, it was hard
to talk when his teeth were grating so. A slow, bitter
smile curved his lip. "How very unusual. Weren't you
expecting me?"

He didn't dare touch her. Not yet. He took the dipper from her fingers, lowered it into the bucket, and
raised the water from her well to his lips. It was cool
and sweet. It did nothing to ease the fire burning ever
more brightly throughout his limbs.

He could see that she was wondering just what
venue his anger would take. That pulse against the
ivory white column was beating every more rampantly.

"No poison? Perhaps some shards of glass?" he
murmured.

He moved more closely toward her. His voice was

husky, low and tense and trembling with the heat of his emotion. "You look as if you're welcoming a ghost, Mrs. Michaelson. Ah, but then, perhaps you had wished that I would be a ghost by now, long gone, dust upon the battlefield. No, angel, I am here." He was still as several seconds ticked slowly past, as the breeze picked up, as it touched them both. He smiled again. "By God, Callie, but you are still so beautiful. I should throttle you. I should wind my fingers right around your very beautiful neck, and throttle you. But even if you fell, you would torture me still!"

At last she moved, squaring her shoulders, standing even more tall against him. Her chin hiked up, her eyes shimmered, and her tone was soft and entirely superior to any of his taunts.

"Colonel, help yourself to water, and then, if you will, ride on. This is Union territory, and you are not welcome."

The back of her hand touched his chest. Head high, she was pushing him out of her way and starting for the house.

"Callie!"

Perhaps the extent of his rage was in his voice. Perhaps there was even more than that in the simple utterance of her name.

She began to run.

"Callie!" He shouted out her name again. Every restraint within him seemed to fail. The bitterness of nearly a year ripped wide, and he didn't know himself what he intended to do.

He followed her.

She had slammed the back door on him, bolted it against him. He hurtled his shoulder against it. It shuddered. He slammed against it again.

It began to give.

"Daniel, go away! Go home, go back to your men, to your army—to your South!"

The door burst open.

She stood staring at him.

Again, he felt a taunting curl touch his lips. He hadn't known what he would do when he saw her again. He still didn't know.

But he was going to touch her.

"What?" he demanded, taking a stride into the kitchen. "Are there no troops close enough to come to your rescue once you've seduced me into your bed this time?"

He ducked quickly. Her fingers had curled around a coffee cup, and hurtled it across the kitchen at him.

"Go away!" she commanded him.

"Go away?" he repeated. "How very rude, Mrs. Michaelson! When I have waited all these months to return? I lie awake nights dreaming for a chance to come back to your side. What a fool I was, Callie! And still, I suppose I did not learn."

He swept his hat from his head and sent it flying to the kitchen table. "Well, I have come back, angel. And I'm very anxious to pick up right where I left off. Let's see, where was that? Your bedroom, I believe. Ah, that's right. Your bed. And let's see, just how were we situated?"

"Get out of my house!" she charged him.

"Not on your life," he promised. "Not, madam, on your life!"

He strode toward her.

"Don't!" she cried out instantly.

Her denial seemed to touch him inside and out, adding fuel to the fire that raged so viciously inside of him. Dear God! Where was everything he had learned through a lifetime? Where was restraint, forgiveness, mercy?

He remembered the chill on his naked back when the Yanks had taken him. He remembered being in love with her. Damn her, but he remembered trusting her.

"This is one invasion of the North that is going to be successful!" Indeed, yes. Let it be a battle.

A battle that he would not lose.

He began to walk toward her once again. Maybe his intent was clear in his movement. Or perhaps she saw it in the cold hard glimmer of his eyes. Some sound escaped her, and she knocked over a chair in his way.

It wouldn't stop him. Not tonight.

"Don't, damn you!" she cried out suddenly. Her breasts were heaving more swiftly now with her growing agitation. Angel, you can falter and fall, and so beautifully. For a moment he almost paused. For a moment it was there again, the silver softness in her eyes, the sweetness in her voice. The plea, the seduction. "You have to listen to me—" she began.

The seduction. Yes, damn her.

"Listen to you!" he exploded. He was shaking. His flesh was on fire. His fingers twitched.

"Callie, time is precious! I have not come to talk this night. I listened to you once before."

"Daniel, don't come any nearer. You must—"

"I must finish what you started, Callie. Then maybe I can sleep again at night."

He reached for her arm and the fire in his eyes seemed to sizzle through both of them.

"Daniel, stop!" she hissed. She jerked free of him and ran.

But tonight, there was nowhere for her to run. He followed her.

She stopped and found a vase and tossed it his way. He ducked again, and the vase crashed against a wall. She tore through the parlor, looking for more missiles. A shoe came flying his way, a book, a newspaper. Nothing halted his stride.

She reached the stairs, and he was there behind her.

She started to race up them and realized her mistake. He was behind her. She reached the landing.

He caught her by her hair. He thought that she cried out, but he didn't care. All that mattered was having her.

He swept her into his arms and strode the last few steps to the bedroom, the bedroom where she had lured him once before.

"Let's finish what we started, shall we, angel?"

"Let me go!" Callie demanded. Her fists were flying; she struggled wildly.

"Let you go?" He heard the lethal roar of his own voice, and it might have belonged to someone else. He'd never let her go. Not now. His words tumbled from his lips. "Once I tried to walk away. To honor both North and South, and everything that we both held sacred. But you raced after me, angel. You could not bear to have me leave. You wanted me here. Remember, Mrs. Michaelson. Here."

He strode to the bed, and tossed her heedlessly upon it. She rose up on her elbows instantly, head proud, chin high, and watched him.

"Don't!" she commanded. "Don't even think—"

He straddled over her. Her eyes widened. He glowered at her.

Her hand connected with his cheek, but he stripped off his mustard gauntlets to catch her wrists when she struggled against him.

"Just what am I thinking, Callie?" he demanded.

He heard her teeth grinding. Felt the defiant flame of her gaze as it met his.

"I don't know. What are you thinking?"

"Ah, if the Yanks but had you in the field!" he murmured. "Maybe you are recalling the last time we met. It was right here. I'll never forget, because I loved this room from the first time I saw it. I loved the dark wood of the furniture, and the soft white of the curtains and the bed. And I loved the way that you looked here. I'll never forget your hair. It was like a sunset spread across the pillow. Sweet and fragrant, and so enticing. Newly washed, like silk. I can't forget your eyes. I can go on, Callie. There's so much that I never forgot. I remembered you in camp, and I remembered you every moment that I planned and plotted an escape. I thought of your mouth, Callie. It's a beautiful mouth. I thought of the way that you kissed me. I thought of your lovely neck, and the beauty of your breasts. I thought of the feel of your flesh, and the movement of your hips. Over and over and over again. I remembered wanting you like I'd never wanted anything or anyone before in my life. Of feeling more alive than ever before just because I breathed in the scent of you as I lay against your breast. And when you touched me, I think I came closer to believing I had died and gone to heaven than I've ever done upon a battlefield. Damn you! I was in love with you. In the midst of chaos, I was at peace. I believed in you, and dear God, when I lay here with you, I even believed in life again. What a fool I was!"

"Daniel—"

"No! Don't! Don't tell me anything. Don't give me any protestations of innocence. I'll tell you what I've thought over all these months. I've thought that you were a spy, and that you deserved the fate of a spy. I thought about choking the life out of you." He released her wrists. His knuckles moved slowly up and down the column of her throat. She didn't move. Those silver-gray eyes met his. Wide. Luminous. Beautiful still. Haunting him. The eyes of an angel.

"But I could never do it," he said quietly. "I could never wind my fingers around that long white neck. I could never do anything to mar that beauty. Then I thought that you should be hanged, or that you should be shot. Through long dark nights, Callie, I thought about all of these things. But do you know what I thought about most of all?"

She was so still. He moved more closely against her.

"What?" she whispered.

"I thought about being here with you. I thought about this bed. I thought about your naked flesh, and I thought about your smile when it seemed that you poured yourself upon me, heart, soul, and body. I thought about the way that your eyes could turn silver. I thought that all I wanted was to be back here."

He had to touch her. He had to finish what they had started.

"I wondered what it would be like to have you when I hated you every bit as much as I had once loved you."

She moved swiftly. Her eyes grew instantly dark, and she swung at him with a wild fury, but he caught her hand. She lashed out at him with venom in her voice. "Hate me, then, you fool! Give me no chance, no leave, no grace, no mercy—"

"Were I to give you more mercy, I might as well shoot myself, madam!" he swore.

"You self-righteous bastard! Hate me and I will despise you. You were the enemy! You are the enemy! This is Union soil! God damn you for expecting more from me!"

She was so furious, the force of her anger was great enough to dislodge herself. But not for long. He hadn't known what he would do. Now he did.

He had wanted some proof of innocence. He had wanted her to plead, to profess her innocence. He had wanted to believe in her.

God damn you, he raged inwardly. He caught her hard, and dragged her back down. He used the length of himself to subdue her when she fought and struggled wildly. He felt the fluid movement of her body, and he wanted her with an ever greater hunger. She was so warm against him. He felt her heart and her breath. Felt the curve of her hip, the length of her thigh. Even the curve of her breast. Her body seemed etched against his. He could feel all of her heat, and against the growing swell of his desire, he could feel the subtle movement at the juncture of her thighs.

In all the heat and tempest there was the pulse of something beside her anger. She wanted him.

"Here we are, Callie. You'll not leave me tonight. And you'll not betray me."

"And you'll not have me!"

But he would. He'd be damned if he'd be a gentleman. He would have her. Now. And in any way.

"I will."

"It would be—rape!" she spat out.

"I doubt it."

"Oh, you flatter yourself!"

"I've waited long and cold and furious nights, Callie. I will have you."

"You won't! You won't hurt me, you won't force me. You won't, because you promised! You won't, because of who you are. I know it, I know you—"

She didn't know him. Not anymore. He didn't know himself.

"Damn you, Callie! You don't know me. You never knew me!"

His lips descended upon hers. With hunger, with passion. With all the longing that had tormented him through the never-ending months. He kissed her with a startling violence, demanding, parting her lips and tasting their sweetness, marveling at the feel of his tongue upon them.

She fought him. Fought his touch; fought the invasion. Fought the sweep of his tongue, the taunt and the fury of it. And then, somewhere within this fury she ceased to fight.

His kiss gentled. His fingers moved upon her. Ached

to touch her. She seemed to give. She trembled beneath him.

"Callie!" he whispered her name. Her gaze touched his. Did she plead for mercy still? Did she seek only to be freed? Was she, ever and always, the ultimate actress? Did she spy for the Yanks, had she done more for her cause than just her capture of him?

"Damn, I'll not let you sway me!" he roared. His fingers bit into her arms. Nothing would stop him, nothing, he swore.

But something did.

A loud, fierce cry suddenly tore through the air between them.

A baby's cry.

He sat back. "What in God's name . . . ?"

"It's—it's Jared." She slipped from beneath him, and he let her go. He stared at her, amazed.

"That's a baby."

"Yes! It's a baby!" She leapt from the bed and disappeared into the hallway.

He followed her down the hall. He watched her pick up the tiny bundle of an infant. Hers. He knew immediately that it was hers.

If the child was hers, who knew how many men she had betrayed. There was the Yankee captain who had taken him, once Callie had disarmed him. How many others, friends, enemies?

He strode across the room.

She hugged the child to her breast, staring at him with the first real fear in her eyes.

He reached for the child. "Give him to me, Callie."

She wanted to fight him; he could see it in her eyes. But she wouldn't hurt the baby. She released him.

Daniel watched with amazement as the baby squalled, little fists and feet flying. He was beautiful. He was amazing. He was perfect in every way. And loud. His screams defied any Rebel yell that Daniel had ever heard.

He was beautiful, perfect, sound. Something welled up inside of Daniel. The fiercest urge he had ever known to protect someone. It was warm. It was all powerful. He looked into the little face. The face of his son. I love you, he thought, amazed at his own emotion. We've never met, until this moment. You are incredible.

And indisputably, my boy, you are a Cameron.

Daniel stared at Callie. Did she intend to deny it? She'd certainly made no effort to tell him about the child. Had she done so, she would have learned that he had been out of prison for a long, long time.

"It's my baby!" he exclaimed harshly.

She didn't answer him. Damn her. She would do so. He turned and started out the doorway.

"Daniel!"

She caught up with him at the foot of the stairway. For once, she was learning how to plead. She was desperate. Tears touched her eyes, making them sparkle an incredible silver. "What are you doing? Give him to me! Daniel, he's crying because he's hungry. You can't take him from me! Daniel, please! What do you think you're doing?"

"He's my son."

"You can't begin to know that—"

"The hell I can't. What a fool you are to try to deny it."

"Daniel, give him back!"

"He doesn't belong here. He belongs at Cameron Hall."

He'd never seen her so stunned. She must have just realized how deeply he felt.

"You can't take him! He's barely two months old. You can't care for him. Daniel, please!" Tears sprang to her eyes. She caught hold of his elbow and held on hard. "Daniel, he needs me. He's crying because he's hungry. You have to give him back to me."

A slow smile curved his mouth despite the baby's hungry screaming. "You didn't even intend to tell me about him, did you, Callie?"

She shook her head fiercely. "Yes, I intended to tell you!"

She was lying. She was still beautiful, and he was still in love with her. No, in hate with her. He didn't know which.

"When the hell did you intend to tell me?" he bellowed.

"You didn't give me a chance. You came in here condemning me—"

"You knew that I'd come back. Maybe you didn't," he corrected himself bitterly. "Maybe you thought that I'd rot and die in that camp!"

"Damn you, Daniel, you can't kidnap my son!"

"My son. And he'll have my name," Daniel said. He realized then that he did intend to take the baby. With or without Callie.

Or maybe he was taking the baby because by doing so, he would take Callie too.

"You can't care for him!" she cried out.

But he could. And he was determined to do so. No, he couldn't be a mother to his son. But Jared was coming to Cameron Hall.

He stopped and turned back with a smile. "Oh, but I can, Callie. I can find a mammy to care for him easily enough. Within the hour."

"You wouldn't!" she breathed.

"He's a Cameron, Callie, and he's going south tonight."

"You can't take him away from me! He's mine!"

"And mine. Created under very bitter circumstances. He's coming home, and that's that."

"This is his home!"

"No, his home is south, upon the James."

"I'll call the law!" she threatened.

"There is no law anymore, Callie. Just war."

She was following him as he strode for the door. Did she know that he was waiting for her? Waiting to see what she would do next, when she would swallow her pride, when she would plead to come with him?

Was this the great cruelty, the revenge he had imagined so many dark nights?

If so, it was not sweet, as revenge should have been.

"No! You cannot take him from me!" she thundered, and she slammed against him, beating her fists against his back.

He spun on her, blue eyes fierce, ruthlessly cold.

"Then you'd best be prepared to travel south, too, Callie. Because that's where he's going!"

She stepped back, stunned once again.

"What?"

"My son is going south. If you want to be with him, you can prepare to ride with me. I'll give you ten minutes to decide. Then we're moving. Who knows, Meade just may decide to chase Lee's army this time, though it seems poor Uncle Abe can't find himself a general to come after Lee. But I'm not waiting. So if you're coming, get ready."

She didn't answer him, but he knew that she believed him—knew that she had only one choice, and it was a simple one. Her lips were trembling.

She reached out her arms to him. "Daniel, give me the baby. Just let me feed him." Her voice rose to a cry. "Please!"

He placed the baby in her arms.

"Ten minutes, Callie," he warned her. "I'll be waiting on this step. For Jared, and you, if you choose to come. But Jared is coming with me."

"But we're enemies!"

"Bitter enemies," he agreed politely.

"I could betray you again, moving through this territory."

She was still threatening him, he thought with amazement. Daring him. Defying him. But he wouldn't be taken in by her again. Ever.

"You'll never have the chance again," he promised her.

She stared at him, her eyes a tempest of her inner conflict. She turned and fled up the steps with Jared.

He watched her go.

He looked down at his hands. They were trembling. In all this horror and bloodshed, here was something incredibly fine and good, a child. His. Callie had betrayed him, and he had lived with the rage and the bitterness building within him for nearly a year.

While she had lived with Jared.

It was astonishing how deeply he felt about this tiny babe. He hadn't even known that the boy existed and now he loved him. Instantly. Completely. He was more important than anything in the world.

Daniel leaned back wearily, and his gaze followed the path that Callie had taken up the stairs.

He loved him. Jared. He loved him with the same deep passion with which he hated his infant's mother.

Hated, loved, which was it? He wasn't sure that he knew himself.

Perhaps he would discover the truth soon enough.

It might be a long, long ride back home. A very long ride for a Yank and a Rebel. And the child born of the tempest between the two.

3

Bittersweet Revenge

Eighteen

When Callie made her final decision and came down the stairway, she found Daniel sitting in the parlor. His arms were spread out over the back of the settee and his booted feet were stretched out before him, resting on the fine cherry-wood occasional table. He appeared entirely relaxed. Rudely so. She was certain that he would never sit so in his own parlor.

She was equally certain that his posture was a definite statement of his opinion of her.

But then again, maybe it was just a bone-deep exhaustion brought on by the war. Yet his eyes were on her like those of a hawk.

"You've been far more than ten minutes, Mrs. Michaelson," he informed her.

"And you're still here, Colonel," she commented in return.

"I told you that I wasn't leaving my son," he said flatly.

"Yes, well your son needed things for the journey," Callie informed him coolly. She wondered why her stomach was winding into such vicious knots. How could she wonder? Daniel was back.

She was suddenly aware that she was still very much in love with him. No matter how condemning his eyes, or how furious she was with him. He was back, and he was in her parlor. The same man who had ridden into her life before, in the same gray uniform. A uniform the worse for wear, ragged, frayed, and even torn in spots. A wealth of unbidden tears threatened to spill from her eyes. She clamped down hard on her jaw.

But no matter how ragged or worn the uniform, the man within it was Daniel. And nothing could change the fact that he wore it well, that he was strikingly handsome in his cockaded and plumed hat, and that when he stood, he was tall and regal in the uniform.

Regal—and menacing, she decided. Against her will, Callie took a step back. He had been an extraordinary lover. Now he would prove to be an exceptional foe, she was certain. He would never believe that she had really been innocent of betrayal. She had no proof to give him. The only proof could come from his heart, and that heart was sealed hard against her.

He stood and walked toward her. She backed away again, warily. She couldn't let him touch her. If he wanted to wage war, well, war it would be.

He smiled, aware that she had backed away from him. She couldn't begin to read what lay in his mind. He ceased to move and contemplated her as if she were a stranger he had been sent to escort south.

"I reckon then, Mrs. Michaelson, that you are accompanying me?"

"I reckon, Colonel, that you've given me no choice," she replied politely.

"There are always choices, Mrs. Michaelson."

"Well, I choose for you to ride on, Colonel, but it doesn't appear to me that you are going to do so."

"Not alone."

"Then it seems that I have no choice. But I wonder, Colonel, if you know quite what you're taking on?" she asked, raising her chin.

His challenging smile deepened. "Mrs. Michaelson, I

regret to inform you that I am well acquainted with infants."

"Really? Well then, you must understand the collection of clothing and diapers that are necessary! And I'm ever so delighted that I shall have help along the way!"

"Where's the baby?" he asked her.

She hesitated. "Sleeping. I set him in his bed so that I could collect his things." Something was at war within her. She was so sorry for his appearance. He looked so exhausted. His handsome features were gaunt and strained. He was thin. The battle he had left had gone so badly for the Rebels. She'd been hearing the tales of it all day from the soldiers in retreat. She wanted to hate him. She wanted to be mad enough to scratch his eyes out.

She also wanted to hold him in her arms, to smooth away the lines of care that haunted his eyes. She wanted to scrub away the dust and grime of battle from his back.

"Daniel, everything has been taken by one army or the other, but I've still some soup left in the cellar. If you want to rest a night I could clean your uniform and you could take a long bath—"

"And you could seduce me and the Yanks could come and take me again. No thanks," he informed her icily.

She felt her back stiffen just as if a rod of steel had been set in it.

"Fine! Go hungry. Go dirty. Be miserable! I never seduced you."

"You did."

"I had no choice."

"Poor Callie. You never seem to have choices. How is Captain Dabney, by the way?"

"I certainly don't know," Callie said.

"Really?" He arched a brow. "I thought you knew one another very well."

Callie took two steps toward him and struck out as quickly as she could. He caught her hand—but not before it connected with his cheek, bringing with it a sharp, startling sound.

Once he had her hand, he pulled her against him, hard. His gaze glittered as it touched hers. "Watch it, Callie. The war has taught me lots of nasty habits. When I'm attacked, I attack back."

He was so hot. Like a fire. And so furious. So many emotions seemed to churn in the searing blue force of his eyes. She wanted to cry out. She could not. She had to keep the battle waging, for it was better than surrender.

"When *I'm* attacked, Colonel, I attack back."

"I asked you a question."

She shook her head vehemently. "No, you haven't asked me a question! You've cast accusations at me, and I find them offensive."

"I found what happened to me here offensive."

"I'm sorry for that. But you don't believe me, so there's nothing more I can say."

"Yes, there is. I've asked you about Dabney. How is he? Is he still roaming the area? Has he ever managed to bring his company into a real battle?"

"I did answer your question! I don't know!" His grip was tight around her wrist, and she was still held close against him. The warmth, the vibrancy of his body seemed to wrap around her own. She needed to break free from him.

She jerked hard on her wrist, backing away once again. "I don't know! I haven't seen him."

He turned away from her. "I want to leave, Callie. Now. Shall I get the baby?"

She felt the blood rushing from her face. She had

known that he meant it. Then why did she feel so frightened now?

Because he was taking her away, and this was home, despite the enemies who had trampled over her land. She didn't know exactly where he was taking her, or how she would manage once he brought her there.

He wanted the baby. He didn't want her. And they were going south. She had brought up the law. Surely no judge would allow a soldier to take a child from its mother. But she didn't know for sure. Perhaps Daniel would take her to a place where the Camerons owned the judges, where her child could be taken from her.

She clenched her fists hard at her sides and took a step back from Daniel, lifting her chin, praying that her voice would not waver.

"I won't leave him, Daniel. I don't know your intentions, but I won't leave my son. I don't care what you try to do."

He stared at her, perplexed, as if she had suddenly lost her senses.

"If you were intending to leave him, Callie, I don't imagine that you'd come with me now."

"No! I didn't mean that. I mean that you—you won't be able to get rid of me."

"Oh, Mrs. Michaelson, I didn't intend to get rid of you," he said, and something about the depths of his voice sent shivers racing along her spine. "I think it's much safer to know exactly where you are at all times. I spent time in a northern prison," he said softly. "Perhaps you're about to spend time in southern incarceration."

She kept her chin high. "Just so long as . . ." Still, her voice broke.

"As what?"

"You don't intend to—force me away from him."

Her voice was a whisper. Soft and desperate on the air. Maybe it touched something within him at last.

"I said that I was taking him home. I told you that you had ten minutes to decide. What are you talking about now?"

She lowered her eyes. "You're taking him to your home, Daniel. This is my home. His home."

He was silent and she raised her head at last. He studied her intently.

"His home is Cameron Hall, Callie. He will be welcome there."

"And what about me? I won't be welcome. Will I even be abided?"

"No one has ever been made to feel unwelcome in my family's house."

"Right. I'm sure your slaves were always welcome."

"I don't own any more slaves, Callie. But if you're interested in your own private shack, it's a very big plantation."

"You're going to put me in a shack—"

"I said you were welcome to one if you want one!" Daniel barked back.

"But what do you intend for me?"

"How prim, how sweet, how innocent!" he responded.

"It's a legitimate question!"

"What do you intend, Callie?" he demanded harshly.

"You are impossible!" she gasped, her fingers curling into the cotton of her skirts.

"No, Callie, I'm not impossible. But I'll never, never be taken in by you again!"

"Taken in! You needn't worry, Colonel Cameron. You'll never touch me again, I swear it!"

"It's far safer to touch a rattler."

"Then how will we live, what will we do?" she demanded.

"What are you talking about?"

She was going to falter soon, she knew. "This is foolish, what we're planning—"

"We aren't planning anything," Daniel said flatly. "I'm taking Jared to Virginia. You're coming with us."

"But we live in a certain society. North or South."

"Society will wait, madam. At the moment, I'm wondering if we'll survive this trip, if I won't waken to find the Yanks at my throat, if I haven't taken a sweet viper to my breast once again."

Scarlet flamed across her cheeks and she felt the simmering growth of fury deep within her. "Sir, I would rather travel with an entire band of Apache Indians!"

"Pity the Indians!"

"Daniel, damn you! How will we live? How can we do this? Are you thinking of this child at all that you're so determined to have—"

"Jesu, enough questions, Callie! I don't intend anything right now. Except to get Jared home!"

"Daniel, don't speak in circles!"

"What do you want from me, Callie? I was chained like an animal because of you!"

"And I have been ostracized because of you! What do you think? That this has been easy? My husband, a good Union soldier lies dead in my yard. When I should have still been clad in black, I was carrying a Rebel's child! Don't you see? You've no right to him at all—"

"I have every right!"

"You don't!"

"Well, I'm taking him."

"How can you just—"

"Callie, I am much bigger and much stronger than you are, that's how. Now, shall I get the baby?"

He didn't wait for an answer. He stared at her for a moment, then started for the stairs.

She raced after him. She was afraid to let him have Jared until they were well under way. "I'll get Jared.

I've packed Pa's old saddlebags with his things. If you'll get them . . ."

She let the words trail away, and she hurried up the stairs past Daniel. She hurried into the baby's room, swept him gently up into her arms, and swirled around. Daniel was behind her. As she had asked, he picked up the saddlebags and threw them over his shoulder.

Oh, how she hated him at this moment! And still . . . She looked at him. He was so tired, so worn. Like a lean, hungry wolf. For a moment she forgot the passion of her hatred and her anger.

"You really should eat something—" she began.

"Not on your life. Let's go."

"Fine. Starve. Don't expect me to be nice to you again."

"The last time you were nice I wound up in chains."

"What you belong in," she informed him evenly, "is a muzzle, Colonel."

She turned around, head high, and started down the stairs. He came behind her.

She walked through her parlor with her shoulders straight. Tears threatened to spill from her eyes again. She was going to walk away from her home. A home she had kept so long and so industriously, waiting for the day when her brothers would come home.

She stepped out on the porch. She didn't look back. She didn't dare. She would see in her mind the warmth and comfort of the parlor, the settee where Daniel had awaited her. She would see the little marble side table with the paintings of her parents, and of Jeremy and Joshua and Josiah. She had never left it before, except for short trips to Washington. Even when she had married, they had come back to this house because there had been more room for them here.

It was where her family lay buried.

She stood on the porch, feeling the slight breeze of

the night stir by her. To her surprise, Daniel carefully locked the door behind them. She smiled.

"What?" he demanded.

"Two armies have come and taken what they want. The windows have been shelled, and there are still cannonballs in the wall. Yet you lock the door."

"Yes." He walked by her, approaching his gaunt horse, a tall roan that waited by the well. He turned back. "Have you any animals? If so, we need to leave them somewhere, though certainly with all these soldiers coming near, anything that walks on four legs will quickly become a meal."

"I've no animals left. Your soldiers have already come through."

"Then let's go."

He strode across the yard to where his roan horse waited. He turned back to her. "Let's go," he repeated, looking at her before tossing the saddlebags over the roan's haunches.

It had grown very late. Despite the heat in the summer days, the night had grown cool, perhaps because of the rain that had made mud of so many of the roads.

In the darkness, near and far, they could see the light of camp fires.

Yanks and Rebs were camped all around them.

Callie swallowed hard. The going would be rough.

"Do you really want to ride out tonight?" she whispered.

"This minute," he informed her.

Reluctantly, she stepped forward. Before she reached the roan horse he turned. His hands spanned across her waist as he lifted her and Jared, setting them both up atop his mount. With an easy swing he was up behind her, and a moment later, he was urging the horse on, into the night, into the darkness.

She was aware of him as she had never been aware before. Aware of the rough wool of his uniform coat, of the heat and movement and muscle play of his body beneath it. His arms were around her, and around their sleeping child as they started off at a slow walk.

Callie wondered if the roan could take more than such a slow pace.

"There are troops camped all over," Callie said softly.

"I know."

"You're worried about my bringing the Yankees down upon you—"

"I know that there are Yankees out there," he said lightly. "It's when I don't expect to find them that they're so dangerous."

He was silent for a second, and she winced when he continued.

"I didn't expect to find them in your bed."

"They weren't in my bed."

"Damned close."

She bit her lip, determined not to make an effort to explain things to a man who would not listen.

The baby began to whimper. She cradled him more tightly against her, and he fell silent once again. She was tempted to try to turn around, to look back.

The sight of the farmhouse would be fading away.

"Oh!" she exclaimed suddenly.

"What?"

"There is something that I need to do. Could we stop—"

She felt his arms stiffen instantly. He would always be suspicious of her, she thought.

"Rudy and Helga Weiss. They'll worry when they find that I'm gone. They might look for me. At a hardship to themselves. Please. Their place is not far off the road."

"And you want to stop? You've become good friends with the Dunkards?"

"The Dunkards became my friends," she said softly. She didn't add that they had done so when no one else seemed to care if she lived or died. "I have to tell them that I'm leaving. There's no treachery involved, I swear it."

"I'll stop, and you may have five minutes to speak with them. I'll keep the baby."

"Helga delivered him for me—"

"I'll keep the baby. It's my last offer. Take it or leave it."

Damn him. She managed to keep her mouth closed, very aware that nothing could deter him when he spoke in that tone of voice. She pointed the way down the road to Rudy's small farmstead.

As he had said he would do, he stopped a certain distance from the house. He dismounted from the roan, and his hands circled around her waist once again. He lifted her down, but once her feet had touched the ground, he released her. The warmth of his touch was gone.

He took Jared from her arms. He did so easily, with no awkwardness. He didn't even waken his sleeping son.

"Say good-bye to them, Callie. Quickly. For all I know, you could be planning on having them send someone after us. I'm warning you. If I have to run, I'll run with Jared. And I'm good at getting where I want to go."

"I'm not warning anyone about anything," Callie said irritably. "I'm saying good-bye to people who were very good to me. And to your son."

She didn't wait for his reply, but hurried toward the small, simple house. She knocked quickly on the door. Rudy answered it, crying out when he saw her. "What's wrong? What has happened? Where is the baby? Are you all right, Frau Michaelson?"

"Yes, I'm fine, and the baby is just outside. I'm—I'm leaving the area for a while. I just came to say good-bye. And to thank you. Thank you so much for everything."

She could see past the plain entryway and into the house. It was barren of decoration in any form, and still it was warm. A fire crackled in the hearth, and simple wood furnishings were set around it. From the kitchen, Callie could see Helga hurrying out to greet her.

"Callie! Where's mein kinder?"

"Jared is just outside. I'm leaving for a while. I'm taking Jared south."

"South!" Helga exclaimed. "But there is so much danger in the South—"

"Helga!" Callie interrupted, smiling. "Twice we have been in the path of a battle here! I don't think that I can find a place with greater danger!" Impulsively she hugged the older woman. "I'll be all right, I promise. I just came to say good-bye, so that you wouldn't worry about me."

Helga hugged her warmly in return. "I will worry about you anyway, child. I will miss you."

"I will miss you, too, Helga. I thank you so very much for all that you have done for me."

"What we have done? Bah. We have all looked out after one another, yes?"

"You are going with the child's father?" Rudy said disapprovingly.

"Rudy! She must do what she feels is right. And surely, it will be right. God will see to it, soon enough. You go, and you take care of yourself." She smoothed her hand tenderly over Callie's cheek.

Rudy sighed. He still didn't like the fact that Callie was leaving. "I will look after the farm, Frau Michaelson. I will look after it carefully."

"Thank you. But you musn't make yourself too much more work."

"Work, what work?" He threw his hands into the air. "There are no animals left to work for!" He took her from his wife's arms, and hugged her warmly. Callie stood on her toes and kissed his cheek. "I'll come back," she promised. "When the war is over."

She turned and fled, amazed at how attached she had become to the elderly couple. It was worse than leaving her own home. She didn't dare take any more time, though. Daniel was waiting.

When she came back into the yard, Daniel was nowhere to be seen.

Fear stormed into her heart, stark and vivid. She swirled in the pale light that radiated from the Weiss home, looking feverishly about her.

He had warned her that he would take the baby. He had threatened to take the baby if she didn't return quickly enough.

No! Oh, God, no! This couldn't be his revenge!

"Daniel!" She shrieked his name, heedless of the sound, heedless of the night. Tears sprang to her eyes and she started to run in the darkness, tearing for the road. "No, oh no, oh no, Daniel!" Her breath came raggedly, desperately. She swirled around in the road again, unable to see him anywhere.

"Daniel!"

She almost fell, doubling over with panic and pain.

She heard hoofbeats, and then the sound of his voice.

"I'm right here, Callie! Would you hush? You'll wake the dead Yanks nearby as well as the living ones!"

She straightened, and blinked away her tears. He had emerged from the side of the road, Jared in his arms, leading his horse. Jared, miraculously, still slept.

Callie rushed to Daniel's side and looked down at

her sleeping son. She itched to snatch him back from his father, but she refrained.

She felt Daniel's fingers on her cheek, and met his gaze, startled. There was a gentleness in his touch. Almost a reassurance.

"You really love him," he said softly.

"More than life," she agreed.

He handed the baby carefully back into her arms. She was silent as his hands slipped around her waist and he lifted her back onto the roan horse. Silently, and with perfect agility, he leapt up behind her. Once again, the lean horse bore them down the trail.

"You said your good-byes?" he asked her.

"Yes."

"And you won't look back?"

"I'm not looking back."

He fell silent. They plodded along.

The night was dark. There were few stars in the skies. It was cool, with the promise of rain, and then it seemed to become hot and muggy with the same promise.

They moved very slowly. Daniel stopped time and time again, listening.

Sometimes he reined in and paused, rising in his stirrups, looking around them. Callie didn't know what he saw. She could see nothing at all, except for the stygian darkness.

They rode on.

Callie grew tired. Jared's weight seemed to grow with each heavy plod of the horse's hooves. She felt her eyes closing, and she fought to keep them open.

She felt herself easing back against Daniel. She didn't want to do so. She wanted to ride with her back straight and her head high. She couldn't quite manage it. She leaned against the warm living strength of his chest, and the warmth and comfort there became more and more inviting. Her eyes began to close. She couldn't sleep, she warned herself. She might drop the baby.

No, Daniel would never let her drop the baby.

A curious sensation swept along her spine. She wasn't alone anymore. There were two of them concerned for Jared.

She blinked hard. She shouldn't sleep.

Daniel reined in. She tried very hard to open her eyes. The darkness remained.

"Where are we?" she whispered.

"We're still in Maryland, Mrs. Michaelson," he said softly. "We'll sleep here tonight."

She tried to open her eyes more widely. "Here? Where are we? We're nowhere."

He dismounted from the horse, and reached for her. "We're in the wilderness, my love. And this is where we shall sleep tonight."

He set her down upon the ground, then immediately turned and began to unbuckle the girth on the horse. "Go ahead and find a tree. Curl up."

Callie stared at him blankly. He turned around, the saddle in his hand, and laughed when he saw her forlorn face.

"Come here, Mrs. Michaelson."

He carried the saddle in his one hand, and with the other, he led her along. From nearby, she could hear the soft sounds of a bubbling brook. Daniel dropped the saddle by the base of an old oak tree. He released Callie and headed back to his horse, brought down the blanket and both his saddlebags and the ones Callie had brought, and led the horse to the side of the road where rich long grasses grew.

He tethered the horse loosely to a tree, and returned to Callie's side once again.

"We needed to leave my house quickly so that we could come and sleep here?" she said.

"There's a beautiful sky for a roof, grass for a bed,

sweet air to breathe," Daniel told her. "And there are no Yankees here. None to have to keep an eye on."

"You're wrong," she reminded him. "I'm a Yankee."

"Excuse me. There's only one Yankee here," he said. He touched her chin. "And I will keep my eye on her," he said, his voice husky.

She turned away from him. He tossed her a blanket and she did her best to stretch it out and maintain her hold on the baby. Daniel made an impatient sound and came and stretched it out for her.

She lay down, her back to him, easing Jared to her side. She stretched a protective arm around him, as if he could roll away in the darkness.

She felt her baby moving. Felt the subtle rise and fall of his little chest. Her fingers moved over the ink-dark hair. He still hadn't awakened. She touched his cheek. She felt the always overwhelming sense of love for him invade her.

She closed her eyes. She was so weary. It had been such a long night. They had ridden so far.

He had come back into her life.

She hated him. She loved him.

The darkness seemed to close in around her. She started to shiver, cuddling Jared even closer. Summer days were hot. It was amazing that night could be so cold.

Her shivers increased. She was shaking so violently that she started to fear she would wake the baby.

She started to rise, but suddenly there was warmth all around her.

Daniel was stretching out beside her. "Dammit, Callie, what is the matter?"

"I'm cold!" she cried softly.

He brought her back down with him, his arm around her, warm and secure.

His hand, so large and bronze and powerful, rested

protectively around her and on top of the blanket bundling their son.

Callie's shivers slowly ceased.

A smile curved her lips. She slept, as easily, as sweetly, as Jared.

Nineteen

The journey southward was long and tedious.

Despite the very late hour at which they had stopped, Daniel woke Callie early. Not long after she had finally fallen asleep, the baby had awakened, hungry, and so she had spent time up with him. She was very tired when Daniel woke her. She had a headache, her throat was dry, and her hair was in a wild tangle. She could barely struggle into a sitting position, bringing the baby up with her.

It didn't help any that Daniel laughed at her when she turned reproachful eyes his way.

"Up!" he commanded her. "If we get going now, I'll make coffee a little way down the road."

He reached for Jared, and Callie surrendered the baby to his father. To her surprise, the baby was awake. He wasn't crying—he watched both her and Daniel pensively.

"There's a creek right down there," Daniel advised her, inclining his head down the slope from the road. With his free hand, he helped her to her feet.

Callie searched through her set of saddlebags for her brush and toothbrush, both of which were showing sad signs of wear, but then again, in comparison to the supplies that Daniel carried, they seemed to be in exceptionally fine condition.

She bit into her lip, not wanting to look back at Daniel. She could too clearly remember the imprint of his body next to her own as they had slept. With the morning's light, she was once again reminded that no amount of wear or tear really seemed to tarnish her wayward cavalier. He had shaven before he had awakened her, scrubbed his hands and face, and doused his ink-dark hair. The hollows in his cheeks were deeper than she had remembered. More tiny lines were etched around his eyes. And still, she loved his face. More gaunt, it merely appeared more noble.

She walked down to the creek, branches catching at her skirt, wondering again how it was possible to hate and resent someone so very much and also love him all the while.

There was little she could do for her own appearance, but the cool water felt good, and she took the time to brush out her hair. When she reached the road once again, Daniel was ready to ride.

The morning passed silently. When she would have spoken, he shushed her. When the baby cried at last, Daniel urged her to quiet him quickly. Lee's entire army might be heading this way, but there might well be Yankee patrols following in its path. Skirmishing was sure to take place, and Daniel was determined to avoid either army.

Biting into her lower lip, she loosed the buttons on her bodice to feed the baby while they rode. She had promised herself that she would demand her privacy in all things. This decision was quickly falling apart. But Daniel seemed heedless even of her presence as she fed the baby. He merely grunted his approval when she whispered later that Jared slept once again.

He had promised her coffee, but she was certain that it was at the very least late afternoon when he reined in on the road and dismounted. He did so easily. When he lifted her down, she staggered and would have fallen with Jared if Daniel hadn't supported her. She was not accustomed to hour after hour in the saddle.

Her stomach was growling. She'd had soup the night before—Daniel, she was certain, had paused for nothing on his way to reach her. How could he go so long and so far on nothing?

The war, she thought. As always, these days, it seemed that the answer to any question was the same.

He had stopped where she could hear the nearby gurgle of a creek once again. When she could stand on her own he led the horse through the trees to reach it, and Callie followed behind with the baby. The water looked delicious and she quickly sat down beside it. Holding the baby close against her chest, she cupped one hand to scoop up the cool liquid.

She looked behind her to discover that Daniel had cleared a spot of ground on which to build a fire. Quickly and competently, he drew coffee and a tin pot from a saddlebag, took water from the brook, and set the coffee to brew.

"Are you hungry?" he asked Callie.

She nodded, aware that he had really forgotten that people usually ate three times a day, beginning with breakfast.

He dug further into the bag, and came out with a pair of heavy square biscuits. He handed her one. Hardtack, she thought. A soldier's staple. But even as she looked at the biscuit, a tiny worm crawled out from it. Then another, and another.

She swallowed hard, allowing the biscuit to fall.

"Sorry," he said huskily.

She shrugged. "I've seen worms before. Just not—just not so many," she finished. She handed him back the biscuit. "I'm really not that hungry."

He stared at the biscuit, then seemed suddenly furious. He tossed it away in a wide arc.

"Jesu! This is what we're reduced to!" He inhaled and exhaled raggedly. "It won't be like this at home. The river is teeming with fish. We've livestock in abundance. So many ducks you can hardly imagine them, and enough chickens for an army—"

He broke off, twisting his jaw. They both knew that if any army had been through the peninsula—even Daniel's own army—there was probably nothing left at Cameron Hall either.

Jared opened his wide blue eyes and smiled at his mother. He didn't seem to care about the food supply. He didn't need to care, not yet, Callie thought. But a few more days of nothing, and she might well fail in her efforts to feed him.

Daniel was watching the baby. Jared flailed out with his tiny hands and Daniel suddenly reached over. Little fingers curled around his larger one. Daniel smiled, much like his son. Callie felt a tug at her heart as she realized that Daniel had never decided to take the baby for revenge. He loved Jared. Maybe he couldn't love the baby the same way that she did. He hadn't borne him, hadn't held him from the very start. But he loved him, nonetheless.

"I think that the coffee's ready," Callie said.

His gaze met hers. Blue. Speculative. "So it is," he said. He went over to the pot, and a moment later he was back with a tin cup. Callie laid the baby in her lap, and took the cup from Daniel. The coffee was curiously good, or else it was simply delicious because it was a different taste from water, all that she had had. She sipped it, savoring it. She looked at Daniel, who was watching her.

"You're not having any?"

He shrugged. "A soldier's mess carries only one cup," he said.

She flushed, passing it back to him.

"There's plenty of coffee in the pot. Finish that."

She did so, then passed back the tin cup. He left her, poured himself a cup of coffee, drank it, then immediately began to put out the fire and return his belongings to his saddlebag. Callie watched him, then realized that he wanted to start riding again and roused herself. "I need to change the baby," she told him, and dug through her own belongings for one of the diapers she had made for Jared. Daniel had moved so quickly, and she tried to do the same. Finishing with the baby, she paused, but just briefly. She set him into Daniel's arms to hurry down to the creek to rinse out his old diaper. It could dry while they rode.

Daniel handed her back the baby, set her on the horse, and they were on their way once again. She realized that they were going very slowly, but as nightfall neared, they had reached the Potomac River.

Daniel halted, staring out over the river. She followed behind him. Despite the war, the view was still beautiful, the mountains rising high over the water and the valleys, the colors of summer so rich and green and blue.

But Daniel wasn't seeing the beauty of it.

"The Yanks must be holding Harpers Ferry again," he mused. "This bridge is out. The water is swollen from all the rain. We'll have to find somewhere else to ford the river."

Callie nodded, but shivered. When night came, so did a chill, despite the fact that it was summer.

"Cold?" he asked her.

"Yes."

"I can't build a fire. It could too easily be seen by night," he told her.

She nodded, understanding.

"You must be very hungry."

She shrugged. Hungry? She was famished.

"You must be hungry too."

He grinned. "I'm accustomed to hunger. I barely hear the growls or feel the claws anymore." He watched her in the fading light. "I can't light a fire by night. In the morning, we'll snare a rabbit or catch some fish. We'll—we'll rest a few hours."

Callie nodded and turned away from him. He passed her by, striding to the horse. "We'll sleep on the other side of the river, over there. There's a feeder creek for water," he told her.

Callie didn't answer. She followed along with him. Daniel left the road behind, leading the horse deep into the trees and down by the creek bed. Jared was starting to cry. She held back as Daniel led the horse onward to drink from the creek.

Finding a tall oak, Callie sat down before it, loosed the buttons of her bodice, and swept her shawl around herself and the baby as he nursed. She felt the familiar tug of his tiny mouth against her breast and closed her eyes, still so grateful for him. Nothing, no horror or war, no comment or fury from Daniel or anyone else, could change the fact that Jared was beautiful, a true gift from God.

The Lord did move in mysterious ways. Helga had assured her that it was so.

She opened her eyes and jumped. Daniel was back, standing before her. He was caught in shadow, and she could see nothing of his face. All she could see was his silhouette, the tall cavalier in his high black books, his frock coat a cape over broad shoulders, his sweeping plume jaunty against the night.

He watched her.

But then he turned away and spoke to her over his shoulder. "The blanket is laid out over here. Get some sleep so that we can rise early."

He walked away from her. Hungry, weary, and very sore, Callie decided that there was little else for her to do. She held the baby over her shoulder, waiting for little burps, and then she rose and walked over to the blanket.

Daniel was still standing there, looking out over the creek.

"What is it?"

"Someone is near," he said. He pointed in the darkness. Callie strained her eyes. She could see the flicker of a camp fire.

"Who—"

"I don't know. Fires don't wear colors," he told her. "Go to sleep. We're safe enough here for the night."

"But you—"

"Damn it, Callie, I'm staying up awhile. Take the baby and go to sleep."

She spun around and took the baby and laid down with him by the tree. But she didn't sleep. She lay there, awake and waiting.

Finally, when it seemed that hours had passed, she dozed off. She woke, time and again, shivering.

Then she slept soundly. She awoke again because Jared was beginning to fuss.

Daniel was with her at last. The warmth of his body had entered into hers, and that was why she had slept so easily.

She kept her back to him while she fed the baby. She kissed Jared's forehead, pleased that he had slipped back to sleep with his little mouth still moving.

She slipped back to sleep herself.

When she awoke in the morning, she was alone. She looked around and saw that Daniel had gathered the makings for a fire, but it seemed that he was waiting to build it.

Perhaps he was off finding something to eat.

She hoped so. The pain in her stomach was sharp and cruel now.

Jared made a gurgling sound, and she glanced at him, smiling as she laid him down on the blanket. She whispered silly words to him, rubbing his tiny nose with her own, watching his smile spread across his face. His arms and legs wiggled and flailed and she laughed. He started to stare at something above her and she realized that he was fascinated with the leaves on the trees. Smiling, she left him and hurried to the water. She was desperately thirsty.

She leaned down and buried her face in the cool creek. The water was cold in the early morning, but it was delicious. She raised her face, and opened her bodice to splash the cool water against her chest. She drenched her gown, but it didn't matter. The sun was going to rise hot and high, and it would dry her.

She reached into the water again, and then she paused.

She could hear movement across the creek.

Frozen, she watched as men began to move toward the river. There were at least ten of them, and all in Federal blue uniforms. Yankees. Her own side.

Her heart seemed to freeze.

She stood quickly, trying to back away from the creek in absolute silence.

She backed against something and almost screamed out loud. She felt hands on her shoulders, spinning her around.

Daniel was back. He held a finger to his lips. His eyes held all manner of warning.

"Don't scream, Callie."

"I wasn't going to scream!" she whispered back furiously. "I was going to warn you!"

She didn't know if he believed her or not. His eyes were cobalt and entirely enigmatic.

They heard voices carrying across the creek, and Daniel pressed on her shoulders, pulling her down low on her knees beside him.

"She can't have gone too far. The old man said that she was traveling with a baby. That will cost our Reb friend some mean time."

Callie's eyes widened with dismay and disbelief as she stared across the creek.

It was Eric Dabney again. He'd stripped off his uniform shirt and was in the creek in his blue breeches, underwear shirt, and suspenders, and he was talking to the man beside him.

"Lieutenant Colonel Dabney, sir!" a soldier called out from the bank. "There's the remains of a camp fire to our immediate east, sir!"

"Lieutenant Colonel," Daniel murmured bitterly into Callie's ear. "So he did receive a promotion out of me." He turned to Callie and stared at her. "And you," he added softly.

She wanted to shout at him, to strike him, to hurt him in some way.

It wasn't the time.

"I think there are about twenty of them," she warned him quietly.

"Yes, I reckon you're right," he agreed. He was still staring hard at her. "And you didn't know anything about them. Or him. And you didn't leave a message with the old folks, your Dunkard friends, when we left?"

Callie gaped at him, incredulous. Her jaw snapped shut with fury. "I could have screamed right now, you fool!" she hissed. "I could have brought every single one of them down upon you—"

"Except that I'm armed now, right, Callie?"

She wrenched free from his touch. To her amazement, he let her go. "You are incredible!" she stammered. "There are twenty of them. One of you."

"Those are the odds we Rebs always did pride ourselves on."

She shook her head furiously. She was so mad she wanted to spit.

She was also afraid. What was he planning on doing?

"Ten to one, Colonel. I've heard all the boasts. The Rebs always claim that one of them is worth ten Yanks. Not twenty." She grit her teeth, still staring at him incredulously. "Do you have a death wish, Cameron?" She demanded harshly.

He smiled, reached for her, and jerked her close to him so that they were hunched down on the creek bank on their knees. His eyes seemed to sear into hers like the heated steel of a sword. His arms were hot, the length of his body was hot, electric, tense, and poised for battle.

"And you're innocent this time, right, Callie? You really haven't seen this Eric Dabney in all this time. He just happened along here today?"

Callie grit her teeth. Obviously, Eric hadn't just "happened" by. He must have gone by the farm. And he must have found Rudy and Helga, and maybe Rudy had thought it in Callie's best interest to say something.

She tried to keep her chin high. "Innocent or guilty, I am condemned in your eyes," she said bitterly.

"You're so treacherous, Callie, and so beautiful," he said softly, and she was startled when he stroked her cheek. "Perhaps you could not be the one without the other."

"I had nothing to do with this!" she insisted.

His reply was a grunt; his eyes were on the Yankees across the creek.

"Would you stop it!" she hissed to him. "I could scream right now if I chose to do so."

Instantly, his eyes were back upon her. Speculative, sharp.

"If you would just trust me—"

"Never. Never again," he said flatly. A startled cry

nearly escaped her, for suddenly she found that his hand was clamped over her lips, only to be quickly replaced with his yellow uniform bandanna, tied tight around her mouth even as she struggled against him. Her eyes widened with alarm as she wondered if he had forgotten the baby, lying peacefully beneath the tree. She fought him like a wildcat then, but he ignored her eyes and the fire of her flailing fists. He even ignored the solid punch she managed against his chest, and the sounds of desperation that sounded too quietly in her throat. He twirled her around, lacing her wrists together behind her back with his uniform sash.

He jerked her back against him, his whisper stinging her ear. "Give me any trouble now, Callie, and I'll take the baby and the horse and ride. I'm damned good at riding. Alone—alone with Jared, that is—I can move like lightning."

She went dead still in his arms. Holding her, he dragged her backward with him from the creek until they were out of view of the Yanks. He brought her back until they were beneath the oak where Jared lay.

He slept. While the world rocked around him, the baby slept, his face as peaceful as that of an angel beneath the sunlight that flickered through the leaves of the trees.

Daniel set her beside him and rose, and she knew that he intended to leave her there.

She was suddenly very frightened.

She tried to make some sound to stop him. Fighting her fury and her fear, she stared at him with imploring eyes.

To her amazement, he paused. His fingers moved gently over her cheek. "Scream now and I really might throttle you," he warned.

He slipped the bandanna from her mouth.

"Daniel, you have to let me go!" she whispered. "What if Jared awakes? He'll cry out—"

"If his mother hasn't done so first."

"I won't. I swear it." She hesitated. "On his life, Daniel, I swear it."

He hesitated only a moment longer, then roughly turned her about. A second later she was free.

She had no chance to say anything else to him. By the time she twirled around, he was gone.

Nervously, she knelt beside the baby and looked past the brush and tall grasses to the opposite side of the creek.

Her hand flew to her mouth as she saw Daniel behind the Yankee troops. One by one, and with a silent agility and speed, he moved from Yankee horse to Yankee horse, freeing them all. The company of Yanks, involved with their thirst and their desire to douse themselves in the cool water, were making a fair amount of noise.

None of them noticed Daniel.

Callie's heart seemed to hammer against her chest. As he neared the end of the line of horses, Daniel held on to the reins of the last pair. Both were tall bays, and both looked healthy, and well fed. Far more so than the pathetic roan they had been riding.

He was coming back around for her with the fresh horses, she realized. She started to rise, but maintained a low position on the balls of her feet. She watched Daniel as he moved far to the rear of the Yankee soldiers, circling them widely. He was well down the creek before he crossed it once again, and then she lost sight of him.

She was still searching for him when she felt his hands on her shoulders. She nearly jumped, but his whisper quickly touched her ear. "Get the baby. I'll get our things."

She did as he told her, quickly scooping Jared into her arms and against her shoulder. She hurried after Daniel in time to see him throwing the saddlebags over the haunches of one of the Yankee mounts, a tall bay that glistened in the early morning sunlight.

"Here!" he called to her softly. She hurried over to him. His hands were on her waist and he lifted her quickly, setting her upon the first horse. She balanced the baby tightly against her chest as she reached for the reins. For a fleeting second his eyes touched hers. "I'll be right behind you," he warned.

She didn't answer him. He didn't deserve an answer.

A moment later, he was mounted himself on the second horse. The Yanks still hadn't noticed that their entire line of horses had been released. Some of their mounts wandered to the high grasses near them; some had ambled clean away.

"Go!" Daniel urged Callie.

It was just then that Jared chose to awake, letting out a lusty and hungry wail.

Callie's gaze met Daniel's once again. "Go!" he roared. Riding up behind her, he slapped her horse hard on the rump. The animal leapt forward, then began to race in a long, clean gallop. It was all that Callie could do to hold the baby and the reins. Foliage slapped her and tugged hard at her flesh and clothing and hair. She was blinded by the branches that tore at her, desperate to shield Jared from danger.

Even as she left the embankment behind, she realized that Daniel raced after her. Her horse, spurred on by the sounds of his behind it, raced on at a frantic pace. They reached the road, and a small bridge that crossed the creek farther down from the bend where they had spent the night.

Her horse tore over the bridge. Daniel followed. She heard him shouting "Woah!" and he reined in his horse.

She brought her own mount under control and turned it around. Daniel had paused on the bridge, she saw, because two of the Yankee soldiers had managed to capture their horses and come in pursuit of her and Daniel.

Daniel drew his sword from its scabbard. A Rebel cry, a sound so frightening it even brought chills to her spine, tore from his lips, and carried hauntingly on the air as he charged his enemies, his sword swinging.

He didn't need to slay either of them. The men were so unnerved by his charge that they backed their horses too close to the edge of the bridge. Callie watched as men and horses went plunging over it amidst the sounds of their own screams. The horses quickly staggered up; the men, drenched and demoralized, barely made it to their knees.

Daniel spun his mount about and started to race toward Callie. There was one more horseman coming up behind him.

"Daniel!"

She shouted his name in warning.

He twirled his mount around once again. The grace of his horsemanship was so fine and deadly that it held a rare and chilling beauty.

The Yankee coming his way reined in.

It was just a boy, Callie thought. He couldn't even really be eighteen, she was convinced.

He faced Daniel and Daniel's very lethal cavalry sword.

No! Callie cried out in her heart. No, please.

But if the boy came after Daniel, Daniel would have to slay him. To defend himself, and her, and Jared. She closed her eyes. She couldn't bear to see it. She didn't want to see Daniel slain, but neither did she want to see this boy fall beneath his steel.

"Stop, son!"

She was startled to hear Daniel's voice, and her eyes flew open. He was sitting still atop his new mount, staring at the boy.

"Come no further."

"Sir, you are my prisoner!" the young Yank said in a wavering voice.

"Sir, like hell I am!" Daniel replied. "Go back, boy, save your fool life!"

But the lad, quivering as he might be, drew his own sword and faced Daniel.

"Daniel, no!"

She didn't know she had intended to cry out until she did so. And then she was terribly afraid. Daniel didn't turn, but apparently he had heard her.

"Oh, the hell with this!" he muttered.

She watched in horror as he pulled out his Colt pistol with his left hand. The boy's eyes widened in fear; his face blanched.

Daniel shot at the bridge, his bullet lodging into the wood barely an inch from the Yank horse's hoof.

The horse screamed and reared, and the boy went catapulting from it.

"Ride!" Daniel commanded Callie.

She turned to do so, giving her horse free rein to gallop down the road. Daniel was behind her once again. Despite the pounding of her own horse's hooves, she could hear that he followed her.

And again, she knew when he paused.

She knew, once again, that they were being followed.

She reined in even as Daniel did. Closing in on them was Eric Dabney himself.

Eric's horse's reins lay idle over the saddle.

Eric held a rifle aimed their way. Callie wasn't at all certain which of them he intended to hit. Her heart thundered hard. He would kill one of them.

She heard the explosion of a shot and a scream ripped from her lips. But Daniel didn't fall, and neither did she. Jared shrieked, but she quickly ascertained that he had not been hit.

A shout of pain and fury reached her ears, and she

saw Eric Dabney fall from his horse to the ground. He rolled, and came to his knees gripping his arm.

Callie realized that Daniel had drawn his Colt once again, and that miraculously, he had beat Eric to the trigger.

"Bastard Rebel varmint!" Eric shouted in a rage. "You'll pay, Cameron! I swear, you'll pay for this!"

"Go!" Daniel commanded Callie, and once again, he gave her mount a firm slap upon its hindquarters. Her horse leapt into flight.

And this time, as Callie raced with the wind, no one followed.

No one except Daniel.

She was running with her enemy.

Twenty

After the incident by the creek Daniel drove them harder than ever. He was too smart a horseman to race the horses forever, but he didn't let up on a continuous movement. They paused only to water the horses once they had cooled down, and then they rode, relentlessly.

It was night before he allowed them to rest, and by then, Callie's stomach was truly grumbling. The day had been hot, and then it had rained, and then it had become hot again. She was exhausted from the hours in the saddle, worn ragged from the heat and the dampness.

When Daniel dismounted at last and came to set her on her feet, she nearly fell over. The look in his eyes, however, kept her standing.

"You—varmint!" she exploded. "You really think that I had Rudy Weiss send someone after us!"

He didn't answer her. He turned away and reached to take the saddlebags from his horse's haunches.

It was the wrong side of enough for Callie. Her limbs found new life. With Jared cradled strongly in one arm, she marched on Daniel and sent a fierce punch into his back with her free hand. It must have packed a certain wallop, for he spun on her with his eyes wide and his teeth clenched. "Bastard!" she hissed. "And you must think that I sat there and pinched my own baby to make him cry out when it appeared that the Yanks might not stop us! I enjoy a reckless gallop across the countryside with my infant in my arms! Arrgh!'' The sound escaped her, a cry, a growl, an emission of her deep-seated rage and resentment. She smashed her fist against his chest with the same fury.

"Stop it, Callie!" he cried in turn, catching her wrist, twisting it, pulling her against him. Her gaze met his, still in a rage. "Stop!"

"You stop!"

"Give me one good reason to trust you!"

She wrenched free of his hold, amazed that she could be so angry and feel the flash of tears burning in her eyes.

"One good reason? All right, Daniel, I'll give you the best. You should have trusted me, no matter what, because I loved you."

"Love is a word, Callie. One you know how to use well."

She inhaled sharply. "I was trying to save your life, you fool Reb!"

"By sending me to a Yankee prison camp?"

"You're not invincible, Daniel. They would have killed you."

He took a step toward her. There was a deep tension etched into his features. "Would that I could really believe that, Callie. Would that I could trust you."

The tears that had burned her eyes threatened to spill over. Maybe she had planted the seeds of doubt within his mind, but he still didn't believe her. Maybe he couldn't. Maybe the war had made him too mistrustful, too bitter.

But she had told him the truth, as simple as it was. And she wasn't risking placing her heart beneath his feet any longer.

She backed away from him, rubbing her chaffed

wrist. "Don't bother to put yourself out on my account, Colonel. You must be a bitter man, dragging me through enemy territory. Don't ever forget, Daniel, that I am a Yankee. I believe in our cause. If you must mistrust me, go ahead and do so. I've never lied to you about my loyalties."

He stared at her. In the night, she couldn't fathom the emotion in his eyes.

Perhaps there was none.

She spun on her heel, and walked away from him. Exhausted, heartsick, and bone weary, she sank down by a tree. Jared was fussy. She tried to feed him and crooned to him softly. She was so hungry herself perhaps she wasn't making decent milk for him anymore. She closed her eyes. Even the extent of her anger was fading. Everything was fading except for the pit of hunger at the bottom of her stomach.

She didn't realize that Daniel had left her until she began to smell something with an aroma so sweet and tantalizing that she thought she had to be dreaming. What a dream. She smelled something fresh-baked, like a pie crust. There was meat in it. Maybe even beef. It had that rich, wonderful scent of beef and gravy.

There was no beef to be had. Daniel hadn't caught and cooked anything because he didn't want to light a fire by night.

But oh, what a dream!

Her eyes flew open.

She wasn't dreaming. Daniel was hunched down before her with a fresh meat pie in his hands. Steam wafted above it, and it was the steam that brought the incredibly sweet and wonderful scent to her nose.

She stared at him, amazed.

He produced the fork from his mess kit, and handed it to her. She kept staring at him.

"Eat slowly, or you'll get sick," he warned her.

"But how—where—?"

"A farmhouse window, a good mile down the road. There were three of them. I only took one."

"You stole this?"

"I confiscated it."

"Stole it."

"Do you want to eat it or not?"

She did. She started to raise Jared to her shoulder, but Daniel reached for his son. The baby began to cry, but for once her hunger was stronger than her maternal instinct. It had been Daniel's idea to drag him through the countryside like this. And Daniel had claimed to be good with babies. He was welcome to be good now.

And he was. He walked away from her, gently rocking the baby on his shoulder, talking to him. Callie couldn't hear his words. She worried for just a second, and then she worried no more. She dived into the meat pie.

The first bite was heaven. The second bite was even sweeter still. She tried to warn herself to slow down, but the food was so good that she began to eat faster and faster. The food hit her empty stomach. Had she been standing, she would have swayed. She bit down hard, fighting a wave of nausea. Slowly, it passed. She looked down at the pie again. She had eaten more than half of it.

She waited a minute, assuring herself that she could stand, and that she wouldn't be sick. Then she rose, and walked the pie slowly over to Daniel.

She wanted to clobber him, but she felt compelled to apologize about the food. She did so, regally, trying to dredge up the best of her prewar manners.

"I'm so sorry. I believe that I've managed to consume a great deal more than my share."

There was the first light of humor in his eyes as they met hers.

"It's all right."

"It's not all right, sir! I had no—"

"Callie, you're feeding a baby. And we're not at a barn dance, or in someone's parlor. It's all right." He exchanged the baby for the pie, plucking the fork from her fingers. She had a feeling he would have lit into the pie with just his fingers if that meant saving some of the juices.

She would have done so herself.

He walked away from her, calling to her over his shoulder. "There's water, just down through the embankment over there. It's a creek, but it's running pretty deep, and there's plenty of rapids and falls along it. Be careful."

She nodded and turned away from him. She found a clean diaper for Jared and one of the few clean sacques she had along for him. She hurried down to the water.

It might be dangerous, she thought, but it was breathtaking. There was a moon out, and it was glittering down on the water that rushed over rocks, creating tiny falls. The creek ran straight to the river, she was sure, and it had some of the scope and power of the Potomac. The water seemed to dance in the moonlight, beautiful, magical.

She set Jared down on the soft shoulder, changed him and cleaned him, talking to him all the while. He smiled and gurgled in turn. She rinsed out his old clothing and diaper, and set them to dry on a rock. They probably wouldn't do so overnight, but in the morning they might.

She drank deeply, and splashed the water over her face and throat and arms. It felt so cool, so clean, after the long day. Days, she reminded herself. She had never felt so sweaty, so dirty. She glanced out over the creek, longing to dive right into it.

Some slight sound came from behind her. She swiveled around on her haunches.

Daniel was behind her. Leaning against a tree, he

watched her. She wondered just how long he had been there. He walked down to her and fell on his knees beside her. He swept off his hat, then buried his own face in the water. He rose with it falling from him in splatters and waves. He cupped his hands and drank deeply. Then he eyed her, speculatively. "Good night, Mrs. Michaelson," he said softly.

He rose and walked slowly up the shoulder. He didn't go very far. She saw that he had led the horses to a nearby tree and tethered them. He had set the blanket down under the shade of a heavy old oak. He stretched out on it, adjusting his hat over his face to cut out the moonlight.

Well, she wasn't going to curl up by him. Not tonight.

She picked up Jared. She whispered to him, playing for a while, and Jared smiled and cooed and played back. He became fussy, and Callie fed him, and in time, he fell asleep at her breast. She adjusted her bodice and turned at last. There was another large oak near Daniel. She could spread her shawl out there for the baby to sleep on.

She did so, curling up beside him. The ground felt very rough and gritty. And dirty.

It was supposed to be dirty, she reminded herself. It was dirt.

But she began to wonder what crawled in it, as she never did when she slept beside Daniel. When she heard the hoot of an owl, she bolted up, nearly dislodging Jared.

Daniel was up, too, instantly alert. He stared at Callie in the moonlight.

"What the hell are you doing?"

"Trying to sleep."

"Why are you over there?"

"Because I don't care to sleep that close to you!"

He arched a brow. "Oh, I see. Fickle. Eat my pie, but eschew my bed!"

He was laughing at her, she thought. She turned her back on him, stretching out to try to sleep again.

He sighed. "Get over here, Callie."

"I will not."

"Get over here."

"I will not sleep beside a bloody Reb who won't even trust me!"

"You've warned me that you're a Yank through and through. I don't dare trust you completely. Now, are you coming over here?"

"No, I'm not!"

He was on his feet, striding her way. She bolted warily to a sitting position. "Are you planning on apologizing?" she asked him.

"No!"

"Then I am not coming over!"

"Give in, Callie."

"I will not. You give in."

"Hell no! I don't give in. It's all we Rebs have got."

"Well then, sir, we are at a stalement, and no one wins!"

He paused, directly above her. She shrieked out as he reached down and plucked her up into his arms. His hold was tight. His eyes were fierce.

"No, Callie!" he corrected her as she stared at him, lips tight, body tense. "I win."

"Why the hell do you win?"

"Because I'm bigger. And stronger. And because you're going to sleep where I put you, that's why!"

He turned around, heading for the tree. "Daniel, don't you dare—Daniel, the baby!" she reminded him.

"I'm going back for him," he assured her, depositing her none too gently on the blanket beneath the tree that he had chosen. As he promised, he turned back for Jared.

A minute later her sleeping child was pressed back into her arms.

She kept her back stiff and hard to him all through the night.

Toward morning he awoke briefly, as she did, when Jared began to cry with hunger. Callie was very aware of him behind her, but she kept silent, her back stiff even then. She felt Daniel lie down beside her again.

She never went back to sleep after that point. She lay there for a long while, just watching as the first faint streaks of dawn began to peek softly through the leaves of the tree overhead. She closed her eyes, and she could hear the light chirping of the birds, and the soft rush of the water in the brook so near them. She opened her eyes again. The light that slowly began to flood around them seemed colored itself, pink and gold and orange and even crimson. It flickered gently, beautifully, over the trees, the earth, and the bubbling water. The earth smelled rich with the coming of the morning. From where Callie lay, it might have been a little stretch of Paradise, rather than a piece of border land, deeply divided between North and South.

For once, it was hard to think of the war. Callie sat up, watching how the light of dawn played over the water. The colors were truly glorious, dancing, playing on the foam that jumped and bubbled over the rocks.

She glanced at Jared. He slept soundly, his little mouth open, his tiny limbs splayed. She smiled. Her smile fading, she glanced at his father. Daniel, too, it seemed, slept peacefully.

Carefully, so as not to arouse either of them, she rose. She walked down to the creek bed. The water was so clean and enticing. And she was so dusty and sweaty and miserable.

She glanced back at the sleeping men in her life. She shed her shirt and bodice and her petticoat and pantalets. She shivered as the morning air hit her, clad only in her long chemise. She wanted to strip it away, too, but she didn't. She glanced at Daniel again nervously, but then she didn't care. The temptation to soak herself in the cool clean water was overwhelming.

She stepped into it. She nearly screamed as the cold first struck her, but she swallowed down the urge. She moved farther across the creek, grateful that it grew deeper, deep enough for her to sink into it to her waist, and filled enough with rock so that her toes didn't sink into squishy mud. She shivered violently at first, but as she came down into the water, her shivering ceased. It was beautiful. It seemed to cleanse away the days of riding, the mud and the dust.

She found a low, flat rock beneath a craggy rapid and sat upon it, delighting in the water that cascaded down upon her head and hair. She scrubbed her face with it, and rubbed it over her shoulders. She stretched out, allowing it to fall over her breasts and belly and thighs. She opened her mouth, and drank it, and she cupped it into her hands and sluiced it over her throat once again.

She looked to the embankment.

Jared still slept.

Daniel did not.

Barefoot and in his uniform breeches only, he was standing on the embankment. He had cast off his frock coat and shirt to bury his torso in the water, it seemed, but then he had seen her. He watched her now, the sun glistening over the bronze muscles of his shoulders and chest, and the lean ripple of flesh that led down to his belly.

His eyes met hers.

She had kept on the chemise for modesty's sake. How foolish. For it was sheer and pale, and it was plastered against her, and it hid nothing of her body. It accented it, she thought, clinging to every curve and angle. Puckering over her breasts. Molding tight to the triangle at her legs.

She needed to do something. To sink low into the water, to cover herself.

But as she watched him, she discovered that she couldn't move.

Daniel had no such problem.

His eyes held hers. With a slow stride, he started across the rushing creek. The water waltzed and danced and rushed around his gray pants legs. It shimmered in droplets on his shoulders and chest. He had grown lean, she thought vaguely. Lean, but hard, harder than ever. A pulse ticked against the cord of his throat, and muscles constricted and rippled as he moved.

Leave, she told herself. Push away from the rock, and leave. Walk by him. He will not stop you.

But she didn't leave. She stayed there, watching as he came. Feeling his eyes burn into her. He came close, closer still. The heat and power of his body became tangible.

And still, she didn't move.

He stood in front of her in his taut, soaked breeches. She raised her chin, to better look into his eyes. She moistened her lips with the tip of her tongue against the dryness that so suddenly and so fiercely plagued them.

He was watching her mouth. He was going to kiss her.

He did not.

He suddenly dropped to his knees in the shallow water, his hands bracing her hips. She should have moved. She should have cried out. She should have denounced him for the way that he condemned her.

She did nothing. She was electrified, caught in his hold, in the staggering heat of his body.

And in the kiss that finally touched her. Not her lips.

Her belly. Through the thin fabric of her chemise, she
felt his lips. Then felt the ragged, searing fire of his
tongue as it moved in a staggering path across the
plane of her stomach. Touching her navel, lowering to
tease and taunt in an ever closer pattern to the heat
and pulse that had now begun to throb between her
thighs.

Cry out, stop him! she warned herself. She opened
her mouth, but no words would come, only a choking,
breathless sound. He stood, rising before her. His
hands moved possessively over the length of her.
Touching her, warming her. His mouth, his lips, his
kiss, focused on her breasts. Closing over the fabric,
heedless of it, no, using it. The movement of cloth and
the heat and dampness of his mouth upon her nipple
were nearly more than she could bear. He tugged
gently, then suckled hard, drawing her into his mouth,
easing his hold, playing his tongue upon her again. He
must taste the baby's milk, she thought, her face flaming, but if so, then he was fascinated by it. For his
intimate touch moved over her breasts again and again.

At long last, his lips found hers. Found them, and
held them. Moved upon them frantically, demanding
more and more. His mouth parted hers, his tongue
delved deeply, plundered, and caressed once again.
She began to shake and shiver wildly, not from the cold
of the water, but from the heat of the man.

His mouth closed over her shoulder, his teeth nipped
lightly, his tongue bathed her. His kiss trailed down the
sodden valley of cloth between her breasts. He created
a line with his tongue. The line began to burn.

And to travel farther and farther down.

It seemed to lazily sear the length of her. Touching
her navel again. Forming a distinct trail beneath it.
Coming lower and lower and then finding the very
heart of the throbbing between her thighs. Touching
upon soft and intimate places with the fabric still be-

tween his mouth's caress and the tender and sensitive and secret regions of her flesh. Had fire been set to dry kindling, no sensation could have been more explosive. Sweet honeyed ripplings of pleasure burst through Callie, and she cast her head back, trying not to cry out with the sheer sensual pleasure that filled her, but emitting soft moans despite her best efforts.

And he kept on and on until she was shivering anew, filled to the bursting point, scarcely able to stand. Perhaps he knew his own power, for the very moment she would have fallen, he was up, scooping her into his arms, carrying her to the embankment. In seconds his breeches were shed, unleashing the ardency of his desire to spring to life before her. She closed her eyes, shivering, wanting him.

He lowered himself upon her. She was barely aware of the earth and sky and the rush of the water, and then again, she had never felt them so keenly. She felt her back, moving over the earth, she felt the hot touch of the sun, she felt the cooling sensation of the water.

She felt the hard burning entry of the man, felt a spasm of pain at first; she almost fought him. But his words were there, as silken and seductive as the movement of his fingers over her bare flesh. "It's the baby, Callie. You've had a baby. It will ease."

She bit into his shoulder, and he moved again. Slowly. Fully. Desire rushed through her again, easing away the pain. Within moments, it was gone.

Blessedly so, for his desire seemed even greater than the other hunger that had plagued them so. He was ever a considerate lover, then consideration fell away. He was the sun itself, burning with a fire not to be quenched. He moved like the impetus of the brook, cascading in a rush upon her. He was as rich, as full, as redolent as the earth around her. But most of all, he was storm, thundering against a windswept shore, and sweeping her into the ardent whirlwind of his deepest needs.

Even as she soared and seemed to slip into some netherland of near darkness, he shuddered violently against her, again, again, and again. She felt the ripple of muscle, the sweet expulsion from his body filling her own, and then slowly, the heat of his weight, descending upon hers. For long moments their breath mingled, their heartbeats thundered and finally slowed together. For long sweet moments she felt encapsulated by warmth, by intimacy, by tenderness.

He held her, his face wet and slick against her throat and breasts.

"Callie!"

She thought she heard his whisper and that something remained in it of the love they had once shared that seemed but a distant memory now. It seemed as if something might be salvaged, as if he might believe in her again.

He rolled from her, breaking the band of heat and the aftermath of tenderness. He lay with his arm cast over his forehead as he stared up at the sky.

Callie felt the cold breeze sweeping around her. His warmth was gone from her. And she realized that although he might be feeling a few doubts, he still didn't trust her. Maybe he wanted to.

But he hadn't really forgiven her. He had come to her because he had wanted her. He had come to her because of the deprivations of war. Just as a hungry man would dine on any meal.

Tears, as hot and vibrant as her passion had been, rushed to her eyes. She would never shed them before him, she swore swiftly. She twisted far from his touch and rose, rushing back into the water.

"Callie!"

He, too, was on his feet quickly, heedless of his lack

of dress. She ignored his call, sinking into the water, glad of the cold, grateful even for the discomfort.

"Callie, damn you!"

He caught her hands and wrenched her up. "What in God's name is the matter with you?"

"Nothing. Will you get away from me, please?"

"Why are you running from me?"

"I'm not running. I'm trying to bathe."

She saw him stiffen. Felt it in his fingers. "Trying to bathe away my touch?" he asked softly.

"You tell me," she replied, her tone as light, "Have you decided that I didn't warn the Yanks? That in that, at the very least, I am innocent?"

He didn't answer. She saw the shadows cover his eyes, the hard subtle twist of his jaw. "You're trying to tell me that you didn't bring me back to your house to be disarmed and taken by your friend, Captain Dabney?"

"Yes! I brought you back! I didn't want them to kill you. You don't want to understand—"

"No, you're wrong. I want desperately to understand. I'd like to understand, too, why Dabney reappeared," he said politely. Something was different. Maybe he did doubt himself. Maybe he was afraid to do so.

She stared at him, frustrated, furious, wishing that she could slap him—and then jump up and down on his fallen body. "Bastard!" She shoved against him so hard that he stumbled.

Trying to pull her drenched chemise down as she moved, she ignored him and started to stride from the water.

His hand fell upon her arm, swinging her back. "I've been the target for enough Yanks, Mrs. Michaelson. Don't push me any further."

"Push you!" she hissed. "Push you! I'd like to take a buggy whip to you!"

"Careful—" he warned, his eyes narrowing.

"Careful be damned! You despise me, you mistrust me, yet you're willing to drag me across the country. Your hatred seems to have little to do with your desires."

"Really, and what of yours?"

"I didn't accost you—"

"Accost?" he interrupted coolly. "I don't think that what I just did could be misconstrued in any way as an attack or an act of force."

Her cheeks flamed. "It surely was not my idea, you Rebel—rodent!"

"Rebel—rodent?" he repeated, just a shade of amusement touching his voice, bending his lips. The amusement vanished. His eyes were intense. "Sorry," he said softly, "I didn't hear the protests."

"Well, hear them now, Colonel Cameron. Stay away from me."

He stared at her, then reminded her quietly, "There was a time, Mrs. Michaelson, when you didn't seem to mind so very much. There was a time when you went out of your way to openly seduce a man. Today you were far more subtle."

"What?" Callie gasped.

He smiled, a casual, taunting smile. He would have tipped his hat, had he been wearing it. And still, not wearing anything at all, he managed a swaggering arrogance as he passed by her.

"Today you were a vision in white, Mrs. Michaelson. From the moment I awoke. White that lay like a second skin over your bare flesh."

"I needed to bathe!" she cried out indignantly.

He walked by her. The assumption was left that it had been her fault. That she had seduced him before, and tried to do so again now.

"Oh!" she screamed out her exasperation and fury. He didn't stop. She stooped down and grabbed some of the mud from the floor of the creek. She sent it flying across the creek to slap hard over his naked back.

It brought him to a standstill. He whipped around, and seeing the look on his face, Callie was ready to run again. She spun, but the creek bottom was slippery. She hadn't managed to take a single step before he catapulted his length against her, bringing them crashing back down into the water.

She struggled to free herself from his hold. He straddled over her, holding her tightly. Panting, she paused and found herself staring up into his eyes again. He was laughing, and suddenly she discovered that she was laughing too.

But then their laughter died away, and once again, a warmth swept through her, one always created by his touch. The cold shadows had slipped away from his eyes and his passion rode hot within them again.

"Tell me that you didn't want me, Callie!" he charged her heatedly.

"I did not set out to seduce you!" she cried. Dear Lord, what did he want from her? "Daniel, let me up, let me be! All right! I wanted you. But this can't happen anymore!"

"Why, Callie? If you're so damned innocent, why is it only all right when the Yanks are around?"

"Stop it!" she charged him. "That's exactly why it's so wrong."

His hold on her suddenly loosened. His fingers moved gently over a wet tendril of hair. "Help me?" he whispered suddenly. "I want to believe! Callie, you do seduce, so help me God, you seduce. You are beautiful. And what if you're telling the truth? I'm still a Rebel. You're a Yank. Not just by geography—by conviction, Callie, I . . ."

His voice trailed away. He started to speak again,

e suddenly interrupted by a loud and furi-

ᴊared.

Callie shoved at Daniel. "I have to get the baby."

He didn't move but stared hard at her. She shoved him again. "I'm begging you, leave me be!" she cried to him passionately. "Leave me be."

He rose, caught her hands, and jerked her to her feet. "If only we can leave one another be!"

She heard the baby's plaintive wail. And still they stared at one another.

She spun around, heedless of his meaning. She rushed back to the river bank to sweep her son into her arms.

If only they could leave one another be.

Twenty-one

Three days later, they managed to cross the Potomac. They were back in Virginia, but it was dangerous territory, and the going was rough. They could stumble upon more troops from either army at any given time.

It was difficult, for they both had little to say to one another. The tension grew between them as the long days and nights passed.

Finally, eight days but a true eternity since they had set out, they reached Fredericksburg. Callie could immediately see the change in Daniel when they reached the city, for it was held firmly in Confederate hands.

It was a beautiful old city, Callie thought. She knew that George Washington's family had lived here and kept property near the Rappahannock. Under better circumstances, she might have enjoyed the travel.

But war had come here and too many times. Many buildings were riddled with shot, and the people bore the haggard look of tenacious but weary fighters.

Callie hoped that they would stay, at least for a few days. She longed for a bath with steaming hot water and for a soft bed beneath her at night. But Daniel was determined to push on. He was able to buy some food, some bread and ham at exorbitant prices, and he procured a wagon so that Callie could ride awhile with the

g in back. But he was dead set on reaching
— nd then his home.

y passed by all the sentries and came into
Richmond, the Confederate capital, the heart of its existence.

Daniel was driving the wagon with the horses hitched to the rear when they first approached the city from a slight ridge. Callie looked down on it. It was large and sprawling with the beautiful capital buildings visible in the sunlight. She could even see the statuary before it. Handsome buildings and beautiful churches surrounded it. It was a busy place, with people moving at a hectic pace.

"Well, you are home," Callie said softly.

He glanced her way. "Not home, but close."

She bowed her head. She was so weary. She prayed he didn't intend to keep riding on tonight. Yet she was afraid to let him know just how exhausted she was. It hadn't seemed that she had slept, really slept, in an eternity. She and Daniel had taken to sleeping at a distance, and the ground—to which it seemed he had grown so accustomed—was hard and cold to her, sending chills into her body every night. And every night she lay awake, wanting the warmth he could give her, more furious with each passing day that she could still desire someone who taunted her so, condemned her so.

She loved him still. As much as she hated some of the things that he said and did, there were other things that reminded her why she had first fallen in love with him. When she watched him with Jared, she knew that he loved the child, that he was the best of fathers, that he would have been this caring with or without the war. He had tried very diligently to see to her welfare, managing to procure more and more food for them as they came closer and closer to Rebel territory. He would never take a portion of food first; he would never even take a sip of water first when they came to a stream. Her cavalier was tarnished and tattered, but underneath the fraying gray, the gentleman remained, no matter what the circumstances, no matter what his anger or his emotion.

Callie's only defense against Daniel were her pride and strength, and both were at a low ebb now.

She sat stiffly, determined that she would not break down and beg for anything at this late date. Perhaps she could make a casual suggestion.

"Have you friends to see in Richmond?" she asked him, feigning a yawn as she did so.

She felt the force of his blue gaze. "Yes, Reb friends, of course," he replied politely.

"People you need to see?"

He laughed softly. "You don't give a damn if I need to see anyone, Callie. You just want a bed for a night."

She gazed at him coolly. "Is that so bad?"

"Not if you come right out and ask for it," he told her. He clicked the reins over the horses' flanks and the wagon began to move more briskly. "Yes, Callie, I have friends here. And we'll stay for the night."

It wasn't quite that easy. By the time they moved into the city streets, Callie saw that they were filled with people hurrying along their way. There were lines in various places where people were trying to buy goods. Inflation was high; the Yankee blockade was doing its damage to the Confederacy with far more efficiency than any of the troops in the field.

A footless soldier in a ragged uniform limped by them on a pair of rude crutches and Daniel drew in the carriage, calling out to him, "Soldier, do you know of any rooms available?"

The man saluted sharply, then came toward Daniel. "Sir! I'm afraid I know of none." He glanced Callie's way. "How do you do, ma'am." To Daniel he said, "Bringing your wife and child into safety, eh, sir? Well,

I'm sure the army can see to something. And you, ma'am, you musn't worry. We won't let the Yankees into Richmond. Ever. We've fought 'em time and time again. Don't fret none."

Callie remained silent. Within another hour, though, Daniel was swearing softly. He'd tried every rooming house and hotel he knew, and all were filled to the hallways. Refugees naturally seemed to flock to Richmond. Once their farms were destroyed, they had to seek some kind of employment. As the war continued, their numbers were growing.

"We should have just ridden home," he muttered.

Callie, with Jared in her arms, stretched her aching back. "I thought that you had friends in the city," she said.

"I didn't think you would want to meet them," he returned.

Of course. His friends would know he didn't have a wife.

"Hell!" he muttered suddenly. "If we're going to go that route, we'll do it from the top."

"Daniel, what are you doing?" she demanded.

He refused to answer. Ten minutes later they were pulling up before a beautiful and gracious white house with a wide porch and huge white columns. There were horses and carriages all around, soldiers standing on duty, and a great deal of commotion.

"Daniel, where are we?" Callie demanded.

"At a friend's house," he said tersely. He caught her hand. "Come on."

"I can't go in there!" Callie said, tugging on her hand nervously. "I haven't bathed, it's been as hot as blazes, the baby's clothes are as filthy as my own. Daniel, let me go—"

But he didn't let her go, and his hold was fierce. Apparently he was well known here, for soldiers greeted him not just with salutes but with warm greetings as they hurried to the entry.

"Daniel, where are we?" Callie persisted.

"They call it the White House of the Confederacy."

"And—and Jeff Davis is your friend?" she nearly shrieked.

"Actually, I know Varina much better," he told her. She blanched. She wanted to hit him, she wanted to run.

"Let me go, Daniel."

"Not on your life."

"You're bringing a Yank to see Jeff Davis?"

"You said you wanted a bed. Varina will find one for me."

"You'd better let me go! I could do horrible things in there, Daniel. I could start singing the 'Battle Hymn of the Republic.' I could—"

"Open your mouth just once at the wrong time, Callie, and you'll be singing it hog-tied in the wagon!" he warned her.

The door opened. A handsome black butler stood there, his face split into a grin. "Why, Colonel Cameron." His smile faded slightly, and his voice dropped to a whisper. "Colonel, I'm mighty pleased to see you alive, sir. We heard all about that battle in that Gettysburg place, sir, yes we did. It's taken a hard toll on my folks in there, what with Vicksburg falling on the Fourth of July, just like a plum into the hands of them Yanks. But you come on in now, ye hear. Lawdy, yes, Colonel, you come on in. And a little one! My, my, you've gone done and got yerself hitched, Colonel Cameron!"

Daniel didn't reply. The butler was now taking a closer look at both of them, staring at Callie's worn shoes and getting a full view of a dusty, travel-stained skirt. He swallowed. "Yessir, you and your lady come on in."

Daniel thanked him and they came into a handsome foyer with statuettes in niches on either side of the main entry into the house. The fine hardwood floor was covered with a thick paper matting in an attractive pattern, set there to protect the floor from the hundreds of feet that must surely pass over it every day. The walls were covered with a beautiful papering that made them appear to be marble.

The butler disappeared ahead of them. A doorway to the right, slightly ajar, led to an immense dining room. The doorway to Callie's left was closed, but the main doorway before her suddenly burst open, and a beautiful woman with haunting dark eyes came through.

"Daniel!"

Her voice was soft, gracious, melodious. She was not a young girl, but a mature woman, probably in her middle to late thirties, Callie thought. She had seldom seen a woman more beautiful.

Or clean, she added, in comparison to herself.

Her skirts rustled with her every movement. Her day dress was demure, cut nearly to the throat. It was a dove gray and shimmering silver, enhanced by rows of fine black embroidered lace. Her hair was neatly confined to a net at the back of her head, and despite the heat of the day, she appeared remarkably cool and poised.

She hugged Daniel. He caught her hands and kissed both of her cheeks.

"Daniel, you've come back from Gettysburg!" she whispered. "Was it as horrible as they say? Oh, dear Lord, what am I asking you? Of course it was horrible, wretched, terrible. But my poor old Banny, so many don't see it, but he dies just a little bit with every soldier out there! Now Vicksburg has fallen too."

Her voice trailed away as she looked past Daniel and saw Callie. If she thought anything at all of Callie's pathetic appearance, she was too well bred to give any sign. "I am so very, very sorry!" She broke away from Daniel and stretched out her hands to Callie. "I am Varina Davis, child, and you appear exhausted. And you've a baby! Please, may I take him?"

The beautiful woman in her crisp elegant clothing swept the baby into her arms, not seeming to notice that his bundling was as dirty as everything else about Callie and Daniel.

Varina Davis took one look at the baby and then not even her immense poise could hide her surprise. "Daniel! Oh, but the war does strange things to people. You've married and had this precious child!" Jared started to whimper and Callie had to fight the impulse to snatch him back. She didn't need to. Varina Davis laughed and set him over her shoulder, patting his back, and he quieted. "Daniel, you must be trying to get your baby and bride home."

Callie waited, holding her breath, wondering if Daniel would blithely mentioned that he hadn't bothered to marry his child's mother.

She thought about mentioning it herself. She opened her mouth to do so, thinking that Daniel deserved whatever she chose to say.

But her mouth closed, for she discovered that no matter what her anger for Daniel, she was entranced with Varina Davis. The lady was truly the heart of the Confederacy, Callie thought. And if the Rebs were her enemies, no one could be more so than this woman, wife of the Confederate president. But she was charming, and she was caring. In her voice was all her passion for the men who had died—and all of her concern and empathy for her Banny. Just a few short years ago—before the war, before secession—Jefferson Davis had been the secretary of war for the United States, and he had been a fairly well-known man. His reputation was that of a cold, hard, unyielding man, one with little charm. And yet, if this woman loved him so deeply, there had to be something good, something warm, about him.

"You all look exhausted and famished!" Varina said. "I've some ladies from the hospital league in the drawing room; come in, please, and join us. They'll all be so delighted to see Daniel, and soon I can be alone—"

"No!" Callie gasped. She realized quickly how rude she had sounded, and she apologized quickly. "I'm so sorry, it's just that we really can't come in." She moistened her lips. That her simple homespun cotton could never compare with the elegance of Varina's dress didn't bother her. Before the war, her family hadn't been rich, but they hadn't been poor, and Pa had always told them that the measure of a man or a woman wasn't in the gold in his pocket, but in the way he felt inside. She had never been intimidated by silk, satin, or wealth.

She was somewhat intimidated here, though. Not by Varina's elegance, but by her poise and her heart. She had never felt more shabby in her life.

"Mrs. Davis, truly, I couldn't possibly come farther into your home than I am now."

"I'm desperate for a room, Varina," Daniel told her. "Richmond has gone insane, it seems. I cannot get a room anywhere."

"Of course!" Varina murmured. "Stay here, I shall be right back."

She smiled, surrendered Jared back to Callie, and disappeared into the parlor for a minute.

"How could you bring us here!" Callie hissed to Daniel.

"You said that you—"

"But to bring us here!"

"Sad place for a Yank, eh?" he murmured. He bent closer. "Jeff receives his official visitors upstairs. If there is anything you wish to plan against the Union, that's the place where you should be."

"It would serve you right if I were a full-fledged spy!" she retorted.

"I must admit, I have given the idea some thought," he said with a slight bow.

She would have replied, except that Varina was returning, stepping back through the doorway into the foyer. She smiled radiantly at Daniel. "Well, Daniel, we're all set. Lucretia Marby is in the parlor and just as I thought, her sister's house is empty, what with Letty and her husband striving so diligently for our cause in England. You know the place, Daniel, it's the brick Gunner Estate. And you know the people, of course. Gerald and Letty Lunt. You've been there for parties, I'm quite certain. Ben, Letty's house servant, is there, and will see to your needs." She passed Daniel a note. "Just hand him this note. He does read, so you'll have no difficulties."

"Thank you, Varina," Daniel told her. "Very much."

He kissed her cheek. She smiled again. "I'll expect to see you before you leave. And that beautiful baby of yours." She took Callie's hand. Her grip was warm and firm. "It's been a pleasure, dear. If you grow weary at that old plantation of Daniel's, come back to Richmond." She sighed softly. "We'll put you to work!"

"Thank you," Callie told her. Varina withdrew, and she turned as Daniel took her elbow and led her back out of the foyer. People were hurrying down the walk to reach the house even as they left it; women who nodded cordially, men who tipped their hats.

They reached the wagon and Daniel lifted her into it. "You were very well behaved," he told her pleasantly.

"Spies need to be," she told him sweetly. He arched a brow, but didn't take the bait. When he was seated again, and flipped the reins, she studied him. "Do all

Confederate colonels know the president and his wife
so well?"

He glanced her way. "My mother was from Mississippi. From near Varina's home. Their families were
friends. But the door to the house is nearly always
open. They entertain frequently. Jefferson is not nearly
so rigid as he is often made out to be; he is an excellent
husband, an adoring father. And Varina . . ." He
paused for a moment. "I think that she is the greatest
lady I have ever met."

Callie listened to the gentleness in his voice, to the
note of reverence in it. He would never, never speak so
kindly of her, she was certain, and for some reason, she
was hurt.

The wagon turned a corner. "Here we are," Daniel
commented.

They had come to a large, Federal-style brick house
with a broad porch. Daniel reined in the wagon and
lifted Callie down with the baby, and urged her up the
walk and steps. He knocked quickly at the door, and it
was answered by a very tall black man in gold-and-
black livery. A bright white smile quickly lit across his
features. "Why, Colonel Cameron."

"Hello, Ben," Daniel said, passing him the note.
"We've come for the night. I hope we're not too great
an inconvenience to the household."

Ben looked from their weary faces to the note,
quickly scanning it. "You didn't need no note, Colonel.
You know you're always welcome in this house," he
chastised. "Colonel, Mrs. Cameron, please come right
in. You just tell me what you want, and it's yours."

They entered an elegant, marble-floored foyer with
ceilings that seemed to touch the sky.

Callie stared about, awed despite her best intentions.
This was a room for the night?

"What would you like, Callie? A nap?" Daniel suggested.

She looked at Ben. "A bath. With steaming water. Please."

"Just as you say, ma'am. It will steam like a kettle, I swear it! Cissy!" Ben called out. He smiled at Callie. "Cissy sure does love little ones. She'll bathe him and fix him up right as rain, with your permission, ma'am."

Cissy entered the room. She was round and plump, with a broad smile. Callie wished that she could curl into the woman's arms right along with the baby.

"I don't need long—" Callie began.

"Oh, he's a precious one!" Cissy crooned. "You go right on, ma'am." Cissy turned to walk away with the baby. Ben clapped his hands and a few boys appeared, tall, wiry youths. He quickly ordered that Miz Letty's big tin tub be filled upstairs in the guest room, then he told Callie that he would show her to the room. Daniel excused himself, saying that he was going to the den, and would help himself to brandy.

After the days on the road, the house was like a buffer of soft cotton. Following Ben up the stairway, Callie was afraid to touch the bannisters. She hated to walk on the crimson carpeting.

When she reached the guest room, her eyes went first to the huge bed with its beautiful quilt. She would sleep on that tonight, she thought, and the very idea of it seemed to be a promise of heaven.

The tub arrived in the room, and then bucket after bucket of steaming water. A young black girl arrived with soap and a cloth and a heavy bath sheet. At long last, she was left alone. She touched the water, and it was steaming, so warm it almost scorched the flesh. It was just what she wanted.

She peeled away her clothing with haste, heedless of where it fell, and crawled into the tub. She almost cried out, but the warmth evened out, and it was delicious. She waited a moment, then sank low into the water, soaking her hair.

She breathed in the soap, then scrubbed it furiously over her body, working the lather into her hair. She rinsed, soaped herself and her hair again, and then sank back, resting her head on the rim of the tub, and simply luxuriating in the feel of being clean.

She could have lain there forever.

Downstairs, Daniel poured himself a large brandy from Gerald's desk-side bar. He swallowed the first one quickly, then poured himself another. This he sipped, slowly savoring the taste. He rolled the glass in his hands. Despite the blockade, the Lunts seemed to be faring well enough. He had heard that Lunt had financed a blockade runner, and that while the ship was bringing in its share of medicines and the more necessary implements of a war-torn society, the ship was also bringing in fashions and colognes and soaps from France from which a tremendous profit was being made. Wars could break men. They could also make them rich.

He set the brandy glass down, noticing that his fingers weren't quite steady. At the moment, he was grateful that Gerald Lunt was doing well. He was desperately hungry, and someone was in the kitchen fixing him a dinner of fried chicken, potatoes, turnip greens, and black-eyed peas. Callie had wanted a bath first. He'd wanted to eat. He'd been so careful never to let her see how hungry he had been while they traveled.

He sat back in a leather armchair. He still wanted to throttle her. Now more so than ever. But he hadn't been able to stand watching her in any physical distress. It had hurt to see her hungry; it had hurt worse to watch her shiver in the night. Especially once he had discovered that he dared not go near her.

Dear Lord, he wanted her still! Nothing had been quenched by touching her.

Was she as innocent as she claimed? Maybe his anger had seized hold of his mind. He still couldn't trust her completely, but doubts as to his own righteousness had set in.

Why was he so damned torn, thinking one moment that he cradled a viper to his breast, and finding the very next second that he could still think of nothing but her. Maybe she was innocent—and he was a fool. He dreamed now night and day of touching her again, dreamed of the way she had looked rising from the water, droplets gliding along the curves of her body, that sheer garment of hers hugging everything that he longed to touch. He hadn't thought that morning, not for a single minute. He had just walked out to take what he wanted.

She was the greatest glory he had ever known.

He raised his brandy glass again. "Angel!" he whispered.

The door opened. Ben brought in a plate of food. The aromas were mouth watering. The tray, with its steaming coffee and well-seasoned food, was set before him on Gerald Lunt's cherry-wood desk.

"How's that, Colonel?"

"Well, I'll tell you, Ben, I don't think that I've seen anything quite so wonderful-looking in my whole life."

Ben laughed. "Get on with you, sir! Why, that little boy of yours has to be the most wonderful thing you've ever seen. He's your spittin' image, sir, that's what he is."

Daniel looked up sharply. "He is, isn't he?"

"A boy to be proud of, sir!"

Yes, he was. Jared was wonderful. Daniel drummed his fingers over the desk, watching Ben. "How is—my wife?"

"Sir, she seems just as pleased as if she's gone to heaven with all the angels! She's a right fine lady you've found yourself, Colonel."

Daniel grunted.

"And she sure done give you one beautiful boy, sir!"

Yes, she had done that. It seemed that she hadn't even intended to tell him about Jared, but that didn't really matter. Not now. He had his son.

What were the laws on the child?

More importantly, what were his responsibilities to her?

"Enjoy your meal," Ben said, and grinned. "Good thing you married her, sir, before she could get away. I'm not so sure I've ever seen a more beautiful woman, white or black! Some other man would have been along for her real quick, that's darned certain, if you hadn't a married her, Colonel!"

Daniel forced his face into a grin. "Right, Ben."

Ben left him. He tried to bite into the chicken that had smelled so damned good just a few moments before.

What about Callie? Did she hate him now, did she fear him? Sometimes she felt the same things he did. He had held her when she quaked within his arms and had flown the ultimate bounds of passion.

She was always fighting him. But she had carried Jared, and she had been determined to come with Daniel when he had said he was taking his son.

He had to marry her. His father would have said so; his mother would have been shocked. Jesse would definitely find it his sworn duty—especially since Daniel had been the one to warn his brother that he had best marry Kiernan quickly if he wanted his son born in wedlock.

It was the only honorable thing to do. And she said that she had loved him. Had. Past tense. Even if those words were true, so very much lay between them. Their worlds were at war.

What were his feelings for her? His real feelings? Just the thought of her made him warm, made him tremble.

He groaned aloud and set down his fork. Once upon

a time, he would have known that it was the only right thing to do, no matter what. But once upon a time he had lived in a beautiful gracious world where men and women knew all the rules, and both lived by those rules. It had been a beautiful time, before hunger, before this awful loss of innocence had befallen them all.

Jesse! He thought suddenly of his brother. His best friend. His companion. The steadying voice in his life for so many years. If only he were here.

But Jesse wore blue. He couldn't be here to listen, to advise.

Daniel leaned back, and the hint of a wistful smile played at his lips. "I do know what you would say, brother. I believe that I do. And maybe that doesn't even matter. I cannot risk losing my son. You should see him, Jess. God, is he beautiful."

His voice trailed away.

He wondered if he wasn't just a little bit afraid of losing *her* now that he had his hands upon her.

Maybe reasons didn't matter at all. Only the deed.

He rose, strode across the room, opened the door, and shouted for Ben. He was going home with a wife.

"Yessir, Colonel?" Ben was quickly before him.

"Ben, I have a little problem with my wife."

"What's that, sir?"

"She isn't my wife."

Ben drew back, shocked. Daniel hid a smile. Even the old-world servants knew that the world had rules. And they insisted their masters know them and live by them.

"Well, it ain't my place to say nothin', sir—"

"Ben, I'm trying to rectify that situation, but I need some help. Could you find me someone very, very discreet, who could arrange to marry us?"

"Here, sir? Now?"

"Right now. Well, say, in thirty minutes."

Ben grinned broadly. "Well, now, sir, I—I'll do my

best!" He stepped back, frowning. He started to walk away, shaking his head. "Brandy, that was easy," he muttered. "A meal, that's easy, too. A bath I can manage quick as a wink. But a minister . . . folks, they just want everything these days!"

"Ben—one more thing. Could I scare up some clean clothes? I can arrange a new uniform at home. Civilian dress would be just fine. And I need something for Callie."

"Yessir!" Ben said. "Yessir." He turned again, shaking his head as he hurried away.

Daniel smiled. With his mind made up, he found that he was famished once again. He sat down to his meal. He'd just eaten the last piece of chicken when there was tap on the door. Ben entered with a large box.

"Colonel, I got here a white muslin with fine little flowers embroidered into it."

Daniel's brows shot up. Ben had worked quickly. "Is it Letty's?"

He shook his head. "No sir, I didn't think that Miz Cameron—that your lady—would be too cotton on taking a handout for her wedding. I bought it from a young lady down the street who's heading back to Charleston to stay with her family. Her man's just been killed at Gettysburg and she's wearing black, so she's no more need of this."

"That's fine. I've not much money on me, Ben, but I'll get the cost back to Gerald as soon as I reach Cameron Hall."

"There's no need, Colonel. I bought it with your horse."

Daniel laughed. "That's fine." The Yankee bay cavalry horses were worth quite a bit. Especially now. But he was going home. No place on earth bred finer horses than Cameron Hall. "What about the ceremony?"

"I went on down to the Episcopal Church, and I

didn't know where to start, so I just set the whole thing right in Father Flannery's lap. He said that it was all highly irregular, that's what he said—irregular—but seeing as how you were a hero in the cause, he could understand how maybe you and the lady were delayed a bit in the sacrament."

Daniel lowered his head. He was certain that he might also need to make a bit of a contribution to the church.

"When's he coming?"

"Within the hour, Colonel. He promised."

"That's good. I thank you, Ben. You're a good man. You ever get tired of working here, and there will always be a place for you at Cameron Hall."

"Lawdy, Colonel Cameron, you know I can't go nowhere, never. I'm Mr. Lunt's personal property."

"Not according to Lincoln," Daniel muttered.

Ben shrugged. "But Mr. Lincoln, he got to make those northerners win the war first, right? And you must own your own houseman, Colonel Cameron."

Daniel stood up. "I don't own any man, Ben." Ben looked at him curiously.

Daniel clamped him on the shoulder. "It's a strange damned world, isn't it, Ben?"

"Yessir, Colonel. And getting stranger by the minute!"

Callie stayed in the water quite some time. Nothing had ever felt so good.

But as the water cooled, she felt the stirrings of hunger. The miraculous thing was that she could eat. Here, in this household, wonderful things like beds and baths and food seemed to be hers for the asking.

She just needed to rouse herself.

She opened her eyes and almost screamed. She wasn't alone in the room anymore.

Daniel had come in silently, as if it were his right. He

stood there watching her, a large dressmaker's box held idly in his arms. His sweeping hat was gone, but he still wore his tattered uniform. The fire that could make him so exciting burned in his eyes. He stood straight, shoulders squared, yet still casual.

And still arrogant.

She swallowed hard, narrowing her eyes. "What are you doing here?"

"How very rude of you," he replied.

"Get out."

"Can't, I'm afraid. It's my room too."

"Your room—"

"Well, you haven't protested being called Mrs. Cameron. They've placed us here together—my love."

"Don't call me that!"

"Is it so disturbing?"

"It's hypocritical."

"Just practicing."

"For what?"

He pulled out his pocket watch. "There's an Episcopal priest coming in about twenty minutes now. If we're lucky. I need the tub. Out."

"What?" Callie's fingers gripped the rim of the tub.

"He's coming to marry us."

Her fingers curled more tightly. Someone was coming to marry them. Daniel was joking. He was speaking too blithely to be joking. And he seriously wanted her out of the tub.

Her heart seemed to catch in her throat. Of course she wanted to marry him. The hope had always been there, she had just never let it rise from the depths of her heart, because she hadn't begun to imagine that he would marry her, not even for Jared, not after what had happened when she had turned him over to Eric Dabney.

She couldn't breathe, because suddenly it all hurt very much. She wanted to marry him because she loved him. She should haved stopped loving him. She should have been able to make her anger into a real hatred and make that hatred stomp out the love.

But she hadn't managed to do so. All that she had managed to do was play a part. What did she want then, she asked herself. Easy, she wanted him to love her.

She bit into her lip, watching him as he stood there, the dressmaker's box in his arms.

She turned her gaze from him to the linen washcloth she had been given.

"No."

"What?"

"I don't care to marry you."

The box went flying onto the bed. She shivered as he strode across the room to glare down at her. "What the hell do you mean, no?"

"I mean 'no.' You haven't even asked me. You're rude and obnoxious. I hate you. You are truly—"

"A Rebel rodent?"

"Precisely," she said pleasantly. "Why should I marry you?"

"Because you have borne my son out of wedlock, madam, and because of him, I am willing to marry you."

"Well, I'm not willing to marry you."

She heard him sigh. "Well, I hope you're willing to receive my hand across your posterior anatomy."

She glanced at him quickly, suddenly afraid of pushing him too far. She had come to know the tone of his voice very well, and he meant the threat.

"Why are you marrying me? What will you tell your family? Am I a suitable wife for a Cameron?"

To her surprise and alarm he knelt down by the side of the tub. She moistened her lips quickly and hugged her knees to her chest.

"I'll tell my family that you were buck naked and I

was overcome," he said flatly. "I fell down on my knees and asked you to marry me. It will be the truth."

"No—"

"It will be the truth. You're going to marry me, Callie."

"No! You haven't asked me!" she cried. "You just keep telling me. And you still hate me, and I'm still a Yankee, and you condemn me for what wasn't my fault—"

"All right. Will you marry me?" he said impatiently.

It certainly wasn't what she had in mind for a proposal. She swallowed hard. "I—I can't."

"Why not? You prefer being an unwed mother? On your own?"

"I can make it on my own, Daniel."

"But do you have the right to do it to Jared?"

She looked ahead of her. Her lashes skimmed over her cheeks. She loved him. And she had to believe that underneath it all, he loved her. "I'll marry you, Daniel. For Jared. But I . . ."

"You what?"

"I can't . . . I mean . . . I don't want—"

"Spit it out, Callie. I haven't seen you shy yet."

"I want you to leave me—alone." He stiffened. His movement was barely perceptible. Had she hurt him?

He started to laugh, and it was a very dry, hollow sound. "Madam, I want my son. Legally. And you might want to recall—I've never forced you into anything. At the moment, you're welcome to any privacy you desire. I give no guarantees for the future—should we have one."

Her fingers moved idly over the water.

"I don't know," she began.

His startling blue eyes met hers. "Take a gamble. You should be pleased. I'll be returning to the war almost immediately. I could very easily be shot or run

through with a sword. You'd have all my money and
my name and your freedom."

"Yes, that could happen," she said coolly. God, but
the water had gotten cold! She was starting to shiver.
The cold she felt went beyond anything she had ever
known.

He stood up. "Your dress is on the bed. I'm afraid
we haven't time for any false modesty now. The priest
will be here very soon, and even if this water is stone
cold, I need a good dousing in it." He stretched out the
towel to Callie. She rose to take it.

It dropped to her feet before she could grab it and
wrap herself within it.

"Sorry," Daniel said idly.

Like hell he was sorry.

She swept the towel up from the floor. She started to
walk away and nearly lost the towel again.

"One more thing, Callie," he called after her.

He was stripping off his dirty frock coat, watching
her.

"What?"

"I don't call any man property—you know that we
freed all of our slaves."

"Yes, you told me."

He smiled. "Well, I just want you to know that I do
consider a wife a man's property. You'll be mine."

"We'll just have to see, won't we?" Callie said
sweetly in reply.

But as she turned to dress, she was still shaking.

Twenty-two

The dress was beautiful. It was unlike anything she had ever owned before.

It came with exquisite undergarments, made especially to enhance the gown. There was a huge hoop and a petticoat with row after row of bristling taffeta. There were fine white hose, shimmer-thin pantalets, a silky soft chemise, and an ivory corset, embroidered with the same tiny red flowers that patterned delicately over the dress itself.

Despite the fact that she was clad in nothing but the giant bath sheet, Callie had to pause to stare at the gown before she could even think of putting it on. Her fingers trembled as she touched it.

"Is something wrong?" he asked her from the tub.

"No," she said quickly. Her back to him—and trying to keep the bath sheet around her back—she began to dress. It was difficult. She managed everything but the corset. It was incredibly difficult to try to tie it on by herself.

She stiffened as she felt his hands on her. "Suck in," he ordered, and she did so. "Oh!" she gasped. He had it pulled taut and looped and tied in a matter of seconds. His touch definitely spoke of experience.

She pulled away from him, spinning around. She

turned around quickly again because he was as naked as a tiger in a jungle and seemed just as dangerous.

"What's the matter?"

"You're extremely competent with women's—clothing," she told him over her shoulder.

"Am I?"

She ignored him, reaching for the elegant dress. She slipped it over her shoulders. It fell about her softly, like angel's wings. She struggled to adjust the back, to fluff the skirt out over her petticoat.

Once again, she felt his touch, his fingers at her back. One by one, he did up the tiny hooks, then shook the skirt out over the taffeta petticoat. He stood back to study her.

"Would you please put something on?" she hissed.

That drew a smile. "You've seen me often enough. Now that we're about to make this legal, you're going to find offense?"

She was determined to ignore him. She snatched the skirt from the adjusting touch of his fingers and strode to the long swivel mirror near the door. Her breath caught at the sight of the gown. It had been made for her. It was exquisite. The bodice hugged her breasts. It was not at all decadently low, but it left bare her collarbone and the first hint of the rise of her breasts. The puff sleeves also bared her shoulders. It was cool and sweeping, a perfect dress for the heat of summer. Her hair was nearly copper against the white, damp as it still was.

Her eyes were very wide and her cheeks were flushed. She actually felt beautiful, dressed in the gown.

There was a sharp rap on the door. She jumped as Daniel strode across the room to open it. He had wrapped her discarded bath sheet around his hips. Ben was there with an outfit for Daniel. There were charcoal-gray pinstripe trousers, a red vest, a gray suit coat with elongated tails. There was a frilled white shirt, a cravat, and even a pair of shining black shoes.

"These should be all right, Colonel Cameron," Ben told him. "They come from Miz Letty's oldest boy, Andrew, and he grew to be right near as tall a man as you, Colonel."

"Thank you, Ben. I'll see that they're returned in as good a condition as you've given them to me."

"Colonel Cameron, sir, that won't matter none. He was killed back at Sharpsburg. His folks would be right proud to hear his clothes were of use to you."

"Thank you, then," Daniel said softly.

"Oh!" Ben said, a grin splitting his face once again. "Why, Father Flannery is downstairs. I showed him into the den, and he's having himself a brandy now. His niece is with him, to witness the ceremony."

"We'll be along immediately," Daniel promised.

He closed the door.

Callie realized that she was really going to get married. She looked at her fingers. They were shaking.

Daniel was already halfway dressed. He needed no help. In seconds he had his cravat tied, his vest buttoned, every piece of his outfit perfectly adjusted. He winced as he slipped on the shoes. "A little small," he murmured. "But then . . ."

He stared at Callie. She had been watching him in the mirror.

"Callie," he nearly growled, "we need to get down there."

She glanced at her own reflection in the mirror again. Her hair was still damp against her head. She couldn't possibly dry it in time, but she could at least brush it.

She turned quickly to find her shoes, but when she did so, she paused, biting her lip. They had been good shoes, serviceable shoes. But now they appeared as rough and worn as burned lumber. They seemed a travesty against the beauty of her dress and the white silk stockings.

"Shoes!" Daniel moaned. "I forgot all about shoes." He shrugged. "Forget them for now. No one will see your feet." He strode quickly across the room, plucking a brush from a dressing table. Before Callie could move he was behind her again, pulling the brush through her hair.

"I can do it myself!" she protested, and he gave her the brush. She could still see him in the mirror. Maybe she couldn't do it herself. Her fingers were still trembling. He was dashing in the civilian dress clothing, so lean, so dark, so fluid still in his movement. The gray, black, and red enhanced his dark good looks. The outfit might have been tailored specifically for him.

"Give it to me!" he commanded, taking the brush back from her fingers, and making quick work with the length of her hair.

"You're awfully good with hair too," Callie commented.

"Experience," he said briefly.

She inhaled swiftly, nervously longing to slap him. His eyes were sharp when they met hers in the mirror. He tossed the brush back to the dresser and took her elbow. "Let's go. We can't keep Flannery waiting."

He was walking so swiftly it seemed that he dragged her along. "Slow down!" she commanded.

"Move faster," he replied.

She stubbed her shoeless toe on the first step. She wasn't accustomed to the huge hoop, and she had difficulty just managing to stay on the stairway with him.

But Father Flannery, white haired and very grave, was awaiting them now at the foot of the stairs, a young, brown-haired girl at his side. Callie refrained from making any comments to Daniel.

"Father, thank you for coming," Daniel told him.

"Well, Colonel, I must tell you, I disapprove of this

haste. I understand, however, sir, that you have been delayed by battle after battle, and so here I am. Sir, you are, I fear, at least better late than never."

"Right," Daniel said briefly. "Shall we get started." He looked at Callie. "My love?"

"Of course. If both parties are of age and entering into this sacrament willingly?"

Callie suddenly couldn't speak. Daniel squeezed her fingers so hard she nearly yelped. "Yes. My love," she squeezed out. Father Flannery turned to give them all room at the foot of the stairs. Callie stared at Daniel. "Bastard!" she hissed.

He smiled serenely. His grip was still upon her and he pulled her close, whispering. "The bastard you are about to promise to love, honor, and obey."

"I don't love you."

"I'm merely shooting for two out of three, and the last two will do nicely."

"Is there a problem?" Father Flannery demanded, turning back to them.

"Not at all," Daniel said. "Would you like to begin?"

Flannery gazed at them both sternly, then sighed. "All right, then. Your name, young woman."

"Calliope McCauley Michaelson."

Daniel swung around and stared at her. Flannery began flipping the pages in his book.

"Calliope?" Daniel whispered.

She shrugged. "My father was very fond of the circus."

He was smirking. She was about to get married, and the groom was smirking.

Flannery settled on a page in his prayer book and began to read from it. She heard the words—they seemed to drone on and on. It was a good thing that Father Flannery had never desired to make his life's vocation drama, she determined, for she had never imagined anyone could make a wedding service more dull or dry.

Perhaps it was her. Her fingers were ice cold. She felt numb from head to toe.

She wasn't sure that they could really be doing this. It was a wedding. When it was over, she would really be Daniel's wife.

Even so, she would know how he felt. Property. A wife was property. He would do whatever he chose. And she would, indeed, be trapped in a southern prison.

"Callie!"

They were all staring at her, waiting. She was supposed to speak. To give her vow. She couldn't do it. She loved him.

He nearly broke the bones in her fingers once again. She must have shrieked out something that sounded like "I do!," because Flannery was droning on and on again.

Then Daniel was slipping his pinkie signet ring over her middle finger, and Flannery was pronouncing them man and wife.

It was done. There was a flicker of fire in his eyes, and she realized that the bars had, indeed, just closed upon her own private hell.

His lips touched hers. Briefly. He turned from her and thanked Flannery and promised that he would send support to the church as soon as he reached home. Ben managed to produce champagne, and Flannery seemed willing enough to share a glass with them. He allowed his young niece a glass, too, and then announced that the papers had to be signed. Callie found herself writing out her name, and then realized that it was different again.

She was a Cameron.

And theirs was, indeed, a house divided.

She managed to write out her name. Just as she finished doing so, she heard a wailing and swung around, feeling a tingling in her breasts. Jared! Ben was bringing the baby forward. He'd been bathed and dressed in a fine bleached white cotton shirt.

For the first time in his short little life, she had forgotten her son.

Forgotten him for the wedding that was taking place because of him.

"Thank you, Father Flannery," she said hastily. Ignoring her husband of a matter of seconds, she took Jared gratefully from Ben, and ran up the stairs with him to the bedroom that had been given them.

She closed the door and sat at the foot of the bed with the baby, struggling with the tight gown to free her breast. Once the baby was situated, she began to tremble again, thinking about what she had done.

She had married Daniel. She was committed to him now. No, she had been committed to him since she had decided to follow him home. No, that had been a commitment to Jared.

He had made her no promises. What would their marriage be? She had asked to be left alone. He would never leave her alone. She was property; he had said so.

She shivered and realized she shivered because she did not know what she wanted from him. Yes, she wanted him to demand everything from her.

But she wanted something too. His love, unconditional. The kind that would allow him to trust her.

There was a tapping on the door. She jumped, staring at it. Daniel? Would he knock? Or would he merely burst in?

"Callie, we'll leave here in ten minutes for supper with Varina. Be ready, please."

It was Daniel. He had spoken politely. It had also been with an implacable authority.

It was the way he had always spoken, she told herself.

No, something was very different. He had married her. And he expected two out of three. Honor and obey.

Jared suddenly sputtered and coughed. Callie swept him up on her shoulder and stood, walking nervously with him as she patted his back. He let out a startling burp for such a tiny being, and she laughed and sat again, stretching him out on her lap. "Just what can he really expect, my love, eh? He married a Yankee. And really, I haven't 'obeyed' anyone since Pa . . ." Her voice trailed away.

She leapt up. Her ten minutes had to be just about up.

She paused, feeling the hard wood beneath her stockinged feet. She still had no shoes.

Well, it was summer; her feet wouldn't freeze. But there was so much mud and dust in the road.

"Callie!"

He called her from downstairs. Her old shoes were too worn and filthy to possibly be on her feet while she wore this dress. She bit into her lip once, then went flying out of the room.

He was waiting for her at the foot of the stairs. His eyes swept over her and he let out a grunt, as if voicing a grudging approval.

"Let's go. Ben will be taking us in the Lunt's carriage." He hesitated. "You could leave Jared with Cissy."

She shook her head vehemently. "He might—need me," she said. Actually, that night, she needed Jared. And she hadn't come from his kind of money. She wasn't accustomed to leaving her baby behind.

It was a brief ride back to the White House of the Confederacy. Night had come, and the house was lit against it and seemed very beautiful as they approached. There were other carriages arriving, and guests coming on foot. Once again, they came in by the pleasant foyer. Varina, gracious and beautiful, greeted them. This time they moved through that central door into a very gracious parlor.

The women there seemed to dazzle, Callie thought. They all sat so beautifully, or stood with such grace, their hair swept up, their fans moving like humming-bird's wings against the heat of the night.

They all seemed to know one another. And Daniel. They flocked around him, talking about the war, demanding to know about this battle or that, then whispering that, of course, they didn't really want to hear.

They were ladies, after all.

They spoke softly, with lovely, cultured drawls, ignoring Callie at first, then trying very hard to appear well bred and not stare too pointedly once Varina had managed to introduce her as Daniel's wife.

Callie felt as if her teeth had been permanently glued into a mask, but to Daniel's credit, he seemed totally unaware of the adulation that had come his way. They were quickly parted, but each time she looked across the room, she found his eyes upon her, cool and speculative.

"Why are you staring so?" she whispered when she had a chance.

"I'm just hoping that no one spills any of the big secrets of the Confederacy while you're here," he whispered back.

"How very amusing."

"It's not amusing at all. At the moment, it seems that we're doing a very good job of losing the war without your help."

He moved on. A blonde caught his arm. She felt a strident pang of jealousy. A dashing young man with a sweeping mustache, dressed in uniform that had surely never seen any duty, struck up a conversation with Callie, assuming that she knew all about Daniel's Tidewater home. She smiled and murmured now and then, and that seemed enough.

One buxom brunet cooed over the baby, but a moment later Callie heard a whisper behind her back that such an infant should have been left with its nanny. Callie didn't care as long as Varina seemed so delighted with Jared.

Daniel introduced her to two men in uniform, a Major Tomlinson and a Lieutenant Prosky. When she turned, she heard the major speak to his wife.

"My Lord, but he did find a stunning bride!"

"Find? But that's just it dear, where did he find her?" his wife replied. "I know nothing of her, or her family. Does anyone know anything about her?"

Callie felt as if her ears were burning. Daniel had been swept away by the lieutenant. She had never felt so very alone, surrounded by so many people.

And all of them Rebs.

The crème de la crème of Rebs, at that!

A soft hand fell on her arm, and she was looking into the warm and beautiful eyes of Varina Davis. "Come, Mrs. Cameron, let me show you the house. The dining room is there, of course, to the left of the foyer. Now, these rooms here you see, the one we're in and the one to the right, can be separated by those doors. Pocket doors. They're so very clever, don't you think? We can break the house up when we're alone, and open it up like this for such an occasion as tonight. It's a wonderful house. We were so grateful that the city should give it to us. I've enjoyed Richmond and the Virginians tremendously. Jeff was inaugurated in Alabama, of course, but I've very much loved this place."

"It's very beautiful," Callie agreed.

Varina smiled. "You'll like Virginia."

"I'm not from so very far away," Callie murmured. "Maryland."

Varina studied her. Maryland. A state more split than the country itself. It seemed that Varina sensed that Callie had come from a home with Federal leanings, no matter where that home stood. But she didn't seem to despise her for it. She seemed to understand.

"It is a very hard war," she said softly. She reached out and stroked Jared's dark hair, for the baby slept against Callie's shoulder. "Come, follow me," she said, leading Callie to a small room that sat straight to the right of the foyer. "If you want privacy with the baby, you must bring him in here. There are a few of Jefferson's books here and my sewing, and a nice comfortable chair. You will not be disturbed."

"Thank you," Callie told her. She hesitated. "I'm sorry. I didn't—I don't—have a nanny. He has always been with me."

"That's very special," Varina said. "Children are precious. Perhaps we forget that too often." She smiled, and started to lead the way back. When they returned to the main parlor, Callie was immediately struck by the tall thin man with the haggard face standing by the mantle, conversing with the major. His hair was graying, but he stood with a striking dignity. There were heavy lines about his eyes, and he appeared a man wearied by a great sorrow. He listened to the major, but as his eyes caught Varina's across the room, it seemed that the weariness he wore like a heavy cloak was somewhat lightened. He smiled vaguely. His gaze rested upon Callie, and his brows arched.

Varina caught her hand. "Come, you must meet my husband, Mrs. Cameron."

Her palms went wet; Callie nearly pulled back. She had just married Daniel, and now she was about to meet the president of the Confederate States.

How could she ever explain it to her brothers?

But there was nothing that she could do—short of

shouting out that she was a Yankee and probably finding herself facing half a dozen swords.

She had to go forward.

But Lord, how had she wound up here, a very part and parcel of the beating heart of the Confederacy.

"Daniel's wife, my love," Varina said. "Mrs. Cameron, my husband, President Davis."

She extended her hand. Very much the gentleman, the president leaned over it with all gallantry. "Mrs. Cameron. You grace us with your presence."

And that was it. Dinner was announced, and now Daniel's hand was on her arm again. In the large dining room, they were seated across from one another. Despite efforts for the conversation to be led along light lines, there could be no conversation that did not include the war.

The gentleman to Callie's left complained about inflation. But the president, helping himself to meat from a platter, did not seem to hear the words. "There have been cavalry skirmishes all the way down, Daniel," he said. "Lee brought the bulk of the army over the Potomac on the fourteenth. Meade is following, so I am told. But he failed as those men always failed—he has not managed any assault on our main army."

"Lee is a wily commander, sir."

"Were it only that all my commanders were so able."

"Yessir."

Davis set his fork down. "Dear Lord, but we are in dark days now. This horrid battle . . . Gettysburg. And the loss of Vicksburg."

"They can't break our spirit!" Varina said softly from the other end of the table.

He lifted his wine goblet to her. "No, they cannot break our spirit," he agreed. He looked to Daniel again. "Nor can those northern fellows best our brave fighting men, like our fine Colonel Cameron. Sir, you will be back with your unit as soon as possible, won't you?"

Callie was startled to sense the slightest hesitation on Daniel's part. Perhaps she had imagined it.

Yet when Daniel spoke, she thought there was a deep weariness in his voice, despite the words. "Yessir. I shall be back as soon as possible." His eyes, deep, brooding, touched Callie's across the table. Yes, he would be gone. Soon. And she would be free of him.

Except for her vows.

"To our brave boys in fine butternut and gray!" someone called out.

The guests stood. Wine glasses clinked.

Callie took that opportunity to flee, excusing herself swiftly to Varina, finding the sanctity of the sewing room where she could be alone.

Yes, Daniel would be gone.

It was truly a world gone mad. She closed her eyes, rocking with Jared. It hadn't been so long ago that she had lived on a little farm and had wanted nothing more than to stay there, with the mountains always in view, for all of her life. Day in and day out, her cares had been the same. She had buried her loved ones, her grief sustained by the firm belief that they had died for something that she believed in deeply—the sanctity of the Union and freedom for all men. A freedom promised in the Constitution of a great nation, but a freedom not yet realized. Still, it had been a simple life.

Now here she was, in silk and taffeta, married to the enemy. And dining with the president of the enemy nation.

She swallowed hard, then pressed her hand against her hot cheeks. She could not stay here forever.

Daniel might well believe she was tearing apart the president's house in search of some vital information.

Jared slept. She rose with him and started out of the little room.

The pocket doors to the right side of the parlor had been pulled over. She could dimly hear the voices still coming from the dining room.

She wasn't alone.

She stopped short, seeing the tall, lean president of the Confederacy slouched by the mantle, his forehead in his hands. Etched into his face was a look of such utter misery that Callie could not help but find a burst of pity swelling within her heart.

He sensed her there and turned.

"I'm—I'm so sorry," she murmured swiftly. "Mrs. Jefferson said that I might use her sewing room. Well, it's your room, too, of course." She sounded so very awkward. "I'm sorry. I've intruded terribly, and I did not mean to do so."

He watched her gravely, then a slow, sad smile touched his lips. "You are welcome here in this house, Mrs. Cameron. Wherever it is that you choose to be."

"But I have disturbed you. I—I'm sorry," she said again. "The look on your face . . ."

"You mustn't worry so. I was merely thinking of the men."

"The men?"

"Those who have died. So many. I read the death lists and I see so many friends have gone on." His gaze met hers suddenly. "From both sides, Mrs. Cameron. The men I fight are often the men with whom I worked for years and years before this all began."

"The lists of the dead hurt us all."

"They must, Mrs. Cameron. Have you still kin in the Union army?"

How did he know? She was certain that Daniel had not announced her status.

"Yes, sir. I do."

"It is very hard to pray for men, Mrs. Cameron, when the ones you love might well face one another. Daniel must face his own brother. And now, perhaps, he will face your kin too. My heart is with you, Mrs. Cameron."

"Thank you," she said swiftly. He was gentle and kind. She didn't want him to be so. She wanted him to be stiff and cold, the president that the northerners so frequently mocked. She didn't want to like him, or feel this empathy with him. "I am sorry that I disturbed you," she said. "The baby—"

"Yes. What a lovely thing to see him with you. May I?"

To her amazement, he reached for the baby. Callie hesitated, then walked across the room. Davis took the child from her gently. Jared didn't protest. He stared up at the tall man in black.

"He's a very beautiful child, Mrs. Cameron. My congratulations."

"Thank you."

A curious, small bubbling sound of laughter came to them. Callie swirled around. From the hallway, where there was a beautiful winding stairway to the upper floors, there was movement.

"Who's there?" The president demanded. He sounded very stern.

But his voice didn't bother the pretty child who suddenly appeared. She stepped out, her eyes alight, her hands behind her back.

She was in a long white nightgown, and she looked very demure at first, then she pelted across the room to come to a swift halt in front of the president.

"Margaret, my eldest," he explained to Callie, and his face softened tremendously, even as he tried again to be stern.

"Young lady, you are supposed to be in bed." His voice was meant to be stern. It was not quite so hard as it might have been, and Margaret, who knew very well she should have been in bed, lowered her lashes, then gave him a beautiful, imploring smile.

"But, Father, what a lovely baby! May I see him?"

"You must ask Mrs. Cameron." Davis said. Callie could not help but think that here was a man, a very powerful and important man, and like all others, North and South, he was blessed or cursed with an Achilles' heel where his children were concerned.

Margaret had wonderful, deep eyes. She was as charming as her mother as she turned to Callie. "May I, Mrs. Cameron? Just peek at him, please?"

Callie smiled. "Of course."

Davis went down on a knee, holding Jared. Margaret touched his cheek, and the baby offered up a coo. "I'm very good with babies, Mrs. Cameron. Truly, I am. I am the eldest, you see."

"And now, back to bed! Before your mother catches us!" Davis said, rising with the baby.

Margaret gave him an impish grin, and turned to flee back toward the stairway. She paused before she reached it, turned and bowed very prettily to Callie. She disappeared once again.

"Perhaps I haven't a heavy enough hand," Davis mused.

"She's a lovely girl, sir."

"Thank you." He crossed the room, returning the baby to Callie. "Perhaps we had best return. My wife will be worried for my state of mind. And your husband will be worried, for surely he must worry every time you are out of his sight."

Yes, that was probably true enough, Callie thought wryly. Daniel would be worried about the state of his beloved Confederacy.

The president took her elbow to lead her back to the dining room.

"I am sorry that you must find yourself here, dear, in enemy territory. It is so very complex, this war. My enemies are so often my friends. Perhaps, eventually, you will be more a Virginian than anything else. Whatever, you must not think yourself an enemy to this house. Come visit when you may, and know that the door will be open to you."

"Thank you!" Callie said. They had reached the dining room, and Daniel's eyes were on the doorway, as they must have been since she had first left the room.

Those sharp blue eyes narrowed the moment he saw her entering upon Davis' arm.

He stood up, walking around the table to seat Callie himself. He stared at her, in question, in warning.

She smiled demurely and dinner continued.

It was a subdued night, because of the battle losses. And because Meade, with his whole army, was moving after Lee's. Sluggishly, perhaps, but still, the Union army would be raping the Virginia countryside once again. Virginia herself was now already long split, with the western counties having voted to join the Union and the Union now having taken them on as a state. Some said that especially in Harpers Ferry, the people had voted to secede from Virginia and the Confederacy because there had been Yankees all around with rifles, watching the voting.

No one really knew.

But it seemed the South had reached a darkest hour, and that was evident tonight.

Yet it was equally evident, Callie thought, that no essence of their spirit was dead. These people were proud, they were honorable. She felt, as she sometimes did with Daniel, that intangible thing they were fighting for. It held them together against loss. It—along with the talent of their generals—kept them strong in battle when the northern numbers should have been overwhelming. It sustained them against loss.

And she thought, it would hold them together as a people when this great conflict was long over.

Despite the losses now coming the Rebel way, victory might still be theirs. Not so much on the battlefront, but in the political arena.

The war had changed dinner conversation. No one suggested that the present situation not be discussed in front of the ladies.

And so Callie listened to the talk and speculation.

McClellan, Little Mac, the general who had so often infuriated Lincoln by refusing to move against Lee, was moving now—into the political arena. If he were elected president of the United States, he wanted to sue for a negotiated peace.

But the elections were still a year off.

Lincoln now had a few great victories behind him.

The South would rise again.

The South would always rise again.

Callie looked up. Daniel's eyes were steadily upon her.

"Tell us, what do you think, Mrs. Cameron?"

Startled, she drew her eyes from her husband's. Down the hall, the young lieutenant in uniform was speaking to her. He continued, "How can we lose, when we have such dashing cavaliers, such splendid horsemen as your husband! He's been known to cover well over fifty miles in a single day, to ride circles around the Yanks! We cannot lose! What do you say, Mrs. Cameron?"

All eyes on the table were upon her. The war was suddenly sitting in her lap.

Once upon a time, she might have engaged in battle. Not tonight. Tonight her enemies were truly flesh and blood. They were people with graciousness, with kindness, with exceptional honor and pride.

They were people who loved their children.

She smiled gravely, and then her eyes touched Daniel's once again.

"I say that, indeed, my husband is a splendid horseman."

Pleasant laughter rang out. The moment passed. Conversation continued.

Daniel's eyes remained upon her, grave, intent.

Perhaps there was even the slightest flicker of approval in them.

She had neither surrendered nor taken up the sword. She was somewhat startled to realize that perhaps, just perhaps, it was all that he wanted of her.

Dinner broke; the men had brandy and cigars, the ladies closed the pocket doors and sipped a supply of English tea which had come through the blockade as a special gift from one of Varina's close friends. Thankfully, they did not tarry long, for Callie was uncomfortable again, aware of the very curious stares that came her way when her back was turned.

But no one was rude now. The ladies, even as they speculated about her, passed Jared from one to another, heaping all manner of advice upon her.

At last, it was time to leave. Varina managed to hold her back until the last of the guests had gone other than she and Daniel.

Even then she pulled Callie back into the little sewing room on the pretext of showing her something.

On the floor lay a pair of red satin slippers. They matched the tiny flowers in her dress beautifully.

"The moment I saw your dress, I thought that you must have these to go with them!" Varina said.

Callie flushed. "Oh, but I can't take your shoes. Oh!" She gasped, aware that she had been in Varina's house all night, shoeless, depending upon her skirt to hide the fact. "I'm so sorry—"

"Please try these on. Our men go barefoot in the field, I am told, and I am heartbroken that I can do nothing for them. At the very least, I can see a pair of slippers on the wife of a dear friend and cavalryman. I shall be truly upset if you do not take them."

Callie stared at her, then tentatively placed a foot in a slipper. It fit her comfortably.

"But I can't—" she began.

"Of course you can! A wedding present!" Varina told her.

She could protest no more, for Varina had opened the door to the foyer, and Daniel was there with the president.

Davis was giving him stern warning. "I am ever on the alert, lest the times grow dangerous, indeed, and it is necessary to evacuate Varina and the children. If you must go home, you must take grave care. It seems we never know when the enemy is upon the peninsula."

"I'll be careful, sir."

"You could leave Mrs. Cameron in Richmond," Varina suggested. "She could travel with me farther south, should it become expedient."

"I'm not sure that would be such a good idea," Daniel said, eyeing Callie. His tone was pleasant. His wry glance was something only Callie could really understand. He turned then to Davis. "Well, good-bye, sir, and thank you immeasurably for the evening. We'll be leaving quite early, and with any luck, sleep in Williamsburg tomorrow night, and reach home the next day."

He kissed Varina's cheek, and shook Davis' hand. Both of them bid Callie good night, both of them kissing her cheek.

Out in the night air Callie and Daniel hurried to the coach. Ben had come for them.

They were silent for a few minutes. Callie sat far to her own side of the carriage, wishing that she could not feel the speculative heat of his gaze so constantly.

He spoke to her dryly. "My, my, Mrs. Cameron, but you were on good behavior this evening!"

She hated the tone of his voice. "The better to steal Confederate secrets," she said pleasantly.

A mistake. She could almost feel the sudden burst of fury within him, despite the fact that he in no way touched her.

He replied softly enough. "At the very least, madam, you were polite."

"Dared I not be so?"

"Of course not." Even in the darkness, she felt the cobalt stroke of his gaze. "Had you been anything less than entirely pleasant, I would have merely excused myself and taken you for a foray into the barn and a lesson with a buggy whip!"

Tremors assailed her. She was suddenly very ready for battle. "Oh, I do think not, Colonel Cameron! Why, every man there would have been totally appalled by your lack of manners and good breeding!"

"They might have been startled, but they would have pitied me, thinking that the hardships of the war were costing me my mind at last."

Callie drew herself very straight in the carriage. "Say what you will. You'll not threaten me."

"I don't really care to threaten. And you need never fear me—my love—action will come far before any words of warning!"

They had reached the house. Callie held Jared close to her and leapt from the carriage before either Ben or Daniel could give her any assistance.

"You fool!" Daniel called after her. "You could have tripped! You could have injured the baby!"

She spun around at the door. "I have become very accustomed to caring for him under any circumstance or physical handicap!" she retorted. "After all, his father chose to drag him through war-torn country."

She hurried into the house and began to race up the stairs. She would reach the guest room, slam the door against him, and bolt it quickly. Surely, not even Daniel would dare to break down another man's door.

She shouldn't have bothered to elude him. Daniel caught her on the upstairs landing.

"What!" she cried.

He dropped her arm. To her surprise, he offered her an elegant—if mocking—bow.

"Actually, madam, I had meant to thank you for your manners this evening in the proximity of your enemies. Perhaps we will change you to our side after all."

She stared at him, at the evocative blue fire in his gaze, at the ebony lock that now dangled rakishly over one eye.

Her husband was indeed a splendid horseman.

A splendid man. She wanted to reach out to him and to be held by him.

They had just been married. It was their wedding night. She should have been able to cry out and fall into his arms.

And whisper, beg, that he make love to her, and in doing so, erase the fact that they were enemies. She wanted so dearly to be held against the darkness!

But by morning's light, they would be enemies again.

"I cannot change sides," she said softly. Neither could she lie at that moment. "I cannot change sides, for you are wrong, sir. And you know it, Daniel. You know that owning another man—be he black, white, or purple—is wrong. Jesu, Daniel! In his will, George Washington freed his slaves! He was a *Virginian,* Daniel. *He* knew slavery was wrong!"

He stared at her. Tall, straight, as proud as the southern cause itself.

He bowed again, graceful and agile.

"Good night, madam," he said simply, and left her.

She didn't have to close or bolt a door against him.

It was their wedding night and he walked away from her.

Twenty-three

Nothing that Callie had ever seen before prepared her for her first sight of Cameron Hall.

It was twilight when they came upon the house, and it seemed to sit atop a glittering hill, the last rays of the sun shimmering on the elegant white pillars. The house was large, rising into the blue and crimson sky, with gentle acres of lawn sloping off from its height. A long, wide, curving drive led to the large steps that ended at the huge sweeping porch. Back upon the porch were massive double doors with brass knockers that, even from this distance, gleamed.

Daniel had reined in the remaining Yank horse and Callie, mounted behind him, leaned around to see his face. He was staring hard at the house himself. For the last several miles, he had been exceptionally tense.

He had seen to it that Ben awakened her at the crack of dawn the day before. If she thought he had ridden hard to reach Richmond, she had not imagined just how anxious he could be to reach his home. He had barely spoken to her the length of the long road home.

He had ridden carefully, always aware that there could be danger on the roads, but he had ridden quickly. She had wondered if he meant to ride through the night yesterday, but he had stopped in Williamsburg, taking a room at an old inn.

Williamsburg had seemed very quiet, depressed. The war had touched the town, and it was obvious. The young men were all gone. There was no bustle in the streets. Fresh Confederate graves lay behind the old Episcopal church. Fields were empty.

The inn, though, was pleasant enough, exceptionally clean, and the innkeeper was a charming man. Callie, exhausted, had eaten and taken Jared up to bed, falling asleep with the baby at her side.

Daniel had known a number of the older men down in the tap room, and found two old friends who had been badly disabled, one without a left hand, and one minus his right leg from the knee down. It had seemed to Callie that they all overindulged in whiskey, yet she had been far too weary and heartsick to care. Lying awake she realized that her stomach was in knots because she would soon reach Daniel's home. Though she had met Jesse Cameron and knew him to be a kind gentleman, it would not be Jesse she would be meeting, but his household, a Rebel household. How strange, though, that she could live there, and Jesse could not.

She was uneasy about the women she would meet, for Daniel had been so curt with her that he had described them very little. There was Kiernan, Jesse's wife, and Christa, their sister. There was a man named Jigger who ran everything in the house, and a woman named Janey who had once belonged to Kiernan, but who was now a free black. They still grew cotton and tobacco, and so far, had managed to survive numerous battles in the near vicinity. The house was very old, he had told her, the cornerstone having been laid in the early sixteen hundreds.

Having awakened later in the evening, she wondered what made him so certain that she would stay once he had returned to war. She felt a set of chills assail her. If

she left, he would come after her. As he had told her
once, there would be no place where she could hide.
He would find her.

She had to write to her brothers, to pray that her
letters would reach them wherever they were. She
would have to make them understand why she was
suddenly living in the heart of the Confederacy.

She would leave out the part about having dined
with President and Mrs. Davis!

Though Jeremy, at least, might understand.

She punched her pillow, and tried hard to sleep
again. She could hear the laughter from below. Damn
Daniel. Well, they would have a late morning of it!

She didn't want him here! she reminded herself. She
didn't want him demanding any rights. She bit down on
her knuckle, remembering the sweet ecstacy at the
creek that had been so cleanly swept away from her
when she had seen the look on his face. He didn't love
her; he had wanted her. Forgiveness was the farthest
thing from his mind.

She didn't want forgiveness. She hadn't betrayed
him. She wanted understanding. She wanted trust.

She tossed and turned. She would fight him tooth
and nail now if he touched her. Yet he made no attempt to come near her. He gave her no chance to tell
him what she thought about his conjugal rights!

Exhaustion overwhelmed her and at last she slept.
Sometime deep in the night, Daniel came to the room.
When he awakened her next morning, she was certain
that he had slept on the other side of the bed, on the
other side of Jared. The pillow was indented, the sheets
were warm.

He was in breeches only, reaching for the white cotton shirt he had left at the foot of the bed. "Get up. I
want to get going."

They had started out with the wagon. They hadn't
traveled very far before a Confederate sentry warned

them there were rumors of a Yankee company moving down the main road.

Daniel decided to leave the wagon to travel through the forest paths.

They had left everything with the wagon. She had left the beautiful white dress with the tiny red embroidered flowers.

She didn't know exactly why, but leaving the dress hurt. Daniel had commented on it.

"I won't be stopped over a gown, Callie."

She had shrugged. "You, sir, are the one bred to wealth. There is nothing that I need," she had told him regally.

But it hadn't been true. The dress had meant a lot to her. It was the first really elegant piece of clothing she had ever owned. And it was matched so perfectly by the red slippers that Varina Davis had given her.

It didn't matter. They had deserted the wagon, and she had cradled Jared into her arms, and mounted behind Daniel on their remaining horse. They were both back in the near rags they had worn from Maryland to Virginia, clothing that had at the least been cleaned and mended during their short stay in Richmond. To Daniel, it didn't matter. He was in uniform again and he was going home.

Along the way, riding through the forests and close to the river, they had come upon the ruins of two great houses. A stairway still extended from one of them, leading straight up into the blue sky. Daniel had paused, stared hard, and then ridden again.

And at last, Cameron Hall seemed to burst and blaze before them.

And Daniel, at long last, seemed to draw in an even breath.

"This is it. Home," he told her briefly. He urged the horse forward, bringing them down the path. When they were still a good fifty yards from the house, he flipped his leg over the horse's haunches and leapt down from the mount. "Christa! Kiernan!" His voice rang out and he went running.

Seconds later the double doors burst open. Callie allowed the horse to amble forward at a slower pace as she watched as Daniel was greeted by the two women.

One with deep, raven dark hair, the other a blonde with sun-bright reddish streaks. The dark-haired girl was in a sunburst yellow gown, and the blonde was in midnight blue. Their gowns were beautiful and elegant, even if they were just day gowns. They were trimmed with fine laces, and both women wore hoops and petticoats.

And both were young, and fresh, and very lovely.

And both were very loving.

Callie felt very much the intruder as she watched the scene upon the grand porch. One by one, the women kissed and hugged him. And one by one he swept them up, swirling them around. There was laughter and chatter and so very much happiness.

The horse was still plodding forward. Callie pulled back on the reins, determined to go no farther for the moment.

But it was just when she did so that the blonde caught sight of her.

In the beat of several seconds, Callie just stared at her, and couldn't help but feel a peculiar little flutter of fear.

She didn't belong here.

But then the blond woman smiled a broad, entrancing smile of greeting. Her eyes fell from Callie's to the bundle in her arms.

"A baby!" she exclaimed. "Daniel, you've brought a baby!"

She came running down the steps, moving as if she glided across the expanse of lawn to reach Callie.

"Hello! Welcome! I'm Kiernan Cameron, Daniel's sis-ter-in-law."

"Hello," Callie said softly. "I'm Callie . . ."

Her voice trailed away. She'd never spoken her mar-ried name; she still couldn't quite grasp that it was re-ally hers, and she knew that she couldn't form the words to explain that she was Daniel's wife.

She didn't need to. Daniel spoke dryly from the porch. "Callie is my wife."

"Wife!" the brunet gasped. But she quickly regained her composure. "How wonderful! And that means that this is your baby, Daniel. But you were just home be-fore Christmas and you didn't mention—"

"Christa!" Kiernan interrupted quickly. She hadn't lost a bit of her composure or poise. Callie was sure that her cheeks were growing pink despite her very best efforts. "Let's get Callie and the baby in, shall we?" She smiled brilliantly. "Daniel has always been full of surprises."

Daniel left the porch, and now strode up to the horse, reaching up to lift Callie down.

"The baby!" Kiernan cried.

"We're quite accustomed to him," Daniel told her.

But when Callie's feet touched the ground, Kiernan was reaching out for Jared. "May I?"

She didn't really expect an answer; she swept the baby up and pulled the cotton bunting from his face. "Oh, you're beautiful!" she murmured to the baby. She glanced up, smiling at Callie and Daniel. "My Lord, Daniel, you would recognize this child anywhere as a Cameron. And he's so young! Callie, how old is he now? Two months old?"

"Yes, just about," Daniel replied before Callie could speak.

"Oh, is he precious!" Kiernan said.

"But Daniel, you were here last fall and you never mentioned a wife. Oh—" Christa began. She cut off

her own words, flushing. Of course, it had to be painfully evident to them both, Callie thought, that if she
and Daniel were actually married at all, the ceremony
had to have taken place long after the baby's concep-
tion.

"Oh!" she repeated quickly. "Where are my manners? You've had a long trip. You must be tired."

"And famished," Kiernan added, "and very thirsty.
Daniel, bring your wife in." To Callie she added,
"We've done our best to aid the war effort, but we've
also been very lucky. We've had friends burned out,
but the Yanks haven't tred this way yet. Of course, my
husband is a Yankee—maybe that's kept some of the
companies from our doorstep—but that's another
story, and a very confused one. Come in. Just leave the
horse, Daniel. Jigger will have him seen to."

Kiernan had the baby bundled in the crook of one
elbow. She linked her free arm through Callie's and
started leading her up the steps. "I don't imagine that
my brother-in-law will be home very long?"

The affection in her voice was warm and genuine
and Callie found herself answering softly. "I don't
think so. He has to return as soon as possible to his
command."

"Well, then, we shall have to make the best of this
time for both of you. Christa and I will not intrude.
Still, first things first!" She had pushed open the doors
to the house. Callie was met by a massive wide hallway
with doorways leading to rooms on either side of the
house. There was a wonderful grand stairway leading
to a landing where, even from here, Callie could see a
gallery filled with pictures. Embroidered love seats
lined the great hallway, and the matching rear doors,
the ones that faced the river, had been thrown open.
Far beyond the house Callie could see the beginnings
of a rose garden.

"Janey, Jigger!" Kiernan cried out. A doorway to

the left burst open. A tiny whirlwind of energy in very small breeches came bursting through first, racing toward Kiernan.

"Mama!" he cried.

"Oh, dear!" Kiernan laughed, scooping down to pick up the little boy. Callie was startled at the boy's appearance, for surely she was looking at her own son, one year from now.

"John Daniel," Kiernan said, "this is your aunt Callie. And your cousin. What is his name?"

"Jared," Callie said.

"This is your cousin, Jared."

"Kiernan, he isn't in the least interested in a cousin, yet!" Daniel said. He came around to sweep his wriggling nephew from Kiernan, holding the little boy up in the air so that he shrieked with laughter. "My goodness, John Daniel, you're getting big!" He glanced at Kiernan. "Has Jesse seen him lately?"

She shook her head. "Not since Christmas. We discussed the idea of my moving up to Washington, but he knew that I would hate it there, and it probably wouldn't help much, he never seems to get any time away." She breathed quietly for a moment, looking at Daniel. "He's back in Virginia, I've heard. In the valley somewhere, with Meade's army."

"Perhaps I'll see him," Daniel said lightly.

"Oh, Daniel, I pray not! When you see him, it is so frequently because you're injured or in some place like that horrible prison!"

"Yes," Daniel muttered, and despite herself, Callie felt herself flushing again. Well, it seemed evident enough that he'd never mentioned her to his sister and sister-in-law before. But she couldn't tell by his manner just what he intended to tell them now that they were here.

He wasn't going to say anything now, for there was

suddenly a cackle of glee. "Master Daniel, you've done come home!"

"Jigger!" Daniel said happily, striding across the hall to hug the tall, lean black man who had just come in, running after little John Daniel Cameron. The boy, caught between the two men, squealed with delight.

"You look wonderful, Jigger. The rheumatism's not too bad, eh?"

"No, sir. The summer weather is kind to my bones! But you, sir, you are looking by far the worse for wear!"

"Well, that's because I do feel so well worn," Daniel said.

Jigger was frowning, looking at Jared, still held in Kiernan's arms, then glancing at Callie, and glancing at the baby again. "Oh, Lawdy! Why, you done brought home a missus, sir. And another little one." He rolled his eyes. "This is going to be one busy household, sir, that it is!" He suddenly stood very straight, and offered Callie an extremely dignified bow. "Miz Cameron, welcome to Cameron Hall!"

"Thank you, Jigger," she said quietly.

His gaze moved quickly over her travel-worn dress. "First things, first, I think. The new Miz Cameron must surely be wanting a bath."

"Of course!" Christa said suddenly. "And you couldn't possibly have carried any of your things. I think we're of about the same size. I hope you won't mind taking a few dresses and things from me?"

"I wouldn't mind at all," Callie said. "But you needn't—"

"Here's Janey!" Kiernan interrupted. A very tall, extremely attractive black woman came walking in from the rear porch.

"Well, I'll be . . ." she began. "Master Daniel!"

A grin broke out on her face, and she ran down the hall to greet him. Callie suddenly felt warm. He was loved here. Dearly loved by his family. He could not be a cold or a cruel man and have earned this love.

She had loved him herself. He was hard, he was a blade honed razor-sharp by the years of war. But she had known that he was admirable, and that was why she had loved him.

Loved him still.

No! Only a fool would love a man who felt such a contempt for her as Daniel did for Callie.

"What!" Janey gasped, listening to something that Daniel had said. She, too, swung around to stare at Callie. "A wife! And a baby! Another boy? Miss Kiernan, when is someone in this house going to produce us a little girl to dress up and pamper."

Kiernan laughed. "Don't look at me, Janey. I haven't seen Jesse since Christmas. Perhaps we can look to Daniel and his bride."

Callie gritted her teeth. If she flushed just one more time here, she was going to scream. Don't look at us! She almost cried. We hate one another.

But, as she had discovered, that very often had little to do with the production of a child. No promises, Daniel had told her. She had agreed to become his wife.

He stared at her now, watching her reaction. Gauging it?

Or mocking her all the while?

She didn't know.

"Let's give the poor woman a chance to breathe," Christa said, laughing. "A bath first! Janey, can you see to it, please?"

"Surely," Jane said. "I'll just take that child for you—"

"No, you will not!" Kiernan protested, holding tight to Jared. "John Daniel has gotten far too big to hold and love like this. I'm going to become acquainted with my new nephew. Daniel, perhaps you should take a walk with yours! Christa can see to whatever you may need, Callie, and then supper should be ready soon enough. How does that sound for everyone?"

"Fine," Daniel said. "Young John Daniel, you and I are going for a walk."

John Daniel wasn't old enough to have much of a vocabulary, but he seemed to like his uncle well enough. "Walk!" he agreed, chubby little fingers winding around Daniel's neck. Without a backward glance, Daniel started out through the back. Kiernan offered Callie a radiant smile. "I'll just take him into the study."

"He might need new—pants," Callie said.

Kiernan laughed. "Why, Mrs. D. Cameron, I'm certainly experienced with changing a baby's pants. Get away with you now!"

Then she was gone, and Christa had taken Callie's arm. They walked up the long winding stairway, with Christa talking all the while, softly, warmly, as sweetly as if she had asked Callie to her home herself.

Callie paused in the portrait gallery at the top landing, intrigued by the portraits. Some of them were very old. All of them were oil paintings, except for one at the end of the gallery.

It was a photograph, a picture of a family. A handsome man and woman sat on a sofa, with Christa, perhaps at fifteen or sixteen, between them. Behind the sofa stood both Jesse and Daniel. Both were dressed in the dark blue of the Union cavalry.

"It's nice, isn't it?" Christa said softly. "It was taken several years before the war. I've heard that it was one of Mr. Brady's finest. Ma and Pa were still alive then. And Jesse and Daniel were both in the U.S. Army. I love this portrait. It means so much to me. Especially when day after day after day goes by and I don't know exactly where either of them might be . . ." Her voice trailed away. "A bath! I know that it is the first thing that I would desire, and I'd desire it with all of my heart!"

Christa led her to a room. Wonderful full-length windows looked out on the garden and the river beyond. Against the inner wall was a cherry-wood sleigh bed, and to the left was a huge fireplace. A desk was situated before the windows to catch the light, and two plush chairs were drawn close by so that someone sitting in them might look out on the beauty of the view. There were also two huge armoires in the room, and a large trunk at the foot of the bed, and a washstand to the left of it.

It was an attractive room, a welcoming one. It was also a definitely masculine one.

Daniel's.

The tub had already been brought, and a golden-colored little servant boy was dumping in a huge bucket of water.

"Just let me get you some things, and then I'll leave you in peace," Christa told her.

She was as good as her word, bringing in a supply of soap and towels, and then being joined by Janey, who helped her carry in all manner of petticoats and pantalets and stockings and gowns. There was such an array of things that Callie began to protest, but Christa ignored her. "There's nowhere for me to wear all of these things anymore! I'm afraid I was terribly frivolous before the war, so I'm grateful now that I can think perhaps it was destiny I was so sadly greedy!" She laughed, and then she was gone, and Callie was alone.

The first thing she thought when she sank into the water was that it was not going to be nearly so terrible as she had imagined.

She leaned back, then bolted up again. This was Daniel's room. She didn't know when he would come back to it. She bit her lip, looking around, noticing the little things she hadn't seen at first.

There was a set of crossed swords on the wall, old swords it seemed, from the Revolutionary War. There was a tintype of Daniel. He was in a Union uniform, and he appeared very young. She wondered if it had been his graduation from West Point.

In the stand beside the bed were several books. Books by Shakespeare, by Defoe. She strained her eyes. A copy of Chaucer's *Canterbury Tales*. There were a few other books. A small handbook on military maneuvers, and one on animal husbandry. On the desk was another photograph. It was one of Daniel and Jesse, arm in arm, in front of the house.

She closed her eyes. The water was growing cold.

How would they bear it here if either brother died?

Don't go back, Daniel, she thought.

But it was wishful thinking. Even if he loved her, even if he adored her, he would not shrink from returning to the war.

I love him, she thought.

No! He would not believe you; he would hurt you worse. Maintain your distance, keep your heart safe and hold on to your pride. And then he will be gone.

But what if he doesn't come back?

With that question continuing to plague her, she rose from the tub. She dried herself quickly, then looked through the array of Christa's gifts. There was a silver-gray day dress, with cream and black lace edgings. She ran her fingers over it, then began to dress. Christa had supplied simply everything. She found stockings and garters and pantalets, and everything fit. She awkwardly tied herself into a corset, then slipped the dress over her head and shoulders, and let it fall. It was beautiful.

She still wished she had the white dress back. It had meant so much to her. She didn't know if it was because it was the first thing that Daniel had given her, or because she had been married in it, or because of the little red slippers Varina had given her to go with it.

No matter. It was gone. And she was surrounded by more luxury than she had ever known.

Christa had supplied her with shoes as well. And with a silver-handled brush.

She finished dressing, aware of the silence in the house. She tentatively stepped into the hallway and walked down the stairs. A door toward the back of the house was open. She could hear voices coming from it and walked toward it.

She paused, for she could hear Kiernan and Daniel. They were talking about her.

"Daniel, truly, I've no wish to intrude in your life, but . . . ?"

"What is it, Kiernan?" he asked dryly, but a warmth and humor remained in his voice. "Please go ahead and intrude now, because eventually you're going to do so anyway."

"All right, where is she from?"

"Maryland."

"Are you really married?"

"Yes."

"Does she want to be here?"

"No."

"Wonderful. You're going back to war and leaving us with a woman who despises us all!"

"She doesn't despise you all. Just me," he said. There was a deep, underlying bitterness there. Callie bit her lip. She had no right to be eavesdropping in the hallway. She needed to make her presence known.

"But that baby . . . Daniel! You didn't—"

"I didn't what?"

"Force her into anything, did you? I mean you didn't—"

"Rape her? Kiernan! How the hell long have you known me?"

"I'm sorry, Daniel. But this baby! He is so beautiful! All that black hair—and the eyes. Beyond a doubt, they are Cameron eyes!"

"Yes, I know."

"Daniel Cameron, you forced her down here because of this baby!"

"He's my son."

"But he is hers too!"

"And she's my wife, Kiernan!" he said, and sounded impatient.

"But—"

"Kiernan, Lord knows how many marriages are arranged with the bride and groom scarcely knowing one another. So ours is not a love affair. She is still my wife."

"Well, you did acquire a striking woman, Daniel. She is probably the most beautiful woman I have ever seen."

Daniel sniffed loudly. Callie could hear the sound all the way into the hallway.

He spoke softly. "Yes, she is beautiful. And she knows how to weave a spell and use that beauty. My wife can be as treacherous as she is lovely, Kiernan. Remember that."

"Where are you going?" Kiernan said.

He must have been rising. Panicked, Callie ran out to the porch.

It was dark now. She flattened herself against the wall. She was breathing far too quickly. She closed her eyes, willing her heart to beat at a more sensible pace.

She opened her eyes. Daniel was standing before her.

He had bathed and shaved elsewhere. His hair was damp, his cheeks were clean and alluring, the fullness of his mouth was twisted in a wry, rueful smile. In the darkness, his eyes were obsidian. His scent was clean and raw, and as he moved closer to her, she nearly cried out.

"Well, well, good evening, Mrs. Cameron. Fancy finding you out here."

She lifted her chin, and hiked up a brow. "Oh? Was I to have been confined to the house, sir? If that is the case, then you should have advised me so."

"Careful, Mrs. Cameron, you'll find yourself confined to your room."

"I haven't a room. It is your room."

"I keep a lot of my personal property in my room," he said casually.

She tried to kick him. He stepped out of the way, laughing, then he caught her arms and suddenly wrenched her toward him.

"I'm going to have one dinner in this house, madam. And it's going to be a pleasant one."

"Perhaps I should beg a headache, and then you needn't fear any disruption."

"No, my dear wife, for if you were so distressed, I would consider it my duty to be with you. And we'd be locked together all of those endless hours."

"Dinner sounds divine," Callie said sweetly.

He took her arm. Warmth danced along her spine.

The moon suddenly appeared, shining down on them both. "You are extraordinarily beautiful," he told her softly.

She swallowed. She wanted to say something. She wanted to beg for a truce.

"Am I?" she whispered wistfully.

"Indeed. We've one night, my love. Just one night."

The warm, dancing shivers assailed her once again.

She didn't know if the words were some kind of a threat or a promise.

Twenty-four

Sometimes, Daniel reckoned, it was possible to forget the war.

Sometimes he could almost half close his eyes, sit back, and imagine that they had gone back to a time when the army rations weren't always riddled with worms, when he didn't have to look at shoeless men in rags day after day.

Sometimes there was a return to events so warm and sweet and gracious that he forgot the screams of the dying as they echoed in his head.

Like tonight.

The older children, Patricia and Jacob Miller, had determined that they weren't going to eat with the grown-ups, but that they'd be responsible for entertaining John David until his bedtime.

Christa had determined they wouldn't sit at the regular dining table, for it was far too large for an intimate dinner of four. The large oak table had been set far down the room, and a small square table from the kitchen had been brought in and covered with a snowy cloth.

The Cameron's best silver was on the table, and their glittering Irish cut crystal. Between the women of the household and Janey and Jigger, they had created a banquet. The meat was only ham, but there was an array of summer vegetables and fruit to tempt even a well-fed palate, let alone Daniel's. He held an orange with amazement, but Kiernan cheerfully told him they'd had a blockade runner tied up at their dock just the week before, picking up raw produce from the plantation in exchange for all manner of commodities. The captain had just been down to Florida, and the fruit he had brought back had been exceptional.

He saw that Callie, too, studied an orange with a certain awe, and he was startled by the depth of feeling that suddenly shook him, a combination of shame and admiration.

Perhaps he really had had no right to drag her through the lines the way that he had. He'd put her through danger, and massive discomfort. She'd never once complained.

He bit into his ham, chewing hard. She'd always had courage. He'd admired it from the start. That was why he had fallen so swiftly and so completely in love with her. That was why he had followed her out of the corn-field that day.

It was why the Yanks had beaten, subdued, shackled, and imprisoned him.

But perhaps she had done it to save his life. If it weren't for the damned war, perhaps he *could* trust her. He wanted to.

She had created the fabulous creature now being rocked by Janey in the kitchen. Jared Cameron. His son. A healthy, beautiful baby boy.

His stomach turned. Who could have ever imagined that it would feel this wonderful to be a father? He'd always liked children; he'd had some time with John Daniel as an infant to learn what they were like. And he'd loved his nephew dearly, just as he loved Jesse and Kiernan.

He'd never imagined what he would feel, looking

into Jared's sky-blue eyes, feeling those tiny fingers close around his own.

They were all here now. He'd wanted his son home. The idea probably hadn't even been rational at first. But he hadn't been about to leave the boy with Callie.

Revenge?

Maybe. Or maybe he had just wanted her here. And maybe he hadn't wanted to marry her because that would hurt her too. She had come with him anyway. She had never suggested marriage. He had.

He sat back. They were all so beautiful. Most men in his position would be convinced they had died and gone to heaven. His sister was striking with her ivory skin, coal-dark hair, and startling, deep-blue Cameron eyes. Even as a child Kiernan had been a beauty, with her classic features and wheat-blond hair, just touched by streaks of strawberry and sun.

Callie sat between them to complete the picture. Delicate, elegant, with the perfect shaping of her face, the large pools of her haunting gray eyes, the lovely bow of her mouth, and the shimmering auburn blaze of her hair to defy even the shade of a perfect sunset. She was dressed in silver this evening, silver-gray, a color that met and matched her eyes, and made them even deeper, darker, more elusive.

She truly was beautiful, he thought, extraordinarily so. In this dove-gray and silver, and in the white gown with the embroidered red flowers that Ben had procured for their wedding.

She'd been upset when they had left that gown behind. It had probably been the first gown of such elegance that she had ever owned. She had come from a small farm. Even the white wedding dress she had certainly worn to her first wedding had probably not been of the same quality.

He could never accuse her of seeking riches of any

kind. She seemed to stand up well against any calamity, be it flying bullets, poverty, hunger, hardship.

But this was the same way that he had been made the fool before, believing in her, loving her. She had the face of an angel.

She caught him studying her as she handled the orange and she flushed, placing it back on the table. She sat very stiffly, so quickly on the defensive.

And why not? Do you ever say anything even remotely kind to her? he taunted himself.

What is there to say? Tell her the truth? I love you, Callie, I love you with all of my heart. I want it just to be Jared, but I need you, I want you. So many times I have longed to bring you close beside me, to speak all that is in my heart.

But then I hear your whisper, feel the softness of your flesh. . . .

They were all talking. His sister and Kiernan, who truly loved him, and Callie, who they were artfully drawing into the conversation. He watched as she became animated, talking about her brothers.

Her smile was beautiful; the sound of her laughter was contagious.

He wanted to love her so badly. But he was afraid. Afraid that he had killed the love between them. Afraid that he could never really trust her, not while the war raged on.

He pushed back his chair. Three pairs of startled eyes were drawn his way.

"Excuse me, ladies," he said with an extravagant drawl. "I think I'll go out on the porch for a cigar."

He bowed abruptly and turned to leave them.

"But Daniel—" Christa began. "Ouch!"

Kiernan must have kicked her beneath the table, Daniel decided wryly. His sister was hurt, he knew. He had so little time with them, and it seemed that he was trying to escape them.

He leaned over the porch rail and looked over the rose garden, beautiful, haunted in the moonlight. Far down the slope of the lawn, the ivory glitter of the near full orb in the sky fell upon the river, the ever moving river. It was beautiful. It was peaceful. It was his home, and he was loath to leave it again.

Far across the yard he saw the old family cemetery, and beyond, the summer cottage. He paused, struck a match to his boot and lit a thin cheroot he had taken from the huge accounts desk in the den. He puffed on the fine tobacco.

He wandered down the steps and began to walk.

Summer was hot and humid. But here, by night, no matter how bad the day had been, nightfall brought a balmy breeze that seemed to caress and envelop him. Had it always felt so good just to walk in the darkness? Or had he learned the beauty of his home once he had been forced away from it so many great lengths of time?

Traditionally, the house would come to Jesse. Cameron Hall had always been inherited by the eldest son. But Jesse had always been more interested in his medicine, and Daniel had been the one who knew the acreage and the livestock. There had never been any reason to worry about who actually owned the place. They both loved it. And the family owned more houses than they might ever need. His mother had hailed from Mississippi, but his grandmother had brought a plantation into the family, a place called Stirling Hall. Kiernan had her own home, too, just up the river, and a doting father with no one to leave the place to except to his daughter and her children. Yes, they were all rich in houses and land.

Now they were rich. But the war would eventually strip them all. So far they had been lucky. Maybe they would stay lucky.

Maybe some Union company that didn't give a hoot

about a colonel named Cameron might come along
and burn down the place.

And any company, Reb or Yank, could come by and
rob it blind, "confiscating" for the troops. Just as they
had confiscated through Pennsylvania and Maryland.

He had reached the graveyard. The shadowy silver
light of the moon fell upon the white tombstones. A
low heat fog lay on the ground, and marble angels
seemed nearly to dance.

Daniel walked through the little gate and wandered
to his father's grave, and his mother's beside it. "Who's
right, Pa? Jesse and Callie, so convinced on the one
side, and Kiernan and Christa and I, ever rebels at
heart!" he whispered to the night. He sighed and continued to speak out loud. "Maybe slavery is wrong, Pa,
but isn't it equally wrong for one set of people to tell
another set how to live? Given time, the southern
states might have begun to free their slaves—they
might have voted it out. I hear tell that Vermont abol-
ished slavery some time ago. Hell, Pa, Thomas Jefferson couldn't deal with the question when he was writing the Constitution. The founding fathers actually left
us in a bit of a bind here. And we're killing one another over it daily now. I had to go with Virginia, Pa.
That's the way I saw it. Just like Jesse had to go
north."

And then there's Callie, he thought, silent once
again.

His father would have liked her. He would have
liked her poise, and he would have liked the way that
her eyes met the world, wide and steadfast. He would
have liked her strength under duress, and he would
have liked the beautiful smile that curved her lips every time she looked upon their son.

"Yes, then there's Callie!" he said aloud. "How do I
know what's true within her heart and soul, Pa? How
do you learn to trust someone again? I want to believe

her, but then I'm afraid. I hurt her, and God knows, I hurt myself. And if she really cared for me once I've managed to turn that love to dust!''

He paused in the moonlight, then smiled suddenly and turned away from the graves. He didn't know what he had expected to find here, but he had found a curious determination.

He walked past the smokehouse and the laundry and the rows of slave quarters until he reached the barn. Quietly and quickly he walked among the horses, talking to them as he passed them, looking them all over one by one.

The Yankee bay had been a decent enough mount, but he was wasn't taking it when he rode back to war. He wanted one of the saddle horses he had bred and trained himself.

He paused, wincing, thinking of the horses that had been killed beneath him. He chose a tall black named Zeus, patting the animal's nose. "Maybe we'll have better luck this time, eh, boy?" he whispered, stroking the fine neck. Zeus was half Arabian, and he had the deep dish nose and flying tail of that breed. He was a large horse, standing nearly seventeen hands high. "The Yanks might be after me just to get their hands on you, boy, but what the hell, sir, they'll be after us no matter what. We'll worry about that tomorrow. Tonight, well, tonight we're out for a ride."

He saddled and bridled the horse, and when he was done, he mounted up and began to ride.

The moonlight was all the guide he needed.

He rode over the plantation, impressed again with the manner with which his sister and Kiernan—and the twins—had managed to keep things going. He rode slowly, determined to drink in the sights and scents and the richness of summer here along the river before he would have to ride away.

But he did not ride idly. He knew where he was going.

An hour or so out he came upon the rough wagon they had abandoned on their ride in. There, in the darkness, he looked through the belongings they had deserted on their trip home.

He found the box with the white dress and its embroidered red flowers, crooked it under his arm, and mounted up once again.

He returned to the barn, watered Zeus and brushed him down well, and strode slowly back to the house.

The house seemed very quiet as he entered it through the back porch. He glanced in the dining room, but it was empty.

Curiously, he walked up the stairs, still carrying the dress box. He strode the few steps from the portrait gallery to his room. He tried the doorknob and scowled, a bolt of fury ripping through him like lightning.

The little witch. She'd bolted the door against him.

He nearly slammed his shoulder against it then and there, determined to break it down.

He hesitated. No, not yet. If she was lying awake, let her brood for a while.

And hell, he wanted to get his temper back under control.

He strode back down the stairway and went back into the den, drew the chair out from the desk, sat down, and propped his feet up. He leaned back, closing his eyes.

He had one fool night home, and he had spent it in the saddle, where God help him, he'd be spending his nights from now until who-knew-when!

And now she'd bolted the door against him. No matter. He'd made her no promises, and he didn't give a damn what the household might think. It was his room. He'd give her a few minutes. But then he was going in.

"Daniel?"

The soft whisper startled him. He glanced up. Kiernan was in the doorway.

"Come in," he told her.

She did so. He'd known her his entire life. She wasn't shy with him.

She sat down across from him, folding her hands in her lap. He smiled. That surely meant he was in for it.

"What, Kiernan?"

"That was rather rude."

He shrugged. "Kiernan, I assure you, my wife would far prefer your company to mine."

"Are you so very certain?"

"Entirely."

"Daniel—"

"Kiernan, I love you dearly," he warned her softly, "but you are treading on dangerous ground!"

"Hmmph! And I used to think that Jesse was the difficult one!"

"He is. You just don't see enough of him to truly appreciate his difficulty anymore," Daniel teased.

"Daniel—"

"Kiernan!"

She sighed. "Oh, all right! But just in case you're wondering about your wife, I'll tell you. She kept up a tremendous front, trying not to appear embarrassed that her husband had but one night with her and his son and disappeared in the midst of dinner despite it. She was in a difficult position, but I daresay she held her temper fairly well the first hour. Then she excused herself, saying that she was exhausted, which I'm sure she is, although I imagine she is presently torn between sleep—and the burning desire to skewer you through."

Daniel arched a brow at Kiernan. "I wasn't wondering about my wife. I know exactly where she is. But thank you, Mrs. Cameron!"

"You don't intend to apologize?"

"No, madam, I do not! I told you," he added more softly. "I don't think she missed my presence. In fact, I can almost guarantee it. And I will be going up. Soon."

Kiernan rose. "Well, I think that you're being as pigheaded as a mule. But still, I want you to know . . ."

"What?"

"Well, I've put both the boys to bed in John Daniel's nursery. John Daniel has graduated from his cradle, and it's just right for Jared. They're both sound asleep. I thought that you should know. Just in case."

It was good to know.

"Thank you," he told her softly.

"Good night, Daniel," Kiernan said softly. "I love you, you know." She came behind him, hugging his shoulders. She kissed him on the cheek.

He held her hand, where it lay against his shoulder. Then he turned slightly and kissed it. "I love you too."

She left him, and he stared broodingly across the room.

He'd married her. He'd brought her home. She was upstairs in his own room, and he was her husband, and he had every right, and he was about to ride away to war. . . .

There was a sound outside. He narrowed his eyes.

Maybe she was bringing the war to him.

But it wasn't Callie.

There was a slight tap on the door, and then Christa poked her head in.

"Daniel!"

"Come in," he told her.

She smiled and came in. "How about a brandy for your sister?" she asked.

Placing his feet on the ground, he pulled out the brandy carafe and glasses. He quickly poured the amber liquid. He didn't comment that a lady shouldn't be so determined on drinking at this hour of the night.

A lady shouldn't be working the way that Christa did to keep a place together, either.

He walked around the desk, handing her a brandy. "To the real Cameron among us, Christa! The one keeping the home fires burning."

Christa smiled. "You've three women keeping the home fires burning now, Daniel! Even if you are atrociously rude."

He sighed. "Must everyone comment on my affairs?"

Christa lowered her head. "No, I won't. Not anymore, not tonight. You're my brother, and I love you."

She stood up abruptly, careless with her glass as she suddenly hugged him, hard and tight. "Oh, Daniel, it's so good to see you, and so hard to know that you'll ride away so quickly again. Every time one of you leaves I feel that more of my heart is torn away. Jesse hasn't managed to come home in more than a year now!"

He hugged her in return, smoothing back her hair. "Shhhh!" he told her softly. "It's all right."

"Sometimes. And sometimes, I'm so scared, Daniel! It will never be the same again. Never, never."

"No, it will be the same! We'll be the same, Christa. Nothing has ever managed to touch the fact that we're a family, that we love one another, that we have one another! We need to hold on to that."

"Yes, of course. Except that Jesse is so far away. He might as well be across an ocean, the chasm is so deep!"

"Christa!" He lifted her face by her chin, searching out her eyes. "What—"

"Daniel, I want to get married. I can wait a few more months, but not forever! I love Liam McCloskey so much, and I'm always so afraid! With—with your blessing, we've set June for a wedding date. I pray that the war will be over. I pray so desperately that it will end!

But if it doesn't, Jesse will be far away! Oh, Daniel, he should be there—"

"Hush, Christa, maybe he will be."

"Kiernan can go to Washington. She can see Jesse there and let him know."

That probably wasn't such a good idea. Kiernan had to be very careful, moving back and forth across enemy lines. Too many Yanks knew that Jesse's family was all Reb, including his wife. The war itself was like that. Families were divided.

But spying was dangerous, and though Daniel knew that Jesse had suspected his wife of spying at one time, they had come to a truce of their own.

"There will be a way to let Jesse know," he assured her. "I'll see to it."

"He won't say no, will he?"

Daniel grinned. There were some things war couldn't change. Christa wanted Jesse's approval. It was only right.

But after their own hasty marriages, Daniel couldn't begin to see either Jesse or himself dictating anything about propriety to Christa!

"He won't say no."

She leaned against his shoulder. "I'm just so tired of it all. Daniel, there was an explosion in Richmond at the munitions factory—someone grew careless—and there were over sixty people killed." She pushed away from him and her eyes welled with tears. "They were mostly women, Daniel, working because the men were all gone to war. So now the ladies die as well as the gentlemen, and still, a generation of boys will be dead when this is done! Are we wrong, Daniel? Have we brought on this bloodshed for nothing?"

"We didn't bring on the bloodshed, Christa. Not you, nor I, nor Jesse. We were swept up into the midst of it, and we all did what we thought we had to do, and that's all that any man—or woman—can do. I pray that we're not wrong, I pray that daily. It's all I can do when I watch men fall, and bleed, and die. And walk barefoot in the snow, looking to me for a guidance I find it harder and harder to give."

"Oh, Daniel, I did not mean to distress you!"

He smiled and touched her cheek. "You never distress me. At least, you don't anymore. You were, upon occasion, a tremendous little hellion years ago."

She grinned. "I've seen to it that you've a fresh uniform to wear back to the front, Daniel. I've sewn on your insignias and bars just today. And I've knitted you a wonderful sash, and Patricia went out to find new plumes for your hat."

"Thank you."

She kissed his cheek. "Good night, Daniel. And don't forget, you must come home next June to give me away for my wedding just in case Jesse can't make it."

"Will your groom be home?"

"Of course. I'm giving you both ample notice."

She blew a kiss to him and disappeared. Daniel sat back down and picked up his brandy glass, swallowing down the contents instantly.

Poor Christa. She could give them all the time in the world, but neither he nor Christa's beloved captain could dictate the course of the war.

Please God, let it be over! he thought.

It didn't seem that God had answered many prayers lately.

The brandy was good. It burned. He poured another quickly and swallowed it down just as fast.

He had a good head for brandy. But he wanted the haze tonight, something to blunt the edges.

What the hell was he going to do? Sit here as the hours passed and want her, ache for her, long to wake her and shake her . . . and have her?

He caught his breath suddenly, for he could see her

through the slit at the doorway. The door to the den stood ajar.

She was coming down the stairs. She seemed a wisp of cloud at first. Ethereal, magical. She moved like a sprite, reaching the foot of the stairs.

She moved swiftly and furtively across the hallway. Still, she seemed to float, in that elusive cloud of beauty, her hair a clean and brilliant fire, the sheer froth of whatever she was wearing swirling with her at every step.

She was wearing something of Christa's.

And Christa had beautiful things.

This concoction of silk and fluff was in softest gray, a color that caught hold of the moonlight well, that shimmered and moved beneath it. It seemed to dance hauntingly along with the swift, graceful glide of the woman. When she paused, it hugged her form, delineating each curve and plane and fascinating hollow.

Everything within him tightened and constricted. Still, he sat motionless in his seat, watching her. What was she up to?

He knew. She had come down to assure herself that he had chosen to sleep elsewhere, that she might find herself in peace for the evening. He sat back, watching, brooding, as she looked into the dining room. She peeked quickly in and quickly out, a wraith in the shadows of the darkened house.

He rose at last, silently leaning against the doorway, watching her still as she moved along the great hall. She turned and started to hurry back to the stairway, and that was when she discovered him standing there, arms crossed over his chest, awaiting her.

"Good evening, Mrs. Cameron."

She stopped dead still. "Good evening," she replied coolly, spinning to skirt around him, having decided, it seemed, that retreat might leave her to battle another day.

Not tonight.

He caught hold of her arm, swinging her back around. "I believe you were looking for something?"

"Yes," she said quickly. "I thought that a sherry might help me sleep."

"No, you didn't. You don't want anything to drink, and you weren't looking for anything to drink."

She jerked her arm free. "Well, the same doesn't seem to be true of you!" she informed him smoothly. She wrinkled her nose as if she were the grandest dame to have ever set a foot on Virginian soil.

"Why, yes, Mrs. Cameron, I have had a drink or two. But rest assured, I am not drunk." He bowed deeply to her. "A southern officer would never overimbibe."

Callie didn't know if he was drunk or not; she only knew that he was dangerous at that moment.

If she came too close, he might touch her. She couldn't allow him to do so. Her pride still seemed ravaged by what he had done tonight, walking away from his own family in order to walk away from her.

"So, just what are you doing?" he asked her.

She felt his tension, felt an anger as great as her own. An uneasy thought struck her. Perhaps he had come upstairs and he knew she had locked the door against him.

"I told you—"

"You didn't come down for anything other than the hope that you would find me sound asleep in a desk chair. I imagine you were hoping I might be well gone into oblivion!"

"Don't be ridiculous," she said. "It is immaterial to me where you choose to sleep."

He smiled, striding toward her. It was probably the moment to run. She couldn't quite do that. He had her angled against the door, and suddenly she was pinned there, his hands on either side of her face.

"Then why was the door locked?" he demanded.

"Oh, did I lock it?"

"Indeed, madam, you did."

His gaze was sharp, glittering in the moonlight. Callie felt the tension that ripped through his body, and she was suddenly more furious than ever.

"Yes, I locked the door! I locked it against the rudest Rebel bastard I've ever met, and I'd do so again."

She slammed her fists against his chest, shoving past him. For a moment he was still, and she thought that she might make the stairway in one piece. If she could just reach the room, she could lock the door against him again. He wouldn't break down a door in his own house.

She didn't dare look back. She fled, running up the steps one by one on bare feet. She burst into the room and turned to close the door.

But he was there. He had followed at her own speed, in silence. She tried to throw the door shut.

He caught the door as Callie tried to slam it against him. He slammed it back open with both palms. The door shuddered and reverberated and Callie wondered if the sound couldn't be heard throughout the entire house.

"You've no right!" Callie hissed suddenly. "No right whatsoever in here—"

She broke off, crying out, spinning to leap away as he strode for her. His fingers knotted into the beautiful silk-and-lace nightgown that Christa had given her. He jerked her back around to face him.

His eyes touched hers, and to her deepest dismay, she felt the fire from that blue stare leap into her trembling frame. He held her shoulders, held them taut. And then he kissed her.

Deeply. With no desire to seek acquiescence, his mouth bore down on hers. He forced her lips to part. She felt the sure sweep of his tongue within her mouth, and each liquid caress seemed to steal more resolve from her pride and soul.

She tried to wrench free, beating her hands against his chest. She turned, but a piece of the gown caught in his hands, and she heard a rip. Startled, she paused, and turned back. She met his gaze again.

This night, he had determined, was his.

And God help her, seeing him stand there, the hot blue resolution in his eyes, the granite determination in the contours of his face, she felt a burst of near desperate desire come sweeping through her once again.

"The gown is Christa's!" she snapped at him. "You've no right to destroy it."

"Then get it off."

In a fit of fury she drew the exquisite piece of fluff and lace over her shoulders, tossing it on the floor. Naked, she lifted her chin.

"We haven't begun to discuss this—"

"And we're not going to discuss it!" he told her curtly.

She backed away with his first stride toward her. "Oh, yes, we are! Don't you ever think that you can just burst into places and behave this way. At the very least, you could have pretended—"

"Pretended what?"

"You're only here this one night! You could have pretended that we had a normal marriage. That if we weren't madly in love, at the least we didn't despise one another. That there was something we each wanted from one another. You know very well what I mean and you have no rights with me whatsoever and you will not—"

"Oh, but I will! Rebels do what they choose, Mrs. Cameron," he assured her.

"No! I won't be—"

"I keep forgetting! This play is to be reserved for those moments when they might suit you well—when your fine noble Yanks are waiting in the closet. Should I look? Have I someone in my bedroom closet already?''

Callie stopped backing away. She struck him across the face instantly, just as hard as she could.

It was all that she could do to keep from crying out, for she was lifted up into his arms and thrown down upon the bed. Dazed, she lay still for a moment. He strode toward the bed. She thought that he was unbuckling his scabbard, but when she tried to rise from his bed she discovered the truth.

He had drawn his cavalry sword.

The point of it lay between her breasts, the steel cold against the bareness of her flesh.

"It's a pity, Callie, that I can't simply split you in two." The steel lifted. Just a whisper above her flesh now, it moved. Along her ribs, low over her abdomen, lower. It rose again. "Tear away the flesh and the outer beauty, and see into the very depths of your heart. I would dearly love to see what lies there. Maybe I should try it. Sever you into two pieces . . ."

He let his words trail. She glared at him shivering.

What would you find, my love? That I want you now, that I love you, that I have so little to cling to when you fight a war against me more bitter than that you wage against the men of the North.

Damn him.

He would never really hurt her. Whether he hated her or no. She had learned that much about him.

She shoved the sword away from her face, and told him exactly that. Then she told him what she thought he ought to go do with himself.

His laughter rang out. His sword, his scabbard, and his clothing fell to the bedside.

"Don't you dare think that you're coming to this bed, Daniel Cameron! If you do—"

He did.

Naked, hot as fire himself, he came upon her with the grace of a great cat, covering her body with the length and breadth of his. She squirmed beneath him, feeling the flush, the fever, seize her. His chest pressed to her breasts, his thighs were hard upon hers.

And his sex, immensely hard and erect and insinuative, lay directly against the apex of her thighs.

"If I do, you'll what?" he demanded, his lips directly above hers, his fingers moving into the wings of her hair at the sides of her head.

"I'll scream."

"Scream."

"I think that I really hate you, Daniel!"

His reply was bitter, but the words startled her. "I wish that I really hated you, Callie." Still, his lips were just above hers in the near darkness. The whisper of his words caressed her mouth. The pulse of his desire lay very naked against her, and she had never wanted him more.

"Well, will you scream?" he murmured.

"Bastard!" she whispered in return.

His mouth touched hers again. This time she did not fight him. She molded her mouth to his; she arched against the imprint of his body, feeling a liquid like lava sweep through her, creating an arousal and a passion both beautiful and painful.

His mouth caressed hers. Savored, touched, licked. The touch came sensually over her shoulders, her collarbones, her breasts.

He moved, still agile, quick, flipping her over in the bed. She felt his lips against the line of her spine and still close to her ear.

"You wanted to pretend. Let's pretend. Let's pretend that you love me. That your heart aches to see me leave. Let's pretend . . ."

Dear Lord, but he knew how to kiss and caress. Straddled easily over her, his hands swept her shoulders and her back, his fingers caressed the sensitive sides of her breasts.

His lips continued their sweet assault upon her senses as he spoke, whispering against her flesh, following the trail of her spine.

"Let's pretend that I am a soldier, going off to your own cause. That you will pine away the hours that I am gone. That you will love me now with all your heart and soul, touch me to remember me, in all the long days that will come to pass."

His kiss fell very low against her buttocks. His fingers swept her flesh. She shivered, alive, quaking with the desire he had so deftly lit and stoked.

He flipped her over again, and his gaze met hers.

"We needn't pretend on one thing, my love. For I do want you. God, yes, Callie, I want you."

His dark head buried itself against her breasts. Against her belly, against the juncture of her thighs. She cried out softly, trying to rise against him, tugging at his dark hair. She brought his lips to hers, and she kissed them in turn, kissed and savored his lips and his mouth.

She rose against him, her fingers tracing patterns over his shoulders, her lips against the muscles of his chest, her teeth nipping at them, her tongue running elusively over every tiny touch. She stroked his body and knelt before him, then dared to let her hands fall. Her fingers curled around the hard, pulsing rod of his sex. His body nearly jackknifed. She grew bolder and bolder, stroking, touching.

His arms were suddenly around her and they fell into the depths of the bed together. Soft, clean, fragrant sheets seemed to reach up and take her in, a contrast to the blinding heat and demand of his body, now part of hers. She bit into his shoulder as he thrust deep inside of her. Deeper. His body moving. A startling, soaring rhythm.

Stars burst, the darkness was broken, and then it fell
again. She felt the sweat-slickened weight of his body
hard against hers, and lay there in silence, still touching
him, feeling his touch. It was good to lie here so, sated,
entwined, as if they loved one another.

Moments later, she gave in to temptation. She
crawled atop him, legs straddled over his hips. She
leaned low against him, her hair teasing his flesh, trailing against it.

"Let's pretend," she whispered softly. "Let's pretend that you love me. That you crave this night before
you ride away to war. That you will hold me into the
darkness, and into the light. That my name will be
upon your lips when you fight a thousand battles. Daniel, let's pretend . . ."

She paused, her eyes meeting his in the near darkness.

"Pretend, my love," he whispered in return.

His arms wrapped around her. He swept her beneath
him, and she cried out softly again with the volatility of
his assault upon her senses, his kisses roaming where
they would, his touch demanding every intimacy.

He was part of her again, one with her. No darkness
of war could enter then within them, for they soared
above any matters of the earth. This time she reached a
pinnacle so high it seemed she lost touch with even the
pale moonlight, and then she was gently, gently falling
again.

She wanted to speak, but her eyes were so heavy.
She wanted to say things, but she didn't want to break
the spell. She lay upon his chest, touching him still, her
fingers lying easily upon muscle and the crisp dark hair
that grew there.

And he held her tight.

Her eyes were so heavy. She closed them.

* * *

He awoke with the first pink streaks of dawn. For a moment, he started, and then he felt her against him. He held his breath and studied her.

The auburn hair, more than a match for those radiant streaks of dawn. Her face, now surely that of an angel, so delicate, so beautiful, half hidden by the profusion of her hair.

The length of her. Ivory beauty as she lay curled against the sheets—and him. Each supple curve seemed both innocent and evocative this morning. Angel.

She slept so peacefully.

He rose, careful not to waken her.

In his wardrobe, he found the clean uniform that Christa had seen to for him.

He would be very well clad and well shod, compared to the rest of his troops.

He buckled his scabbard around his waist, and stood at the foot of the bed. He wondered if he should wake her and apologize for being a horse's ass.

Sorry, Mrs. Cameron, but maybe we southern gentlemen do overindulge upon occassion.

No.

He wouldn't awaken her. Their world of pretend was far too sweet.

He hurried downstairs and into the den, finding the box with her dress. He came back up and hesitated. No, he could not wake her.

He had to touch her, though. He bent, smoothed her hair away, and kissed her forehead. Still, she didn't rise.

And so, regretfully, he left her.

Down the hall, he entered the nursery. He was tempted to sweep his tiny son into his arms, but he refrained from doing so.

Like his mother, Jared slept peacefully.

Janey came in to tell him that she had food ready. He nodded absently and said that he would be along.

The sun rose higher.

It was time to go.

It was several hours later when Callie awoke.

She did so abruptly, with a jerk, instinctively reaching out for Daniel.

He was gone.

The white dress with embroidered red flowers lay spread across the foot of the bed.

4

When Johnny Comes Marching Home Again

Twenty-five

During the fall of 1863, Daniel felt as if they played a game of cat and mouse with the Yankees, covering a great deal of Virginia, pushing forward, being pushed back, skirmishing.

Both sides were becoming quiet once again.

As always, silence was ominous.

Daniel hadn't been back long with his regiment when a lull in the fighting brought him a visit from a tall cavalry captain with the Virginia militia. Daniel was busy with a group of maps when the man stepped into his tent and saluted sharply. Daniel gazed at him, thinking that he somewhat resembled George Custer, for he had long blond hair, a curling mustache, and a neatly clipped beard. He was young, in his early twenties, and for a moment Daniel stared at him blankly, wondering just who he was and why he was disturbing Daniel when he was so engrossed in the geography of the area they were trying to hold.

"Colonel Cameron!"

"Yes?"

The man was stiff and straight, and seemed somewhat nervous. Odd, for he looked like a strong fellow, one quite confident in himself. Daniel gave him his full attention, noting that he would probably be considered a very handsome lad by the ladies, and that he also seemed determined.

Daniel sat down behind his field desk. "Yes, Captain. Just what is it that I can do for you?"

"My name is Liam McCloskey, sir. I have been trying to find you for quite some time. I . . ." He took a deep breath, then spoke in a rush. "I wish to ask for your sister's hand in marriage, sir. I understand that you are not the eldest male member of the family, but since that man is a member of the enemy's army, I have come to you."

Funny, he didn't like to hear Jesse called an enemy. Even if it was true. But the look on the young man's face was so earnest that Daniel bit back a retort.

"Ah, Liam McCloskey." He rose and came around his desk, offering the man his hand. He studied him carefully once again. The earnestness remained.

"I meant no offense, sir. Christa has made it quite plain to me that she loves her family intensely, and I have assured her that whatever my mind concerning the North, my thoughts will be kept to myself should the Yank Colonel Cameron and I manage to meet. Truly, Colonel, I mean no offense."

"None taken." Obviously, there were no split loyalties within McCloskey's family. He was suddenly reminded of what Jeb Stuart had told him he'd written to a family member when he heard his father-in-law was determined to stay with the Union. "He will regret it but once, and that will be continuously."

But Jeb had also said upon a number of occasions that he would rather die than lose the war.

He had been so furious with his father-in-law that he had renamed his son, since the boy had been named after his grandfather. Philip St. George Cooke Stuart became James Ewell Brown Stuart II.

Daniel was no longer certain what he felt. He'd

never hated Jesse. He'd never even been angry. He'd often seen Jesse's side.

In the long days and nights, Daniel could too often remember Callie's words, telling him that he knew slavery was wrong.

The North had made it a question of slavery. He believed with his whole heart that he and the state of Virginia were fighting for states' rights.

But he had to admit that the southern states were fighting for the right to keep their way of life.

And that way of life meant slaves.

"Sir?"

"Yes, yes, I'm sorry."

"I believe that Christa might have mentioned—"

"Indeed, sir, she did."

"Colonel, I must tell you that I hail from a decent-sized farm down Norfolk way. I'm never quite sure of what is going to be left of it once this thing is over and the Yanks are beat back, but I can promise you this—I will love her with every breath in my body, from now unto eternity!"

Daniel lowered his lashes quickly, not wanting the very passionate young McCloskey to see his amusement. Yes, he did love Christa. He seemed to embody all the right virtues for a young man.

And Christa loved him.

"I'm glad we've met, Captain. Christa has expressed a desire for a June wedding."

"Yes, sir. With your blessing, sir."

"You've got my blessing, Captain. I've promised to do my best to be there to give my sister away."

"Thank you. I've requested my leave for June fifteenth, just in case we don't get a chance to whip the Yanks by then, sir. Again, I thank you so much." He saluted and turned sharply, striding out of the large field tent. He paused at the flap. "Rest assured, sir. I do love her!"

The words were so soft and so fervent Daniel couldn't help but smile as the young man left at last.

For days, the fervent passion in McCloskey's voice haunted Daniel and left him thinking of his own wife again. Sometimes speculating, sometimes hurting, and always wishing that he could get home again.

The skirmishing dragged on, the Yanks and the Rebs skirting one another.

On the western front, great armies clashed at Chicamauga and then at Chattanooga, and southern casualties were high. Those losses brought further weight down upon the laboring shoulders of the Confederacy, and yet few men spoke of a true defeat.

Daniel's forces battled fiercely at Bristoe, then the armies shifted again.

By December 1, the Union army moved across the Rapidan.

Southern commanders were wary, and Daniel knew there would be no way he could take another leave to go home for Christmas.

He managed to get a letter through to Jesse, assuring him that his wife and child were fine, and telling him about Christa's wedding plans. "She would dearly love to have you there, but God alone knows when this war will end. I believe she knows her own mind and is determined upon marriage now. Don't risk yourself."

He had not heard back from his brother, and he was worried.

He ached for home.

Or maybe it wasn't home that he pined for anymore. He lay awake each night and relived every last moment he had spent with Callie.

He had tried to write to her but his notes never sounded quite right, and so he had given up the effort, addressing his letters to all three of the women in his household and keeping them as light as he could.

She did not write in return. Christa wrote, and

Kiernan wrote, and sometimes when he was lucky, mail came through.

But Callie did not write.

She remained at Cameron Hall, and must have been resigned to life there, for Christa and Kiernan both mentioned her and the children constantly. John Daniel was speaking more clearly daily, and Jared was tearing around the house on his knees. Ships were still managing to come and go on the river, despite the Yankee blockade. They hadn't heard of any troops anywhere near them for quite some time.

On Christmas morning, Daniel was in a command tent along the Rapidan River when one of his sergeants made an appearance before him.

"Yanks across the river, sir!"

"Yes, I know," he said dryly. "They've been there for quite some time. I don't think they're planning on any hostilities today. It is Christmas day." Sometimes fighting did break out on Christmas. Both sides tried to avoid it.

"No, sir. They aren't planning any hostilities. Come on out, sir. I promised that I'd bring you down to the river."

Curious, Daniel rose, buckled on his sword, and followed his sergeant.

Far across a new layer of snow and ice-clogged water, he could see a detachment of mounted soldiers, Yankee cavalry.

One of the mounted men raced forward, close to the glistening river, and shouted out.

"In your honor, sir! Your brother, Colonel Jesse Cameron, has recently heard of your marriage, and the birth of your son. He—and many other officers with whom you studied at West Point and rode with in Kansas—now salute you, sir! Also, sir, Colonel Jesse Cameron sends his love to his wife and his sister, and congragulates the latter on her upcoming nuptials, sir!"

And there, on Christmas day, guns exploded into the air and a series of cries went up.

Daniel grinned broadly, shouting back to the Yank across the river. "Tell my brother, and the other gentlemen, thank you, sir!"

They both saluted. The Yankees rode away, disappearing into a haze of snow.

"Well, Jess," he murmured to himself, "at least I know that you are alive and well."

Daniel turned, startled to discover that he was more weary than ever and returned to his tent.

It was Christmas. A dark day for the men and women of the Confederacy.

With a new, dark year stretching before them.

As yet, they couldn't guess how dark that year would be.

Christmas came to Cameron Hall.

By that time, Callie was very comfortable in her new home and with everyone in it.

During the long fall, she had earned herself a place there, startling both Kiernan and Christa with her abilities with both the plantation livestock and the garden planting.

She didn't know anything about cotton at all, but that didn't matter because both Christa and Kiernan did, as did the very able ex-slaves who had served the Camerons for years.

Christa told her that there had been a time when she had worried deeply about running the place herself, because a number of their freed people had determined to move to the North.

But a large group of blacks from Cameron Hall had been in New York when the draft riots had exploded in mid-July of '63. In a period of four days, mobs had burned the draft office, the offices of the *Tribune,* and other buildings. The violence had turned toward the blacks—held to be responsible for the war by many of the northerners. White men had died, too, but it had been mostly blacks killed, and in that four-day period, nearly a thousand people had died or been wounded.

It had been a dark day for the North.

But it had brought a number of Cameron Hall's freed slaves back to work her fields, and Christa had been relieved to have them return.

Before the war, there had been nearly a hundred field hands at Cameron Hall. Now there were only thirty-eight, but before the men had made their way back from New York, there had been a scant twenty-two.

In November they had acquired some more help, in the form of Joseph Ashby, a Confederate soldier honorably discharged after he lost his left leg at Gettysburg. Joseph was as cheerful as the day was long—still convinced that the Yanks would never win—and the best overseer any plantation had ever seen. With Joseph up every morning at the crack of dawn to hobble along on his wooden leg, life became much easier not just for Christa, but for all of the Cameron women. Not that Callie had ever minded work—work kept her mind off the future—but Jared was constantly changing now, learning new things, and she cherished her time with him. The household could also be fun, with John Daniel running about everywhere, and Jared now trying to keep up on his knees.

Callie discovered that she liked both of her sister-in-laws very much. They were both headstrong, and determined, but also very kind. While Callie could make a garden grow under the most difficult situation, Kiernan and Christa knew every little nuance of proper dress and society, and even in the midst of war with her own inner conflict almost always raging, Callie learned that her sisters-in-law could make her laugh, exaggerating the proper way to hold a teacup, to walk, to laugh, to flutter eyelashes, to lift a chin imperiously, in short, to charm a man—or stop him cold.

They lived for the days when a letter would come through, brought more and more often by passing friends or even strangers as the war disrupted regular mail service. Letters came most frequently from Daniel, but they were never addressed to Callie alone, and she tried to hide her feelings of both embarrassment and desolation that he would not make a special effort to write to his own wife.

Two letters came through from Jesse, and they were for Kiernan alone, although she assured both Christa and Callie that he had sent them both his love. After the first, Kiernan had seemed strange for a day or two, and then she had come to Callie's room one evening to ask just how Callie had come to know Jesse.

Callie explained that he had come by after the battle of Antietam, when he had been looking for Daniel. And that she had known, of course, where Daniel was.

Kiernan watched Callie as she spoke, then she exclaimed softly, "That's it! Daniel thinks you were responsible for his being in prison!"

Callie looked down at her hands. "I was responsible," she said quietly.

Kiernan gasped. "Dear Lord, I could have sworn that you cared something for him!"

"I do," Callie told her. She shrugged and added, "I love him. That's why I did what I did." She tried very hard to explain everything that happened. She couldn't quite meet Kiernan's eyes when she told her almost exactly what she had done, but she stuttered through a story very close to the entire truth. "They would have killed him, Kiernan. I didn't want him to die."

Kiernan sat beside her and hugged her tightly. "Oh, Callie! But if you've explained things to Daniel the way that you've explained them to me—"

"I've tried, but I don't think he believes me. Maybe he can't believe me. And maybe it's just the war that now makes enemies of us."

"And maybe he ought to be smacked right in the face," Kiernan said determinedly.

"I've tried that too," Callie admitted, smiling ruefully.

"Perhaps if I were to intercede—" Kiernan began.

"No," Callie told her. "Kiernan, don't you see? He has to believe in me again, or nothing will ever be any good. The fates don't seem to be looking on me very kindly. As soon as we started heading for Virginia, the same Yankee came after us again. He's Lieutenant Colonel Dabney now—he received a promotion for bringing Daniel in. What's worse, he was a friend before the war. I had asked Daniel to stop to say goodbye to the people who had helped me when I was alone. Dabney came after us because one of the Weisses—concerned for my welfare or that of the baby, I'm sure—told him where I had gone."

"I see," Kiernan murmured.

"And there's more, of course."

"What's that?"

"*I am a Yankee,*" Callie said. "Oh, Kiernan, I'm sorry, I know how you love your South! But I believe in the Union, I believe that as a whole we can be great, I—"

"Wait! I've heard it!" Kiernan interrupted her. She smiled. "You forget, I've a Yankee physician for a husband. Callie! I've seen Virginia ravaged, I've seen men die—God, help me! I've assisted in removing their limbs. I cannot bear what has happened here, the rape of the land, the cruelties that exist. But I have discovered more than ever that the war has brought out the best in good men, and the worst in those less noble, North and South. I don't want to see this, my home burned, nor my father's home burned. What I want, more than anything, is for the war to end."

Callie smiled, and hugged Kiernan fiercely. "It's what I want too."

Kiernan sat back, studying her. "Daniel does love you, you know."

"Once, I think that he did. Sometimes now I'm convinced that he hates me."

"No. I've known Daniel all my life. I have never seen him so intense before, so passionate, so torn. Don't you see, Callie, if he did not care, his manners would be far better!"

Callie thought of the beautiful white dress with its red flowers, left at the foot of the bed.

Let's pretend . . .

"But I can't tell him that I love him—he does not trust me. And I try so very hard to keep my distance, because I am lost if I ever surrender—"

"I agree! You can never, never surrender to Cameron men," Kiernan assured her. "But you can sue for a negotiated peace."

"Perhaps," Callie agreed.

"Time will tell."

"And the war will end!"

But the war didn't end.

Christmas day brought the three Cameron women outside, despite the cold. They sat on the porch, watching the drive, all praying that a loved one would come to them.

No soldiers came home that day.

Callie prayed for safety, for Daniel, for Jesse, for her brothers on some distant front. She wrote to them time and time again, but so far, had received no replies. Maybe her letters had never reached them. Maybe they didn't know where she was. She could only pray that they were safe.

In early February, Kiernan received a request to come and help one of the matrons at the military hospital on the outskirts of Richmond. Again, she sought Callie out at night, reading the letter.

"I know, dear, that some of our Richmond ladies have been less than kind since hearing of your marriage to the Cameron who turned his back on his people, but as I knew your heart to be strong and true—and at the utmost, loyal—I am begging you to suffer their slings and arrows, as it were, to come give me some assistance here. Supplies are woefully low, and the men are dearly in need of good cheer. I have heard from a young man your husband assisted (an officer injured and imprisoned and exchanged) that you are an excellent nurse, with better qualifications gained at your husband's side than many a man who titles himself 'doctor.' Please come. But take extreme care. Yankees are ever trying to reach our dear capital!"

"What will you do?" Callie asked her.

"I will go, of course."

"I'm coming with you," Callie determined suddenly.

"To save Rebel lives?" Kiernan asked her.

"To save human lives."

Kiernan grinned. "Good! I was hoping you would come!"

Yankees were very near the capital.

At the end of February Daniel was summoned to a meeting. A courier had arrived with dispatches warning of the discovery of a planned raid on Richmond. Federal General Judson Kilpatrick and Federal Colonel Ulric Dahlgren were leading forces that would separate, meet, seize the capital, distribute amnesty proclamations, and free the Federal prisoners in Richmond.

Daniel, who knew the countryside like the back of his hand, was ordered to leave his troops to ride communications for the troops who would defend against these raiders.

By nightfall of the first of March, Dahlgren and his men were within two and a half miles of the capital. Daniel was there with the Confederate forces who fought him.

Riding around Dahlgren's forces, Daniel discovered that he had ordered a retreat.

The next day, the Confederates pursued him. Late that night they set up an ambush. In the fighting that followed, Dahlgren was killed.

The raid might have been considered a minor incident in a war in which thousands sometimes died in a battle, except for the fact that startling documents were found on Dahlgren's body.

There were orders to his men—signed by Dahlgren—that they must burn Richmond, "the hated city," to the ground.

A second paper, unsigned, said that they must find Jeff Davis and his cabinet, and kill them.

Daniel returned to his command with the couriers carrying the photographic copies of the letters to Lee. Word was out about the letters, and emotions were running high against the Union. Southerners, on the field of battle and off, were outraged.

Lee sent copies of the letters to Meade. In turn, Meade replied to Lee assuring him that the United States government had never sanctioned such orders, had indeed, sanctioned nothing but what action might be necessary by war.

Whether it was a cover-up or the truth, no one knew.

Beauty Stuart had summoned Daniel when the reply

came in. He showed him a copy. "Well, what do you think?"

"I think it's a good thing that Dahlgren did not succeed with his raid," Daniel said.

"And what of our one-time friends in the North?"

"I cannot believe that they would condone murder."

Stuart shrugged. "Perhaps not." He gazed at Daniel sharply. "Well, did you see your wife in Richmond?"

"What?" Daniel demanded sharply.

"I'm sorry, you didn't know? Flora mentioned in a letter to me that she had heard both your sister-in-law and your wife were working at the hospital. You know that I'm not a man to take leave often, and that I don't appreciate time taken by my officers. But as you were so close . . ."

Daniel gritted his teeth. He hadn't known that Callie was in Richmond.

Callie didn't write.

But he hadn't heard from Kiernan, either.

"As we are still so close," Daniel said, "when you feel that I might be spared again, I would highly appreciate just a day or two to see to her welfare, and that of my sister-in-law and son."

Beauty acquiesced.

Once again, Daniel bided his time.

Winter was fading; spring had come. With warmer weather, the fighting would intensify.

He wanted to see Callie. Soon.

Callie's first days in the hospital seemed to bring her from one horror to the next.

She had seen men die before. She had seen them die all over her yard. She had nursed Daniel when he was wounded, and she had feared for her life.

None of it had prepared her for the hospital.

There were not enough drugs, and now there was

barely enough whiskey to be prescribed for the patients.

Amputations were the order of the day. By the end of her first week, Callie couldn't count the number of operations in which she had assisted. At first, she had nearly passed out. Kiernan had warned her to pinch herself, and thus save herself such an embarrassment.

There was much more to helping in the hospital than the horror of seeing whole men lose their limbs. Some soldiers tried to bring their whole families in to sleep, and she had to part clinging wives from their soldier husbands and insist that the hospital was for the sick. She read until she was hoarse, and she wrote endless letters.

She wrote letters for men who died before they finished dictating them.

She and Kiernan and Janey had rented a small row house right by the hospital for themselves and the boys, and while Kiernan and Callie put in their endless hours with the wounded, Janey minded the boys and did what she could to put food on their own table.

Callie couldn't have said that she was happy. To live in the midst of such pain and misery could not make one happy.

But she felt useful.

She was also, upon occasion, able to visit Varina Davis. One evening she and Kiernan both stripped off their worn work gowns and attended one of Varina's receptions. Kiernan tried to tell Callie that she was really not very welcome because of her marriage to Jesse, and Callie commented that it was very strange that she—the one who was the Yank—seemed to fare better than a full-blooded Confederate like Kiernan.

"I'm afraid it's a man's world," Kiernan said. "And we are judged by our men." She grinned. "You, at least, are thereby a national hero."

"I don't think that Daniel would agree."

"But you must take advantage of his situation, right?"

It was impossible not to come to love Kiernan dearly, and Callie was very grateful for her. No matter what other women might be saying about Kiernan, Varina was, as always, the ultimate hostess.

Varina was expecting another baby that spring, and despite the lines drawn into her beautiful face by the tensions of her position, she seemed to hold a special beauty.

"You manage to be happy, despite it all," Callie told her.

"And you seem to serve us well, even if your heart lies elsewhere!" Varina told her. She smiled a beautiful smile, even if her slender face seemed drawn. In her way, Varina was happy. She loved her husband, and she loved her children. She was willing to ride out any storm with him, to rise to the heights, to endure any hardship.

Callie was suddenly very envious. She could suddenly see clearly what she wanted more than anything in the world.

A love so simple, and a love so complex.

It might well be something she could never have. She and Daniel might never come to an understanding. He didn't trust her; there was the possibility that he never would.

It was a division every bit as deep as the Mason-Dixon line.

Kiernan had told her that Daniel did love her. Maybe in time.

She smiled ruefully and told Varina, "I'm glad to be at the hospital. Well, I think I am. It's terrible to watch the men suffer. Sometimes, it's pure agony to write their letters, and help them say good-bye, telling their mothers or wives or children that they love them so. But when they're in the hospital, it doesn't seem that

they are Yankees or Rebels anymore, it just seems they
are men, God-fearing and all alike."

"And once we were," Varina murmured. She flashed
Callie a smile. "I have a wayward child slipping down
the stairway once again. Excuse me!"

Callie laughed. Through the open foyer doors she
could see a dark-haired little boy with a brilliant smile
to defy any mention of warfare, inching down the elegant stairway.

Again, she felt a little tug of envy for Varina Davis.
The world, it seemed, was crumbling down around
her. But she had her "dear old Banny," and her beautiful children.

Callie and Kiernan enjoyed the evening, but retired
early.

Richmond was crawling with refugees. Even in the
late evening, the streets were filled with people. Many
of them were living on the streets, Callie had heard.
They had been burned out of their homes, or were in
the way of a northern army determinedly destroying
any source of supply it could.

The Yankees were very close. And still, the southern
spirit was a determined one.

The Yankees might come close, but they wouldn't
take Richmond.

Working in the hospital again, Callie discovered that
more and more of the injured men were coming in
from skirmishes extremely close to the capital. She was
startled to discover that she was hanging on every word
that the soldiers told her.

She began to hear about her husband. He was close
with his flamboyant commander, that dashing cavalier
Stuart, and they were keeping close tabs on Union
General Custer's troops now.

Callie felt her heart beating quickly as she cooled
fevered foreheads and tried to make men more comfortable. She realized that she was longing to see Dan-

iel again. But as Kiernan had said, she could not surrender. But she could sue for a negotiated peace.

But war gave no quarter to the wants and desires of the contestants locked within it.

Daniel remained on the battlefield, and Callie remained in Richmond, praying that he would come for a day, an hour.

Deeper tragedy struck.

On April 30, the precocious little boy with the beautiful smile, Varina's Joey, fell from the porch of the Confederate White House.

A servant brought news of the awful event to Callie at the hospital. An old, gaunt black man, tears running down his face, told Callie the tale.

"Miz Varina, she had just left the children playing in her room, and she done bring some tea or some-such into the president. Next thing we all know, that boy— her very pride and joy—why he done crawl up on a bannister and then . . . then he was on the ground and there was all manner of screaming. Miz Varina, why, she done reach her child mighty quick, and he died in his mother's arms. She was overcome. Just overcome. But the army, ma'am, it had dispatches coming in for the president all the time, even as he was kneeling there, bowed over his son in grief. He done told them at last that he had to have one day with his child. And there she is, Miz Varina, expecting another babe, weeping over this one, and trying to hold up her husband all the while. She's strong, Miz Cameron, but Lawd almighty, how strong can a woman be? She sets a store by you, ma'am, and I thought that maybe . . ."

"I'll come right away," Callie promised him.

And she did.

It seemed that there was so little that she could do. The Davises were closeted with their grief.

Callie tried to help with the weeping babes who were so lost and confused at their brother's death, and she tried to greet the mourners who came to the door. She sat numbly as she saw the small boy dressed out for his burial, and she could think of no words to say when Varina was before her.

There *were* no words to atone for the loss of a child. Callie thought of how recently she had seen little Joey with his beautiful smile.

And after all the death she had witnessed time and time again, she turned away and wept.

The thunder of cannon fire could be heard as the little boy was laid to rest.

Within days, the Union and Confederate forces were engaged in fierce fighting in the Wilderness. Callie had never seen anything more terrible, for the forests caught on fire, and men brought into the hospital were sometimes little more than charred corpses. And no one knew if their uniforms had been blue or gray.

Then came the battle of Yellow Tavern.

A little less than two weeks after the death of little Joe Davis, the thunder of cannon fire could be heard again as Callie stood in Hollywood Cemetery, eyes glazed as she watched another burial.

James Ewell Brown Stuart, the flamboyant, defiant, passionate, dashing cavalier, was dead.

He had been mortally wounded in battle with General Custer's forces. An ambulance had been found to bring him back to Richmond.

Jeff Davis had come to his side; some old friends and comrades had come to do the same.

They had sung "Rock of Ages," his favorite hymn. He had asked the doctor if he might survive the night, just long enough for his wife to arrive.

But Flora Stuart had arrived to a house of silence, and no one had needed to tell her that her husband was dead.

The Yankees were so close that there was no local

militia to form an honor guard—the city's forces were all out fighting for the city's defense.

Callie attended the church service, her heart heavy. She'd never met Stuart—she had known that he had meant a great deal to Daniel. Stuart had known he was dying; he had ordered his officers not to follow him to his deathbed, but to see to their duty.

So Daniel must be seeing to his duty, collecting bullets. Like Stuart. Like Stonewall Jackson. Like so many others.

Callie didn't hear the service at the cemetery. She heard the burst of shells, a not too distant sound. She saw the slopes and curves and sections of the cemetery, and she gazed at the place where Jeb's little daughter —Flora, for her mother—had been reinterred just a year ago. He had accepted his death, they said, because he whispered that he would be with his Flora again.

Callie looked at the sky, and she thought that soon it would rain. She couldn't pray for the man being buried.

She could only fervently pray for Daniel. He would never falter if asked to lead a charge. All these years, he had been in the thick of things. The fighting was growing more and more fierce daily.

Dear God, don't let him die.

She could hear Flora Stuart, sobbing softly.

He wouldn't die, she told herself. Not now, not today. Little Joe had died, and Jeb was dead, and no matter what his general had ordered, Daniel had thought the world of Jeb Stuart. He would leave the front lines; he would come home to be here now. She would close her eyes, and open them, and Daniel would be there, across the crowd.

She closed her eyes, her lips moving in prayer.

She opened her eyes.

But Daniel was not there. He was not coming. He

was still in the battlefield, where he had been ordered to stay.

The minister finished the service.

The sky suddenly seemed to burst open, and it began to rain.

Twenty-six

June 7, 1864
Cold Harbor, Virginia

Since the third of June, Daniel was certain that he had done nothing but listen to the moans and cries of the wounded.

They were mostly Yanks out there now, but since battle had been engaged here, the Union man in charge, General U. S. Grant, had refused to seek any parley to remove his dead and wounded from the field.

Perhaps it was because the commanding general who asked first to bring his wounded from the field was customarily the general admitting to defeat.

Grant had been defeated here, whether he wanted to admit it or not. In these days of almost constant battle, from the Wilderness to Yellow Tavern to Spotsylvania, and now here, at last, to Cold Harbor, Grant had been defeated. Richmond, once again, had been saved.

Grant's forces were still in their trenches and so were Lee's. The southerners watched carefully, wondering just what Grant would do next.

Riding in back of the curiously quiet lines, Daniel wondered why he felt no exuberance.

Perhaps there was none left to feel.

Beauty was dead, dead and buried. Daniel still felt numb when he thought of it. Stonewall a year ago, Beauty now, and so many others in between.

Now they had beaten back even Grant, but Grant didn't retreat. His men lay on the field, screaming and dying, but he didn't admit defeat.

The Confederates had brought in a number of the Union wounded with their own, risking forays out into the field of battle. To listen to the men scream was torture; it was no hardship to bring them in, be they Yanks or rebels.

Everyone seemed to be waiting.

Daniel reined in. He still smelled like soot and ashes, he thought, and that from the Wilderness.

Never had he seen anything like it, or imagined anything like it. Smoke and fog so thick that Union troops fired on Union troops and southern troops did the same. Then the forest burst into flames, and then again, the horrible screams of men and horses trapped in fallen foliage or wounded too severely to try to escape the lapping flames of the fire.

So much bloodshed in so very few days.

The problem was that they could lick the Yankees. They had licked them time and time again. But more of them came. No matter how many they battled and how many they killed, there were always more.

They were outnumbered and outgunned.

"Colonel Cameron, sir!"

A young soldier on horseback came riding up to him. "We've stopped a conveyance on the road, sir. There's two ladies, two children, and a black woman in it."

"Yes?"

"Well, the women claim to be kin of yours. Your wife and your sister-in-law."

His heart suddenly slammed against his chest. Callie, here?

He was instantly torn in two. He had wanted to see her so damned badly for so very long!

They couldn't possibly be such fools, riding around the countryside with battle waging like this!

"Where is this conveyance, soldier?" Daniel asked. He called to one of his lieutenants to take charge of the forces directly beneath him, and he rode swiftly behind the soldier back to the main road. The Yankees were well to the other side of it, but the fighting here had been so fierce and so vicious that he felt ill thinking of Callie and Kiernan stumbling upon it.

With the children!

It couldn't be the two of them. Surely, Kiernan would not be so foolish.

But it was them.

He reined in his horse and leapt down from it at the road, staring at the wagon.

Callie and Kiernan were both in the front, waiting. Daniel was startled at their appearances, for though nothing could take away the extent of their beauty, they were far different from the women he had last seen at Cameron Hall. Both were in black, the color of mourning. In honor of Beauty, or perhaps in honor of little Joey Davis. They were minus their hoops, their gowns were simple, and they were both very thin.

"Jesu!" Daniel breathed. His eyes fell upon his wife, and only his wife. His stomach and heart seemed to catapult together. His fingers were shaking.

No black costuming could take away the radiance of her color. Silver-gray eyes fell on his, and warmth surged through him. Dear God. It had been so long since he had seen her.

Pretend that you love me!

He had pretended through all these awful months of warfare. Dreamed of her through the nights when he had managed to sleep through the screams of the dying.

And she was indeed before him now.

All he could think of was the dangerous mission they had set upon, and how she dared risk herself so!

There were Yanks everywhere!

She was a Yank!

It wasn't so much that she might have run into Rebels or Yankees, it was the fact they might have stumbled upon deserters, as they had once before, in nearly this same place, and at nearly this same time, years before.

Before he had met Callie, before he had loved her.

Temper! he warned himself. For those silver eyes were on him, brilliant, beautiful. He wanted to crush her into his arms, and hold her so tightly.

But he didn't embrace her; he was shaking too hard to do so. Long strides brought him to the wagon.

"What in God's name do you two think that you're doing?" he thundered.

He reached for Callie, grabbing her around the waist, and bringing her down against him. The warmth of her body seemed to explode against him. Her toes touched the ground, and he met her angry eyes.

"We're trying to get home," she informed him.

She had called Cameron Hall her home.

"What?" he said incredulously. He looked from Callie to Kiernan, and back again. "Haven't you heard? The fighting has been constant here!"

Callie was still against him. She'd made no attempt to fight his hold. He looked down into her eyes again. She smiled suddenly.

Smiled, and the anger faded from her eyes. The silver light was in them once again. Without conscious thought he touched her face, his thumb tracing over her cheek. She really had the face of an angel. She was hatless, and her hair streamed down her back in all its glory, the deepest, richest fire imaginable. *I love you,* he thought. *I have loved you for years now.*

"You could have been killed, you little fools!" he murmured.

"Daniel, Kiernan and I must get home. Christa is going to be married, remember? And . . ."

"And we didn't know if you or Jesse would manage to get there, and so we decided that we had to," Kiernan finished from the wagon.

"Jesu! Christa would understand. We're in the midst of a war!"

"Mum?"

A sound from the back of the wagon suddenly distracted Daniel. He looked around the rough wood exterior and jumped.

His son was standing, holding on to the wagon. Bright blue eyes looked at him with no recognition. A second pair of blue eyes stared at him, too, as John Daniel leaned up to see what was going on. Except for the difference in their ages, the little boys might have been twins.

Like Jesse and I, he thought. And then emotion seemed to rush in on him. My son is standing, maybe walking. He forms words now, and he doesn't know who I am. He has gotten so big, and I haven't been there to see him stand, to take his first steps.

This was war. He could still remember Beauty's strong feelings on the subject. Duty came first. House and home came later.

Still, how could a man make house and home come later when his family was sitting in front of him, and the war itself was all around them?

He decided that he didn't give a damn about the war for the moment. He left Callie's side and walked around to the wagon.

"Hello," he said softly to the boys.

"Mum," Jared repeated.

"He doesn't say very much," John Daniel advised his uncle. "He's just a little over a year, you know."

Daniel grinned, tousling his nephew's hair. "And you're just over two, young man!" He reached out to his son. Jared observed him with wide blue eyes. Don't shy away from me, he thought. Please, don't shy away from me!

For a moment, he was certain that Jared would. Then the little boy reached out with his chubby little arms and Daniel swept him up, hugging him fiercely.

Callie had come around the wagon. He saw her over his son's dark head. She watched him gravely, and he wondered for a brief moment just what it might be like if they could only have a normal relationship, if they could only have a life! She was so beautiful. And she had given him this child, and so far she had cared for his child alone, and she had done so in his home, or in Richmond.

"He's big now," Daniel told her softly.

She smiled. She'd never seemed to begrudge him Jared, or to begrudge him any of his son's affections. She'd been so independent, but she'd bowed to him in so many things. Yet, he'd been stronger, he'd had the ability to take Jared and make her come south.

But he'd never forced her to stay, yet she had done so anyway.

"Very big," she agreed.

"Why in heaven did you come to Richmond?" he asked her.

She shrugged. "They needed help at the hospital."

"So you came to Richmond to patch together Rebs."

"Rebels, Yankees, whoever came in," she agreed.

He buried his face against his son's throat. "You were there for little Joe's funeral?"

"And Jeb Stuart's," she said softly. "We could hear the cannon through it all."

"What did you two think that you were doing, riding out with the children like this?"

"Daniel, I'm not afraid—"

"Callie, you should be afraid!"

He gritted his teeth. They hadn't been so far from here a little over two years ago. Was it two years ago? It felt as if he had been fighting forever. He had been injured, Kiernan had been expecting the baby, and the ride home had seemed endless. We're going in circles! he thought, feeling they were back to that time. Somehow, he had to get them home. Grant's forces were quiet at this hour, but that could change anytime.

He handed Jared to Callie. "I'll ask for time to bring you home," he told her.

"Daniel, we are capable—"

"Callie," he snapped roughly, "you're taking my son and my nephew through battle lines!"

She stiffened. Dear Lord, why was he always yelling? What little ground they had made toward one another in a year of absence and a smile seemed suddenly to be swept away.

"I have never risked our child!" she said. He thought that the brilliance in her eyes might be that of tears. "But take time, Daniel, yes, please, take time! It's a way to get you out of the front lines of this war!"

She sounded bitter, ironic.

Almost as if she had missed him.

He turned away from her and mounted his horse, anxious to find his superiors. Had it been just two days before, he knew he never would have been given any leave to travel.

But now Grant was ominously silent.

He was able to find both Wade Hampton—Stuart's successor with the cavalry—and Fitzhugh Lee, Robert E.'s talented nephew. Both thought him insane at first, but the explanation that his wife had simply appeared in the road was taken well by both men, and he was granted leave to escort his wife and son back to Cameron Hall.

Signing a pass so that Daniel could move unharrassed through any Confederate lines, General Hampton warned him, "Make haste. It seems that the Yanks have started terrorizing all of the countryside, and I must have you back. On your honor, sir!"

He left his lieutenant in charge, and begged his men to obey him as they would himself, promising to return swiftly.

He came back to the wagon, tied his horse to the back, and urged Callie to move over so that he might take the reins.

He met Kiernan's eyes over Callie's. They both remembered the last time they had taken such a ride. They both remembered the dangers they had met along the way.

He urged the horse forward. "Home, horse!" he told the nag. And they started off.

They rode for miles in near silence, Janey in the back with the boys; Daniel, Callie, and Kiernan in the front. No troops accosted them.

The cannons were quiet. Along the lush and beautiful countryside, they heard no sound of guns. Summer had come to the land beautifully. The foliage was brilliantly green, and there was a soft breeze as they rode. Upon occasion, they passed a burned-down house, or a field stripped of any good supply it might have carried. Only then did it seem possible that there was a war.

How quickly the land made up for the things that befell it! Daniel thought. For once they passed by such a place, the deep forests took over once again.

By nightfall, he moved into one of the forest trails, glad that he was in a place he knew so well. He was determined not to go into Williamsburg, but to skirt around it, and thus come home that way.

He jumped down from the wagon, and reached up for Callie. She hesitated, then set her hands upon his shoulders and allowed him to lift her down. He released her quickly, though, and reached for Kiernan.

"We're staying here tonight?" Callie asked.

He nodded. "You two and Janey can sleep with the boys in the back. I'll keep watch now. Try to get some sleep. I don't know if I can stay up the whole night. If not, the two of you will have to stay up together. Can you do it?"

Callie nodded. "Yes, of course we can."

"Then get some sleep."

He sat down before the wagon, and loaded his guns. He had two Colts, and a Spencer repeating rifle that he had taken from the ground at the Wilderness.

The gun hadn't saved its previous Yank owner from the fires of hell, but Daniel prayed that now it could keep them all safe.

Callie didn't go to sleep right away. He was startled to find her by his side, offering him a cup of water and some bread and dried beef.

Rations had been more than slim since their last campaign had begun. He didn't hesitate, but took the water and the food from her.

While he ate, he watched her. She seemed to have acquired a composure and a serenity since he had seen her last. Her eyes met his, then fell, rich sweeping lashes creating shadows on her cheek. She sat close to him, nearly touching him. The sweet feminine scent of her was nearly more than he could bear.

He touched her cheek. Her eyes, gray and silver and luminous, came to his once again. "How have you been, Callie? Tending to the sick and wounded, how have you been yourself?"

"Well," she told him. She poured more water into his cup. "Except when we read the death notices. I always knew that I would not find your name on the list. I felt certain that I would hear if you had been injured, if you had been . . ."

"Killed?"

"Yes," she said flatly.

He caught hold of her wrist. "I'm not going to die, Callie. I'm good, I'm careful."

"No. You're a colonel. I know you're probably reckless! I . . ."

Her voice trailed away, for his eyes were so hot upon her.

He watched her mouth, and suddenly, he could bear it no longer. He leaned forward, pulling her into his embrace, and kissed her. He touched her lips with his own, ground down upon them. He parted her lips with his tongue, and he felt her give to him. He filled her mouth with his kiss, tasting, savoring, needing. She gave fully to him. Their tongues met, wet, hot, touching, dancing, needing more.

Then out of the near darkness, he heard a warning cry.

"Daniel! There's someone on the road," Kiernan cried from the wagon.

He pressed Callie from him, leaping to his feet. Kiernan was right and he should have heard it. There was a horseman coming nearer and nearer. He backed behind the tree that blocked the wagon and tried to look around it. Darkness had come, and there was very little moon. What there was seemed to be behind a cloud.

The cloud moved and he saw a Yankee horseman coming.

Daniel strode quickly down the road, keeping to the shadows. He shimmied up the trunk of a tree just in time to see the shadowed rider pause.

The rider had heard him. The rider had sensed danger.

He urged his horse forward, closer.

Daniel leapt from the tree and onto the horseman. He swept the rider from his horse, and together they rolled and rolled on the dark ground, both grunting, both breathing hard. An elbow caught Daniel in the ribs. He nearly cried out. He shoved a fist into a muscled gut.

He briefly obtained the upper hand, straddling over his enemy.

The cloud moved completely.

"Jesse!"

"Daniel, Jesu, you scared the damn hell out of me!" Jesse swore.

"You're lucky I didn't shoot you!" Daniel stood quickly, stretching down a hand to his brother. Jesse stood. For a moment they stared at one another in the moonlight. Then they stepped forward and embraced. "How the hell did you come to be here?" Daniel demanded.

"Mutual friends," Jesse said dryly. "I heard that my wife had passed by Cold Harbor, and that my brother was taking her home."

"And you got leave?"

Jesse shrugged. "There weren't many wounded left alive after Cold Harbor," he said bitterly.

The two went no further in their conversation, for they were suddenly interrupted by a shrill, glad cry. They started and turned, and Kiernan came leaping out of the darkness, running like a bat out of hell to reach Jesse.

She catapulted into his arms. Daniel stepped aside as the two of them greeted each other with one of the most tender and passionate kisses he'd ever witnessed. A throat cleared softly, and he realized that Callie was on the other side of the entwined pair, a child in either arm.

Jesse and Kiernan split apart. Daniel could hear his brother inhale sharply. "John Daniel and Jared, is it?" He took his son from Callie, staring at the little boy. "John Daniel . . . you've gotten so big! Do you know who I am?"

John Daniel surveyed him studiously. "He's Uncle Daniel. You're my father."

"That's right," Jesse said. He hugged the boy, and he glanced at Callie again, grinning. "Welcome to the family," he told her.

"Thank you," Callie replied. She glanced nervously at Daniel. "If Jesse came upon us so easily . . ."

"Then we need to be very careful, because anybody could. I'll take the first watch, and Jesse can take the second," Daniel said.

"Who are we watching out for now?" Callie asked softly. "The Yanks or the Rebs?"

"Either," Jesse and Daniel answered together.

"All of you, go and get some sleep," Daniel said. He glanced at Callie. He could still taste her kiss. It had been sweet, so much so that if Kiernan hadn't been on guard, he wouldn't have heard Jesse coming.

"Everyone, go to sleep," he persisted. "I'm best on guard by myself."

Callie turned away, hugging Jared to her.

Kiernan's eyes still shimmered as she looked at Jesse. The two of them, with John Daniel between them, walked away.

Stiff as a poker, Daniel sat down to keep guard.

There were no other interruptions. He sat awake and alert for hours, but nothing moved but the breeze through the trees. At about three, Jesse came and tapped him on the shoulder. "Go get some rest. I'll take it from here."

Daniel nodded. He rose, stretched, and yawned, and started for a tree. "Over there," Jesse directed him.

Daniel looked where Jesse pointed. Callie was there. She was sound asleep, but she had stretched out a blanket that was plenty large for them both and Jared.

Jared was in his mother's arms. Daniel stretched out at her back and held her tenderly. It wasn't exactly what he wanted. Not when the scent of her was so intoxicating. It was good to hold her. To hear her sigh softly and curve against him, even as she slept.

When Callie awoke, she felt his hand on her upper arm. She started and turned, and found his enigmatic blue gaze upon her. "We've got to go," was all that he said. He had slept with her, she thought. He had held her through the night, given her his warmth.

Pretend that you love me.

He was quickly on his feet and reaching a hand down to her. She accepted his help to rise, then turned for Jared, who was still sleeping. Daniel leaned past her, picking up their sleeping son. He nodded toward the wagon. Jesse and Kiernan and Janey were there, waiting for them.

"I'll ride on ahead and scout the road," Daniel said.

"I can do it—" Jesse said.

"It's still supposed to be Rebel territory," Daniel reminded him. "I'll go." He handed Jared to Callie, then untied his horse from the back of the wagon and mounted up. Callie watched him ride ahead.

There was a difference in the brothers now, she thought sadly. Jesse's uniform was in sound shape. Daniel was in near rags again.

Yet no matter how tattered his uniform became, there was still something majestic in his appearance. The plume remained high in his hat, his shoulders were broad. He still seemed a part of some sweet chivalry gone past. She wanted to reach out and hold on to that chivalry.

"Let me help you up," Jesse told her. "Kiernan, ride with me up front?"

"Of course," Kiernan said softly.

Callie was still tired, and Janey seemed weary herself. Callie lay in the back of the wagon with Jared, closed her eyes, and dreamed.

It had been something to see Kiernan and Jesse as they had spotted one another. Something to watch their every step as they moved toward one another. Something to watch their kiss.

She wanted Daniel to love her that way. Whole-heartedly, with no reservations. Without the terrible mistrust that always stood between them.

She must have dozed, for she could see the long, long drive to Cameron Hall. Daniel was coming down that walk, her tattered cavalier. She saw him, and he saw her. His eyes lit up as his brother's had done for Kiernan. Her hand flew to her throat, her heart quickened. Suddenly she was running, running . . .

He was running, too, to greet her. He reached her, and she was in his arms, and then his lips were on hers, and he was spinning with her, spinning beneath a beautiful, red setting sun.

She awoke with a start. Janey was sitting up in the back of the wagon. She looked at Callie and smiled. "Home, child. We're home."

Christa came running out to the steps. Daniel was dismounting, and she threw herself at him, hugging him first. She went on to Jesse, and then to Kiernan, and then she came to the rear of the wagon. "Oh, you came! You all came, every one of you. Give me the boys, Callie, one by one. There we go, you scamps. Janey—"

But Daniel was there, lifting Janey out, then reaching for his wife. She slipped into his arms, watching his eyes as he slid her down to the ground, his movement slow, his touch warm.

"Let's get in," Christa said. "We don't want any of the neighbors to notice Jesse."

Their nearest neighbor was acres away, but it seemed they all believed that Christa had a point. Callie found herself back in the house, greeting Jigger once again, and Patricia and Jacob Miller. It seemed that they all talked forever, avoiding the war, and then

Daniel rose, saying that he was going to go and find their new overseer.

Callie watched him rise and impulsively asked Patricia to take Jared, and she followed her husband out.

He wasn't in any great hurry to find the overseer. He had headed straight for the old family burial ground, and was standing broodingly by the fence. He heard her coming, and his back was still to her when he spoke. "What is it, Callie?"

She paused, then kept coming. "You tell me, Daniel," she said softly. "What is it?"

He turned and stared at her hard. "What do you mean?"

She lifted her hands, tears making her eyes glisten silver. "I came here, I married you. I lived here, among all my enemies. I waited for months. I served the enemy. I mourned for you, Daniel. For Joe, for Beauty. Jesu, Daniel, what more do you want from me? Why can't you—"

"Why can't I do what, Callie?"

"I love you, Daniel. I've tried to show you that in every way that I know how. Why can't you love me?" she said softly.

It seemed he stared at her the longest time, his gaze nearly cobalt.

"I do love you," he said, the words so quiet they might have been a rustling in the trees overhead. His voice was deep when he continued, "I love you more each day this wretched war keeps me from you."

Stunned, she heard the words tumbling from her. "But you hold me at arm's length! You don't really believe—"

"Callie, I was hurt. It takes time to heal. To believe."

"I swear, Daniel, I only ever wanted to save your life. I love you. I loved you then. I never stopped."

"You denied it well!" he whispered.

"Pride," she admitted ruefully.

"Come here," he murmured. She couldn't move. He caught her arm, and he pulled her close against him. He gazed down deeply into her eyes, and his fingers threaded into her hair. His lips touched hers, softly. Yet they spoke of a deeper passion, of a hunger. They stirred and stoked and kindled sweet fires and hungers deep within her. She parted her lips to his kiss. Tasted it. Savored it.

Callie thought she would die with the sweetness of his kiss. Then suddenly, he broke it. He stared off around the corner of the house.

"Daniel, what is it?"

His eyes focused on her. "You don't know?" he said sharply.

"What are you talking about?" she demanded, confused.

He shoved her forward. "You love me, yes! And the damn Yanks are heading straight for the house!"

"What?" she said incredulously.

"There was a man in a Yank uniform who just stepped onto the front porch."

"Daniel, damn you, it's probably Jesse."

"I don't think so."

He was staring at her, hard. She trembled. Could he doubt her still? "You said that you loved me," she reminded him harshly.

He nodded, still watching her. "I do. But, Jesu, Callie, why is it that every time you whisper words of love, I am plagued by blue uniforms?"

"I'm telling you—"

"I do love you, Callie."

"Daniel—"

"Get to the house!" he thundered, shoving her forward. She tried to swing around, to protest. It was too late, Daniel was gone. She didn't know which way he had disappeared, but he had slunk into the forest, and she was very afraid.

Jesse. She had to reach Jesse. Maybe he could make some sense of this. Her feeling of danger was acute.

She went racing full speed back to the house. Maybe the man in the uniform was Jesse. Maybe he had gone back outside for some reason.

She burst through the back doors and stared around the hallway. Christa was just walking back toward the den and she stopped, startled by Callie's appearance.

"There's a Yank in the front. Is it Jesse?"

"What?" Christa said.

Callie shook her head, racing down the length of the hallway, throwing open the doors.

There was a Yankee soldier there. A cavalry officer. He was bent over, dusting the dirt from his boots. "A Yank!" Christa whispered. "You're right! My Lord, I'll get my gun."

"It could be Jesse—"

"I know my own brother!" Christa cried.

Callie gasped suddenly. "No, no! You can't get your gun."

"I'm telling you, it's not my brother!"

"But it *is* mine!" Callie told her. She cried out, "Jeremy!"

The soldier stood and smiled and came hurrying toward her.

Within seconds she was in his arms, laughing as he swung her around the porch.

Then her laughter was suddenly caught short as Jeremy's circle brought her around to face Daniel as he stepped from behind a pillar, his hands on his hips, his eyes as sharp as razors.

"Excuse me, Mrs. Cameron, but just what is going on here? Do I pour brandy, or draw my sword?"

— Twenty-seven —

Callie felt Jeremy tensing beneath her fingers. Daniel looked as if he were ready to explode.

Suddenly Christa Cameron was out on the porch. "My Lord, Yanks are just springing up all over!"

"You're on my porch in southern territory, Yank," Daniel stated. "And worse than that, sir, you've got my wife. You've about five seconds left for an explanation!"

"Me!" Jeremy exclaimed. Callie could feel her brother's temper beginning to seethe. "Insolent Reb! You came north and kidnapped—"

"Kidnapped!" Daniel exploded. He was about to draw his sword.

"That's right," Jeremy stated.

Daniel let out a warning oath. Steel was going to flash any second.

"Wait!" Callie cried, pushing away from Jeremy, and standing before Daniel. "Daniel, stop! This is my brother!"

Daniel gazed from Callie to the stranger on his porch, then back again.

"Brother?" Daniel said.

There was chaos on the porch, with everyone talking, and everyone wary.

"Did he really marry you, Callie, or is he talking through his teeth?"

"Don't you dare accuse my brother of lying, you northern varmint!" Christa put in.

"Christa, please, I told you, he's my brother—"

"Your *brother*? Really?" Daniel demanded.

"Yes, I have three of them, you know that."

Everyone fell silent. Jeremy and Daniel were still looking at one another suspiciously, and Callie thought that with the drop of a hat they could be at one another's throats.

A new, amused voice interrupted them.

"I think that brandy might be a good idea." Jesse had come out to the porch.

Jeremy swung around and looked at him. He saw the colonel's blue uniform from the medical corps, and he instantly saluted, then dropped his hand.

"My Lord, he's a Yank!" Jeremy stared at Callie. "Who is he?"

"*My* brother!" Daniel offered, then brushed past them all. "If I'm not drawing my sword, then I'm pouring the brandy. Anyone care to join me?"

"Indeed, sir, I would!" Jeremy announced, following closely behind him. Callie started to follow the two of them. Jesse caught hold of her arm, gently pulling her back.

She stared at her brother-in-law. "Jesse, they'll kill one another."

He shook his head, and smiled. "Give them a chance."

She looked to Christa for help. Christa shrugged. "Daniel is hotheaded, but you know that, you married him. You ought to know, too, that he's not a murderer, and that he's sick and tired of death and violence. He'll be all right." She paused. "What about your brother?"

"He's not a murderer!" she said quickly, indignantly. "But they've both been shooting people in uniforms

just like one another's for three years!'' Callie added
miserably. "Are they going to know the difference
now?"

"Give them a chance," Jesse told her. He released
her and opened the door for her, following her into the
main hallway.

Down that hallway, the door to the den was closed.

She walked down to it, and stood very still. She
could hear nothing.

She glanced to Jesse, but he shrugged and grinned.

Callie began to pace the hallway.

Inside the den Daniel was beginning to wonder how
he had ever missed the fact that this man was Callie's
brother, except that his wife was so beautifully feminine it was, perhaps, difficult to transfer her coloring
and attributes to a man.

This soldier was tall, his own height. His eyes were
so similar to Callie's eyes only a darker gray. His hair
was an even deeper auburn than Callie's, and his features were more ruggedly hewn. But he was a striking
man, just as Callie was a beautiful woman. Nor did he
seem afraid of Daniel, or of the fact that he was facing
an enemy in enemy territory. Maybe it was because he
had already seen a fellow countryman in uniform, as
unlikely as such a presence should have been at this
southern plantation.

Daniel poured brandy and handed one to Jeremy. So
far they hadn't exchanged a word.

Daniel asked one question, and the words began to
flow between them like wildfire.

"Why did you come here?"

"To bring her home. I heard that she had been spirited away—to the South."

"Well, she wasn't spirited away. I came after her.
And my son," he added softly.

"Where the hell were you when she was expecting
that son?" Jeremy demanded heatedly.

Daniel arched a brow. "In Old Capitol Prison," he said briefly.

"Oh," Jeremy murmured. "Well, then, perhaps . . ." He shrugged. "She is my sister, sir. My father is dead. Her welfare is my concern."

Daniel smiled suddenly and lifted his glass. "Sir, I see your point, truly, I do. And I assure you, we are legally wed." Yes, they were wed, but was Callie where she wanted to be? He hadn't actually kidnapped her, but then again, he had given her little choice.

"I think, sir, that we must ask Callie where she wants to be," Daniel said softly.

Jeremy arched a brow, watching Daniel. But Daniel frowned suddenly.

"How did you know where to find your sister if you heard only that she had been spirited away?"

"That was easy enough. An old friend of the family did some research for me, Eric Dabney. He knew who you were, and he found out where you lived."

Dabney!

"You know the name?" Jeremy said.

"Oh, yes." Daniel ran his finger around the rim of his glass. "I know the name well. Lieutenant Colonel Dabney was responsible for my stay in Old Capitol."

"How curious!" Jeremy said. "I was always convinced that Dabney was in love with Callie himself. He was close to her husband, but you could always see that look in his eyes . . ." He shrugged. "I'm surprised he would want to make her miserable. Maybe he didn't know that there was a relationship—"

"He knew," Daniel said flatly. He rose to pour Jeremy another shot of brandy. "Excuse my curiosity, sir, but it has been some time since Callie and I left Maryland. Why has it taken you so long to come here?"

"I've been on the western front of this war, under Grant. When Grant was ordered east, I received papers soon after to come this way. I didn't want to fight here," he said regretfully.

"Because?"

"Because I've too many good friends in Virginia and Maryland companies—fighting for the South."

Daniel nodded wearily, taking up his seat behind his desk. "I understand," he said.

Jeremy grinned. "So the Yank out there is really your brother?"

"Yes, sir, he is."

"And you're still speaking to one another?"

"Any time we come across one another, which seems to be about once a year."

Jeremy grinned slowly. "How interesting."

"Too interesting," Daniel said softly. "You're regular cavalry, aren't you?"

"Yes," Jeremy answered. His grin faded. Jesse was with the fully established medical corps now, he would never face Daniel in battle.

Jeremy very likely could.

"Jesu!" Jeremy breathed. He started to speak again, then the door suddenly burst open, and in came Callie, breathing hard, her eyes silver and as wild as her hair. She stared at them both. "I'm—sorry!" she murmured. She tossed back that wild mane of hair. "No, I'm not. I was worried sick about the both of you!"

Daniel walked around and leaned on the edge of his desk, watching her. "Why would you be so worried?" he asked her.

Jeremy, in turn, stared at his sister. "Indeed, Callie! We're both quite civilized."

Civilized! They were so civilized she wanted to smack them both.

Where was the brother who adored her, who should have gone to battle for her with a vengeance?

And where was her enemy, her husband, who had

brought her here? If the love between them had all been pretend, at least the passion had been real.

Wives were property, he had told her!

Would he fight for the plantation before he would fight for her?

What was the matter with her? Did she want a fight between Daniel and Jeremy?

No. She just wanted Daniel to care.

"I was worried," she said quietly.

Daniel stared at her. She'd have given anything to read what lay behind the brilliant blue fire in his eyes. What emotion lay within his heart?

Fight for me, dammit! She thought. Fight for me as you do for this place, as you do for those other things in your heart that mean so very much to you.

Ebony dark lashes fell over his eyes, and then he was staring at her again. She could still read nothing in his eyes.

"Your brother came to rescue you, you know," he told her.

"Oh?" she murmured, looking at Jeremy.

"He seemed to have been under the impression that you were kidnapped."

She didn't respond; she didn't move. What in God's name was Daniel doing?

"I thought that I should give you the choice, Callie. I don't want you to be miserable here, in the South. Or with me." The last was spoken so softly that she wasn't even certain that she heard him correctly. Did he want her to stay, or did he want her to go? What was he doing? She wanted to cry out, and she wanted to scream and beat against him.

She stood silently at the door, returning his stare, trying to keep her chin very high. She had told him that she loved him. She had given him everything.

"Callie?" he said.

Pretend. Pretend that you love me.

She opened her mouth, but she never had a chance to speak. The door opened again suddenly and Kiernan, smiling brilliantly, stuck her head in.

"We've a supper on, of sorts, gentlemen, Callie. Janey and Jigger—and I, of course, would be delighted if you'd join us." She extended a hand to Jeremy. "I'm Kiernan Cameron. Welcome to this house, just in case the other residents have neglected to say so. I'm sure you're anxious to meet your nephew. He's right out in the hallway here."

"Supper sounds fine to me," Jeremy said, rising and bowing very politely to Kiernan. He gazed at Daniel. "If I'm truly welcome in this house."

Daniel threw up his hands. "The odds, as always, are against me. We've two men in blue tonight, to one in gray."

Kiernan lowered her lashes, hiding a grin. Jeremy followed her out. Daniel kept studying Callie. "Well?" he said softly.

He never gave her a chance to answer. He took her elbow and led her toward the hallway. "I'm sure Jeremy can be convinced to stay the night. And—" He paused slightly. Callie heard a note of bitterness in his voice. "I'm equally certain that we'll all be riding back to war in the same direction very soon. We can all give it until tomorrow, don't you think?"

"Daniel—"

"No! I don't want you to say anything now." His hand on her elbow, he led her out into the hallway.

Jeremy was busy meeting Jared, and Kiernan was still trying to usher everyone into the dining room. Jesse and Jeremy arrived in uniform blue, Daniel in his tattered gray, Kiernan and Callie in their mourning black, and Christa a burst of summer in a dazzling yellow gown. Patricia and Jacob Miller were also at the table, scrubbed and clean, nearly fourteen now. They'd grown accustomed to Jesse, but Jeremy was a new Yank, and they eyed him very cautiously.

Callie wondered how the meal would go when, before they even sat down, Jesse told Jacob how big he was getting and Jacob stated that he was near big enough to be going off to war. He didn't make any comments about killing Yanks, he cared too much about Jesse to do so, but it was plenty clear just who's side Jacob was on. Kiernan told him he was nowhere near big enough to go off to get killed.

"Soon. Another year, maybe," Jacob said, setting his jaw stubbornly. "There's boys younger than me out there fighting, isn't that true, Daniel?"

It was pathetically true. The South was drawing deeper and deeper into her reserves, though by law, no boy Jacob's age should be fighting. But when the enemy neared Richmond, time and time again it seemed that the soldiers marching out from the city were growing both older and younger—the graybeards came out, and then the boys who couldn't quite grow whiskers yet.

"Jacob, don't go making Kiernan unhappy tonight," Daniel warned the boy. "There's no need for you to be coming to war for some time, and God knows, it has to end soon enough."

"But Daniel—"

"Jacob, see to the young ones at that end of the table, will you?"

The older children watched the younger ones, but Jigger, trying to serve the meal, grinned from ear to ear. "It's near like before! A party this size. And we have excelled, yes, we have!"

"It's certainly the finest meal I've had in some time," Daniel assured him.

And it was. The table was filled with vegetables, string beans, peas, turnip greens, summer squash, sweet potatoes, and tomatoes. There was a smoked ham, rich with the taste of hickory, and there were several fat chickens, too, for someone had decided that this would be a real feast.

As if a prodigal son had returned home.

Which was the prodigal, Callie wondered, Jesse or Daniel?

Conversation flowed easily throughout the meal. The men seemed to be all right about the color of their uniforms, even if the blue at the table didn't seem to set well with Christa. Still, there was laughter at the table. More than Callie had heard in a long time.

She saw Jesse looking at Daniel. "I understand that Jeff Davis passed a suspension of habeas corpus a while back. We could all be in trouble here."

The adults all grew silent.

"What does that mean?" Patricia Miller demanded.

Jesse hesitated, then answered her. "Men—and women—are granted certain rights by the constitution. Your constitution, and our constitution," he added. "You have the right to privacy, and no one should be able to arrest you without proper cause. But in the case of war—"

"Lincoln suspended the right of habeas corpus very early on in the north," Daniel commented.

"But what—"

Daniel set down his fork. "It means we're in trouble if we're all caught," he said flatly. "It means Jesse and Jeremy could wind up in Andersonville, and it means that I could be arrested for consorting with the enemy."

"We could all be in trouble for having dinner?" Patricia said incredulously.

No one answered her. She stared at Jesse. "The South isn't wrong, the North isn't wrong—the war is wrong!" she exclaimed.

Everyone around the table had grown very tense.

A pea suddenly sailed across it. It smacked Jeremy right in the face and he jumped.

Startled, they all looked down the table. John Daniel grinned at them happily, and sent another missile flying.

"My Lord!" Jesse exploded. "The war better end quickly! I've a child with no table manners!"

Callie couldn't help it. She burst out laughing when a third flying green missile caught Jesse square in the left cheek.

"John Daniel!" Kiernan cried in dismay, leaping to her feet. But by then, Jared, entranced by his cousin, was attempting the same feat. He hadn't really the co-ordination to balance the pea in his spoon, so he merely toppled over his entire dish, stared at them all with deep pleasure, laughed, and offered the table a beautiful grin.

"Jared!" Callie moaned and jumped up too.

Christa laughed. "Really, why be so distressed? The two of them at least know they are supposed to be hurtling their shots at Yanks!"

"Christa!" Daniel exclaimed.

"Never mind, Daniel. I shall get the children and myself away from this meal! Patricia, care to join me? Do excuse me, all of you!" She said the words sweetly, but her eyes were afire. Patricia, serene and mature far beyond her years, rose and grinned. "I'll take the young masters Cameron out into the kitchen with Christa," she said. "Please, enjoy dinner, all of you."

When she was gone, there was silence at the table. "I shouldn't be here," Jeremy said.

"Jesu! This is our home!" Daniel exploded. "I'm calling a truce, North and South, for tonight. Let's eat, shall we? We've no time, we've never any time. We're all here now, for the love of God, let's enjoy what we have."

"Yes," Jesse agreed. "Kiernan, sit. Pass the peas, please."

"The normal way, if you would, please," Daniel suggested.

Kiernan sat, laughing, excusing her son's bad manners to Jeremy.

Callie watched them all in silence, so very aware of Daniel across the table from her.

They ate. The conversation was polite. There was a silence again until Jesse asked Daniel, "When are you going back?"

"Tomorrow," Daniel said briefly. He shrugged. "We don't seem to know quite what Grant is doing, and we need to keep a close watch on him." He paused. "When are you going back?"

"Tomorrow. I don't know what Grant is doing either, but he's giving me plenty of wounded, that's for certain." He hesitated, looking at Daniel. "What about Christa's wedding? We're just days away. Liam Mc-Closkey should be arriving any time."

Daniel exhaled slowly and miserably. He shook his head. "There's nothing I can do," he told Jesse softly. "Kiernan will be here. And Callie . . ." He paused again. He had given Callie permission to leave in the morning if that was her desire.

He suddenly determined that it wasn't going to be her desire.

Or if it was, she wouldn't be able to forget him once he had gone.

"Jeremy?" Daniel said suddenly.

"Sir, I'm on leave, but I hardly think that your sister would want me attending her wedding!"

"No, no, that's not what I meant," Daniel said. "I'm glad that you're on leave. You can stay the night," Daniel said. He rose suddenly, walking around the table behind Callie's chair. "My sister will see to a room for you. Now if you'll all excuse the two of us . . ."

Callie's chair was abruptly pulled back. He had her hand, and she was on her feet. She felt a flush flaming her cheeks, and she wanted to protest his sudden and so obvious command, but she had a feeling that she'd be leaving the room one way or the other. If she went out hectoring she'd risk a duel between her brother and her husband once again.

But she did protest as soon as they reached the hall. "Daniel, what do you think you're doing? We were in the middle of a meal—"

"I ate, thank you."

"We weren't alone!"

"Ah, but we're going to be."

"Daniel—" She paused, tugging back on her hand. He paused, but only to scoop her up into his arms and head for the stairway.

"What are you doing?" she demanded angrily.

"What do you think I'm doing?" He cross-queried almost savagely, his eyes cobalt as they touched hers.

She knew what he was doing. His eyes, and his touch, both were so explosive when circumstance had again separated them for so very long. Rivers of excitement began to stream within her. She clenched down hard on her teeth, trying to understand him. Not an hour ago he had been telling her that it was her choice if she wanted to leave him. And now . . .

"Daniel, put me down."

"No."

"You were just saying that I could leave—"

"Not now. In the morning."

"Well, if you want me to leave—"

"I don't want you to leave."

"But you said—"

"I said that it would be your choice."

His long strides had taken them up the stairs now and below the portrait gallery. Long-gone Camerons looked down upon them. Some of them sternly, some of them with mischief in their eyes.

Eyes as blue, as startling, as deep and dark and demanding as those that focused upon her now. "You said that you loved me."

"And no matter what I say," she challenged him heatedly, "you never really believe me, you don't fully trust me!"

They had reached his room. He shoved open the door with his foot, and walked into the darkness.

She wanted him more than she had ever imagined that she could. In the darkness she felt electric. His calloused hands upon the bare flesh of her arms seemed to light swift burning fires just beneath her skin. They raged down the length of her, they tore into her. Sweet, wonderful. He could do this too easily to her.

And leave her so swiftly when it was done.

"Daniel!" she cried. Not tonight. There could be no "pretend" tonight. She wouldn't allow it to be so.

He dropped her down upon the bed. She felt the fall of his weight beside her and then she felt his fingers moving impatiently upon the topmost button of her gown.

"Stop it!" she cried and tried to twist away.

"Callie! We've one night!"

"One night!" She moistened her lips. "Do you believe me?"

"Does it matter so much?" He paused in the near ebony darkness, and all that she could see of him was shadows and a silhouette. She loved that silhouette, the plumed hat gone, the soldier tall and straight as he stood now, looking down at her. What did he see in the darkness? she wondered.

Did any of it matter? If only he would lean down and touch her lips, and make the world go away.

"Yes, it matters!"

His lips came close to hers. She felt the warmth, the whisper of them in the night. "You are a Yank. *Would* you betray me now?" he asked softly.

"Daniel—"

"Callie—"

"Daniel, no!" She found an extraordinary strength, pushing him aside and leaping to her feet. She stared at him, trying to discover something of his features in the darkness. "No, Daniel, I would not betray you now! I would not have betrayed you before, except that I was desperate to save your life. I've told you," she cried out, "that I love you. What more would you have from me, Daniel? I've lived here, without you, all this time. I went with Kiernan to Richmond to be near you. I learned to love my enemy so well that it broke my heart to see that poor child, Joey, die, and still you ask these things of me! I've loved you from the beginning, Daniel. I never ceased to love you. But now! Well, sir, I have had it! I have—"

She gasped, her words breaking off, for he had come for her. Hands upon her upper arms, he dragged her against him. His mouth bore down on hers in a fever; his body, touching hers, was electric. His hands were upon her face, his lips seeming to devour hers. His lips touched her throat, her cheek, her lips again.

"Daniel—"

"I love you, Callie," he said softly.

"But—"

"And I believe you. Forgive me. I was afraid to believe you, but I do. And I love you."

"Oh, Daniel!"

"Make love with me, Callie?"

She paused, her arms around him, meeting his eyes. "There are Yanks downstairs, you know."

"Are there any in the wardrobe?"

She smiled and shook her head. "The only Yank in the room stands before you, waiting."

"Kiss me, Callie?"

"Seduce you?" she queried. "You'll not blame the Yankees being in Virginia on me?"

His fingers threaded into her hair and gave a little tug. She cried out softly but his lips found hers, hungrily, eagerly.

"I said," he whispered just above her mouth, "that I believe in you. And I love you, Callie. More than you'll ever know. More deeply than I'll ever be able to say."

She had never heard words so sweet. She was barely aware when he kissed her again.

"Try . . ." she murmured, smiling, when his lips lifted from hers.

"I love you more than life, more than limb, more than heart or soul . . ." he began, and kissed her again. He began to speak once more, but only slowly did she become aware of his whispers, for she was so acutely aware of his touch upon her clothing.

He whispered of how he dreamed of her in the long nights away. How he closed his eyes and saw her in his dreams, walking toward him. He whispered of how he had longed to believe.

So many times she was there with him. With the breeze from the river lifting her hair, the gently rolling water lying far below them. Honeysuckle was lightly on the air, and there in the rich green grasses, she would shed her clothing and lie down beside him.

In the darkness, the black dress she had worn was suddenly at her feet. She felt her own fingers moving, trembling, upon his scabbard. His weapons were set aside.

The tattered gray uniform lay on the floor.

For a moment they stood together, naked, and the moon came out at last, casting a dim and ivory light over the room. Callie felt the touch of his flesh against the whole of her body, and then she pressed him toward her. Her love . . .

He was tautly muscled and lean. More so every time that she saw him. She pressed her lips against his collarbone, then against the rigid muscle of his breast, then against the bone of a rib. The sleek touch of his hands moved up and down her arms. Whispers, kisses, pressed into her hair. She rubbed her face against his belly, her lips pressing there. She came lower and lower against him until his hoarse cry would allow her no more. She was swept up again, into his arms, and laid down upon the bed in a tempest.

Within seconds he was a part of her, and their magic had begun. The emptiness of lonely nights was filled, just as the thrust of his body filled her own. Hands, limbs, whispers, and kisses entwined as each strove for more of one another, hungry, near bursting, longing for the pleasure—and the love—to go on and on.

Daniel felt the fierce shuddering of her body, the tightening of her slick passage as it grasped his sex. His hands moved deftly over her shoulders and arms, caressed and grasped her buttocks. Climax, sweet and violent, flooded through him and from him and he held her very close, feeling her heart, feeling his own. Her breasts continued to rise and fall. He laid his head against them and touched them tenderly.

At last he rose and kissed her lips. She smiled and quivered. He pulled away. In the moonlight, she was exquisite. Naked ivory flame, her perfect face encompassed by the shimmering auburn of her hair. Hair that waved and tangled around her, beneath the curves of her body, her beautiful breasts, her hips, her thighs. Her eyes were as silver as the moon, and he suddenly found himself shaking.

All these long months of war. He had dragged her here. He had cast her in among her enemy. And she had stayed. She had come to Richmond. Her heart had never faltered in her belief in the northern right, and yet she had cast it aside for him.

All this time he had hurt her so badly with his doubt. He trembled and laid his head against her breast again. "Forgive me," he whispered.

She rose up next to him, throwing her arms around him, holding him again. "Oh, Daniel!" She leaned back. The darkness had been dispelled. Their shadow land was really magical. "Oh, Daniel, I love you so."

Entwined, upon their knees, they began to kiss one another again. He told her that she was beautiful, and she laughed and whispered that he was beautiful too.

"Rebel soldiers are not beautiful," he told her.

"Oh, but you are!" she protested, and despite his indignation, she began to tell him about the time when he'd had his fever. "I had to cool you down. I had to get rid of your uniform. I hadn't been a widow long enough then, but I was so fascinated with your shoulders." She stroked them. "And I needed to . . . to taste you!" Her lips touched down on his flesh. Her eyes met his again. "You were beautiful. Very male and very beautiful. I thought that you had the most beautiful shoulders I had ever seen, the leanest, tightest belly, the trimmest hips. The most beautiful legs . . ." Her voice trailed suggestively. She leaned close and wickedly whispered precisely how beautiful the extraordinary piece of his anatomy that lay between them was, too, and how she had longed to touch that . . .

She had him laughing, and then she had him on fire again.

In the ivory light, they were both very beautiful, he decided, and he made love to her with a driving, desperate passion once again.

And so went the night. They dozed, they awakened, they made love, they dozed.

For the first time, Daniel was truly bitter that he would have to return to the war.

They were losing it. No, it was already lost, he decided. They could hold the Yanks from Richmond.

Maybe they could outfight the Yanks. They were naturally better horsemen. So many of them had military educations. But the Yanks weren't cowards, they never had been. And there were so damned many of them. The South would be starving soon. She was nearly in a death grip now. There would be no help from Europe.

I have admitted that I am losing, but I will go back, I know that I will, he told himself.

His arms tightened around his wife. Dear God, let me come home. Let us survive this. Let us live.

She moved against him. Slowly, erotically, she began to make love to him. Sensual, seductive in her every movement, she rose above him. She bent to kiss his lips. She began to move, oh, so slowly. Like a dance engaged . . .

Until the flames caught, and he could give her the lead no more, but became the aggressor, until he fell beside her, spent once more.

He held her very close, breathing in the fragrance of her hair. He trembled, thinking of how deeply he loved her.

It was morning. The first rays of light were just beginning to streak into the room.

Daniel frowned suddenly, certain that he had heard something outside.

Callie slept. Naked, he slipped quietly from the bed and strode to the window. Carefully, he pulled back the drape and began to watch.

Callie awoke with a start, aware that he was no longer beside her. She sat up, running her hand over the bed where he should have been.

"Daniel!" His name formed on her lips, but something had warned her, and she barely voiced it aloud. She saw him. Naked, silent, he was by the window, looking down. He saw her, and pressed his finger to his lips.

"What is it?" she mouthed.

He walked back to the bed, looking down at her. "Yanks," he said softly.

Yankees. Not her brother, not his brother. Every time he trusted in her, every time he made love to her, the enemy appeared.

Callie leaned up to him, gasping. "Daniel, I didn't—"

"Hush!" He pressed his lips to hers. With sadness, with regret? With a poignant bitterness? "Get dressed, Callie, quickly." He was already dressing. Even as he spoke again, he was pulling on his cavalry boots and reaching for his sword and guns. "I've got to rouse the house, and I've got to get out there."

"Get out there? Daniel, you need to stay in here! Jesse can speak with them, he can—"

"Callie, these aren't friends of Jesse's. These men are definitely the enemy. They're trying to fire the house," he said softly. "I've got to stop them."

"But how—"

"Callie, your old friend, Eric Dabney, is down there. I saw him. Now get dressed. Hurry."

With those last words, he turned and left her.

Twenty-eight

Callie managed to dress quickly. With her blouse barely buttoned, she ran out of the bedroom and raced down the hall, determined first to see to the children.

Janey, her beautiful silk-black flesh paled to an ashen shade, was standing guard over the cribs where the youngest Camerons were sleeping unaware of any danger.

"They're fine, Miz Callie. No one will touch these boys, by my life, I swear it!" she promised.

Callie felt as if she were choking. "We may—we may have to move them out quickly," she advised Janey. "Where has my husband gone?"

"He's gone down, Miz Callie. Move soft, and move quiet, he's got to take them by surprise."

Her heart slammed hard against her chest. Eric Dabney was here. Trying to burn down Cameron Hall. And it was her fault. He had come because he hated Daniel and that hatred was because of her.

She hurried out into the hallway again. Maybe she could speak with him. Maybe she could ride back with him. Maybe she could do something!

She gave Janey a fierce hug. "Please, Janey, please, do watch out for the boys!" she said, and she hurried out.

She reached the portrait gallery. All those long-gone Camerons seemed to look down on her with reproach.

At the foot of the stairway, she nearly cried out as she crashed into a tall, rocklike body. Arms gripped her. But they weren't Daniel's. They were her brother's.

"Jesu, Callie, that's Dabney out there!"

"I know," she whispered miserably.

"I'll talk to the son of a bitch!" Jeremy exploded.

"It won't do any good," a voice suggested softly. Daniel emerged from the shadows in the hallway. "Jeremy, how many of them have you counted?"

"At least a company. There won't be many of us against them—"

"You can't shoot at them," Daniel said flatly. "Neither can Jesse."

"But—"

"Unless we kill every man in that company, the two of you could be hanged as traitors at a later date, assuming you survived the fighting."

"Sir—" Jeremy began. He was interrupted as Christa came running down the stairway with a large, lethal-looking revolver in her hands.

"Daniel! There are dozens of them out there!"

"Not dozens," Jeremy corrected, his eyes raking her length. He looked to Daniel. "I know Dabney; I knew him before the war. He has a company, but no more than twenty. He can't seem to keep much of a command around him. His men ask to be transferred. And they die. Frequently."

Daniel nodded. "Thanks," he told him.

"Wait!" Jeremy said. "This is my fight too!"

"Jeremy, it can't be your fight. And Christa, have some faith in me! Put that damned gun down until I tell you that I need it."

"There's Yankees inside, and Yankees out!" Christa protested. "I wonder what happened to the overseer!"

she cried. "He would have warned us if he could; he would have fought them . . ." She broke off, biting into her hand, misery clear in her features.

Jesse Cameron came hurrying down the stairway, loading a cartridge into his revolver. Daniel stared at his brother and then whispered, "What the hell do you think you're doing?"

"They're attacking my home!" Jesse said flatly. "And I know damned well they haven't been ordered to!"

"You can't shoot at them! They're still Yanks! Someone will have you court-martialed if you fight your own kind."

Jesse Cameron was going to ignore his brother. Callie was glad of it—there was no way that Daniel could take on a company by himself, and she was becoming more and more aware of the furtive intruders herself. She could hear the creaks on the porches, hushed whispers near the windows.

Daniel was striding toward his brother.

"Jesse!" he said suddenly.

Jesse looked up. Daniel caught him in the jaw with a clean right hook.

Jesse Cameron slumped down to the floor.

At the top of the stairway, Kiernan cried out softly. She came running down the steps. "Daniel!"

"Jesu, Kiernan, I had to! He could be shot for what he was intending to do!"

"If we survive this!" Kiernan moaned. "Daniel, they're preparing to light fires out there. They mean to burn the house down."

"I know," Daniel said. "I'm going to take care of it."

"It's twenty to one out there!" Callie cried to him. "Don't be a fool, you can't—"

"I can't have my brother hanged, Callie, and I will not have you and Christa and Kiernan endangered. And I'd just as soon not see your brother hanged either. For the love of God, will you all have some faith in me?" he demanded. "Stay here!"

Christa had found herself a position at one of the windows. The revolver was still in her hands. She was as ready to defend the place as her brothers.

"Kiernan, get that damned gun from Christa, will you? If I don't come back, Dabney will have what he wants, and you won't need to defend yourselves."

"Daniel!" Christa protested. "We're the Rebels! And you can't knock me out like you did Jesse."

"I would," Jeremy muttered.

Daniel cast them both warning stares. "Leave me to this, damn you, both of you! Christa, put the gun down! If I am killed, don't you go trying to shoot them! Jesse can negotiate something for you."

"No!" Christa protested.

"Cameron, whatever your plan is, I'm going with you. Damn it, if Dabney is here now, it might well mean that he followed me, and that I brought this on," Jeremy insisted.

"I brought it on!" Callie said softly.

"If you want to help me, keep an eye on my sister," Daniel told him.

"What?" Christa demanded, indignant, incredulous, and furious.

But Daniel paid her no heed. He was staring at Callie. Suddenly, he wasn't there at all anymore. He had slipped through the door.

"What is he doing?" Callie demanded desperately.

Kiernan, holding Jesse's head in her lap, sighed softly. "He's gone to war," she said.

"He can't fight them alone!" Callie said.

Christa still had her gun. "He isn't alone," she murmured.

Callie bit her lip and moved toward Kiernan. She curled her fingers around Jesse's gun. "I'm going with him!" she whispered.

"The hell you are!" Jeremy growled behind her. He grabbed the gun from her, and sighed, looking at Jesse. "They can sure punch, huh?"

"Yes," Kiernan agreed.

Jeremy tried to lift Jesse to something of a sitting position, but it was true, Daniel knew how to knock out a man.

After all, Jesse had taught him just how to do it.

"He's going to wake up madder than a hornet," Jeremy said. He pressed a finger to his lip. They could both see a shadow by the window in the dining room.

There was silence, then a big thump.

Daniel was out there, all right. But what was he doing? Callie wondered.

Jeremy's eyes met hers. He winked.

Then her brother was off to join her husband, and she was left behind.

To worry. To wait. She gazed at Kiernan and Kiernan at her.

"Oh, dear God, please!" she whispered aloud. The tension mounted.

It was not difficult surrounding his own house in a sure, silent movement. Daniel knew the exact placement of every small bush and trellis.

He stayed low on the porch, moving on the balls of his feet to come around to the north wing of the house. Two men were busy by a dining room window, stuffing straw against the base of it. Daniel rose and padded softly to them.

"Hey!" he said.

They turned to look at him. He caught the first with the butt of his gun in the jaw. He brought the second down with the return thud of the barrel.

He paused long enough to look them over well, stripping them of their weapons. One of them was carrying a Spencer repeating rifle. Daniel acquired that as his own.

He began to inch around the house again. In the rear were three men, setting dry twigs. It seemed that Dabney still considered himself safe from sight. Or maybe he thought Daniel was the only male in residence. That couldn't be true, if Jeremy was right, and Eric Dabney had followed him out. No, Dabney had to think that he had been quiet enough so that the household still slept. That was to Daniel's advantage.

He dropped down below the porch level to the ground, coming around the back. He waited for one of the men to near the edge, then he jerked him over by a foot. The flailing man cried out. Daniel belted him in the jaw, and he crumpled like a puppet. But he'd been heard.

"Jace, what's going on down there!" someone hissed. Footsteps came to the edge of the porch. A wary soldier looked over.

Daniel jerked him down too. This fellow fell with a crunch to his arm. Daniel heard the bone snap.

He didn't have to hit the fellow. The soldier opened his eyes once, stared at Daniel with alarm, and passed out cold.

Daniel looked up. The third Yank was staring at him. He was going to have to pull his gun and shoot. He hadn't wanted to make that kind of noise and alarm the others.

But he didn't pull his gun. To his amazement, the soldier's eyes flew open wide and then closed, and the man toppled over the porch.

He looked at the fallen man, then looked up. Jeremy McCauley was grinning down at him. "Want a hand up?" he mouthed.

It seemed there was no point talking sense to Yankees. Daniel reached for his hand, and Jeremy helped him leap up to the porch.

He tensed as he realized that someone was coming around the corner. He started to cock his Colt, then realized that it was his brother.

Jesse was rubbing his fist, as if he'd just given somebody a good knocking with it.

"Can't talk sense into Yankees, and can't knock it into them, either!" Daniel complained.

"I'm going to knock some into you, little brother, when this is over," Jesse warned him.

"Christ among us!" Daniel complained. "I'm trying to keep the two of you from a hanging!"

"Fine," Jesse said. He hunkered down low, rubbing his sore jaw. "There were two on my side," he whispered.

"Two on the north side, three back here," Daniel said.

"Seven," Jeremy murmured.

"And the rest . . . ?"

"The barn," Jesse suggested. "It will burn like a hellhole!"

It would, Daniel thought quickly. He rose. "If you're with me, come on!" he told his brother and brother-in-law.

They started to move off the porch. It was then they heard a shot fired and then a bloodcurdling scream from the front of the house.

Christa was by the front door, sunk down by the narrow strip of etched glass on the side of it. Kiernan stood on one side of the great hall, watching the dining room windows, and Callie stood on the other side of the hall, looking out through the parlor.

"I hear . . . something!" Christa whispered.

Both Callie and Kiernan hurried toward her. Callie stared out, searching the frozen scenery, feeling as if her heart had lodged permanently in her throat. Kiernan was beside her, and the three of them searched the front in the morning light that grew ever brighter.

Callie felt something cold and sharp at her spine. She swallowed down a gasp, turning around.

Eric Dabney was there, holding a pistol to her. He had come in from behind them. Instinctively she looked toward the stairway, praying that no one had reached the children.

He saw the way that her eyes moved. He smiled, his eyes bright, amused.

"I haven't been up there, Callie, not yet. And I won't go up there. Maybe I won't even burn the house. Not if you come with me. And not if you help me bring in Daniel Cameron."

"Help you?" she queried, fighting desperately to remain calm. "There are any number of you here, Eric. Daniel is out there alone. You need my help?"

"He isn't alone," a man behind Eric said, and Callie realized that he had entered the house with two of his soldiers. "Why, we got men down—"

"Get away from Callie," Christa interrupted the man, aiming at him.

"I'll get her—" Eric's man began, taking a single step.

"Stop!" Christa warned.

But he didn't heed her. Christa fired her gun and Callie heard a long horrible scream. No, it was two screams combined, for the wounded man had screamed, and so had she. The second of Eric's soldiers hurtled himself toward Christa, wrenching the gun from her grasp before she could fire again. Christa swore savagely, something not at all ladylike.

"She's killed him," the man said to Dabney. "She's done killed Bobby Jo."

"He's not dead; he's still breathing," Dabney said. He stared at Callie, twirling the fine end of his mustache. Heedless of the fallen man at his side, he grinned slowly, having seen Callie about to reach for Christa's fallen weapon. He took careful aim and a shot exploded by the gun, which forced her to wrench back her hand and stare at him furiously.

"Come here, Callie. And say thank you, will you? I've come to bring you home."

"I am home," Callie told him. "So you can just get your men—"

"I'm taking Daniel Cameron again, Callie. Dead or alive. Preferably dead. He tore up half my company the last time we met. Cost me good horses."

"Cost you a promotion again too," the man holding Christa supplied.

"Shut up, fool!" Dabney hissed. "This time, Callie, that Reb is going to die."

"You didn't best him before, and you won't best him now!" Callie told him heatedly.

He kept his gun trained on her and walked to the window where his man now held Christa in something like a death grip.

"What have we here?" Eric asked softly.

Christa spit at him. He laughed. "Why, Callie, after I finish with you, I just might have a talk with this little lady. . . ."

"Touch my sister-in-law," Kiernan warned, "and my husband will see to it that you hang."

"And just who might your husband be?"

"Colonel Jesse Cameron, Army of the Potomac," Kiernan enunciated sharply.

"Well, Mrs. Cameron, I imagine that he's far, far away—"

"He's right outside with his brother," Kiernan said.

"There's another Yank with the Reb too," Eric's man muttered.

Eric looked at Callie. She smiled grimly. "Jeremy's out there too, Eric. You're going to war against him?"

Eric Dabney's handsome face seemed to darken.

"Why, damn you, Callie! You've made a traitor of your own brother. You deserve to pay and pay dearly!"

He caught hold of her, swirling her out in front of him. Before she was aware of what he intended to do, she was staggering to her knees, taken unaware by the force of his blow. She swallowed hard, determined not to cry out. But then his fingers entwined in her hair, wrenching her back to her feet, and a cry did escape her lips.

Fury ignited within her. She swirled, despite her pain, kicking him with all of her strength and managing to draw a groan from his lips. But it was to no avail, for too quickly he had her hair again, and she was wrenched so tight against his body that she could scarcely scream.

"You and that damned Rebel! You turned me away to bed down with him! Well, that's all over now, ma'am. This hellhole of traitors is going to light up the sky, and Daniel Cameron is going to die. I'm going to cut his throat in front of you, Callie. I'm going to let you watch your hero beg for mercy."

Callie bit her lip. "You're sick!" she told him.

"Maybe I am." He turned around, suddenly taking careful aim at Kiernan. Her eyes widened, but she didn't let out a sound. "I'll shoot her, Callie. I'll shoot her right now unless you start being a little helpful."

"If Daniel doesn't kill you, you're going to hang," Callie promised him softly.

"Maybe. Let's go. You come with me now, and these two ladies will have a chance to save your brats before the flames become an inferno."

"Light the fires!" He bellowed out the order.

Nothing happened.

Callie smiled, hating him, and wondering what could have gone so wrong with his mind that he could hate her so.

"Don't look at me like that!" he ordered her. He

jerked her close against him. "It's you, Callie, always you! From the beginning. You wouldn't look at me because you had to have Michaelson! Well, lady, place that at your feet too. No battle killed him."

She stared at Eric and gasped with horror. "You killed him! You murdered your best friend! Dear God, you bastard—"

"Just so long as you know there is nothing I won't do, Callie," he interrupted softly. His voice rang out again.

"Light the goddamn fires!" Eric exploded. He jerked on her hair again. "In a moment, Callie, you'll smell the smoke."

But there was no smoke. No sound, no fire.

"Let's go out and get your husband, shall we, Mrs. Cameron?" Eric said to her.

Callie felt ill. She could scarcely stand. All these years she thought that she had been fighting the South.

But during all these years, it had been Eric who had declared war on her. He had killed her husband.

And now he wanted Daniel.

"Eric!" she cried suddenly. "Forget this! Forget the house, forget Daniel. Let's forget the whole war. I'll go with you. I'll ride with you—"

"Too late, Callie," he said softly. "It's too late now. I've got to kill him."

Eric dragged Callie to the doorway. He stroked her cheek with his gun.

"Keep quiet, and I may let you live. Jensen, you stay here, and keep your gun on these two." He indicated Kiernan and Christa. "The others will be out in the barn. I'll get help once I've gotten Cameron."

Dragging Callie tightly along with him, he threw open the front door.

"Call your husband. Tell him that you need him."

His fingers were tight on her upper arm. In a moment he would force her to do something.

To betray Daniel again. . . .

No, Daniel would understand this time.

If he lived.

Callie couldn't risk his life. She closed her eyes for a moment. It might not just be his life. It might be Kiernan's and Jesse's and Christa's and her brother's and John Daniel's and . . .

Jared.

She twisted her head, sinking her teeth hard into Eric's hand. She didn't care about the rifle in his hands —she just bit down. As hard as she could.

Eric screamed out. But he didn't release her.

She cried out, "Daniel, don't come! It's just what he wants you to do. Daniel, stay away—"

She saw Daniel. He had moved around the house, sneaking up on Dabney's men, one by one. They littered the area around the house, some slumped over, either unconscious or dead, and several of them tied up like hogs.

Now he stood just below the porch in plain view. His gun was trained on Eric.

"Let her go. Now," Daniel commanded, his tone deathly quiet.

"I'll kill her first," Eric said. "You drop the gun. Then she lives."

"No!"

Callie kicked him hard, and he lost his grasp.

"Callie, no!" Daniel shrieked to her.

But she had to reach him.

She ran.

She heard simultaneous explosions of gunfire. There was a sting, high up on her temple, just like that of a bee.

She reached for her face, and her fingers came away red. She tried to turn. She didn't need to run anymore. Eric was dead. Daniel had taken him down even as she had burst away from him. Sightless now, Eric Dabney stared up at the sky.

Callie stumbled. She looked before her.

Daniel was running to her. His blue eyes were suddenly naked. Brilliant with color. She wanted to smile; she wanted to touch him.

She had never seen such concern. Such love. In all of her dreams, she had never imagined him looking at her as he was looking at her now.

She couldn't quite touch him. Her fingers were numb.

"Daniel!"

She called his name again, and then she felt herself falling into his arms.

"Callie, Jesu, Callie! You're hit!"

"There's another man in there, Daniel. He has Christa and Kiernan—"

"Shh," Daniel said softly, still holding her. But Callie realized that he was taking aim, that the soldier had brought Christa and Kiernan out to the porch, and was trying to use them as shields.

He fired. The man fell. Christa shrieked as he nearly dragged her down.

"Callie!" Daniel said. She could hear him, hear his voice, but he seemed very far away. She touched his cheek. It felt as if it was wet. She marveled at the feel. He did love her.

In the distance, she could hear the sounds of more gunfire. It was coming from the barn, she thought.

"I'm all right," she told Daniel. She tried for a smile. "Flesh wound." She grabbed onto him. She managed to stand.

"Callie!" Kiernan was there, and Christa was at her other side.

Callie forced a smile to her lips, praying that she could stand long enough to convince Daniel that she was all right. "Go."

"I can't—" Daniel began.

"Daniel, you must!" Kiernan urged him. "It's Jesse and Jeremy against how many?"

Anguished, Daniel kissed Callie's forehead, and left her in the tender care of the other women.

He dashed off toward the barn.

"Can you stand?" Kiernan asked Callie.

"No!" She laughed. "Oh, God, Kiernan, what's going to happen now?"

"Now there are three of them, against ten," Christa said miserably. "We should go—"

"I can't walk!" Callie told her.

"Jesu, but are you bleeding!" Christa murmured, and she tried to dab at Callie's forehead with her hem. She ripped up her petticoat, creating a bandage. "Jesse will see to it!" she said, worried. "As soon as he comes back!"

The firing was becoming far more fierce at the barn. Dabney was dead, and they still might lose, Callie realized. There were just the three of them, Daniel and Jesse and Jeremy, and there were Eric's men, entrenched in the barn, with rapid-fire weapons and plenty of ammunition.

They heard the sound of a bugle. Troops were coming.

"My God," Christa whispered. "Are they ours?"

Callie wondered if it mattered. She closed her eyes, fighting to remain conscious.

For a moment, the firing increased, then all was silence.

"Oh, Kiernan!" Callie cried, and holding tight to her sister-in-law, she watched.

Moments later, Jesse, Jeremy, and Daniel were marching her way. Her brother and her brother-in-law in blue, her husband in gray.

Behind them rode a small group of Confederate horsemen.

Daniel was alive; Eric was dead. Rebels were here now, and so were Jesse and Jeremy.

"Colonel Cameron!"

The bewhiskered head of the Confederate soldier called to Daniel. He didn't pause, not until he reached Callie. He put his arm around her, then turned back to the Confederate militia captain.

"Colonel Cameron, just what is going on here?"

"They attacked our house. We fought them," Daniel said simply.

"But what about—these two?" the man demanded. "I'll have to take them with me, sir—"

"No," Daniel said firmly. "Not unless you want to arrest me too." He hesitated. "Captain, these men chose a different side, but this was a private war."

The captain stared at Jesse. Obviously, he had known him at some earlier, different date.

"Colonel Cameron, have you—become a Reb?"

Jesse shook his head. "No, sir. I can't say that I have. But these men attacked my house. I fought for it."

"They attacked my sister," Jeremy exclaimed.

"Well, then—" the captain began.

"Sir," Daniel said, "On my honor, nothing was exchanged here. No information. Nothing. We brought down twenty Yanks. You can bring them all in. But couldn't we just pretend that you didn't see these two? On my honor, sir, I'll have them back with their own armies by tomorrow!"

"On my honor, sir!" Jeremy said.

"On my honor," Jesse agreed. "We'll be gone. Sir, we were fighting for my home!"

The captain, still confused, sighed.

At his left, one of his men murmured, "This is highly irregular, sir—"

That comment seemed to make up the captain's mind. "I have never doubted the word of a Cameron, ever. Be he my countryman, or my foe. Gentlemen!"

He turned to his troops. "We'll clean up here and leave these people be!"

A cheer went up. A Rebel yell. Callie smiled. "Oh, Daniel!" she whispered.

The darkness she had fought so strenuously came crashing down upon her. Despite her very best efforts, she fainted in his arms.

Minutes later—or eons later?—she opened her eyes. A pair of brilliant blue eyes met hers, but they weren't Daniel's. They were Jesse's.

She was no longer on the ground in front of the house. She was lying on a plump sofa in the parlor.

"There, I told you! She's back with us," Jesse said.

The room ceased to spin. She hadn't died, it wasn't heaven.

It was the next best thing. It was Cameron Hall. Still standing. And there were faces within it. Faces that stared down at her with grave concern. Kiernan's face, and Christa's face, and her brother's and Janey's. Even Jigger was there, watching over her too.

She tried to smile. Where was Daniel?

Behind Jesse. Jesse suddenly moved, and Daniel was there, sitting beside her.

She stared into those eyes searchingly. He bent low and kissed her forhead. "Jess said it was just a flesh wound. It scared the hell out of me, all right."

"Daniel . . ." She whispered.

"She's going to be fine, trust me," Jesse told the others. "She needs rest." He cleared his throat. "That means you, too, Daniel."

Daniel nodded, but he didn't move. The others cleared out of the room.

"Daniel . . ."

"Don't talk."

"I love you, Daniel."

"I know that you do. I love you too."

She smiled, feeling her eyes flicker shut again. "It doesn't really matter what we are, does it, Daniel?"

His fingers smoothed more hair from her forehead, and he smiled tenderly. "What we were today mattered," he told her softly. "We were a family, all of us. Brothers again, not enemies, Jesse and I. Even Jeremy. Protecting the house and those we love."

"But it's my fault that he came here—"

"No more than it was my fault for bringing you here, Callie."

She shivered, violently. "No, Daniel, you don't understand! Eric hated me. Because I spurned him, I suppose. I didn't even realize it. Daniel, he—he killed my first husband!"

"Shh. I know. Kiernan told me."

"You could have lost Cameron Hall."

"I could have lost you."

"I nearly lost you! Daniel, you went after so many of them—"

"But my brother stood with me. And your brother stood with me. And it's going to be all right. Sleep."

Tears touched her eyes. "I can't sleep. You're going to be leaving too soon."

He hesitated, wishing that he could lie to her. His fingers curled around hers. "I have to go back, Callie." He hesitated another moment. "Callie, you're right. I've always known that slavery was wrong. But I also believe that each state should have decided upon emancipation, that we should have managed it with our laws—"

"It wouldn't have happened, Daniel."

"Hear me out, Callie, please. I want you to understand. I have to go back. I have to see the war through. There are men beneath me, and men above me, and I owe them my loyalty and my service. I have to, Callie. To the bitter end."

She was blinded again. Not by blood, by tears.

"Callie, don't you see? If I don't remain loyal to my cause, to my country, I will never be able to be the father that Jared deserves?"

She nodded. She did understand him.

"Sleep, Callie."

She shook her head. "No! You're leaving!"

He kissed her forehead. "I will wait. One more day will not win or lose the war any faster."

She closed her eyes, believing that he would stay. He had said that he would. He had given his word.

Daniel was glad that Callie slept. As Christa had assumed, their overseer had been killed by Eric's men, shot in his bed before he'd ever awakened.

Daniel, Jesse, Jeremy, and Christa saw to it that he was buried in the family cemetery in the back.

The Yanks, the living and the dead, Daniel turned over to the Rebel captain.

He spent the early afternoon with Jesse, and it was damned good just to talk with his brother again.

They were going to stay another night. Kiernan was awaiting her time with her husband, so Daniel excused himself on some pretext or another. Despite the fact that he was leaving, he couldn't bring himself to wake Callie.

He had been too terrified when he had seen the blood on her forehead. And now she needed rest.

In the late afternoon, he left the house. Daniel came to the slope of grass by the river, his favorite place on the plantation. It was where they had come as children. It was where the grass grew the richest, where it was such a dazzling green it was extraordinary.

It was summer, but the breeze, as always, was soft. The river gave the breeze that brush of velvet. The roses from the garden made it redolent and sweet. Far up on the mound, he could see Cameron Hall, still standing. White, stunning, beautiful in the sunlight.

He smiled. None of it mattered, he knew. None of it. He could live in the snow, in the desert, if he lived with Callie.

But this had been the dream, he reminded himself.

He had lain in the grass, felt the soft kiss of the breeze, heard the endless rush of the river. And then he had seen her. A slow smile on her face, coming toward him. Her hair, catching the sunlight. Her eyes, a silver dazzle.

He blinked.

She was there.

Her hair was pure fire, caught by the last rays of a setting sun. And indeed, her eyes were silver. Her face, her angel's face, had never been more beautiful.

She smiled, standing above him. She lowered herself to her knees. There was a white strip of bandage across her forehead. But her color had returned, and his heart raced as he realized how very well she looked. There had been those awful moments when he hadn't known how seriously she had been injured, trying to keep him from danger.

He smiled, tossed aside the blade of grass he had been chewing, and reached for her. "Come down here, angel!"

She knelt down before him.

"This is a dream, you know," he told her.

"Really?"

He nodded. "In the middle of countless battles, I would see this place with you. Right here. By the river."

"And then?"

"Then you stripped off all of your clothes, and we made love."

"Like this?"

She was all seductress, slowly loosening one button after another.

"Mmmmm," he agreed, but frowned, determined that two could play a game.

"What's wrong?"

"The bandage wasn't in the fantasy," he said.

"Oh! Well, you Rebel varmint!" she began. But by then he was laughing, and he swept her into his arms.

The kiss was far better than any fantasy, any dream.

The sun set, lower and lower. Rays of gold and crimson streaked out over the river and over the grass.

And still, Daniel held Callie in his arms. As he had done as a child with Jesse and Christa, he now spun dreams with Callie.

"When the war is over . . ." he began.

She turned to him, fiercely, passionately. "Oh, Daniel, yes, please God! Let it be soon! When the war is over!"

"My love, our war is over," he whispered and kissed her in return.

But in the morning, he kissed her again, and rode away once more to battle.

At the end of the long drive, he embraced his brother and said good-bye to him.

He turned back and looked to Cameron Hall. "When the war is over, please, God, yes! Let it be soon!"

Twenty-nine

The war would not end that soon.

In the North, George "Little Mac" McClellan lost his bid for the presidency, Lincoln was reelected, and hopes for an end to war by a Union peace effort perished.

Just as thousands more soldiers perished on the fields.

Liam McCloskey never appeared for his wedding— he was killed at Cold Harbor. His name didn't appear on the lists of the dead for weeks, but from the moment that he failed to appear at Cameron Hall, Christa knew. Kiernan and Callie comforted her the best that they could, but there was little to be done. She cried once, then never again, turning her sorrow into supplying the Rebel troops with the very best that she could.

In Richmond, Varina Davis gave birth to a baby girl. She was named Varina for her mother, but they called her "Winnie," and to many she was the "daughter of the Confederacy," for she brought life and hope to a time of loss and desolation.

Spring brought new life and hope to Cameron Hall. On March 14, Kiernan gave birth to a second son. Five days later, Callie had her second child, a little girl.

She was the most beautiful infant Callie had ever

seen, she was convinced. More beautiful than Jared, but Jared, of course, had been handsome. Her daughter was born with a full mop of deep red curls and brilliant blue eyes.

And the face of an angel, Callie thought.

She prayed ever more fervently that Daniel would live to see her.

For Daniel was with the battle to the very end, with Lee at Petersburg.

And the South tried. She fought hard, she fought valiantly, she fought with the life's blood of her sons and daughters.

It wasn't enough.

Grant surrounded Petersburg, and the city was under seige.

Sherman moved steadily forward on his "march to the sea," destroying everything in his path in Georgia.

The Confederacy staggered and fell. She struggled to her feet again. Rebel cries resounded in battle, and some men never gave up.

But in the end, none of it mattered, for the South stumbled and went down again, and this time she was on her knees.

Petersburg fell, and Lee had to warn President Davis to flee from Richmond.

They circled around their enemy. Lee planned to make a last stand near Danville, joining his army with that of Johnston, moving northward from the Carolinas.

But desperately needed supplies did not arrive. Unlike many of his predecessors, Grant could move quickly. One quarter of Lee's men were captured; he was left with a ragtag force of thirty thousand while Federal forces blocked his only avenue of escape.

On April 9, Lee tested Grant's line. It was far too strong to break through.

And so they came to a little place called Appomattox Courthouse.

On the afternoon of Palm Sunday, Lee met with Grant at a farmhouse. It was a curious place, for its owner, a Mr. McClean, had moved to Appomattox Courthouse when his first home had been in the path of some of the opening shots of the war at Manassas.

Lee rode to the meeting upon Traveler, straight and poised in his saddle.

Silent groups of men awaited the outcome.

For all practical purposes, it was over.

Lee didn't formally address his troops until the next day. He told them that he had done his very best for them. And he told them to go home. He told them to be as good citizens as they had been soldiers.

Daniel watched the man he had followed for so very long, and his heart was heavy. The war had taken its toll upon him. His marvelous face was lined with sorrow and with weariness.

The great Army of Northern Virginia was done. There were other forces in the field, still fighting. But they couldn't last long. It was over.

Some of Daniel's men shouted that they would fight on and on. One of them called out to him in dismay. "He's done surrendered, sir! What are you going to do?"

Daniel mulled it over and then smiled with a bittersweet curl to his lip. "I'm going to find my brother. I'm going to embrace him. And I'm going to go home."

It wasn't that easy, of course. The formal surrender of the troops came on the following Wednesday, April 12, 1865. Neither Grant nor Lee was in attendance. The surrender was to be accepted by Major General Joshua Lawrence Chamberlain, a man who had held his positions at Gettysburg, who had been wounded time and time again.

And a gentleman without thought of revenge.

For as the conquered troops moved by him to lay down their arms, Chamberlain ordered his men to salute them.

And salute them they did.

The men were allowed to keep their horses or mules and their side arms.

They were allowed to go home.

Daniel was promoted to brigadier general in the final days of conflict. It was not so easy for him to leave as it was for his men, and there would be all manner of things that he must clear up, but he knew that Jesse was with the Union troops, and Daniel was anxious to see him.

It was Jesse, though, who found him. Daniel was bidding Godspeed to a young major from Yorktown when he looked past the man to see Jesse standing there, waiting silently for him to finish.

Daniel grinned and strode the distance between them, pausing just a second as his brother saluted him.

He saluted in return.

He grasped Jesse, and the two held tight for a long moment.

"I'm sorry, Daniel."

"So am I. Can you get leave?" One good thing about losing, Daniel decided, was that you didn't need permission to go home anymore. Jesse was still in the military.

"Yes, I've already arranged it."

"Good," Daniel told him. "We rode away separately. I'm glad to ride home together."

"Congratulations on your daughter."

"And on your son."

"And we haven't even seen them," Jesse murmured.

"Soon enough, we will."

Jesse held him tight one more time and left him. Daniel returned to the command tent to finish with the business of losing.

His heart should have been heavier. There were still forces in the field. He'd heard that Jeff Davis and the cabinet were in hiding, trying to decide whether to surrender themselves, hide out and fight on with guerilla warfare, or try to escape the country.

Daniel was sorry for all of them, but as Lee had known, to go on was foolish. Lincoln had already been in Richmond. It was over.

And he wanted to go home.

Janey brought the paper with news in it to Kiernan, handing it to her in silence. Kiernan quickly scanned the sheet, then sank into an armchair with it. "We've lost," she said softly. The paper fell from her hands and wafted to the floor. She put her head in her hands, and she began to sob.

Christa walked over to the parlor window and stared out in silence.

Callie thought of the hundreds of thousands of men who lay dead, and she thought of the devastation of the countryside. Kiernan wasn't sorry that it was over— Callie knew that. It was just that intangible thing, that essence, that something that had been the cause itself, a way of life, of acting, of being, was over. Never to come again. She understood. They both understood.

She walked over to Kiernan and put her arms gently around her sister-in-law. "Kiernan, it means that they'll be coming home now!" she told her. "They'll be coming home."

Shocking news reached the country by the morning of April 15. Abraham Lincoln, the greatest single force behind the Union victory—and the sanctity of the Union—was dead. He had been assassinated at Ford's Theater, shot in the back of the head by a man named John Wilkes Booth—an actor, a southern sympathizer, a man who had attended the hanging of John Brown all those years ago at Harpers Ferry. There had been a conspiracy, and officials were in a fury to arrest anyone involved.

Booth had escaped, but he was soon hunted down, and killed.

Daniel, hearing the news, mourned Lincoln's death as deeply as any northerner could.

Lincoln had been as dedicated to repairing the great schism in his country as he had been to preserving it. The Rebels could always claim that they had produced some of the greatest generals to ever live.

The North could claim one of their country's greatest men, for the rail-splitting lawyer from Illinois had proven with tenacity, dedication, and wisdom to be just that.

With Lincoln gone, who knew quite what would befall the South?

That all remained to be seen.

Daniel just wanted to go home.

Early on a late April morning, he rode out into a field of mist and he waited. Minutes later, another horseman appeared. Jesse.

They *were* going home.

Christa was the first to see them. She started screaming from an upstairs window.

Callie heard her and rushed to the porch. She could see them both, the Cameron brothers.

The one in blue.

And the one in gray.

They had dismounted from their horses, and they were walking down the long drive together toward the house, weary, arms linked, leaning upon one another.

Callie cried out.

Daniel lifted his head, and he saw her. A broad grin

touched his face. He turned to Jesse, said something, and broke away from him.

And then he was running to Callie.

And she left the porch behind, running to him.

The distance was not far. It seemed forever. Her feet moved so fleetingly over the earth.

Once upon a time she had dreamed of this. Of seeing Daniel before her, so hungry to meet her, to touch her. Once she had dreamed that she could run to him, with all her love naked in her face.

She catapulted into his arms. She felt them surround her. She caught sight of the blazing blue of his eyes. Then his lips were on hers.

His kiss was eternal. So hot, so sweet, so hungry. A touch that tore away, and fell again. Trembling. Deep. Lifting once again so that he could meet her eyes.

"Jesse! Oh, Jesse!" Callie was dimly aware that Kiernan had raced on by her. Farther down the lane, another sweet homecoming was going on.

But now Daniel was before her.

"Oh, Daniel!" she whispered softly. "I am so sorry!"

He pressed his finger to her lips. "Hush. I am not, Callie." His finger rimmed her lips. "I've a son to raise, a daughter to see. Oh, Callie!"

His mouth seared down upon hers once again. Fierce, poignant, giving, seeking. His eyes rose to hers once again.

"I love you, Callie. The war is over, but"— He smiled, a crooked, rueful, tender smile—"my life is just beginning," he told her.

And arm in arm, they walked back to the house.

And to a new life, together.

About the Author

Heather Graham lives in Florida with her husband and five children. Formerly a professional model, she has written thirteen bestselling historical romances, including the *New York Times* bestseller *And One Rode West*.

Just fill in the coupon below, return it to us, and you will receive exciting information on **HEATHER GRAHAM**. Her novels have captured the hearts of readers and catapulted her into the ranks of America's most beloved bestselling authors.

JOIN THE

HEATHER GRAHAM

FAN CLUB